THE MEMOIRS OF MARY

QUEEN OF SCOTS

Also by Carolly Erickson

THE

MEMOIRS OF

MARY

QUEEN OF SCOTS

Carolly Erickson

ST. MARTIN'S GRIFFIN

NEW YORK

This is a work of fiction. All of the characters, organizations, and events portrayed in this novel are either products of the author's imagination or are used fictitiously.

THE MEMOIRS OF MARY QUEEN OF SCOTS. Copyright © 2009 by Carolly Erickson. All rights reserved. Printed in the United States of America. For information, address St. Martin's Press, 175 Fifth Avenue, New York, N.Y. 10010.

www.stmartins.com

The Library of Congress has cataloged the hardcover edition as follows:

Erickson, Carolly, 1943–
    The memoirs of Mary Queen of Scots / Carolly Erickson.—1st ed.
        p. cm.
    ISBN 978-0-312-37973-5
    1. Mary, Queen of Scots, 1542–1587—Fiction. 2. Scotland—History—Mary Stuart, 1542–1567—Fiction. 3. Great Britain—History—Elizabeth, 1558–1603—Fiction. 4. Queens—Scotland—Fiction. I. Title.
    PS3605.R53M46 2009
    813'.6—dc22
                                                                      2009013190

ISBN 978-0-312-65273-9 (trade paperback)

10 9 8 7 6 5 4 3

Out of the shadows and mists of time, figures are taking shape, and walking across the grand stage of imagination. . . .

THE MEMOIRS OF MARY

QUEEN OF SCOTS

PROLOGUE

FOTHERINGHAY, FEBRUARY 1587

I saw it all. I was standing at the back, in a group of men I didn't know, who like me were shivering in their woolen cloaks as it was as cold as a witch's dug and the big fire in the middle of the room gave us no warmth.

I was there to watch her die, the woman I had loved and hated, wanted and rejected, fought for and nearly died for a dozen times. My wife, my joy and my burden, my sovereign, Mary, Queen of the Scots and Queen Dowager of France and rightful Queen of England too, though it was for that she had to die.

I was impatient. I wanted it to be over. Already I could tell that there would be shouts and a rush for the blood-stained block as soon as the axe fell because many of the men around me had their handkerchiefs out, ready to dip them in her gore. For as everyone knows, the blood of a beheaded criminal works wonders.

The thought of it, the mad rush of the men running past me, shoving me out of the way, the stink of the blood, the twitching body—for I had seen many an execution, and I knew that it takes a long time for a body to give up its last struggle and lie still—made me swear under my breath. I wanted no part of it. I didn't even want to see it, or to feel what would happen around me as the men crowded to get up onto the platform to wipe up the bloody mess.

Lord, let it be quick!

Despite the cold I felt my forehead growing damp with sweat. It had to be the waiting, all the tense waiting, that was making me feel hot. I had known for weeks that it would happen soon, that she would have to die, but no one would say when, what day or what hour. Queen Elizabeth could not make up her mind to choose a day, and so poor Mary and her grieving servants were forced to drag out their mornings and afternoons and long weary evenings, never knowing when the dreaded message would arrive. Finally it had come, and here we were, waiting out the last cold hours of Mary's life, stamping our feet and slapping our arms in a vain effort to get warm. Meanwhile I was sweating.

At last a small door opened and Mary came in.

There was a hush, then a murmur from the hundreds of men in the room. I heard the words "martyr" and "whore," and "murderess" and I stopped my ears, not wanting to hear more. I glanced at her. Her long years in prison, as I knew well, had turned her from the lithe, graceful, slender beauty I had first met when she was seventeen into a stout grandam with wrinkled cheeks who walked with a rheumatic limp, leaning on the arm of her escort, her sad-eyed old equerry Erskine. She still had the husk of beauty, and her eyes, as she searched the crowd, were still a lovely shade of golden brown, though lighter than they had been when we first met.

She had on a worn black gown that had once been costly, and as she walked she fingered a golden rosary tied around her waist and the miniature I had sent her, of myself and our daughter. I recognized the small suite that followed her: besides poor Erskine, there were her surgeon Gervais and her physician Bourgoing, the steward of her household Adrien de Guise, a man she had known in her youth in France, and her favorite tirewoman Margaret Hargatt.

None of the men around me uncovered when she came in, but kept on their high-crowned black hats. Not wanting to be conspicuous, I did the same. The murmuring stopped. Mary sat down in a chair draped with black velvet, the low velvet-covered block in front of her.

The death warrant was read. She was attainted of treason. She had conspired to kill Queen Elizabeth, the warrant said, and had exhorted others to kill her as well. She had to die.

Then a cleric preached to her, and afterwards knelt and began to pray in English after the Protestant fashion, for we were in England, after all, and England is a Protestant realm. But Mary, abandoning her chair and kneeling with difficulty, opened her Latin prayerbook and began to say her Catholic prayers, her voice carrying even more loudly than his, and some among the spectators crossed themselves and mouthed the old Latin words along with her.

At first I thought someone would silence her, and I looked around at the soldiers who stood by, and the sheriff's men arrayed around the edges of the newly built wooden platform, their halberds at the ready, their faces expressionless. But no one in authority moved or spoke, and so she prayed on, her high voice broken but brave, until she reached her amen.

I saw now that one of her hands was trembling, and I could not tell if it was from the cold or from fear. I had an impulse to rush up to her, to put my own warm cloak around her, though I knew I didn't dare. And in that moment she paused once more to look around at those gathered to watch her, and she met my gaze.

I knew at once that she recognized me. A light came into her eyes, and there was the faintest smile on her pale lips. I even thought I detected a flush on her cheeks, though it might have been a mere trick of the wintry sunlight that was beginning to filter in through the high windows.

"Orange Blossom!" I wanted to cry out. "My dearest! I tried! I did my best!"

But she had already begun to forgive the executioner Bull and his burly assistant for the bloody work they were about to do, and to hand them the token coins that were the symbol of her forgiveness.

It would not be long now, I thought. Only a moment and then those brave, loving eyes will close forever. Now I was the one who trembled, and I am not a cowardly man.

I turned aside, I could not watch. When I found my courage again and looked in her direction I saw that her women had taken off the black outer gown she wore to reveal the dark red gown she had on underneath it—red as dried blood, red for martyrdom.

Then I heard a silence, and then a swish of cloth, and in a moment, a dull thud. A shiver passed through the crowd. I looked up—and saw that the first blow of the axe had not severed her head, but sliced into it. A clumsy, crude blow, unpardonable! The knave had missed his target entirely. Vowing to slice him to ribbons once I found him, after the gory day was over, I watched as the next blow cut deep into her neck, but still did not sever her head entirely. Her blood gushed out, quantities of blood, and I could not help but gasp and try not to sob at the sight of it.

At the very last, before she died, she saw me. I swear she did. I saw her lips mouth the words "Jamie. My Jamie." Her lips went on moving even after they held her head up, first by the red-brown wig that soon parted from the head and allowed it to bounce grotesquely along the floorboards, and then by her true hair, lank and gray and dusty from the dirt of the floor. Margaret told me afterwards that she thought Mary had been trying to say "Jesus" when her lips moved. But it wasn't Jesus, it was Jamie.

Even in death the queen was afraid of her. Afraid of what the people would do when they learned she had been killed. So a huge bonfire was made in the courtyard, and every scrap of clothing with blood on it was burnt on that fire, and every relic of her found and destroyed. Even the executioner's apron was burnt to ashes, against his protests. No one was allowed to leave Fotheringhay to carry the news of Mary's death for days afterwards, and the huge iron gates of the castle were shut and closely guarded.

I left as soon as I was able, for I was no one important, just a peddler of potions, and no one wanted to keep me from delivering my oil of vetiver and larks'-tongue balm. Besides, I was eager to get to the coast, where the *Black Messenger* waited, her crew eager to sail to Lisbon and join the Most Fortunate Fleet. There I would tell the story of Mary Queen of Scots to whomever would listen, and I would boast that I, James, fourth Earl of Bothwell, had been fortunate enough to love her, and to watch her die, and to live on to tell the world about it.

ONE

*T*HE trumpets sounded a brilliant fanfare, the shrill high notes soon lost in the bright April air, and the jousts began.

It was my wedding day, I was fifteen years old and quite content to be marrying the dauphin Francis, the boy prince I had known since we were both very small children. The elaborate, lengthy wedding mass at last over, the jousting to celebrate it was about to begin. Francis and I sat together under the roof of the wooden spectators' pavilion overlooking the tiltyard, watching as the armored jousters rode in one by one, the crowd cheering and clapping for each.

Francis and I stood, and clapped with the others, but I stooped a little, for I was so much taller than my new husband that it was embarrassing. I was much admired in my lace-trimmed gown of ivory silk, my long reddish hair coiled like a crown on top of my head, my throat wreathed in diamonds, a long rope of large pearls dangling from my belt to the hem of my gown. My new father-in-law King Henry called me his "petite reinette," his little queen, and said that I was the loveliest child he had ever seen. Only I was no longer a child, I was far too tall for that, and growing taller every day. While my new husband Francis, poor boy, was pathetically stunted in his growth, quite the runt of his parents' royal litter.

The cheering grew louder as King Henry rode into view, magnificent in his gleaming armor of chased silver, his metal helmet with its tall waving white plume, his long lance pointed upward.

I looked over at Francis, and saw that his small face was pale, slightly greenish. He appeared bilious. Knowing him as well as I did, I was aware that uncomfortable situations always made him nauseous. He was very uncomfortable now, aware that those seated near us were nudging each other and tittering, murmuring to one another that he was a coward.

The king had announced that Francis would join in the jousting, but at the last minute Francis had become frightened and fled to the spectators' pavilion, humiliated and miserable. I felt sure that he knew, better than anyone, how futile it would be for him to take the field against the older, stronger competitors, how he would have difficulty couching the heavy lance, aiming at his opponent's helmet (he was squeamish about hurting anyone or any thing), how if struck himself he would fall heavily from the horse and might well be trampled.

"Fight, boy, fight!" his father was always shouting at him. "How can you be a king if you can't even be a man?"

But he couldn't help his size, or the fact that he was cursed with a slight, weak body or that he was a poor athlete quick to tremble and run when chased by an opponent. I felt protective toward him—I was two years older after all—and had always defended him, ever since we were children together. I was still defending him on our wedding day, glaring at those around us who were smirking and making insulting comments and wishing, as we stood up there in the pavilion, that I had worn slippers rather than shoes so that the difference in our heights would not be so obvious.

With a thunder of hooves the king rode down the length of the narrow tiltyard, making us all gasp in admiration. He took up his position at the far end, away from us. We could see his splendid mount tossing its head and skittering and shying nervously, waiting for his full speed and power to be unleashed. The challenger now rode toward the near end of the long corridor of combat, his armor too shining in the sunlight and his charger strong and full of spirit and power.

King and challenger faced one another, the grooms who had been holding the horses loosing their hold and scurrying away. Drums rolled. Another fanfare sounded. Then, as Francis reached for my hand and we both held our breath, the jousters rode at breakneck speed toward one another, lances lowered and pointed at one another's heads.

There was a sickening thwack as the king's lance struck the challenger's visor, shattering into a dozen pieces, and the hapless challenger fell over sideways off his horse.

Grooms rushed to the armor-clad figure lying prone and tried to revive him. When they failed, he was dragged off out of sight and the earth was quickly raked to evenness where he had lain. It all happened so fast that I could almost believe I had imagined it— except for the red stain in the brown earth, and the deep tracks leading off toward the stables.

I looked at Francis, and saw that his pallor had increased. He looked ill. Was he about to throw up?

I reached for my handkerchief. If the worst happens, I thought, I will cover his mouth with my handkerchief. Maybe only those in the very front of the crowd will notice.

At that moment I heard my new mother-in-law's low, syrupy voice.

"If you spew," she said in Francis's ear, leaning down from where she sat behind us, "I swear I'll turn your head into a boiled cabbage."

At this Francis seemed to straighten up a little.

"Courage!" I whispered to him. "Only five challengers more."

"Leave me be!" he said sharply, both to his mother and to me. I felt relieved. He was irritated. His irritation would preoccupy him, I felt sure, and would prevent him from disgracing himself by being sick.

My mother-in-law the queen, Catherine de Medicis, now leaned over me.

"That's the way, little reinette," she said with a smile. Her round, jowly face had the heaviness, her leathery, pockmarked cheeks the roughness of a peasant woman in the marketplace. Her small dark eyes were shrewd. "Encourage him! He will need all his courage tonight."

I knew very well what she meant. It was widely rumored that my husband was impotent. There were no pregnant serving girls claiming to be carrying his baby, as was often the case (so I was told) with princes. Francis was timid with everyone, even the serving girls, and seemed to shrink from the grown men and women around him.

I heard another voice, a much more welcome one, and turned to see that my grandmother Antoinette de Guise was coming to sit beside the queen, shooing away one of the latter's attendants with a wave of one beringed hand and settling her ample self on the cushioned bench.

"I doubt that the prince will accomplish much in the bedroom tonight," she remarked.

"Hush, grandmamma! There is already too much talk of these very personal matters!" I knew I sounded prim, and regretted it, but the truth was, I shared my grandmother's views. Yet I wanted to be loyal to Francis.

"I pray that we will be worthy to bring sons into the world for the honor of Scotland and France," I said stoutly, at which Grandmamma Antoinette lifted her fan to her mouth and made a sound that was somewhere between a sneeze and a snort.

"We must all pray for that," Queen Catherine added immediately, and when I turned to look at her I saw a gleam—was it a gleam of avarice?—in her small eyes. It was the same gleam I had seen on the morning I signed my marriage treaties several days earlier. On that morning, after Francis and I had signed our names on the documents prepared by the court lawyers, the queen had drawn me aside. She had shown me other documents, secret ones, which my mother had prepared without telling me. What these documents said was that, if Francis and I had no children, Scotland would belong to France.

Young as I was, I understood quite well what was at stake in our marriage. Francis and I had to have a son, if possible several sons. It was vital. Scotland's future was at risk. I did not doubt that I was strong and vigorous enough to become a mother. But could he become a father? My household physician, Dr. Bourgoing, thought so, and I trusted his opinion.

How I wished, at that moment, that my own mother could be with us, watching the wedding joust. My widowed mother Marie, who was Queen Dowager of Scotland and who continued to live among the disorderly, treacherous Scots—yes, that is what they were!—in an effort to preserve some sort of harmony and peace among them. How I missed her! I had not seen her in so long, not since her last visit to France when I was seven years old. If I closed my eyes I could see her dear face, hear her voice.

She was a Frenchwoman, she belonged among us. Like Grandmamma Antoinette, she had the royal blood of the Bourbons in her veins.

The spectators were stirring loudly to life once again as a fresh challenger came riding against the king. Once again there came a thunder of hooves, a clashing of lances, and although the king took a blow to his shoulder, his opponent was unhorsed and fell heavily.

On through the afternoon the king continued to be victorious, tiring four mounts and shattering many lances. He seemed invincible. Only the challenger, a tall, burly knight who smashed his lance into the king's chest and a second one into his helmet, appeared to offer real opposition. But in the end the king struck a disabling blow and the man went down.

Francis, sitting quietly beside me, began to sniff and wipe his nose on his sleeve. His attention wandered from the tiltyard.

"Only a few minutes more," I said to him. "Then the banquet will begin."

"I'm not hungry," he whispered. "I want to leave."

"We can't leave. Not until the prize of arms is awarded."

At last twilight began to descend and the king, triumphant, came forward to receive the prize, to the applause and cheers of the on-lookers. Francis and I stood, paying him homage as the undefeated champion of the joust, but Francis was yawning, and we had no sooner returned to the palace than he went to bed, without even waiting for his servant to take off his boots.

I found him there, alone in the immense bed we were expected to share for the first time that night as husband and wife. He was sound asleep under a layer of down, a weary boy at the end of a long and tiring day.

I kissed his cheek and went back to my own apartments, eager to have my attendants dress me in the lovely gown of pale blue satin that my grandmamma had chosen for me to wear that night. I did not want to miss the banquet—or the dancing that would follow it. I loved to dance and besides, it was my wedding day. I would simply explain that Francis had felt ill and needed to take some physick. Everyone would understand. And even if they didn't, they would not dare to complain. For was I not Queen of Scotland and, as of today, dauphine of France?

TWO

WHILE I was becoming accustomed to being a wife and hoping to become a mother, I had many letters from my own dear mother in Scotland. A courier arrived nearly every month with a new bag of documents for me to sign and messages, often hastily scrawled and heavily blotted, signed "from the queen," or simply "Marie," with my mother's special insignia, the silver eaglets of Lorraine, added at the bottom of each page.

She was in trouble.

The great and quarrelsome Scots lords, the most powerful of them as mighty as kings in their own lands, were fighting, and though they often changed allegiances, and clashed fiercely with one another, there were always many of them who were fighting against the crown. I was queen, but my mother was regent, holding authority on my behalf, and try as she might to hold it, that authority was rapidly slipping away.

It did not help that she was ill, and that her illness was slowly growing worse. Her legs and feet swelled until she could barely walk, and her face, she wrote, looked like a sheep's bladder that someone had blown up and forgotten to deflate.

"The doctors shake their heads, and soak my blankets in lime juice, which is supposed to take away the swelling. But all the lime juice in the world can't make my belly flat again," she told me in one letter. "They really don't know what to think, or what to do. Young Jamie—that's the young heir to the earldom of Bothwell—thinks it's witchcraft, and he's brought me a charm stone to keep in my bed."

From the letters, and the visits of mother's couriers and ambassadors to the French court, I was able to follow what was going on, after a fashion. Mother's illness was getting worse, the hostile Scots (she called them wolves) were pursuing her from one castle to another, and despite the aid of "Young Jamie" and others who were faithful to her, it was taking all her courage and the last of her strength to resist them.

Meanwhile here in France a sudden, unexpected event changed the direction of our lives.

The king was once again taking on all challengers at a joust—and Francis, as before, was watching from the spectators' pavilion instead of joining in. The afternoon sun blazed hot on the horses and riders in the tiltyard, and the king, performing with athletic grace as he invariably did, and triumphing over each challenger that came forward, drank deeply and frequently from the goblets that were handed up to him by the grooms.

It seemed to me, by the time he spurred his mount against the fifth challenger, that he rode unsteadily, and appeared to falter, but I quickly dismissed the thought. I had to be mistaken. He was a great champion, I had to be wrong.

Yet his opponent's lance struck him heavily in the chest and he nearly fell from his horse. A gasp went up from the onlookers, many stood, some cried out, "Lord King! Lord King!" in anguish. Francis looked down at his lap, unable to watch.

But within a moment King Henry managed to right himself, and waved to the crowd, and there was applause, and loud cries of relief.

Still, I watched with apprehension as the next challenger took his position and the king, swaying slightly, drank again from a proffered goblet.

This time, having finished off the liquid, he flung the goblet into the crowd—a gesture I had never before seen him make—and I thought to myself, he has drunk too much wine. How will he judge his blows accurately, or evade those of his challenger? I held my breath as he spurred his mount and closed the distance between himself and the other rider, the dust rising under his horse's hooves.

There was a clash—and suddenly both men were on the ground, their mounts shying and snorting in protest.

Grooms rushed to the aid of the fallen jousters, but while the challenger was helped to his feet, and staggered off the course, the king lay where he was, unmoving.

As quickly as I could, I helped the trembling Francis to make his way down from the pavilion and back to the palace, where we went at once to the royal apartments, through corridors crowded with weeping servants and officials.

The hubbub in the king's bedchamber was loud, the courtiers and retainers frantic with worry. Queen Catherine rushed in with three of her ladies, all of them in great distress.

"He's injured!" she shouted to the cluster of physicians who were conferring nervously. "He's covered in blood! Why aren't you treating him? Why are you just standing there, doing nothing?"

The king lay unmoving under the linen sheet, one eye bandaged, the other closed but covered in bruises. Another bandage that covered his throat and ear was red with what looked to me like fresh blood.

Francis trembled and knelt by the bed, grasping his father's hand.

"I warned him not to go," the queen was saying. "I had a bad dream last night. I saw the accident. I saw the horse veer. My husband ran right into the oncoming lance."

It was well known at the court that Queen Catherine had prophetic dreams, and that she kept in her household a physician who was also an astrologer, Michel de Notredame, who foretold the future.

"What shall I do?" Francis murmured to me, shaking his head. "How shall I manage?" The look on his face was piteous.

King Henry lived for ten days after his accident, on the eleventh day he died, and my husband Francis became King of France.

THREE

HE dressed in cloth of gold, he wore immense rubies in his caps and even his shoes had jeweled buckles. Everywhere he went he surrounded himself with an escort of handsome, sturdy young men and when he dined in public he made certain that there were beautiful women adorning his table.

He tried to look like a king.

But no amount of finery or outward show could make Francis kingly, and day by day his misery and fear deepened. He was only happy when away from the court, and his refuge was the hunt.

When autumn came we went to stay at the beautiful new palace of Fontainebleau, where the hunting in the surrounding forest was at its best. Francis rode off happily into the woods early each morning and each evening his foresters brought back many handsome stags and does, all dead by his royal hand (or so they assured everyone), and laid them out on the grass under the light of the torches.

There was a chill in the air, and intermittent rain, and by the fourth day of our stay at the palace I noticed that Francis, who was forever sneezing and having to wipe his nose no matter where we were or what season it was, was sniffing more than ever and blowing his nose noisily and complaining that his ear hurt. When I suggested that he stay indoors rather than ride out in the rain, he snapped at me irritably—and then began coughing as if he could not stop.

On the following morning, despite the dark clouds and sharp wind, he went out to hunt as usual, and all his retinue with him, only to come back a few hours later, soggy in his velvets (Francis loved his finery!) and holding his hand to his ear. Dr. Bourgoing gave him a purgative and sent one of the grooms to the kitchens for a roasted onion to place in his ear to draw out the poisons.

My mother-in-law's astrologer Michel de Notredame also arrived, sent by the queen to examine Francis. He was a dark-haired, heavily jowled man of medium height, well advanced in age (though everyone looked very old to me then, young as I was), with a serious expression and a look of great intelligence, such as I had seen on few faces in my brief life.

He bent over Francis, who had been ordered to bed by Dr. Bourgoing, and listened to his chest and looked into his ear.

"The king has a worm in his ear," he told the doctor. "It has bored its way in, deep into his head. It cannot be dislodged. The onion will not cure him. However, the king will recover—this time."

I was very relieved to hear the astrologer's words, so relieved that I ignored the subtle warning in what he said, the implication that there might be another illness from which he would not recover.

"Monsieur de Notredame," I said as he was preparing to leave, "would you please read my palm?"

He looked at me searchingly. "Are you certain you want me to?"

I hesitated a moment, then nodded.

"Very well then. I should like you to stretch out your hands, palms downward."

I did as he asked.

"Very pretty. The long fingers very elegant. But the nails—"

My nails were bitten down to the quick. My tirewomen soaked them in rosewater each night and rubbed scented oil into the raw edges, but they looked ragged and injured nonetheless. When I attended banquets or masques, I wore gloves—tight, soft dogskin gloves—to hide my nails.

"Please turn them over."

I had had my palms read before, it was a common enough pastime at court, but when Monsieur de Notredame inspected first my left palm, then my right it was with a degree of scrutiny and thoughtfulness I had never encountered. He took his time, tracing the significant lines with one finger, frowning occasionally and slowly shaking his head.

"What day were you born, and at what hour?"

I told him. He remained quiet for a time, then motioned me to sit on a bench near the fireplace.

"More logs!" he called out to the groom who stood nearby. At once the boy ran out of the room and before long came running back in with an armload of wood, which he proceeded to add to the fire.

"Little queen, I would like you to remove one of your bracelets."

I unfastened the clasp of a gold bracelet with rubies set into its intricately carved tracery and slid it off my hand. He took it and held it, keeping his eyes closed. Then he opened them and spoke a single word: "Baleful."

He began pacing up and down in front of the bench where I sat, speaking rapidly, looking not at me but at some object in the distance, as if I wasn't even there. He was near the fire, rivulets of sweat ran down his face as he walked back and forth across the uneven gray stones of the hearth.

"I see that you play the spinet, though not very well, and that you have many little dogs, and one of them, a spotted bitch, has one short leg and cannot run very fast. I see that you work at your lessons but they do not come easily to you. You are kind to your husband and wish him well, but you do not love him and you never will. I see your favorite roan, and your mother—she is ill, is she not?—and—that is all I see."

He stopped pacing and the intensity drained from his face. He relaxed, shrugged, and sat down and handed me back my bracelet.

"Tell me, Monsieur de Notredame, what did you mean by 'baleful'?" The word lingered in my mind, troubling me.

"I would rather not say more. You are too young."

"Please."

He took his time before he spoke, and chose his words with care.

"When you were born," he began, "you were meant to die. You nearly did die. You were born at a savage time. Someone else—your father—died instead. You were given up for dead as well. It was your fate to die, yet you perversely survived."

"How can it be perverse to survive?" I asked. "I know my mother was very glad I did not die, as her other children had."

"There is an order to things," the astrologer said, his tone suddenly severe. "You upset that order. You were not meant to live, to have children."

At the mention of children my nerves were set on edge. I was constantly being reminded of my duty to produce an heir to my husband's throne—and of what my mother-in-law referred to as my barrenness.

"What do you mean, I was not meant to have children? Why else would I have survived? I carry my father's royal blood in my veins, strong blood, rich blood. I am as sturdy as the next girl. I can run, I can ride—even though my mother-in-law does not like me to. I can hunt as well as any boy, draw a bow, shoot a gun. I have brought down a stag. Clearly I am meant to have my husband's child. I have been *spared* so that I might have that child. Spared, do you understand?"

"I understand," Monsieur de Notredame replied calmly, "far more, and far better, than you, little queen. And all that I have said is true. Do not blame me, blame the fates, the blind destiny that governs our lives. I am only the messenger."

He looked at me, and his expression was very grave.

"I tell you this for certain. Something has gone wrong. You endure, but so does the force that assaulted you and brought you low as soon as you were born. The struggle you knew as a weak infant will go on throughout your earthly life."

I was both angry and puzzled by the astrologer's enigmatic words. Until that time I had not had to struggle, everything had always been done for me, my path had been made clear, my every need filled. Was there not fine food on my table at every meal, and a dozen servants to bring it to me? Were there not entire rooms filled with my costly gowns in rich brocades and satins and even cloth of silver, my petticoats, my fans, my hats, my gloves, my jewels? I had only to ask, and whatever I called for was brought to me. I had always been treated like the queen I am.

I got up from the bench and went to the window, looking out to the immaculate, luxuriant gardens.

"If what you say is true," I managed to say, doing my best to keep my tone even, "then why is it that I have been brought up in luxury, with my every request filled, and married to the highest-born man in the land?"

He shook his head. "That was illusion, and will soon end."

I bristled, and turned back toward Monsieur de Notredame. "I don't believe you," I said.

But he only shrugged. "It is written in the stars."

FOUR

THE clashing of swords rang out across the courtyard, and I heard shouts of alarm from the Scottish Archers who formed our royal Garde de Corps. We ran to the windows to see who was fighting. Francis and I were staying at a château near Soissons, on our way northward; the last thing we expected to hear in this out-of-the-way place was the clangor of metal on metal and the grunts of men in combat.

But there they were, two stalwart, strong-looking young men, both swinging heavy broadswords, shouting insults and challenges at one another between blows and panting from their exertions. Neither appeared to be injured, though it was impossible to be sure from the window where I stood and so I made my way from my upstairs room down to the story below and out into the mud and muck of the courtyard.

By the time I reached it, however, the two combatants had begun to laugh, though the insults continued. Finally both men threw down their swords and began playfully buffeting one another, more like boys than men.

"Good sirs," I said, going up to them, "dueling is not allowed within the precincts of the court. What do you wish here?"

The taller of the two, his vest of burgundy velvet askew, his linen sleeves pitted with mud and his soft leather boots black with grime, turned his ruddy bearded face toward me and smiled. He wore a jeweled earring in his left ear and diamonds sparkled from his beribboned codpiece.

"James Hepburn, Earl of Bothwell, Your Highness." He bowed, so elaborately that I wondered whether he might be teasing me.

His companion followed suit. "Cristy Ricarton, Lord of Faskally."

I addressed the earl. "You are my mother's man. The one she calls 'dear Jamie' in her letters."

"Does she now? And did she tell you I was coming to see you?"

"No. But our court has been traveling for many days. Her letter may be following us. Tell me, have you finished your contest of strength?"

The earl looked at his companion, then down at their two discarded swords. "Are we finished, Cristy?"

"For the present." Both men chortled. "Especially since we have been cautioned."

"Then come inside and refresh yourselves."

I felt the earl's dark eyes on me, and could not help but be pleased. I liked the humor in his eyes, his curling beard, the strength of his body, so different from Francis's slender white tapering form. I did not mind at all that he showed me so little ceremony. After all, we were not in a palace, but a country château. And I have never been one to demand deference from my inferiors—unless I feel it is being deliberately withheld.

Francis did not join us for supper, he was still recuperating from his illness. I dined with the two newcomers—Francis not being well enough to join us—and two of Francis's councilors, the garrulous, pop-eyed Comte de Dampierre, who I had always found irksome, and the milder, more thoughtful man of law Augustine de Roncelet. My equerry Arthur Erskine stood behind my chair, Adrien and a dozen of the Scottish Archers formed an honor guard at both ends of the long room.

Insofar as we could, we dined in state, on the best gold plate our traveling chests could provide. I had my tirewoman Margaret Carwood fasten me into a silken gown with ropes of gold embroidery and wide sleeves trimmed in silver lace, and my long red-gold hair was looped and braided almost as elaborately as if we had been at Chambord or Fontainebleau.

No sooner had the first course been set before us than I asked the earl about my mother's health.

"I trust I may be frank with Your Highness," he said, after taking a swallow of wine from his glass.

"Of course you may. Indeed you must."

"She cannot last. The dropsy. Arran and his bastards have laid a spell on her, and it is killing her." The Duke of Arran, my nearest male relative, was of the Scots blood royal as I was, and it was no secret that he coveted my throne. He had made himself my mother's sworn enemy. "My sister and I have kept her alive until now," the earl was saying. "We know a bit of sorcery."

The Lord of Faskally choked on his food, and coughed noisily. "A bit!" he managed to say when he had recovered. "Jamie and Jane could enchant half of Scotland!"

"Cristy! Don't forget where you are, and at whose table you dine."

"I ask your pardon, Your Highness," the lord said, then resumed eating greedily.

"The swelling—the pain she endures—I'm only glad Your Highness cannot see it. It would rend your heart." The earl shook his head sadly as he spoke.

"I wanted to send Dr. Bourgoing to her," I said. "He says he has cured the dropsy with a decoction of black nightshade and he knows of others who have used lady's glove to arrest its worsening. I wrote to her about sending him to Scotland, but she said no."

"The English would never let him through to her. Their ships block Leith harbor."

"I could send him down into Edinburgh from the north. He could go by ship to the Isles, then down through—"

"Through Campbell country! Hah! They'd hack him to pieces as soon as spit on him. Savages, all of them, savages."

The Lord of Faskally nodded vigorously at this, and echoed "savages," and went on eating.

"I will miss your mother when she goes," the earl went on. "A lion of a woman! She's got the heart of a man of war. The English besieging us on one side, the mad Scots rebels on the other, with the villain Arran at their head, and she herself sick as a dog—and still she never gives up." He shook his head in wonderment. "She sent me here to ask for troops and money. Only we both know it won't do any good. She can't last. And when she dies, Scotland will be a land of chaos."

"But my husband did send reinforcements months ago. I know he did."

The earl nodded. "I told you, the English ships block Leith harbor. Those men he sent were waylaid and attacked. They never set foot on Scottish soil."

For a time there was silence while a fresh course was served. Then, as we ate, my husband's councilors questioned our guests about the English, how many ships they had in the harbor, how many men came ashore when they attacked, what sort of armaments they had.

I listened, doing my best to eat a little, though my appetite had left me. Talking of my poor mother and her severe illness made me sad and tense. I drank a little wine in an effort to calm myself.

The councilors droned on, the Lord of Faskally continued to eat and drink heartily, but the earl, while he answered all the questions put to him ably and knowledgeably—or so it appeared—often met my eyes, with a searching look that puzzled me.

Then the conversation turned in an uncomfortable direction.

"You know, of course, that our king is unwell," the Comte de Dampierre said, addressing the earl, "and many believe he will die without an heir of his body."

"To speak in my presence of my husband's infirmity, and of our childlessness, in such a callous way is discourteous," I interrupted. But the count went on, as though I had not said a word.

"His brother Charles will succeed, which will mean that our queen dowager will be regent, which will no doubt inflame the Protestants—"

"I must ask you to guard your tongue, sir," I said, aggravated at the count, "or leave the table."

The count glanced at me dismissively, then went on.

"Adrien!" I called out, addressing the captain of the Scottish Archers. Almost before I had finished speaking his name he stood beside me. "This gentleman has had too much wine. Will you please escort him to his room?"

"I obey only the king's orders," the count snapped.

"And I the queen's," was the captain's retort, and he took a menacing step toward the count.

Monsieur de Roncelet got to his feet. "If you will excuse me, Your Highness, I believe these matters can be left for discussion another day. Come along, Dampierre."

For a moment I thought the count would challenge my authority again, but instead he threw down his linen napkin and turned to leave the room.

In an instant the Earl of Bothwell was on his feet, kicking his chair noisily aside.

"Monsieur le comte! You will ask the queen's permission to withdraw, or you will answer to me!"

Slowly the count turned, bowed in my direction, and murmured, "With your permission, Your Highness."

"You may go."

The earl sat down again. "Now perhaps we may finish our meal in peace. And then, Your Highness, if I may, I would like to see the king."

FIVE

EVEN before we entered Francis's bedchamber we could hear him coughing. I went in first, telling the three Gentlemen of the Bedchamber who were in attendance on him that he had a visitor.

"A visitor?" Francis croaked. "What visitor?"

Though the hearth fire blazed high and the room was hot, he was swathed in a woolen blanket, his feet wrapped in warm leggings. He shivered—or perhaps he was trembling in fear. Visitors frightened Francis.

"It is the Earl of Bothwell, my mother's man. A friend."

"A parasite, you mean. Dampierre has cautioned me about this friend, this friend wants money."

The earl came in then, and at his first sight of Francis, could not help but whisper, "By all that's holy!"

My poor husband was indeed a ghastly sight. His dark, stringy hair stood out around his pale, thin face with its startling gashes of red where the skin disease that tormented him had broken out. With every rasping cough he brought up green sputum, which he wiped away impatiently with one wet hand. His wild eyes were full of fear and bad temper, and the sight of Bothwell, with his twinkling earring and sparkling codpiece, made him cackle.

"A cockscomb then! As well as a parasite!"

Bothwell bowed.

"Your Highness," he said. "I am James Hepburn, Earl of Bothwell, come to bring you greetings from the Queen Dowager Marie of Scotland. She wishes you a quick recovery and fortunate prospects for a long and happy reign."

A thin smile crossed Francis's moist lips.

"Does she indeed? And does she add her apologies for cursing me with a barren daughter for a wife?"

"He doesn't mean that," I said, moving closer to the earl. "He is only echoing his mother. When we are alone he doesn't speak to me like that."

"Sire," the earl went on, "both our realms, Scotland and France, are under siege from the English enemy. It would be well for us not to insult each other or provoke quarrels, but to combine our strengths to fight off this scourge."

"Well said, for a borderer," Francis sniped. "But as you see, I am under siege from quite another source." A spasm of coughing interrupted him. I could hardly look at him, he was so wretched, and I so helpless. At length he went on, his voice low, his head bent toward the floor.

"I refer to my mortality. Now leave me. There is no money for you here."

The earl bowed again, and murmuring, "I am sorry to have found Your Highness in such an unwell state," left the bedchamber. After a moment I followed him.

"I have a great and sudden thirst," he said as I came up to him in the dim torchlit corridor. "Seeing death face to face puts me in need of drink."

I was glad that he made no pretense, that he said what we all saw—that my acid-tongued husband was not likely to live much longer.

"It isn't true, is it?" he asked. "The rumor that he has leprosy? Because if it is, then you probably have it too."

"No. But a worm has bored deep into his ear and Michel de Notredame says it cannot be gotten out. It is rotting him from the inside. The cough, the rheums, the terrible rash—all are caused by this deathly worm."

The earl shook his head. "Poor girl, it must not be easy for you. You must try to have a child, you know. That is your only hope. Otherwise—"

I took a deep breath. I knew what the alternative would be.

"Otherwise," I said, "the queen dowager will send me back to Scotland. Back to the wolves."

The earl's smile was rueful. Yet I saw sympathy in his eyes. "You sound like your mother. But now I must go. No doubt Cristy has already found the nearest tavern. I'll join him, with Your Highness's permission."

"Of course. Thank you," I added.

"For what?"

"For your truthfulness."

He nodded. "And I thank you for yours." We looked at each other then, and smiled, and let the moment linger. I felt something stir deep within me, a sensation for which, then, I had no name. A slowly spreading warmth, a comfort, a sheltering peace. And I was aware once again, as I had been when I first saw him in the courtyard earlier that day, of his bodily strength and vigor.

"Let's hunt tomorrow," he said, "if the day is fine."

I nodded.

"Good night, Your Highness."

"Good night, my lord."

SIX

EARLY showers of rain had left muddy patches in the little wood, and as the kennelmen in their leather breeches brought out the hare hounds they splashed through freshets that ran between the chestnuts and the old hornbeams. The dogs yapped as they leapt through the brushwood, and my little roan tossed her head and skittered nervously under me as we waited for the hunting party to assemble.

I felt a bit guilty, leaving Francis in order to course hares, especially since, of the two of us, he was the one who most loved to hunt. But he was hardly able to leave his chair, much less ride, and I told myself that I was not merely seeking fresh air and exercise, I was taking counsel with my mother's most faithful supporter, the Earl of Bothwell. Whatever conversation we had, whatever further rapport we developed during the day's sport, would benefit France and Scotland—and my husband as well.

"There now, Bravane," I called to the horse, reaching down to pat her neck, steadying myself on the planchon under my feet. My skirts were damp, the morning had not been kind to my riding clothes. Yet as I looked down at the sadly rumpled taffeta the air seemed to brighten and the sun came out, its sudden warmth cutting through the early morning chill. All around me wet leaves glistened as they trembled in the breeze, and the rich smells that rose from the moist earth seemed to grow stronger. Grooms were loading up the horses with baskets of food, and the huntsmen, stamping their feet and flapping their arms, their breaths steaming in the cold air, were signaling to the beaters to begin thrashing the undergrowth with sticks in order to drive the hares toward the open field beyond the wood.

Just as the horns sounded I glimpsed the earl, cap-a-pie in burgundy velvet and mounted on a dark jennet, riding up to join the party. Then we were off, as one great gray hare after another broke free of the scrub and darted off ahead. Slipped of their collars, the dogs raced after them, barking excitedly, and we on our mounts raced after the dogs, coming to a halt now and then when the clever, nimble hares bounded out of sight and the puzzled hounds paused, yapping and circling, until they caught sight of fresh prey.

For two hours and more we rode, in and out of copses, through wet expanses of fern and moss, over bare heath and across fields already shorn of their harvest. Hare after hare fell to the kill, though most, it seemed, escaped. They were vermin, they ate the crops and unless they were hunted, their numbers grew far too great. Still, I was glad when they flew across the fields, veering away from the hounds, turning with dizzying speed, their angular movements impossible to predict or follow. I was glad each time the dogs gave up, baying, for I knew that meant another hare had gotten away.

Escape was much on my mind in those days. For had Michel de Notredame not told me that my entire life was an escape from a dark fate? And were not my mother and my husband seeking to escape death?

Riding at full tilt across the sun-drenched fields on that morning, feeling Bravane's strong muscles moving rhythmically under me, taking risks as I rode—for I have never been one for prudent coursing—I felt that escape from dark premonitions was indeed possible, and I laughed aloud as I went.

Suddenly I heard strengthening hoofbeats and felt Bravane shudder as another horse passed her, nearly colliding with her in its mad gallop.

"You there! Watch out!" I shouted. But the swift rider did not pull up, or even turn to acknowledge me, he merely raised one gloved hand and shouted, "All for risk, woman! Arise and away!"

I looked more closely at his back. It was the earl! The burgundy doublet and feathered cap, the dark jennet, surely there could not be another member of our party that resembled him so closely.

The sun was nearly overhead, and I was both hungry and thirsty. I could tell from the cries of the dogs and the way their heads drooped and their tongues lolled that they too needed rest and refreshment. We came to a brook and I stopped to let Bravane drink her fill, standing in the long grass that grew at the water's edge. Up ahead there was a patch of shade where a grove of beech slanted down a sloping hillside. The grooms were there before us, spreading linen cloths and laying out the contents of hampers.

"There are snakes in that grass," came a low warm voice. I looked around, and saw the earl, approaching on his weary, sweaty-flanked horse, which moved up to stand beside Bravane at the edge of the brook, drinking from the swiftly flowing water.

"You nearly knocked us over," I said irritably. "Your jennet owes my Bravane the courtesy of an apology."

The earl removed his cap, revealing tousled light-brown curling hair.

"We beg your royal pardon. We were chasing the fastest hare ever born."

"And did you catch him?"

"Alas, no." He looked down into the water. "I fear I am not at my best. The tavern last night was well stocked, the drink flowing, the company—"

"Yes, I can imagine the rest."

He chortled. "I am short of sleep. But not too drowsy to offer to bring Your Highness some food." He dismounted, letting the reins of his horse go slack across its broad back, and strolled off in the direction of the grooms in the beech grove.

I dismounted and stretched my stiff limbs. Leaving Bravane to drink, I took a few steps along the water's edge. It felt good to move, to feel the breeze on my cheeks, to loosen, slightly, the tight lacing of my bodice (after all, Margaret was not there to notice and tell me I looked disheveled). I took off my cap and let down the braids of my high-piled hair, feeling the coolness of the wind and closing my eyes for the sheer pleasure of it.

I walked back to where the horse waited and secured her to a tree trunk. The earl had returned with a groom who carried a basket of food and a cloth, which he laid out for us to sit on. When the plate and cutlery had been arranged, the metal trenchers and goblets, I thanked the groom and told him he did not need to stay to serve us. He bowed and, jumping across the brook at a bound, departed.

I noticed the earl watching him, with what I thought was a look of envy.

"He is younger, after all," I said.

"Hah! Am I old? I am not yet twenty-six."

"I imagine my groom is all of, perhaps, sixteen. He plays tennis well. I have played with him, when no one was watching. It is not thought proper for a queen to compete against men—or boys," I added by way of explanation. "Especially servant boys."

"And did you win?"

"Once. I think he let me win. But win or lose, I was good competition."

"I notice you ride well too."

"You noticed?"

"Of course I noticed."

A comfortable silence fell, while we ate and drank. As during the supper the previous night, he ate heartily while I nibbled.

He picked a juicy red strawberry from a bowl and held it out to me. I started to reach for it, then, rather daringly, took it with my teeth, making the earl smile, watching me.

"Now where, do you imagine, are ripe strawberries to be found this late in the year?"

"My mother-in-law has them brought from the south. She says greenhouse strawberries are not as sweet."

"How far south, I wonder? Africa?" We both laughed.

"No. Only her monkeys come from there. Or do they come from the New World? I can't remember. Messy things, monkeys."

After eating several more strawberries and drinking another goblet of wine, the earl began humming. It was a dance tune, one I remembered from my early childhood in Scotland, before I came to France.

"I remember that tune," I said.

"A song from the borders. My father used to play it on the pipes. He tried to teach me to play, but I was never any good."

The earl lay back on the linen, his hands underneath his head, one booted leg crossed over the other. After a time he looked over at me.

"My father loved your mother, did you know?"

"No."

"When they were very young. He was Patrick Hepburn, the Fair Earl. He wanted to marry her—before she was matched with your father the king, that is. I think she secretly loved my father. Still loves him, perhaps. I know he went on loving her, right up until he died. I think the reason she likes me so well is that I remind her of him."

I listened with interest. I had never before thought of my mother as a woman in love, only as a widow, a woman alone. She rarely mentioned my father, and never with affection.

"What was he like, your father?"

"Handsome. A good swordsman."

"Honorable?"

"He upheld the honor of the borders."

"What does that mean?"

He thought for a moment. "It means, you can't trust anyone. A year ago your mother sent me south to make peace with the English. The treacherous, thieving, murderous English. I went. We signed an accord: no more fighting, no more skirmishes along that thin invisible line that separates our two kingdoms.

"We all agreed, made vows, and went home. And do you know what happened next? The lord Arran, your royal kinsman, takes money from the English and does their bidding. He comes to my castle at Crichton with fifty men and two English bombards and breaches the walls, steals everything inside, then sets fires in the ruins. And all, he says, because I broke the peace by brawling with my men on his lands. Brawling, mind you! Not doing anyone or any thing any harm."

Warming to his tale, the earl got to his feet.

"I sent him a challenge. He didn't even answer! He knows I can outfight him any day. But he's still a coward! A weak, sniveling coward.

"I went after him. I made him beg for his life. I wanted to kill him, but I knew your mother wouldn't like it. So I made him pay me a hundred crowns instead and forced him to give me his hand in peace. I left. And do you know what he did then?"

"I cannot imagine."

"He betrayed me to your mother. He went to her and sat in her council chamber and swore that he and I were plotting to kill her and seize the kingdom, and that I put him up to it!"

"I know from mother's letters that Arran is not to be trusted."

"He's not to be borne! I would gladly hunt him and not these silly hares. Set the dogs on him, and let them tear out his black heart!"

The hunt was reassembling, the grooms packing up and preparing the horses. I got up and went over to Bravane, untied her and stroked her neck and asked the earl for his help in mounting her.

"At least," I said as he offered me his arm and I stepped up onto the planchon, arranging my skirts as I took my seat, "Arran is no longer regent."

"No. It is much worse now. He heads the rebels, those pernicious Lords of the Congregation, who have been fighting your mother. Your cousin Elizabeth sends him money. Sometimes my spies catch her messengers riding up from London with bags of gold, meant for Arran and his Lords. As much as a thousand pounds."

He mounted his jennet. The horns were beginning to blow and the beaters to thrash the bushes. We urged our mounts across the brook and joined the other riders, our eyes on the hounds, waiting for the signal to resume our headlong gallop, the swift, elusive prey ever in view.

SEVEN

THEY brought her poor swollen body back to France in a gilded coffin, painted with the silver eaglets of Lorraine.

I watched from the harbor as the great Flemish galleass that bore her hove into view, under full sail, and wept as the ship rode at anchor and her privy councilors lowered the coffin into a small boat and then hoisted it up onto the pier.

I had known that my mother was dying, yet I was not at all prepared for the news of her death. It was the Earl of Bothwell who told me—he had rapidly become my closest adviser, the one man at the French court I felt I could fully trust. Shortly after we returned to Fontainebleau from our northward progress the earl received a message from Edinburgh, telling him that despite the rhubarb poultices and the strong spells his sister cast to counteract the sorcery of the Earl of Arran, the great Queen Dowager of Scotland had died.

She had died, valiant and undefeated, surrounded by traitors and wolves, and as soon as the earl told me of her death I vowed I would avenge her.

I balled my fists as I watched her coffin being carried into the wharfside chapel. I vowed I would fight my villainous cousin Arran, and his rebellious Lords of the Congregation. That I would resist the traitorous Scottish Parliament that had abolished the mass and declared Scotland to be a Protestant kingdom. And I would fight the English too, though how I would manage that, I couldn't for the time being imagine.

For Scotland, without my mother's guiding hand, was a kingdom adrift. I was Scotland's queen, I reigned—but could not rule, not as long as the petty lordlings such as Arran continued to fight like snarling dogs for the bone of power, and I stayed on in France by my husband's bedside.

I had wanted to bury mother among those she loved, at the convent of the Poor Clares in Pont-à-Mousson where she lived as a child. But my uncle the Duc de Guise, as head of the family, prevailed on me to order that she be interred at Rheims, the royal city, as befitting one who had been the wife of a king and the mother of a queen. I was in mourning, I did not insist. I deferred.

I wore a medallion with mother's portrait on it to the requiem mass, and tried to remember her face, not as it was painted on the circlet around my neck, but as it was the last time I saw her, when she came to visit me many years earlier. I remembered that she smiled, and hugged me, and that she cried when she left to return to Scotland, though she tried not to let any of her servants see her crying. I remembered the sound of her voice, and her laughter. But I could no longer see her face clearly, the intervening years had taken it from me. And it was all I could do, as the priest recited the words of the Dies Irae, those terrible words about the day of wrath and destruction, to keep my trembling knees together and prevent myself from falling. For I was an orphan now, an orphan queen, and there was no one I could go to any longer for succor.

EIGHT

AT my suggestion Francis appointed the Earl of Bothwell to be one of his chamber gentlemen and he became a member of our court. His friend Cristy Ricarton stayed nearby, though he had no official court appointment. He seemed glad enough to undertake occasional responsibilities when asked, though what he liked most was to go out with the earl on his nightly excursions.

What must it be like to be a man, I wondered, with the freedom to spend the evening however he liked? Highborn or lowborn, it seemed, men caroused with their friends and hangers-on. They drank, they gambled, they brawled on occasion—and they enjoyed the company of women. Not the sort of women I was forced to spend my evenings among, my ladies and relatives, my Guise cousins and aunts, my grandmother (whose company I always enjoyed), my mother-in-law (whose company I generally shunned). No: men sought another kind of women entirely, ones to be found, I assumed, in taverns or in brothels, in attic rooms or in dark alleyways. Or, as I was well aware, men had mistresses, or visited the luxurious residences of courtesans, like Diane de Poitrine. Diane had several such houses. I had visited them. There amid beautiful, tasteful surroundings, her lovers could indulge themselves to their hearts' content in sensuous pleasures.

Drinking, gambling, brawling, wenching. It was a world closed to me, yet I was curious about it, and I had the strong feeling that men were allotted by nature a generous measure of freedom and enjoyment which was denied to women, and I envied them.

The truth was, I was curious about how the Earl of Bothwell spent his evenings with his friend Cristy, and I asked Adrien to try to find out.

A few nights later Adrien came to tell me what he had learned. I had him escorted into my private apartments and then told my women to leave us—even my tirewoman Margaret Carwood, who knew nearly all of my secrets and who was both surprised and offended to be excluded from my interview with the handsome Scots Guards officer who was coming to be one of my most trusted servants.

"He plays cards, Your Highness," Adrien said simply once we were alone. "He gambles with dice. He is lucky. He wins."

"But to win, one must have a large stake," was my immediate response, "and I thought the earl had no money. At least, he convinced me that, like many Scottish nobles, he has an honored title but no wealth to go with it. In fact he told me outright that he is very short of funds. That was one reason I convinced my husband to appoint him to his household. And beyond that, I gave the earl a purse of coins—six hundred crowns—to reimburse him for his services to my mother, and as a memorial to her."

Adrien looked uncomfortable. "Six hundred crowns is a great deal of money, indeed. However—Your Highness may not wish to hear this—I assure you the earl wagers even larger sums than that with abandon."

"Does he indeed? And when he loses?"

"His friend Lord Ricarton produces from his own purse whatever is needed to make up the losses."

"Ah, so Cristy has a fortune. He is the earl's bank."

Adrien smiled. "I wish I had such a rich friend."

"So they drink, and the earl gambles, and—what else?"

"There is something else. Something that puzzles me."

"And what is that?"

"There is a woman. She is not French. She speaks a language I can't understand. She shouts it, in fact."

"Describe this woman."

"She is not young, she is not beautiful, she does not have a sweet face or a sweet nature. She is very sour, in fact. Very loud and demanding. More like a fishwife than a wellborn lady. And yet—"

"Yes?"

"And yet, her clothes are fine. Not quite clean and certainly not of the newest fashion, but fine nonetheless. She appears every night, wherever the earl and his friend go. They know her—or at least, they are not surprised to see her. The earl glowers when she comes near."

"Is she alone?"

"As far as I can tell, yes."

"Plain, aging, foreign, and alone. And dressed in shabby finery. How very strange."

I pondered Adrien's words for the next few days. I could not help noticing that whenever I went into my husband's apartments and found his chamber gentlemen there, they were idling away their hours playing cards or dice—the Earl of Bothwell among them. He usually appeared to be winning, with a high pile of coins at his elbow and a broad smile of triumph on his face.

I noticed this—and tried to put it out of my mind. But for some reason my knowledge of his gambling, and especially of the odd foreign woman, nagged at me, until in the end I summoned Adrien again.

"I want to see for myself this woman you described," I told him. "I need you to escort me to the tavern where the earl and Lord Ricarton go."

"But Your Highness cannot visit a low tavern! There are thieves and spies there, and women of the streets—and murderers!"

"I shall not go as the queen, but as—as your sister. Are there no mothers or sisters in taverns?"

Adrien thought a moment. "I have seen travelers take their womenfolk now and then."

"So we shall be brother and sister, traveling together. Bring two horses into the stableyard tonight. If anyone asks, say you are being sent on an errand for the king. What time shall I meet you there?"

"Ten o'clock."

"Very well."

As afternoon wore into evening I could not wait to meet Adrien. I listened eagerly for the chiming of the clock, I could hardly sit still. At nine o'clock I retired to my room, telling my bedchamber women that I felt unwell and asking them not to disturb me. Once again, Margaret was offended—and aggrieved. As a rule she slept on a trundle bed at the foot of my own large high four-poster bed. I could tell that my request to be left alone puzzled her. I had never excluded her from my room at night before, though etiquette demanded that whenever Francis came into my room after dark my women left us alone together.

Waiting for the hour of ten to arrive, wearing a borrowed plain gown of homespun stuff, a patched cape with an ample hood enveloping me, I trembled with excitement. Adventure! It was something I had had very little of since my marriage. And now, tonight, I would surely have my fill.

NINE

ADRIEN knew an unfrequented way out of the least used castle gate, a way favored by peddlers and servants, and as I kept the hood of my cape low over my face, no one we passed recognized me as we guided our horses out onto the road that led to the nearby village.

The moon had risen, but dark clouds soon came up to obscure it, and we had not gone far when it began to rain.

It was hard rain that came down in sheets, and I was soon drenched.

"Shall we turn back, Your Highness?" Adrien asked, shouting over the noise of the downpour.

I shook my head and we continued. I could not have said why, except that my blood was pounding in my veins and after all the anticipation of the afternoon and evening I did not want to be disappointed of my adventure.

I did not give a thought to whether or not my absence from the palace would be noticed, I merely assumed that for the next few hours I would be free. And for those precious hours I would not be Mary, wife of the king but someone else entirely: I would be merely the sister of one of the Scots Guards.

By the time we arrived at the Inn of the Three Barrels and Adrien helped me down from my horse I was completely soaked from head to foot. My gown clung to my body in wet lumps, my cloak hung dripping from my shoulders, the hood so low over my face that it covered even my wet untidy hair that drooped in wet ringlets across my cheeks.

Our entry into the noisy, candlelit tavern was inconspicuous, so engrossed were the drunken men inside in their goblets of wine and their raucous singing and laughing. There were a few women among them, and I glanced at the women, though I did not see anyone who looked like a foreigner wearing what had once been costly clothing. I did see the Earl of Bothwell and Lord Ricarton, however. They sat with four others, playing cards.

At first I was all but overcome by the reek of liquor and sweat, damp unwashed clothes and unwashed bodies. Only once before, when entering a soldiers' barracks, had I encountered such a strong odor. I restrained myself from holding my nose and, keeping my head lowered, managed to follow Adrien as he made his way through the room.

We seated ourselves at a table in a dim corner of the tavern and from somewhere Adrien produced a dry cloth with which I dabbed my dripping face and hair. We were served with wine. As I sipped from my goblet I glanced over at the earl's table. He was completely absorbed in his game. Every roll of the dice was greeted with loud cries of dismay or rejoicing.

Suddenly two men sitting near us began shouting at one another and then fighting. Adrien stood, shielding me from the mayhem, and the burly tavernkeeper came up to the table and roughly ordered the men to go outside. They stumbled out. As they reached the doorway they nearly collided with a remarkable figure coming in—a tall woman all in scarlet, from her feathered headdress to her gilt-edged cloak, muddy at the hem, to the embroidered gown she revealed as, throwing aside the cloak with a theatrical gesture, she strode into the room.

"It is the Skottefrauen," I heard someone say as the woman walked up to the Earl of Bothwell and, putting her hands on her hips, spoke to him in guttural tones.

Her words were forceful, but I could not understand them. He ignored her, as did the others around his table, though I heard a few groans and snickers.

She resumed her harangue but was drowned out as some of the men began singing, and soon most of the others in the room joined in. They were singing in French, a gutter French spiced with filthy words.

Big woman with the ugly face, go home!
Big woman with the ugly voice, be still!
*Sit on your ****
Make us all laugh
*Big woman no one wants to ***** you!*

Adrien looked very uncomfortable and pretended to put his hands over his ears.

Big woman where has your husband gone?
Out to find a prettier one, with a sweeter voice
*To sit on her *****
To take his pleasure
*Big woman no one wants to **** you!*

Her cheeks as red as her gown, the woman picked up the goblet from which the earl had been drinking and threw it against the wall. At this Lord Ricarton got up from the table, went to her (I held my breath; I was afraid he was going to strike her), picked her up and carried her back outside. She shrieked and beat on his chest with her fists, which made the men erupt into song and laughter once again.

I looked over at Adrien.

"Is she mad, do you think?" I asked him, though in truth her eyes were not the wild eyes of a madwoman. I had seen madwomen, chained to walls, screeching and tearing their clothes. Or else crouching or lying on the bare ground, looking out from lifeless, closed faces, seeing nothing.

"I think she is very angry."

"Is her name Skottefrauen? Or is that some insult I have never heard before?"

Adrien shrugged and shook his head.

"Will she be back, do you think?"

"She always comes back."

There was a shout of dismay from the earl's table and the room fell silent.

"That whore has brought me bad luck!" I heard him cry out. "Damn her to hell!"

"Damn her to hell!" came the echoing cry from the men around him. "Damn the Skottefrauen!" All of a sudden there was more noise than ever, the men stomping their booted feet on the wooden floor and banging on the tables with their fists.

The mood in the room had grown ominous, and for the first time since entering the tavern I felt cold and wretched in my wet clothes. I wanted to be gone from that place, wearing warm dry clothes and on my way back to the palace at a gallop. I opened my mouth to shout to Adrien over the stridor but before I could say a word the strange foreign woman was running back inside, a dagger in one upraised fist. She ran at the earl, whose companions quickly deserted him. Lord Ricarton was nowhere to be seen.

With the swiftness of a fine swordsman the earl drew his own weapon—a long knife—parried the woman's strong but clumsy dagger thrust and skillfully grabbed her wrist and twisted until the blade fell from her hand with a clatter. She cried out in pain.

"I should make you pay for my losses tonight, you wretch!" he said to her through clenched teeth. "Next time it will be your rings, your necklaces, everything you possess! For now I will settle for—your jeweled buttons!"

At a stroke he slashed the front of the red gown with his knife, severing the many flashing ornamental buttons from the bodice. They spilled out across the filthy floor. Instantly the men were on their knees, grabbing for the jewels, fighting one another, whooping and snorting with hoarse laughter.

I looked across the table at Adrien and he understood at once that I wanted to leave. We got up and hurried out, picking our way among the scrambling men on the floor, Adrien pressing a coin into the tavernkeeper's outstretched hand as we passed him.

I thought I saw the earl, seated once again at his table, glance briefly in my direction as we crossed the room, but I wasn't certain. He gave no sign that he had recognized me—if indeed he had. Just as we went out I heard the sound of dice landing on a wooden table, and knew that he had resumed his game.

Outside the air was fresh and sweet after the rain. I took a deep breath and then another, waiting for Adrien to bring up our mounts.

Where would the Skottefrauen spend the night, I wondered. Who would prepare her bed? Who would repair her gown? I could still hear her harsh, loud voice—more a man's voice than a woman's, I thought—shrieking in her unknown tongue.

I was glad when Adrien and I had gone far enough along the muddy road so that we could no longer hear the noise from the Inn of the Three Barrels, and there was quiet once again as we rode, under the moonlight, back toward the castle.

TEN

WHAT under heaven were you thinking, child? To go out alone, at night, to a place full of thieves and murderers! Be glad I'm the one who found out about your foolish excursion and not Queen Catherine!"

It was the morning after Adrien and I had gone to the Inn of the Three Barrels and my grandmother Antoinette was sitting in my bedchamber rebuking me, frowning in irritation, her wide, generous mouth turned downward even as she tossed her thin leather gloves from hand to hand across her broad lap.

"I wanted an adventure, grandmamma," I said. "That was all."

"An adventure! You are a queen, child. You are not supposed to be off on adventures, you are supposed to be decorous. And docile. And above all, fertile." As she said the last words she sighed, her voice dropping. "Not that there seems to be any chance of that now. Francis is too ill."

"He may yet recover," I said softly, though I knew that neither my grandmother nor I believed it possible that my dying husband would ever regain his vigor.

My grandmother was returning to the subject of my late night wandering.

"From now on you are to stay where the court is, do you understand? You are never to go outside at night, even if you have an escort. When the court travels, you will travel with it. Otherwise you will stay where you are."

"I understand. I will obey you."

But grandmamma was still agitated. Instead of leaving my bedchamber she continued to sit where she was, slapping her gloves against her palm, rolling her eyes, her breathing rapid.

"I promise not to go out again," I said, hoping this repeated reassurance would calm her. Instead it brought out more exasperation.

"There is a problem," she snapped. "You were seen."

I was astonished.

"One of the servants was in the tavern last night. He recognized Adrien. And he heard Adrien speak to you in a respectful tone. As you were both leaving, he saw your shoes, and recognized them too."

My shoes! I had taken care to keep my face well hidden, to wear modest clothing, a modest cloak, I had removed my jewellery so that no one would suspect that I was anything other than Adrien's humbly-born sister—but I had not thought about my shoes, accustomed as I was to assuming that my long skirts always kept them covered. Yet my shoes were very distinctive, made of soft kidskin and trimmed in golden filigree with bright jewels twinkling from within the swirls of the design. They were the shoes of a highborn woman, costly things that belonged in the royal court and not in a rural village.

Remembering all that had happened the night before, I thought I knew when my shoes would have been seen and my identity revealed. It must have been when the earl stripped the gleaming buttons from the Skottefrauen's bodice and all the men got down on their hands and knees and scrambled for the brilliant stones.

"You can imagine what is being said, and how quickly the story is spreading. That the queen has a hidden life. That she keeps low company. That she seeks out places where her favorite the Earl of Bothwell goes."

"But I did not speak to him," I protested. "Nor he to me."

"It is enough that you were nearby. Or so the story goes. I imagine it becomes more scandalous with every retelling."

I insisted that I was blameless but I knew that the damage had been done. And I feared that my mother-in-law was already at work spreading gossip about me. Saying that I was not only unfaithful, but mad. That I ought to be chained up in a dark place, or worse— condemned to die. For in France, as I knew, wives who committed adultery were often killed, though highborn wives were shielded from this brutality.

I sat down beside my grandmother, close to her, close enough to smell the rich odor of the perfumed pomander she wore at her waist, a mixture of violets and gillyflowers. I needed to feel the reassurance of her presence. I needed her support.

She shook her head.

"I would not be in your place for anything," she said, patting my knee. "You must keep your wits sharp, and your friends close by in case of need."

She stood up then, kissed me and started for the doorway. Before she reached it she paused and turned back toward me again.

"Be careful of that astrologer of hers," she said. "She has brought him back to court. Heaven knows what ghoulish plots he is devising."

The vultures were gathering. I could sense them circling over the court, over my husband's sickbed, over me.

Not my Guise relatives, they were slipping from power. But the others, the Comte de Dampierre and Monsieur de Roncelet, the high and mighty constable Anne de Montmorency, the queen dowager's advisers. The members of Prince Charles's household, Francis's little brother Prince Charles who was next in line for the throne. The clergy waiting to hear of deathbed benefactions. And the ever hungry, ever hopeful courtiers who were always to be seen when momentous events were about to occur, men who watched for opportunities and seized them.

The vultures could smell death, and fresh meat. They meant to gorge themselves. They meant to feast on the entrails of power.

I did not count Michel de Notredame among the vultures. He was not greedy to advance or enrich himself, nor did I think he wished anyone ill. But he valued being high in my mother-in-law's favor, and each time I entered my husband's bedchamber and saw him there, sitting quietly or consulting his books or talking in low tones with Queen Catherine, I remembered what he had said about the deathly worm that was burrowing its way deep into Francis's ear, and how nothing could stop it.

I knew that the best way to counteract the damaging gossip being spread about me in those dangerous days as my husband's life ebbed was to stay close to Francis and show my concern for him. Hour after hour I sat at his bedside, talking to him when he was awake and watching him when he slept. From time to time I knelt on the prie-dieu in one corner of the room, repeating familiar prayers and asking for grace. I asked that Francis be freed of his deep-boring worm, that he might be restored to health, and that I would be guided to do and say the right thing. I prayed for my mother's soul and that my kingdom, Scotland, would be spared destruction.

I watched the royal doctors when they came in to examine Francis and stood together afterwards, whispering and looking as doctors always look when they do not expect their patients to survive: they looked grim. The apothecaries were dosing Francis with rhubarb and the stench of the herb permeated the room.

Poor Francis slept most of the time. I did my best to ignore the others who came and went, peering down into Francis's pale face and asking the doctors how he was—by which they meant, of course, how much longer was he likely to last.

Mine was a harrowing vigil. For poor wretched Francis was not only mad with the terrible pain in his head, his mind too was in

CAROLLY ERICKSON

torment. Everything and everyone terrified him. When he was awake his eyes were wide with fear—fear of shadows, even.

"Assassins, assassins!" he cried weakly as he flailed his arms to beat back nonexistent attackers. He lashed out at me, no longer knowing who I was. I had to duck to evade him. Even when his mother came in, wearing mourning black and bringing rhubarb tea, he did not recognize her and practically knocked the tray she carried out of her arms. To my horror, I saw the ghost of a smile cross her plain features when she looked down at her son, helpless and in the grip of his fears. Soon she would be in full control, as regent for the new King Charles. In her mind she had already moved from grieving the loss of Francis to triumphing over her enemies, the Guises, over me, over the entire court. She was about to become sovereign in all but name. And I, Queen Mary, was, I feared, about to become her first victim.

ELEVEN

FRANCIS'S funeral was magnificent even though I heard it whispered that Queen Catherine had had to borrow heavily from her Italian bankers to afford it. All the nobles and officials, both old and new, now clustered around the new king, young King Charles, and crowded his bedchamber. I was ignored, which suited me, except that I continued to fear the queen and to recall the dark future her astrologer had predicted for me.

I wore black to honor my late husband and to follow court etiquette, but inwardly I was not in mourning. Francis's long illness, and his increasing bitterness, had driven away any sorrow I might have felt at losing him. And there was another force at work as well: the strong and forceful Earl of Bothwell was more and more on my mind.

I went to the earl for advice after Francis died and found him, not in the comfortable lodgings he had enjoyed as one of the king's bed-chamber gentlemen but in a cold bare room over one of the stables. He was sitting on the floor, meanly dressed, rubbing a piece of leather with a cloth. He did not seem surprised to see me.

"I wondered how soon you would find me here, Your Highness. As you see, I have been removed from the palace. I no longer have an official position, and I am apparently not welcome as a guest. My mother-in-law the queen is not pleased to honor me with an invitation to stay on."

"In that, I fear, we are the same. She would rather I did not stay on either. Will you go back to Scotland soon?" I asked after a pause.

"If I must. I have a ship in the harbor. My own ship. The *Black Messenger*. She can be ready to sail on very short notice."

"Why delay?"

He put down the piece of leather he was polishing and looked at me through half-closed eyes.

"Because of you, madam."

I felt a jolt, a pang.

"Me?"

"You are my queen. I am Scots, and you are Queen of Scots. You are my concern."

"You are gallant."

"I serve the Scottish throne. Against Arran and the Protestant lords, against the English, even against the dark arts of a certain Michel de Notredame who, if I am not mistaken, wishes you ill."

This comment about Monsieur de Notredame took me aback.

"I was not aware of any ill will from Monsieur de Notredame. Are you certain this is not mere servants' gossip?"

"There is certainly plenty of servants' gossip making its way through the palace. It has even reached the stables. For example, Your Highness, there is a story about you. About you going to a certain tavern on a rainy night and observing what went on there. This story, it seems, is reliable."

So he saw me there, I thought. Had he too recognized me by my lovely shoes? I felt a sudden surge of indignation.

"If you are indeed a servant of the Scottish throne, then you will not sit in the presence of your queen."

He got to his feet.

"Pardon me, Your Highness." He swept me a bow—such an

elaborate bow, there in the dark dirty room, that I could not help but feel that he was mocking me. Why was it that the earl's signs of regard invariably seemed to have an edge of contempt?

I ignored the insult.

"If I had gone to that tavern, I might have seen a very alarming sight. The sight of a certain woman. A frightening woman. A woman who made a nearly fatal attack with a knife on a Scots nobleman who was lucky to escape with his life."

The earl sighed and spread his hands in a hopeless gesture. There was no longer any hint of insult or contempt in his manner.

"Well then, let us speak frankly. You came to see me at the Inn of the Three Barrels, I recognized you, we did not communicate—at least, not directly."

Our eyes met. All of a sudden he looked older, more burdened. I felt a stronger connection to him than ever, though I could not have given that connection a name.

"Let us speak frankly, Jamie," I repeated, my voice low. "As friends?"

"Very well, Your Highness, if you wish it. As friends."

"My name is Mary."

"I cannot call you that."

"What then?"

He laughed. A small, soft, intimate laugh. "Orange Blossom," he whispered.

"What!"

"It is how I think of you."

I shook my head, smiling. Such a sweet, intimate name.

"Then I command it," I said, laughing. "When no one else can hear, I permit you to call your queen Orange Blossom. Now then, who was that fearsome woman in the tavern?"

Once again Jamie—I thought of him from then on as Jamie— gave a hopeless shrug.

"I am being pursued by a Fury. I won her in a card game. Now I can't get rid of her. I call her the Encumbrance."

"You are speaking in riddles."

He sat down again on the floor, and I looked around for a bench, but there was none. With a grunt of exasperation he sprang to his feet again, went out of the room and down the stairs. I heard voices. In a moment he had returned, carrying a saddle, which he put down on the floor for me to sit on. I thanked him and sat.

"Last year your mother sent me to Denmark, as her envoy," he began when he had resumed his own place on the floor. "I had business at the court. I stayed on for a month or so. There were many Norwegians there as well as Danes (Norway being ruled by Denmark, as you know) and in the evenings they liked to drink and play cards. I won many a game. I won nearly enough to buy my ship, as it happens."

"The *Black Messenger.*"

"Yes. She used to be called the *Whale of Trondheim*, but—well, a change was necessary—"

"I can understand that."

"One night we played until dawn," he said, chortling at the memory. "We drank so much we could hardly see, our heads were spinning so fast. One of the players was a young Norwegian, a nobleman, hopelessly beside himself with drink, with no skill at all in his play. He lost all his money, and then began betting his possessions—his horse, his rings, even a lock of his dead mother's hair. Can you imagine! He actually bet a lock of his dead mother's hair!" He shook his head, amazed at the memory.

"Finally, when everything else he had was gone except his title, he bet his betrothed, his bride-to-be from a rich family. She wasn't there in the flesh, of course. Well, I thought it was nothing more than a bizarre jest. I didn't care. I grinned, drained my goblet, took the bet, and won. I certainly never expected to see the young nobleman again—or his fiancée."

He looked up at the ceiling, shook his head, and went on. "I was wrong. The woman came to find me, and said she was my betrothed now, and that I would have to marry her. The nobleman had abandoned her, she said, and had gone away to Iceland. Her family had renounced her. She is the daughter of a Norwegian admiral, and as I am hereditary admiral of the Scottish fleet I must keep her father's goodwill. We rely on the Norwegians to crew our few ships, as you may know."

"What a cruel dilemma! But you are unmarried. Why not just marry the woman, rather than become her victim?"

"You have seen her. You know why."

"She is certainly plain, and graceless, but not hideous."

Jamie looked as if I had just handed him a plate of stinking rot from the refuse pile.

"She is not only plain as a pikestaff, but a violent, vengeful scold. Even though she does have a dowry of seven thousand ecus. And I have half of it—at least I did have half of it until I lost it to a Dutchman who, I'm sure, was cheating." The last words were mumbled, his voice dying away as he spoke. He did not meet my eyes.

"No wonder she follows you. She wants her dowry back."

"Let her take it! I told her the Dutchman's name. It's Lukas Korthals. I wish to God she would follow him and not me. She says she prefers me. Besides, she claims she is carrying my child."

At that I began to feel wary. Had Jamie slept with the woman who called herself the Scottish wife? And if he denied it, could I be certain he was telling me the truth?

"And is she?" I asked, trying to keep my voice even.

He spat. "Of course not. If there is a bastard, it belongs to that drunken young lord who gambled her away. Or some blind man."

I thought for a moment. "She must be paid off."

"If only I could—"

"Can you borrow from your friend Cristy?"

"He only lends me gambling money. And he takes more interest than the Italian bankers."

We were both silent for a time. Jamie went back to polishing his bit of leather, and I began to ponder. Jamie had a dilemma to solve— but so did I. And mine, it seemed, was on a vaster scale.

Leaving him in his room over the stables, I returned to my bedchamber, the bedchamber of an eighteen-year-old widow and dowager queen whose prospects were unclear and whose ability to choose her path was about to be tested.

TWELVE

IT was not long after Francis died that I received a letter from my half-brother Lord James Stewart in Scotland. I had a dim memory of him, from the time when I was a young child, before I left for France. He was much older than I was, already a tall, good-looking, solemn young man. Now, as I knew from Jamie and from my mother's letters, he was even more solemn, with an air of religiosity ("terribly full of himself," in Jamie's words) and a sense of mission.

Lord James was writing to me, his queen, yet the tone of his letter was that of a ruler, not a subject. (Nor was it that of an affectionate brother writing to his younger sister.) He was graciously inviting me to return to my realm, the invitation extended on behalf of the Protestant lords.

I reread the letter several times, reading the Scots with ease—for Scots is very like English, and my English is good—and looking for clues as to his purpose in writing. I found none.

I did not send a response right away, for I had not yet decided what my best course of action was. It was clear to me that my troubled realm of Scotland needed a firm ruler. No doubt my presence there would help to shore up the waning power of the throne. That was a reason to accept my half-brother's invitation and go to Scotland as soon as possible—which, I knew, would please my mother-in-law no end.

Had Lord James written because he wanted me to give him the power to rule in my absence? Not as regent, perhaps, but as my delegate? And if I were to make him my delegate, what then? Might he seek to overthrow me, Scotland's anointed queen, and establish himself and his heirs as rightful rulers?

This possibility worried me, and led me to thoughts of England, where my cousin Elizabeth clung to power against much opposition and where, if I had the armed might, I could challenge her and take the throne as my own. Could I do such a bold and aggressive thing? Part of me thought I could. But I had no army, only what aid I could expect from the Scottish lords and from the French, whose military help to my mother had not been sufficient to keep the English out of my realm.

While I was mulling over these questions my practical grandmother put a quite different set of thoughts into my head.

"You must marry, and soon, my dear," she advised. "The Spanish prince Don Carlos is unmarried. He is Catholic, and rich—at least his father King Philip is rich—and one day he will rule over much of the known world. Of course," she added, "I have heard there are disadvantages."

"And what are those?"

She rolled her eyes.

"They say he is hunchbacked and crippled and disturbed in mind and that he has a fondness for roasting small animals alive."

"Oh. I think I will look elsewhere than Spain for a husband, thank you."

"Just as well. His father Philip is a terrible man, from all that I hear. Not at all amusing company. And then there is his great-grandmother Joan the Mad, who carried her husband's corpse around with her wherever she went—"

"Please, grandmamma, I have heard more than enough about that family—"

"You have a great many Guise cousins, you know. You could do worse than choose from among them."

"But they have no royal blood."

She could think of no answer to that, and so we spoke no more of marriage, though the subject was much on my mind.

Meanwhile I decided to do what I could to eliminate the more immediate problem of the so-called Scottish wife, who continued to pester and threaten Jamie. It ought to be easy enough to convince her to leave him alone, I thought, if only I could offer her enough money. Unfortunately I had no money of my own, and as a rule I needed none. In the past whenever I had wanted a few coins I had always gone to Francis's treasurer, who had supplied me with funds. But now Francis's household was disbanded. There was no treasurer any longer, and no treasury.

So I went to find King Charles.

It took me quite a while to discover where the young king had gone. His bedchamber was full of people as usual, but he was not among them, and when I inquired where I might find him I was given only evasive answers or blank stares. I knew that he liked his dogs and horses, and so I set off for the kennels. But the kennel master had not seen him, and none of the grooms could tell me where to find him either.

I was just about to give up when I heard my name called in a childish voice.

I looked around. There was a low storage shed nearby, its interior too dim for me to tell whether there might be anyone inside. I went up to the door. The hasp was open.

"Mary!"

I peered inside. There, sitting on a sack of oats, was the twelve-year-old king. He was wearing his long thick hawking glove and perched on the glove was a sleek bird that turned its head toward me when I entered the shed.

"Your Majesty," I said, with a bow. A gleeful smile lit up his small face.

"Don't tell them where I am," he whispered loudly. "Come in and close the door." I did as he asked.

"I won't say anything," I said. "Why are you hiding?"

He sighed. "They are always after me. Especially my mother. I have to get away. I come and visit Esme, and feed her mice." He stroked the falcon's head gently. I saw then that a rodent tail dangled from her sharp beak.

"Your Majesty, I must ask a favor."

"Ask whatever you like, Mary."

"When your brother was alive, I would go to him when I needed money. Now that he is in heaven, I must turn to you."

"My mother keeps all the money. In a big chest under her bed."

"Do you have no treasurer of your own?"

He shook his head.

"Well then, I suppose I shall just have to ask your mother."

The king frowned. "No, don't do that."

"Why not?"

"It would not be safe. You are not safe."

"Is your mother's astrologer casting spells on me?"

"Perhaps. But I know that she asked her chef to feed you something that would make you sick."

The suggestion alone was enough to make my stomach start to churn, there in the dark little shed.

"I hope you are not sick, Mary."

"No," I managed to say, holding my stomach. "Now that you have warned me, I will be fine. Thank you, Your Highness."

"Would you like to watch Esme fly?"

"Very much, but it will have to be another day. Thank you, I'll be going now. I hope no one finds you."

"Goodbye Mary."

His tone was plangent. I made certain to close the door of the shed as I left.

With the young king's revelation all became clear to me: I had to get away from Queen Catherine before she poisoned me. I had to get as far away as I could, as quickly as I could. I would go to Scotland. I would be safe there, among my relations. Until I left I would eat nothing that had been prepared in the royal kitchens.

I went to my mother-in-law's moneylender and made over to him one of my estates in Poitou. He gave me ten thousand gold ecus. Then I went to Jamie and spilled out some of the flashing, glittering coins across the floor of his dingy room.

"Here," I said. "Here is enough money to pay the dowry of your tormentor, the one you call the Encumbrance. Your troubles with her are at an end. As for me, I am bound for Scotland, if you will take me, aboard the *Black Messenger*."

THIRTEEN

I had to wrap two warm woolen blankets around my shoulders when we entered the fog-shrouded roads of Leith harbor and Jamie took the pilot aboard. It was still summertime, in that August of 1561, but it felt like winter to me, accustomed as I had been for so many years to the sunny summers of France. A cold wind whipped through the shrouds of the *Black Messenger,* and before long a cold rain began to beat down, forcing me to go below and drink a goblet of heated wine with cinnamon and sugar to try to warm myself.

Our welcome to Scotland was only slightly less chilly than the weather. My half-brother Lord James Stewart did manage, after several hours, to come to the harbor bringing half a dozen others with him and a ragtag cordon of mounted soldiers. But there were no crowds to greet me, no pageantry, no choirs singing or musicians playing or fountains overflowing with wine. There was not even a coach waiting to take me to Edinburgh.

"My dearest sister," brother James said in his deep, grave voice, bending low in a bow, "we did not expect you for several more days. I know the French think of us Scots as barbarians, and I am afraid this poor greeting will only make you think less of us."

"I am one of you, am I not?" I responded, taking Lord James's hand and raising him up. The men with him were looking at me appraisingly.

"Our brothers Robert and John," Lord James said, indicating a grinning, supercilious-looking young man and a shorter, darker companion. I barely recognized Robert, and John was a stranger to me. Our father King James had had many children, most of them bastards; I knew I was going to need to become acquainted with them.

"The Earl of Arran, whom you know by his French title as the Duke of Châtelherault." I felt my hands close into fists at the sound of the name. So this was the infamous Arran, the man who had put a spell on my mother and made her so terribly sick, the man who had led the rebellious Lords of the Congregation in fighting her and her French soldiers. The man who had burned Jamie's castle and torched his fields. The traitor to Scotland—and to me.

He was stout, round-faced, aging. When he bowed to me, his legs were a little unsteady under him. His face wore a bland smile of welcome. I stared at him stonily.

"And this, Your Highness, is our famed man of God, the reverend John Knox."

Now there stepped forward a tough-looking, black-clad man whose eyes burned with a furious energy. He was not young, yet he had the feral force of youth, and I sensed no reverence from him, no acknowledgment of my authority, in fact. He did not bow, or even remove his hat.

I smiled courteously and extended my hand. I expected my smile to melt the sharp disapproving frown chiseled on his features, but there was no change.

"Jezebel!" he cried, ignoring my outstretched hand. "Puppet of the Roman Antichrist! Repent or face eternal torment!"

Jamie, who was standing to my right and slightly behind me, let out a bellow of rage and lunged toward the preacher, but my half-brother James intervened.

"Can we not restrain ourselves in the presence of the queen?" he said blandly, placing himself between Jamie and Knox.

"I am not accustomed to being insulted by clergymen," I said, standing my ground, "though I understand Protestants have few scruples in that regard."

"Judgment is mine, saith the Lord," roared Knox.

"I believe the verse reads, 'Vengeance is mine,' not judgment."

"Vengeance follows judgment, as night follows day," Knox shouted. He stood squarely before me, as threatening a presence as I had ever encountered. He was not armed, he did not point a pistol at me or raise a sword. Yet there was a terrifying strength in him, or running through him, and I felt the menace of that strength. I felt my heart beating rapidly, my breath coming quickly. There was a low rumbling sound in my ears with every beat.

"If I have sinned, sir, it is because all men are cursed with a sinful nature. 'For all have sinned and come short of the glory of God,' as the Bible says. As a good Catholic it is my custom to confess my sins often, and humbly. I do not need you to point them out."

"Aye, all men sin—and all women sin twice as often, and twice as wickedly. It is an abomination for such wicked sinners to rule over men!"

"I am well aware of your vitriolic book on that subject. In it I believe you vilify my late mother, who was as good a woman as God ever made."

"That's not saying much," I heard the preacher mutter.

"I caution you, Mr. Knox. Do not speak ill of my mother in my presence, or you will regret it."

My mother had written to me about the book preacher Knox had written, a book in which he denounced what he called "the monstrous rule of women," and criticized several queens and regents, including my cousin Queen Elizabeth and my mother-in-law Queen Catherine.

The sky had darkened, a dense black storm cloud was approaching the harbor. Once again my brother James intervened, suggesting that we make our way to the royal palace of Holyrood before it began to rain.

Horses were brought and we started off, though we hadn't gone far before our progress was halted by a commotion in the street.

Hundreds of people were gathering to watch what appeared to be a procession making its way down a dirty road whose gutters stank with sewage. I am tall, I can see over the heads of others—even other mounted horsemen. What I saw, moving along that street at a marching pace, was a boy—he could not have been older than my brother-in-law King Charles in France—dressed in the highland blanket they call a plaid, and carrying a ghoulish trophy.

It was a pair of legs.

Bloody, severed legs.

"Hear all people!" the boy was shouting, holding the legs high so that everyone could see them. "And hark all ye nations! These be the limbs of Red Colquhoun, who lay with the wife of the Great MacNeil! Let all men take warning!"

"The MacNeil, the MacNeil." The words were repeated, passed from spectator to spectator. Here were the people of Leith, my subjects, speaking in tones of eerie awe about a distant Highland laird. Far from being horrified at the sight of the mangled legs they were struck solemn, revering the Great MacNeil and the evidence of his power to take vengeance on an enemy.

Vengeance. I had thought, coming to Scotland, that I would be the one seeking vengeance, against those who had hounded and betrayed and cursed my dear mother. But I found myself surrounded by others far more vengeful than I, first the unholy reverend Knox and the offending Lords of the Congregation (whose faint welcome had insulted my majesty) and now, by the brutal MacNeil and the townspeople who venerated him.

The boy with the legs had passed, and the women in the crowd began an uncanny wailing, an unearthly sound that I recognized from my childhood as a lament for the dead. I signaled for my escort to hurry on past and we made our way toward Edinburgh and Holyrood.

That night, settled in my bed in the palace, I dropped off to sleep almost at once. The events of the day had tired me, and left me wrung out with many concerns. My faithful Margaret Carwood had seen to it that the fire in my room was piled high with wood, and had warmed my bedlinens and put out a thick nightgown for me to wear, and with it a pair of knitted short stockings to keep my feet from freezing.

I was dreaming—and then I was awakened. I was awakened by singing. But it was not the lament for the dead, it was a psalm tune. A Protestant church tune.

I got out of bed and went to the window. The courtyard below was full of people, carrying torches and Bibles. All appeared to be in somber garb, long dark plain robes with no adornment. They stood there, a solid phalanx of worshippers, as if in church, intoning the dirgelike notes of the psalm. It was a mournful scene, all the more mournful in that it was being staged for my benefit.

For these people of Edinburgh were, like the reverend Knox, giving me a very pointed message. That I, a Catholic and a sinner, must repent. That I must become one of them, no longer a queen in her colorful bejeweled finery, living her life of vice, but a robe-wearing, humble penitent, carrying a Bible and singing a dirge to the Lord.

I threw up the window sash and looked down on my people. My congregation, as I thought of them at that moment.

"I am your queen!" I shouted over the strong roar of voices. "I am your Catholic queen, Mary, daughter of King James and rightful ruler of this realm! And I command you to go to your homes and leave me in peace!"

I sent the guards down into the courtyard to break up the demonstration, and as I watched from my window the sober penitents, still singing, began to make their way out of the courtyard and back along the road that led toward Edinburgh Castle on its crag. They did not hurry their departure, nor did they take any notice of me, there at the window, so absorbed were they in their song.

I went back to bed, and tried to get to sleep, but for a long time I continued to hear, in the distance, the doleful melody of the psalm.

FOURTEEN

FROM the start, there was never any question of my trying to please the Lords of the Congregation or any of the great clan chiefs—who held the highlands in thrall—or the frightening John Knox.

I went my own way, ignoring what those who opposed me said and thought. For was I not Queen of the Scots, of the blood royal, anointed and sanctioned by God and the church? The true church, I mean, the Roman church, not the rebel church of the Protestants.

I did what I liked, boldly and—as I see it now—rashly and blindly, confident that as queen I could do anything I wanted to do, confusing majesty and authority with real power. It was not that I forgot everything my mother had told me about the wolves, the savage predators that invaded the court (and were often to be found within it). It was more that I was young and arrogant, full of myself and my own exaggerated importance. I had no one to restrain me, or advise me wisely and impartially. My half-brother James cared more for the rights of the Protestant church—and for his own advancement—than for the rights of the crown. My shrewd grandmother (how I missed her!) was too far away to serve as my councilor. Jamie was preoccupied with his feud with Arran and in fact I expected any day to hear that the two of them had fought a duel.

"How I hate that weak, conniving bastard!" Jamie spat, glowering as he paced restlessly in my small presence chamber at Holyrood. "He won't even fight me! I sent him a challenge but he declined. He's a poor swordsman, they say. He's only good at wrecking other people's castles. I ought to wreck one of his!"

He stopped pacing and glared at me.

"You know what his plan is, don't you? He wants you to marry that daft son of his."

I shuddered. I knew only too well that young James Hamilton, Arran's son, was an erratic, weak-minded man, completely unsuited to becoming the husband of the queen. And I wanted nothing to do with him.

Feeling oppressed by the somber, angry men around me, the mournful singing of the Protestants who continued to serenade me night after night, the harangues of the reverend Knox and the schemes of Arran and the other Scots magnates, I obstinately followed my own path of pleasure.

I played tennis with the servant boys—and sometimes won. I rode Bravane through the green countryside, uphill and down, even daring, at times, to ride like a man with one trousered leg on each side of the saddle. Men's clothing served me well when I went in disguise along the narrow wynds of Edinburgh and up and down the hill paths that ringed the town. I danced, lustily and with abandon, to the music that was played in my chamber, the drums thumping and the lutes and pipes and sackbuts blending in raucous harmony in measure after measure. The more the Protestants sang, the more I danced, leaping and twirling with vigor as if to affirm life and joy in the face of their endless wailing.

And I indulged my delight in beautiful, fashionable clothes, for I was then (if I do say so myself) coming into that span of years when a woman's beauty is at its peak, and I was—everyone agreed on this—a very lovely woman.

I ordered my dressmaker Mr. Skut to create for me dozens of gowns in shades of fiery red and russet velvet, golden amber and rich blue and green satin and taffeta, with costly trims of pearls and Hainault lace, gold and silver embroidery and wide ermine-cuffed sleeves. I sent to France for the newest styles in headdresses, some steepled, some heart-shaped, all sparkling with jewels and designed to flatter even the plainest face. My wardrobe trunks overflowed with gilded gloves and net stockings, thick sables and long ropes of pearls—all of which I wore, even on the meanest occasions, my colorful adornment in sharp contrast to the stark black robes of the devout.

My extravagance was much talked of, and before long I had a visit from John Knox.

"Forty gowns!" he said as he swept unceremoniously into my presence. "Nor four, but forty!"

"Forty-two, to be exact," I heard Margaret Carwood murmur as she folded some pairs of sleeves and laid them in a basket.

"Waste! Luxury and waste! And how do you think to pay for it all, girl?"

"I am not a girl, I am your queen. I feel certain the Scottish treasury will pay Mr. Skut's bills."

"And where do you think you are then? In France? That rich land? Scotland is poor! Look around you! There is no wealth here!"

I had noticed that there were no swarms of Italian moneylenders in Scotland, and I thought that significant. (It is no paradox that moneylenders gather where the landed rich are short of cash.) I had no idea how much was in the treasury, no one told me and I had not asked.

Knox raved on, castigating me for putting rouge on my cheeks and marring my face by plucking my eyebrows and torturing my hair with curling tongs.

"I know of your light ways," he thundered. "And I know that you read pagan books, and visit low taverns, and keep company with a man who is not your husband—"

"What man?"

"What man? Why, the one who put a spell on you, enchanted you. The sorcerer Bothwell."

This made me laugh.

"The Earl of Bothwell serves me, as he served my mother. He is liege man to the crown."

"He is your partner in fornication!"

"That is your perverse imagination and nothing more."

But Knox would not be swayed from his conviction of my trespass. "Your sin is known to the world!" he shouted, shaking his fist. "And to God. You will be punished! You will be cast into the flames of hell!"

As irritated as I was alarmed, I waved the preacher away, and he left, escorted by the guards captain Adrien and another of my guardsmen. But his tirade worried me, for if gossip against me was spreading, especially gossip about my chastity, then it would be harder for me to maintain my authority.

I could already see that the forces arrayed against me were gathering strength. When I went to hear mass in my private chapel, my priests were assaulted and the service disrupted. Voices were heard claiming that subjects did not owe obedience to their ruler—if the ruler did not behave properly. And most ominous of all, the strongest of the clans in eastern Scotland, the Gordons, had begun a rebellion against me and I was going to have to fight them.

It took a month and more for our military expedition to get under way.

With the aid of my brother James I assembled the crown troops, Scots and French, and summoned the fighting men of the loyal clans, oversaw the gathering of horses and foodstuffs, the tents and wagons, the guns and other arms. James was to be my commander, he was experienced in battle and had a personal grudge against the Gordons which made him all the more eager to punish them.

At last all was ready and we set out, making our way slowly northward, a long procession of riders and carts and marching men on foot and on horseback. Blocked and damaged roads held us back, and bad weather delayed us, there were bands of thieves who attacked stragglers and I slept every night with a loaded pistol under my pillows. My shoes were full of mud, I felt sticky and dirty all over and my hair (oh! if my grandmother could have seen it! How horrified she would have been!) was full of dust and dirt. (I did not bother dressing it, I merely pulled it back under a simple cap such as shepherd girls wear.) I was often hungry and thirsty and cold, and so tired, so very tired at the end of each long day.

And dear Mother of God, how I loved it all!

It was exhilarating, being out in the wild country, in danger, never knowing when the Gordon men or their clan allies might descend on us, erupting out of the misty hills in their hundreds, never able to be certain of the loyalty of my own fighting men who might, without warning, decide to join the enemy. My brother had cautioned me that George Gordon, clan chief who was known as the proud Cock of the North, had sworn to kidnap me and carry me off to his captured castle of Inverness, and that many men were coming to join his fighting force.

"If we can take the castle, and seize his guns, that should stop him, at least for awhile," James told me. "I pray every hour that he does not have help from the English." Every time a clan rebelled, it seemed, they made a bargain with the English, who were ever hungry to take over my kingdom and who sought whatever allies they could buy. My brother knew this very well, having joined with the English himself when he led the Lords of the Congregation against my mother.

I was doing my best to get used to the rapidly shifting alliances that were the essence of Scottish political life; the monarchy, I was beginning to believe, was but one among a host of factions, each bent on defending its own interests—no matter what the cost to others. Lasting loyalties were unknown, all bonds were temporary and fleeting.

Amid a torrent of rain we assaulted Inverness Castle, and even though half our guns refused to fire because of the bad weather, our forces proved stronger than those of the Gordons, who after a brief defense, ran like hares fleeing the swift hounds, and deserted their commander, whom we hanged as a traitor.

But the defiant Cock of the North, George Gordon himself, was not in the castle, he had taken many of his men to Corrichie and so we pursued him there.

I begged my brother James not to hinder me in my desire to take the field along with the men.

"I can fight!" I swore. "I can draw a bow, I can ride well, and Bravane is a courageous mount—"

"But can you wield a sword? If you are unhorsed, can you fight on foot against a man twice your weight? I think not. And I would be a traitor if I allowed the Scots queen to risk her own fragile life on the battlefield. Especially when she has no child to succeed her."

I had to give in to James's logic. I stayed out of the fighting, watching from a high point, cringing and crying out as fatal blows were struck, urging my men on even though I knew they could not hear me. I was with them in spirit, and when the noisy melee was over, and my men chased the last of the surviving Gordons away, I went down onto the battlefield and walked, feeling an unfamiliar mixture of triumph, pity and sorrow, among the fallen.

I had never seen a battle before, nor the gruesome aftermath of one. Holding my scented pomander to my nose, I stepped out onto the sodden ground, averting my eyes at first from the still, staring faces of men past help, holding my ears when the poor dying horses snorted and screamed in agony, pawing feebly at the air, wishing I could ease the pain of the wounded who lay in their own blood, coughing and choking and calling out for aid.

I saw to it that all possible aid was given, not only to my own men but to the injured Gordons, and that the throats of the wretched horses were slit.

Before long I was trembling and weeping even as I tried to minister to the suffering around me.

"Here now, this is no place for a lass." My brother James put a kindly arm around my shoulders and began to lead me away from the carnage. I confess that it all upset me far more than I had thought it would.

"It is a victory, is it not?"

"It is. Clan Gordon will not rebel again for awhile."

We walked on, then James stopped abruptly.

"My Lord," he murmured, then began reciting the twenty-third psalm in Scots.

"What is it?" I asked him when he had finished his brief recitation.

He pointed to a body, the body of a grossly fat old man wrapped in a plaid, a tall bonnet with three feathers on its head, the neck and chest deep red with blood.

"It's the Cock of the North himself," James said. "The old warrior. Many a time I've fought with him. Oh, he was a fierce one, when the battle rage was on him. God rest his soul."

Just then a boy came by with a basket.

"Here, lad," James called out to him. "I've got another for you." He took a long knife from his belt and, walking over to the corpse of George Gordon, lifted one stiff arm and deftly cut off the thumb of the pale hand. He tossed the thumb into the basket—which, I saw to my horror, was full of thumbs.

My stomach lurched. I put my hand over my mouth.

"Yes indeed," James was saying. "A fierce one. But now he's just another thumb in the basket."

FIFTEEN

He burst into the banquet like an angry bull. Flanked by his friend Cristy Ricarton and another man, the unsavory Red Ormiston of Liddesdale, he strode past the long tables of merrymakers, alarming them and bringing the noisy revels in the room to a sudden halt.

He and the others were armed, and he wore his customary jeweled earring and jeweled codpiece. He came rapidly toward me and swept me the swiftest and most shallow of bows before shouting, loudly enough for the entire room to hear, "You killed my father-in-law!"

Startled by the sight of him, and unnerved by the suddenness of his appearance in the hall along with his armed companions, I nonetheless sat where I was, calmly eating a piece of chicken and taking a sip of wine from the goblet at my elbow.

At length I responded.

"My Lord of Bothwell, we celebrate tonight our victory over the rebellious Gordons. You are interrupting our celebration. Remove yourselves."

"Not until someone accepts my challenge!"

"There will be no fighting here tonight."

Jamie drew his sword, and in the same instant Cristy and Red

Ormiston drew theirs, and into the banquet hall came a dozen others, shouting, swords raised aloft.

I stood then, and called for the swordsmen to leave, my words drowned out by the clangor of metal and the noise of my guardsmen engaging Jamie and his followers.

In an instant the banquet was ruined, the long tables overturned, the heaping platters of meat and fish, the puddings and bowls of sauces lying in aromatic heaps atop the rushes, the wines running out and staining the table linens.

Jamie, more belligerent than I had ever seen him, was fighting with the guardsmen, swinging his heavy sword like a madman. What possessed him, I wondered. He had not been seen at court for many weeks. He had been noticeably absent from the fighting force that I had taken northward against the Gordons, even though I had summoned him to join it. What had he meant about my having killed his father-in-law? He was not married. And why was he keeping company with the notorious Red Ormiston, said to be a thief and a cutthroat, an outlaw and a receiver of stolen goods?

The banquet had become a brawl. Objects were flying through the air, some quite near me. I heard Adrien's voice.

"Your Highness, come away." His hand on my arm was firm and reassuring. I let him lead me out of the room, shielding me with his body. He took me to my apartments and left me there, secure behind two thick oaken doors. An hour later he returned, this time leading a snarling Jamie.

"We have restored order," Adrien announced through the door. "But the Lord Bothwell demands to see you. He says you won't deny him."

I wanted to shout, "Take him to the dungeon," I was furious, but something held me back. I hesitated, I could hear Jamie alternately moaning and cursing.

"Take him away," I said sharply, but almost immediately I changed my mind. "No, bring him in. What of the others who were with him?"

"Most have been caught and put under guard. Red Ormiston got away."

"Damn!"

"Shall I bring the earl in now?"

I straightened my shoulders and prepared myself. I was still very angry, yet at the same time I was aware of feeling something else. Something softer. Something that made me vulnerable. This irritated me.

"Let him come in," I said, putting a cold steely edge on my words.

Jamie stumbled into my bedchamber, his clothes torn and stained, his jewel-encrusted codpiece awry, his breathing ragged. He coughed and sputtered. His forehead was bleeding, and a strip of dirty linen had been wrapped clumsily around the wound. His hands were tied together behind his back.

I resisted an impulse to undo the crude bandage and tend his injury. Instead I glared in angry silence at this man who I had thought was my friend, and who had been my mother's staunch friend and supporter, but who now seemed like a stranger to me. A dangerous, brawling, destructive stranger.

The silence lengthened.

"Hell and damnation, woman, my head feels like a burst cannonball. Just go ahead and hang me, or whatever gruesome torment you have in mind, and get it over with!"

I continued to stare at him angrily, but said nothing, while Jamie, his pain evident on his grimacing features, continued to spit out oaths and talk wildly of my putting him to death.

"I ought to have you thrown into a dungeon for what you and your minions did tonight. And for your failure to answer my summons to join with the army."

"Do it then," he muttered, his voice low, its tone less wild.

"I think perhaps I shall. But first you will tell me what you imagined you were doing, bringing an entire band of armed retainers into your sovereign's court, a notorious thief and murderer among them."

Jamie shook his aching head.

"Ormiston brought me the news that the great George Gordon is dead. I sent up a mighty wail of outrage at that news, I can tell you. I rode here to take revenge. My men followed me."

"You are not a Gordon. Why should you want revenge?"

He sighed. He was obviously suffering, and not only from the pain in his head.

"If you will unshackle me, and let me sit, I will tell you."

"Tell me first."

He was suffering, and I was glad of it.

"I am a Gordon." He looked at me for the first time since entering the room. In that look I thought I saw, not defiance or belligerence, but defeat. And with it, sorrow.

"I am pledged to marry Jean Gordon, daughter of the great Gordon you killed."

At first I reacted only to the accusation that I had unjustly taken the field against a declared enemy, and not to the revelation of Jamie's betrothal.

"He was a rebel. He meant to dethrone me. I had to stop him. It is what my mother would have done," I added.

"And with less success," he conceded, wincing as he spoke.

"I needed you to ride with me, to help me."

"I could not."

We were speaking plainly. What Jamie was saying was no more or less than the truth. Clan loyalties ran very deep, and could not be betrayed without great cost. He had chosen to align himself with the Gordons. Therefore he could not fight against them.

"Please," he said.

"Sit," I told him. Gratefully he sank down heavily onto a bench, his hands still tied awkwardly behind him.

"It's my sister. She insisted. If I didn't pledge myself to Jean, she said, then Jean would marry a McCloud. She threatened to use her powers on me. I didn't dare go against her. And she is my sister, after all. What she's saying is for my own good, much as I hate hearing it, being forced to do it."

He ended in a spasm of coughing.

My anger had lessened. I went over to my wash basin, took a cloth and dipped it in the water. Then I went to him and gently wiped his bloody forehead. He winced at my touch, but I continued, pausing to untie his hands. When I had cleaned his face I undid the crude bandage and tried to clean the wound as well. He will have a scar, I thought. Not a battle scar, honorably won, but a scar from a brawl. A brawl he provoked.

He fights when he is frustrated, when things go against him, I thought. When things happen that hurt him. What was hurting him now?

"I am not going to have you tortured, or kept in the castle dungeon. You must ask my formal pardon, on your knees, in the presence of the court, however."

"And Cristy too? He means you no harm. He is merely loyal to me."

"Yes, Cristy too. But the others must be punished."

He nodded.

As I bent low over his forehead, he surprised me by reaching up to my face with one hand, and rubbing one knuckle against my cheek. He drew it along, slowly.

"So soft, so soft," he murmured.

I knew in that moment that there had been much more between us all along than friendship. I knew what was hurting him. He was fond of me. Very fond. He did not want to marry another woman.

I caught his hand in mine.

"Orange Blossom," he said, "you know as well as I how it is with us. We highborn folk cannot follow our inclinations. We must do as our honor requires. As our families dictate."

"Must we, always?" In that moment I wanted more than anything to kiss his rough hand, to kiss his poor injured face.

We looked into each other's eyes.

"Ah! If only . . ." he began. Then the oaken doors opened and my stepbrother James was ushered in.

I quickly let go of Jamie's hand, but not so quickly that James was unaware of the intimate exchange between us.

"James," I said, clearing my throat, "the Earl of Bothwell has asked for my pardon, for what he and the others did tonight, and I have agreed to grant his request, provided he humbles himself publicly. He has also explained to me that he is pledged to marry Jean Gordon. That is why he did not join with us in fighting the Gordon clan rebels."

James sneered. "You acted like a Gordon tonight," he said to Jamie. "You disgraced yourself. You dishonored this court."

"I very nearly got myself killed too," Jamie retorted. "See for yourself."

My brother glanced at Jamie's wound. I noticed that he himself was unscathed. Either he had not taken part in the fighting or he had acquitted himself expertly. I did not know which.

"Your Highness," my brother said, pointedly turning away from Jamie, "I came to tell you that there has been—an unpleasant incident. A madwoman in a red gown has been seized at the palace gates. She is raving in an unknown tongue. What shall I do with her?"

I looked at Jamie.

"The Scottish wife," I said.

"No, God help me," was Jamie's plangent cry. "Not now!"

"James, will you please take the earl to Dr. Bourgoing. Then go to the kitchens and find me a girl who speaks Norwegian. Then bring the girl and the madwoman to me—along with Adrien."

My brother looked at me, incredulous.

"You are going to interview this madwoman?"

I smiled as Jamie hurried toward the door. "We are old friends," I said. "We met in France. And we have urgent business to conduct. We shall conduct it tomorrow. Now go!"

SIXTEEN

WHEN the following morning the tall, thin, wild-eyed Norwegian woman was brought into my presence chamber, her dirty red dress frayed and torn, the yellow petticoat underneath it ragged, her stockings full of holes and her shoes so worn she could hardly keep them on her large feet, I could tell at a glance that what she needed most was food, a bath and a change of clothing.

I told my tirewoman Margaret Carwood to provide these, and she took the Scottish wife away.

When I saw her next I was amazed at the transformation. Instead of an embattled amazon the woman who now appeared before me was almost stately, much more self-possessed and well groomed. Margaret had helped her bathe, and had dressed her in one of my gowns, a blue one with delicate lace at the neck and sleeves. In it she seemed far less a wild creature possessed by rage and more a lady who had met with an undeserved blow of fate. But she still had a look of desperation in her pale blue eyes, and as I began speaking with her—my words and hers translated by the kitchen maid from Trondheim—I discovered that her situation was a very precarious one.

"She says that her father is an important man in Norway," the kitchen maid said. "A commander of ships. He has money. Lots of money. But he will not speak to her any more. Her mother will not see her or speak to her. Her brother spits on her. Her sisters call her a whore."

"Tell her I know what happened to her. I know her fiancé wagered her dowry in a game of cards and lost. Say that I am prepared to repay her what was lost."

I opened a small chest and showed the Scottish wife the gold coins inside—the remainder of the money I had received from the sale of my land. (I had not given Jamie all of it.) I pushed the chest toward her.

Much to my surprise, she shook her head violently and pushed it back toward me, speaking quickly and vehemently as she did so.

"She says," the kitchen maid explained, "that she does not want money. She wants the man. The man who won her. He must marry her."

I thought quickly. "He is not free," I said. "He has a wife already." It was not strictly true, but soon would be, when Jamie married Jean Gordon.

The large, awkward, anguished woman began to cry. A great, gushing flow of tears that told me she loved Jamie. What had he done to call forth such love? Had he been her lover? Was she carrying his child, as she had claimed?

"Ask her," I said to the kitchen maid when the flow of tears began to subside, "whether she is going to be a mother."

The question was put—and more tears followed. At length there came an answer.

"She says her child was born dead. No one helped her when he was born. She wrapped him in a rag and buried him in an old churchyard, at night, in secret." In saying these words the kitchen maid was moved.

I laid my hand on the Scottish wife's arm, meaning to comfort her, but only making her jump in alarm.

"Tell her I am very sorry."

Even as I spoke I could see that something had shifted behind the woman's eyes. She was suddenly wary, a trapped animal. I felt a tremor of fear. Was it possible she might attack me, the way I had seen her attack Jamie in the Inn of the Three Barrels?

"She says he must leave his wife and marry her."

"Tell her that is not possible. That will never happen."

"She says he owns her. He has won her. Now he owns her, and must be her husband." I saw anger flash in the foreign woman's pale blue eyes. Her body was tensed.

I had an inspiration.

"Tell her he won her—but he lost her again. He bet her and her dowry in another game of cards, and another man won. That man is gone."

I watched while the kitchen maid explained this to the Scottish wife. She was surprised, confused, and then despondent. She lowered her head and shook it slowly, saying a few words—soft words.

"She says her own luck is always bad."

After a pause I said, "Perhaps her luck is changing. Tell her that she is welcome to stay at my court until a husband can be found for her. Until then she is my guest. But she must promise not to bother the Earl of Bothwell in future."

Apparently I was wrong in thinking that the Scottish wife was in love with Jamie, for when the kitchen maid translated my words, a huge smile lit up the plain face of the unfortunate woman, and for a moment she looked almost pretty. What she wanted, clearly, was a husband. Just a husband, any husband. Suddenly all became clear to me. If she married, she would redeem herself. Her family would accept her once again. That was what she cared about.

"She will promise. Will the husband come soon?"

"As soon as it can be arranged."

Hearing this the Scottish wife dropped to her knees, seized my hand and kissed it. Once again there were tears on her thin cheeks.

"Takk, takk, takk," I heard her saying, and I knew, though I had never learned any Norwegian, that she was expressing her heartfelt thanks.

SEVENTEEN

*T*HE first time I saw Henry Stewart, Lord Darnley, was in the cold, snowy February of the year 1565. He was in a firelit room, sitting on a bench covered in deep blue velvet, his long legs folded under him, his thick curling blond hair gleaming, playing the lute.

Sitting beside him was my Italian singer David Riccio, who watched Henry's slender white fingers as he plucked and strummed, occasionally humming along in harmony.

Neither man looked up as I quietly entered the room, so intent were they on the music they were making together. Outside the windows snow had begun to fall, a veil of white descending over bush and tree and rooftop, and the soft, plangent notes of the music fell like a veil over my senses, lulling and enchanting me by the sound, the mood, and above all, by the lute player.

When the song ended Henry looked over at me, a languorous look in his hazel eyes, a lock of his gleaming hair falling across his forehead, and I could not help but catch my breath at the beauty of him.

Henry is my cousin, I reminded myself. His mother and my late royal father were first cousins. His father is the Scottish Earl of

Lennox and his mother is the granddaughter of King Henry VII of England. He has royal blood. He can trace his descent from Queen Margaret of Scotland. He is perfect.

No wonder I feel an affinity with him, I thought as I let my eyes linger on him. It is an affinity of blood. Yes, he is as slender and handsome as the statues of Adonis in the gardens of Chambord, yes, he has inviting red lips. But he is also my kin, naturally I am drawn to him.

I thought these things—and then I ceased to think. I only felt as though I wanted to go on looking at him, and listening to him play his lute, forever.

It was a very cold winter, as I have said, when Henry came to my court, sent there by our cousin Queen Elizabeth. He was not used to the dank chill of Scotland. He suffered from the cold and, being very young (he was a mere nineteen, I was three years older), he caught an ague. He shivered and sweated, coughed and sneezed, but he would not stay in bed. Instead he went out night after night, with David Riccio and my drunken half-brother Robert and other young roisterers of the court, and I was told he often did not come back until nearly sunrise.

I always was courteous to him and made him welcome, and he seemed to take my welcome as no more than his due. He spent time with me, conversing, playing his lute for me, even reading Latin books with me (for which I truly admired him, Latin being difficult for me to read though I had been taught it since childhood). We laughed together over my small dogs, and he helped me teach them tricks. He brought his more genteel companions into my apartments and I assembled my ladies and we all danced—he was a fine and agile dancer—and afterwards we ate dainty cakes and drank wine from a set of small pink fluted glasses he gave me as a present.

I had not enjoyed such refined companionship since I left France, and it was very welcome. Henry behaved like the highborn lord he was, demanding that others accord him the dignity due to his royal breeding and at times becoming quite ferocious when they did not. He slapped his servants until they bled when they disobeyed him and shouted vile names at the members of his household. But I told myself, this is how princes behave, this is how they maintain their authority over their inferiors.

The one person Henry spared was David Riccio, who seemed always to be in his presence or nearby. Like the rest of us, David watched and admired Henry, I could see the admiration in his eyes. He too is worshipping at the shrine of beauty, I thought—and why not? He is a fine musician, he appreciates fine art. And Henry was nothing if not a masterpiece.

If Henry was the most beautiful man at my court, David Riccio was surely among the ugliest. Was it this contrast that led David to stay near Henry?

I was finding, day by day, that I too wanted to be near him, as often as possible. I invented excuses to invite him to my apartments, ordering more new gowns, jewels and headdresses to enhance my own attractions and even trying—in vain—not to bite my nails so that my slender white hands would appear at their best when I prepared myself to encounter him.

Those were giddy days. I was so enraptured that I neglected meeting with my councilors and my brother James chastised me for that. I not only neglected the everyday business of ruling, I neglected to listen to the voices around me telling me of Henry's sins and shortcomings.

One of the loudest of the voices was that of John Knox, who thundered on in his usual overblown fashion about how Henry was a vice-ridden drunkard who went out every night searching for girls to seduce and during the day, played catamite to David Riccio. (I had to ask my brother James what a catamite was, for it was not a word I knew, and he frowned and told me that such things were not fit for ladies to know.) But I refused to listen to anything the preacher said, and reminded him that he had recently disgraced himself and caused much gossip by marrying my sixteen-year-old relative Margaret Stewart without asking my permission (I would naturally have denied it) when he was fifty years old!

I don't believe I would have listened if the Lord God himself had come down from heaven and declared Henry to be a great sinner. I did not want to hear anything but praise, though the truth was that the longer he stayed at my court, the less praise I heard of Henry, and the more he was vilified.

The long cold Scottish winter of that year of 1565 at last began to give way to spring, and I was growing restless. Henry was making himself at home in my palace, he visited me most afternoons. As the weather warmed we went riding together. He wrote verses and gave them to me—though, looking back, I have to admit that they were not verses celebrating my beauty, or declaring his love for me, but rather sonnets in praise of love itself, of its delights and raptures.

Yet surely, I told myself, Henry intended to ask me to marry him. Surely I had captured his heart. We were both of royal blood, I reminded myself again and again, and suitably matched in age and even in height (Henry was one of the few handsome men I had ever met who was taller than I was). The only hindrance to our marrying that I could think of was that because we were close relatives the pope would have to give us his special permission before we went through the wedding ceremony. But that could easily be obtained.

When doubts about Henry's plans for our future arose in my mind I had only to remember what he had told me, in one of our afternoon conversations, which was that Queen Elizabeth herself had said that she would favor a match between us. He had told me this quite matter-of-factly, to be sure, and not romantically, yet he had said it. It was undoubtedly true. But why, oh why, was he taking so long to fulfill the queen's wishes?

As the days warmed and lengthened, I paced fretfully, wishing I could talk to Jamie about all that was on my heart. But Jamie was far from the court, in Gordon country, staying with his future in-laws, and the only other person I could talk to freely, without veiling my deepest thoughts, was my tirewoman Margaret Carwood and hers was one of the voices I was doing my best not to hear. Margaret was a woman of few words, and never forgot the great gulf that separated us, but her curt replies to my remarks about Henry made it very clear that she did not like him, and that she thought I was foolish for being so smitten with him—something I could not possibly have hidden from her.

One afternoon Henry came to my apartments as he so often did, and he brought David Riccio with him. My heart sank. He was not likely to propose to me with David there.

"Are we going to have some music then?" I asked, trying to keep out of my tone the exasperation I felt.

"Your Highness," Henry began after we had settled ourselves, "beyond the pleasure of your company, and perhaps to offer a serenade or two, I have come to ask a favor. I have heard that your French secretary Monsieur Bonnet has gone back to France. You will be needing someone to replace him. May I suggest Davie here?"

At this David Riccio smiled and inclined his head.

"For a generous wage, of course," Henry added. "He has a large family to support, you know. Twenty-seven in all."

I had known that David had a great many relatives, and that some of them hung around the court, running errands, holding horses for visitors, doing odd jobs in the stables and kitchen. But twenty-seven? He was not married; all these relatives had to be sisters and brothers and cousins and their children.

"I pay him well already, for singing."

"But his needs have grown," Henry responded, with one of his most angelic smiles. "And I have assured him that to please me, you would not refuse my request."

There was a subtle undertone of coercion in Henry's words, and I sensed it, and it troubled me. Instead of coming to me, cap in hand, with an offer of marriage Henry was requiring me, indeed almost coercing me, to do his bidding, to benefit his friend. He was threatening to withdraw his amiable companionship if I declined, and he was well aware of how much I desired that companionship.

"But if David becomes my secretary, who will sing the high countertenor parts? No one else at my court can sing so sweetly, or so high."

"I can both sing and write letters, I assure you," David Riccio said smoothly. "I am at your service at all hours."

I thought I saw the two men exchange smiles, and I suddenly felt left out.

"Let me speak to Lord Darnley alone about this," I said. Immediately Henry shifted his tone, ordering David to leave the room in his haughtiest manner.

What had just happened? Why did I feel so worried and uncomfortable, so confused?

Presently I tried to find my way back to familiar ground.

"It is good of you to be so concerned for a man who is so far beneath you, and a foreigner at that," I began when we were alone. "I have had some dealings with Italians," I added, thinking of my former mother-in-law. "They can be slippery."

"Davie is a good fellow, and honest enough."

"He worships you. He is as enamored of you as any girl," I said, laughing, "even though he is old enough to be your father."

When Henry made no reply to this I went on.

"I imagine that you are pursued by many girls and women. Yet you remain unwed. Surely you don't shun the admiration of women?" I smiled flirtatiously.

"I find both men and women to be delightful companions," was Henry's neutral response.

"They say David sings so beautifully because he became a castrato as a boy in Italy," I said after a time. It was well known that Italian boy singers were caponized—a word I preferred to "castrated"—so that their voices did not change, but remained high and pure.

"Indeed," was all Henry had to say.

"He is really not a man at all. He will forever be a boy."

I searched Henry's face, to gauge his reaction, but his features remained blandly composed.

"It must be a cruel fate for a man, to be deprived of the pleasures of manhood," I ventured.

"But if, as you say, he remains a boy, then he must not miss what he has never known," Henry said at length with a wan smile. "Now, about the vacant post of secretary—"

"Yes, yes. He can have it, if it would mean that much to you. You have never pressed me so hard on anything before this afternoon."

"Perhaps we are on a new footing."

I pricked up my ears at this. Did he mean what I hoped he meant?

But he seemed eager to change the subject.

"Do you know, Your Highness, I believe you and I share the same birthday. The seventh of December." He was suddenly all smiles and charm, his tone bright and open.

"Why, yes."

"It must be fate," he said. "Our fates are linked."

Michel de Notredame came into my mind, with his pronouncements about the inescapability of fate and my own baleful destiny. Was Henry, Lord Darnley to be a part of my future? I hoped so. I wanted him to be. I had never wanted anything more. But why oh why was it taking so long to happen?

EIGHTEEN

I was ready to burst.

I thought, if I have to endure one more endless afternoon with Henry, watching him smile at me, hearing him hint that our fates are linked, trying not to shout aloud my feelings for him, I will surely go mad.

Then I heard a clatter in the courtyard below, and saw, from my bedchamber window, that a ruddy-faced, bearded man was riding in on a limping roan, scattering the grooms and chickens that lay in his path. He reined the horse in, and one of the grooms came forward swiftly to hold the bridle while he dismounted.

It was Jamie! I looked in my pier glass, smoothed my hair and adjusted my bodice and skirt. I waited for him to come to me.

But he did not come. After half an hour I sent Margaret to inquire where he was.

"The Earl of Bothwell is with the Lord of Faskally," Margaret said primly when she returned.

"And where is the Lord of Faskally?"

"He has been taken to the Dominican friars to recover from his wounds."

"His wounds? What has happened?"

"I can't say, Your Highness."

I waited another half-hour, then called for Margaret to help me dress. I put on my least uncomfortable gown, and a light cloak—for it was a warm day—and my riding boots. Then I called for Bravane and, with Adrien and six other guardsmen escorting me, rode to the nearby Dominican monastery of Our Lady of Grace. There I found Jamie, in a dormitory room with a dozen beds. In one of the beds was Cristy Ricarton, thin and wan. Jamie sat beside his bed, talking to him in a low voice.

I went in and politely but firmly shooed the monks out. They did not demur; I was their benefactor, after all. I offered them the protection of my soldiers when the angry Protestants had tried to destroy the old religious house the year before, and threatened to burn the monks out.

"Do you see what that swine Darnley has done?" Jamie said to me as soon as I approached the bed. "He's attacked Cristy. Wounded him so badly he can't walk. He may never walk again. And do you know why he did it? Because Cristy had the misfortune to enter a room ahead of the high and mighty Prince Henry, that's why. Prince Henry. That's what Darnley demands to be called now."

"They fought?"

"No, they did not fight. Darnley clouted Cristy from behind, breaking his legs and his back. Poor Cristy will never be able to fight again."

I sat silent, looking down at the suffering Lord of Faskally, remembering how skillfully he swung his broadsword, parrying Jamie's murderous blows, when the two practiced their strokes against one another, how strong and agile he had been.

"Henry thinks too highly of himself," I said. "He punishes others when they fail to honor him."

"He is a brutal maniac." Jamie looked at me, a look of disgust. "But you honor him, don't you? They say you will be his wife."

I shook my head. Jamie's words pained me. "He hasn't asked me," I said softly. "I fear he never will."

"It would be a poor enough bargain, lass, if you made it."

I swallowed. I could not keep the tears out of my voice. "But you see, I love him."

Cristy had gone to sleep. Jamie got up from his bench beside the narrow bed.

"And does he love you?"

At this I began to cry, I couldn't help it. I was glad there was no one else in the room besides the sleeping Cristy, no one to witness my shameful weakness.

"He teases me with talk of our future, he smiles at me like an angel—"

"Has he said that he loves you?"

I shook my head. I could not look at Jamie. I was in agony.

"But oh Jamie, I am dying of love for him!"

"By all the saints, woman, look at yourself! He's turned you into a sniveling, quivering mound of pudding! Where is your dignity! I thought you were a queen!"

This angered me. "But it is as a queen that I desire him! He has royal blood. Our children will rule Scotland and England too, perhaps, if our cousin Elizabeth does not marry. Besides, I know full well that men often do not love the women they marry. Can you tell me honestly that you love Jean Gordon?"

"Pah! That match was never made for love, but for lands. We both know it. And we are not married yet, only promised."

Jamie came over to me and, as he had done once before, softly stroked my cheek with his rough knuckle.

"Don't try to pretend, Orange Blossom. You are just being stubborn. I know you. I have seen you in all your moods. Clearly this man Darnley has bewitched you. He is toying with you, making you miserable, so that he will get what he wants."

"And what is it that he wants?"

"Why, your kingdom of course. Can't you see he is just the tool of the English? Of that fiend Elizabeth? She wants Scotland, just as her father did! She means to get it—not by sending her armies to fight us, but by sending Lord Darnley. He is the beautiful bait she wants you to swallow. Once you become his wife, he will take all your power and authority for himself—and rule here, as Elizabeth's deputy."

It made sense—yet I resisted believing what Jamie said. I did not want my dream of love to wither.

He saw the willing disbelief in my eyes, and it exasperated him.

"He is English!" Jamie shouted. "We Scots despise him! We do not want him for our lord and master!" His words echoed in the old dormitory, making Cristy stir in his bed and moan. Then Jamie added, in a mumble, "And not just because he is English, but because of what he is."

I waited a long moment before replying.

"Well then," I said at length, "if he is as calculating as you say he is, why hasn't he asked me for my hand in marriage?"

"Can't you see why?"

I thought of David Riccio, of all the times Henry and David came to my apartments together, of the music they made and their close friendship. Of how I felt left out when they were with me. Of the words of John Knox, words which I had dismissed when he said them but which now seemed important.

I lifted my eyes to Jamie's bearded face. "What is a catamite, Jamie?"

"Who used that word with you?"

"John Knox."

"He would." He sighed. "A catamite is a boy who serves a man's lusts."

Unwelcome thoughts and images rushed into my mind. The beautiful boy Henry and the ugly middle-aged David. Inseparable. So comfortable together, almost like brothers. Only not brothers—

I pushed the thoughts aside.

"I have been foolish. I have let my desires confuse me. I have forgotten that a queen cannot daydream about love the way a milkmaid or a peasant girl can. Thank you for reminding me."

I heard myself speaking, yet the voice I heard was not my voice. It was too harsh, too real, too sensible. It was not I but the Scots queen who was speaking, my outward self. I knew it, and Jamie knew it too.

"Now now then, Orange Blossom. You may yet find a man who loves you—if you are very lucky. Your mother did: and it was my father."

"But they couldn't marry!"

"No," he said softly, "but they could share a dream."

NINETEEN

AFTER my talk with Jamie I tried my best to put Henry out of my mind. I saw as little of him as possible. I gave orders to my equerry Arthur Erskine, who stood at the door to my rooms during the day, that Henry was not to be admitted to my apartments. That he was to be told that I was ill—and in fact I did suffer, for my efforts to forget him gave me headaches and took away my appetite.

I wrote to Queen Elizabeth thanking her for sending Henry to Scotland for a visit and hinting strongly that it was time he returned home. I waited for a reply, but never received one.

I thought of leaving the court myself for a time, in hopes that while I was away, Henry would order his trunks packed and leave.

But he did not—and despite all my efforts, I could not put him out of my mind. Every time I glimpsed him the old enchantment was revived. I tried to keep in mind all that Jamie had said about him, but in the end I lost the thread of reason and gave in to the strong pull of my desire.

When Margaret Carwood came to me and told me that Henry was buying aquavit from a blowsy vendor who sold it near the Tollbooth, and that he was flirting outrageously with her, I was overjoyed. How could he be a catamite if he was so enthusiastically pursuing this woman?

Jamie was admitted to my apartments about a week after I had talked with him that day in the monastery dormitory. He was brusque and businesslike.

"I've come to say goodbye. I'm taking Cristy back with me to Huntly."

"How is he?"

"He will live—but he will never be whole again."

"Please tell him that I am truly sorry for his injuries."

A curt nod was his only reply.

There was an awkward silence between us, and though Jamie had said he was leaving, he seemed to linger. He fidgeted.

"You were wrong about Henry, you know," I said after a time. "He likes girls. Women. Margaret has seen him with one. She says she is sure there have been others."

Jamie scoffed, then laughed. "I fear to tell you, lass, that this Henry of yours has a wide palate of sexual tastes. Men are his favorites, but he likes sex with boys, with girls, with women, probably with sheep and goats. He has a reputation as long as my arm!"

He spoke harshly. He meant to wound me with his words. I stepped back as if slapped.

"That's one reason the hateful English queen sent him here among us, to your staid court. He was making a spectacle of himself at hers!"

"I don't believe you!" I cried. "I can't believe you!"

"Hell and damnation, woman, how can I make you see that this worthless lout you think you are in love with is simply beneath you, in every way? That if you were to marry him, as you plainly want to, he would make you miserable." He was pacing as he spoke, accentuating his words with every long stride. "He would take his pleasures with others and leave you lonely and wretched. Believe me, I have known others like him. Heartless men who take all that a woman has to offer and then throw her aside to suffer."

Warming to his urgent plea, he grasped my hand.

"Mary, I have heard him speak of you. He ridicules you! Do you know what he calls your court? The Crib of Chastity. Believe me, he does not speak or act like a man in love."

I shook my head and began to turn away, not wanting to hear his hurtful words. But he grabbed me by my shoulders.

"No! You must listen!"

And then, suddenly, impulsively, he kissed me.

Oh, how he kissed me! I was lost in that kiss. I drowned in it, I yielded to the immense tide of feeling that flowed over me when I felt the pressure of his warm, soft lips on mine.

Then, just as suddenly as he had grabbed me, he released me.

"There," he said, his voice rough, even angry. "That is what a man in love would do. Has your Henry kissed you like that?"

Catching my breath, I barely managed to say "He hasn't kissed me at all."

"And what does that tell you then?" he said as he turned to walk out of my chamber. "Don't make this mistake, Mary. Don't be led astray by your lusts!"

"And shall I see you at your wedding then?" I managed to say as he was leaving, my voice weak.

"Eventually. As you can tell I am putting off the evil day for as long as I can."

"While being led astray by your lusts?"

He turned back toward me. "As often, and as fully, as I can," he said evenly, then with a curt bow, walked out.

On an impulse I summoned Henry into my presence.

He did not come for an hour or more, and when he did arrive, clad in a doublet of purple velvet and with a gold chain around his neck that must have weighed half as much as he did, he was not alone. David Riccio walked in after him, keeping a respectful distance. David too was regally clad, in a gold and lilac doublet lavishly embroidered with silver threads and shoes with gold buckles.

"Lord Darnley, I would speak with you alone." My heart was pounding, but I maintained my outward reserve.

"As you wish." Henry gave a swift half-turn, lifted one elegant leg, and kicked the startled David in the groin. Moaning, David went.

I thought, this is not happening the way I dreamed it would. But I must do as my heart leads me.

I came forward and extended my hand toward Henry. He took it, solemnly. His hand was cold and clammy.

"Lord Darnley, it would please me if you would become my husband. Are you agreeable?"

His expression did not change. The light from the high window played on his fine white skin, his candid hazel eyes with their long lashes, his perfectly molded features.

"I assume you are offering me the crown matrimonial? I think any other course would not please our cousin Elizabeth."

His response was such a surprise that I did not know how to answer. I had never thought of anything besides marriage itself, our wedding, our rapturous joining. But of course there were other considerations. When I married the dauphin Francis I had spent an entire morning signing documents that spelled out in great detail just what my status would be after we became husband and wife. All of a sudden I realized what was at stake, that what Henry was asking was that I would make him not only my husband but my royal consort—and king in his own right, should anything happen to me.

I looked at him. Was this the moment he had been waiting for since the day he arrived, I wondered. Had it all been calculated, every word, every gesture? Was Jamie right about him? Did he want nothing from me but my throne?

"We can leave that decision to my councilors and lawyers," I said.

"This is a decision for us to make, and no one else. Am I to be merely your husband, or am I to command the dignity that is my right by birth, the dignity and honor of a royal prince?"

I very nearly refused. I very nearly said, let us consider this and talk it over tomorrow. How close I came! But my cheeks burned with the excitement and tension of it all, and his response was so cool that I feared he might refuse me. It was so hard to think clearly when I was near him. Here we were, on the brink of agreeing to what I had been longing for for so many sleepless nights, so many restless afternoons. I could not risk losing him. I could not.

"Yes, yes of course then. Anything you like! Only say that you will marry me!"

He smiled then, with satisfaction though not with joy, and kissed me on the lips—a surprisingly dry, swift kiss. Those sweetly curving red lips that I had yearned to kiss were at last on mine. Yet their touch was not at all as I had dreamed it would be. I clung to him, wanting more, wanting to be overcome by a passion so exquisite it would surely be unbearable. But I felt no passion. It was nothing like Jamie's kiss, that remarkable kiss that had shaken me to the depths of my being and moved me so beyond myself that I was lost.

No, it was nothing like that. It was, I realized, a chaste kiss. Chaste and dry and empty. What was it that Jamie said Henry had called my court? The Crib of Chastity? How ironic it would be, I thought with a tremor of fear, if my marriage to the man I desired most turned out to be devoid of lust, devoid of passion, worst of all, devoid of love.

TWENTY

O N our wedding morning I was shrouded in funereal black.
A long cloak of black taffeta covered my dark gown, and
its large wide hood came down over my bright reddish-gold hair
and nearly hid my face.

I would have liked to wear bridal white, as I was still young and
very nearly virginal, Francis having been so immature and inept as a
lover, but it was traditional that a widow wear black on her wedding
day, and so I did.

The windows of the chapel at Holyrood had barely begun to be
illumined by the first pink rays of the rising sun when I gave my arm
to my father-in-law to be, the proud, beaming Earl of Lennox, and
we walked down the aisle, with the Earl of Argyll on my other side.

Henry stood waiting at the front of the church, before the altar,
looking as tall and straight as I had ever seen him—I believe he was
the tallest man in the room—and as we approached him he smiled—
and, very quietly, hiccupped.

Most of the members of my court were in attendance in the chapel,
though nearly all of them, I knew, were opposed to my marriage to a
man they considered to be an Englishman and a very high and mighty
one besides. However my half-brother James Stewart, to whom I had

given the title Earl of Moray, was not there. Brother James, who had led my armies against the rebellious Gordons and had been my principal adviser ever since I came to Scotland following my mother's death, was now a rebel himself. My half-brother Robert, on the other hand, was very prominent, standing beside Henry and looking very pleased with himself in his wedding finery.

My escorts and I reached the altar and they stood back to let Henry move into place beside me. The priest began to repeat the opening prayers, the choristers sang, we said our vows and Henry slipped a gold band onto my finger—and then he left me, whispering that he would see me later on.

He left me there, in my black cloak, to hear the mass on my own. He had not warned me that he intended to do this, and for an instant I thought he meant to abandon me, to go back to England and never see me again. I nearly panicked. But then I came to my senses, and realized what he was doing. I remembered that he had been seen attending John Knox's long Protestant sermons at Knox's church near the palace. Henry was Catholic, but his Catholicism was not very firm or constant. He wanted to appease the Protestant Lords of the Congregation, who had been the loudest to shout their opposition when I announced that Henry and I were to be married. By leaving the chapel the way he did he was teasing the Protestant lords, the way he had teased me ever since the previous winter. And he was doing it at my expense.

I was glad to reach my apartments after the ceremony ended and throw off my black cloak and hood. My tirewomen helped me undress and brought the lovely lace gown I was to wear for the bedding ceremony. Henry appeared, looking amiable but hardly amorous, and when I had changed into the beautiful gown, the two of us took our places in the wide canopied marital bed, while the courtiers filed in to witness our coupling.

It was an old ceremony, and a quaint one. I had been through it once before, with Francis. While the members of the court looked on, Henry solemnly put one naked foot against my ankle, and this touching of flesh to flesh symbolized the consummation of our marriage. A sullen cheer went up from a few throats. Then we were left alone.

We were left alone, and nothing happened.

A painful silence enveloped us, broken only by the ticking of my clock and the faint noise of distant voices in other parts of the palace and of cart wheels passing over the worn cobblestones in the courtyard below.

Then Henry spoke.

"There is a pretty saying in the north of England," he said, not looking at me but speaking to me in quite a normal tone of voice. "It is this: Birds of a feather fly together. You and I, my little wife, are not birds of a feather, though we come from a common lineage. We were not meant to share a nest."

It was by far the longest speech he had ever made to me, and the cruelest, though I did not think then that he meant to be cruel, only bluntly truthful.

"Rather than pretend otherwise, let us agree to go on as we were when I first came here. I will join you in the afternoons, from time to time, and we will endeavor to be pleasant companions. There is a suite of rooms below this one, is there not? The two suites connect by a private stair. I will take the lower rooms as my own, and you will stay here, in comfort and in peace."

I heard a moan of anguish erupt from my lungs.

"No!" I screamed. "You cannot do this to me!" I raised my hand to slap him but he caught it in midair.

"And what have you done to me? Made me your caged pet, your chirping canary, your gallant—"

"My husband, whom I love so dearly, so very dearly." I sobbed then, I couldn't help it.

He got up from the bed, and went to stand at the window. I could not stop weeping. I thought I would sob my heart out.

"You are older than I am," he resumed after a time, "but I have known much more of the world, and of the pleasures of the flesh. You have not yet learned how to take your pleasure. It will not be difficult for you. You are beautiful, fragile. You must learn to seek out the birds of your feather, Mary, and fly with them."

"You speak in riddles," I said, my voice ragged, "to hide your beastly cruelty."

He turned and faced me. "Then let me speak more plainly. You are much admired. Do as the French do, as it is said our cousin Queen Elizabeth does, and choose a lover. Choose more than one. Satisfy yourself. But do not expect me to be what I cannot."

"So Jamie was right about you, all along," I whispered. "And all the gossip I have not wanted to believe is true."

He shrugged. "Who knows what lies are told by the envious? Your own reputation is far from pure."

He took a silver flask from his pocket, opened it, and drank from it, then handed it to me.

"Shall we have a toast then? To our future."

Despite the pain I felt, despite feeling cheated and full of a growing rage, my courage did not desert me. I seized the flask he offered, and drank the fiery liquid in it to the dregs. Then I flung it as hard as I could toward the window, breaking the pane and causing Margaret to come running in from the next room, looking worried and shaken, as Henry bolted down the stairs.

TWENTY-ONE

I was furious. I was enraged. I was murderous! I wanted to kill my husband, to pursue him and kill him. So strong was my lust for revenge that I really believe that if it had not been for all the sermons I had heard and all that I had been taught since childhood of Christian charity and forgiveness, I might well have done so.

Instead, I took my revenge by denying Henry the thing he wanted most: the crown matrimonial. I denied him the right, which only I could confer, to rule the kingdom of Scotland in his own name and not by virtue of being my husband.

And I had another weapon in my arsenal. Because of the haste in which we married, soon after I proposed to Henry, there had not been time to obtain a dispensation from the pope, the dispensation that would have made marriage between us as cousins valid. To wait for a dispensation would have meant a long delay. It would have taken many months for a messenger to travel from my court to Rome, then wait there for the papal chancery to draw up the proper documents, then travel back to Scotland. So I decided to go ahead with the wedding and request the dispensation later.

Henry was not aware of this; he assumed the pope had removed any hindrance to the validity of our marriage under church law. But I knew otherwise. I knew that, until the proper documents were obtained from Rome, we were in a kind of limbo, married yet not married—which meant that Henry had no rights at all as my husband, not even under Scottish law.

It pleased me to ponder this, as thoughts of revenge burned themselves into my aching mind on long sleepless nights—nights I spent listening to the raucous shouting and laughter in Henry's apartments below mine and wanting to drive the occupants out with a bullwhip.

For Henry had wasted no time in filling his suite of rooms with the riffraff of the streets: sailors from Leith harbor, roughs from the taverns of the Royal Mile, brigands like Red Ormiston and his thugs, low women of the sort that hid in the shadows of the wynds and let men take them for a few coins. I could hear them, night after night, laughing and shrieking at all hours, their bawdy singing keeping me awake.

Finally one night I had had enough. I commanded my guards to drive every one of my husband's ragtag companions out of the palace, even though the result, as I might have expected, was an icy confrontation with Henry.

"I am king here," he said. "I shall do as I like, and keep what company I like, and you will never interfere with me again."

"I am queen here, and my guards do as I command them. You may not turn my palace into a den of vice." (I could not believe my words, I was sounding like John Knox!)

"And since you are king," I went on, "then you will command our men when we take the field against the rebels. My brother James has turned against me, with five hundred men. I need you to lead the loyal troops against him."

It was another act of revenge. I knew that Henry had never been a warrior. He had never even ridden in a tournament, much less led men in warmaking against an enemy. I ordered my armorer to provide him with a heavy suit of armor, splendidly gilded so that it shone brilliantly in the sunlight, and I gave him a huge strong warhorse to ride.

The gilded armor was fastened on, and he was hoisted up onto the warhorse, but as I had expected, Henry could barely hold his seat in the saddle. He lurched embarrassingly from side to side, and nearly fell off.

The men ridiculed him, and I did too, shouting taunts at him and calling him a coward and saying—I was to regret this—that he was not a man. In the end he simply gave up, humiliated and angry, and had to be helped off his horse and into his tent, where he promptly drank himself into a stupor. I managed to find one of my brother James's former lieutenants, one who had stayed loyal to me when James left my court, and put him in command of my royal army. Under his leadership, and with me, clad in my steel helmet and breastplate, riding with my men and urging them on, we defeated James's force, took our grisly trophies, and returned home to Edinburgh victorious.

As before, I found the warmaking exhilarating, despite the carnage. But in the aftermath of the conflict there was, for me, a terrible price to pay.

One night soon after our victory over the rebels I was awakened by Henry, coming up the private stairs into my bedchamber, accompanied by two lithe, handsome young men, both stark naked.

Before I was fully awake I felt Henry's cold, clammy hand over my mouth. With his other hand he pulled my nightdress up to my waist.

"Here she is then," he was saying to the boys, "the warrior queen. The one who wears a man's armor and thinks she can fight like a man—and thinks I am less than a man. Well then, I'll just have to show her that she is wrong."

Kneeling above me, he spread my legs apart and pulled out his penis. While the boys stood by watching, he thrust himself inside me and, with a stream of insults, came to a climax.

The pain was sharp and terrible. This was nothing like Francis's feeble attempts at lovemaking. I tried to scream but his hand was smothering me so that it was all I could do to keep breathing.

"There now," he said when he had finished. "What do you think, was she worth a kingdom?"

I was terrified that the two boys would use me for their pleasure as well, but they did not. Instead Henry released me roughly and all three left the way they had come, leaving me panting and weeping from pain and shock, and doing my best to call out weakly for help.

TWENTY-TWO

BY the time the first frosts came, I was feeling ill in the mornings and Margaret Carwood called Dr. Bourgoing to come and examine me.

He came, along with the midwife Mistress Asteane, the midwife who, many years earlier, had brought me into the world in those sad days following my father's death.

"There is no question about it," the doctor said after he had examined me and after Mistress Asteane had put her hand briefly on my belly and looked into my puffy face. "You will soon be a mother." The midwife nodded.

I had suspected this, but on hearing the doctor say the words I felt weak and began to weep.

"There now," Mistress Asteane said, bringing out of her bag a leather pouch of some stinking herb. "Women who are with child tend to weep a lot, and rage a lot, and just generally feel miserable and unlike themselves." She looked at my broken, bitten nails. "You are nervous," she said. "Nervous mothers have weak babies. You need to be calm. Make a tea from these herbs and drink it three times a day. It will help you. And I will help you too, if you need it." She patted my hand, just as if I had been a woman from the town or a girl working in the fields, and not a queen.

Everyone was smiling at me encouragingly, sympathetically. I was carrying the heir to Scotland's throne. I had to be joyful.

"Be glad you are not barren," Dr. Bourgoing was saying. "Everyone in France assumed you were."

But what none of them knew, for I had told no one, was that the child I was carrying had been conceived in hatred, not love, and (I can hardly bear to write this) by a man who required the presence of naked boys to stimulate his desire.

It was all too painful, too shameful, to reveal to anyone. I resolved to keep my terrible secret to myself.

For the next several months I brooded, drinking my stinking tea three times a day, sleeping far too much, eating a lot and gaining weight, and still biting my nails.

I had a great deal on my mind. I would soon have a child to care for and worry over. A child! An heir to my throne. A strong boy, I hoped, who would in time be able to bear the rule of Scotland on his broad shoulders. Would I survive the ordeal of his birth? Many women died in the travail of giving birth. Even strong, young women. Would I be able to govern my quarrelsome subjects until he was born? I could not very well ride at the head of my army while I was pregnant, though I had heard that other women had performed this feat, Queen Isabella for one, the courageous mother of Queen Catherine of Aragon. Would my subjects rebel while I was in my unwieldy, semi-invalid state, and unable to control them? Who would serve as my deputy while I was ill?

Henry spent his days hunting, staying away from court, avoiding me. I had sent Dr. Bourgoing to give him the news that we were to be parents but had heard no word from him, not even by messenger. I knew from my equerry Arthur Erskine that Henry had quarreled with his former boon companion David Riccio, and that he was seen more often than ever in the company of the outlaw Red Ormiston, that brigand who had been with Jamie on the night he disrupted my banquet; Henry had often brought Ormiston to Holyrood since our wedding.

What was Henry up to? I drank my tea, and it dulled my mind a little, but my worries remained.

The Christmas season was approaching, my twenty-third birthday came and went early in December of that year of 1565 (the celebration soured for me because I knew that it was also Henry's birthday) and the palace was decorated for the nativity feast. David Riccio offered to take charge of the Christmas festivities, and I did not demur. For weeks David and his many relatives were to be seen throughout the palace rehearsing masques, practicing their songs, putting green boughs around the windows and removing the old rushes from the floor and bringing in fresh ones.

Spiced wine and new pomanders were prepared in the palace kitchens, and the smells of pine and holly, cloves and cinnamon filled the rooms, lifting my spirits and making me long for the Christmases I had known in France, when my grandmother had given me lavish gifts and the entire court had banqueted for weeks on roast swans and peacocks, capons and jellies and pies and glazed fruits hung on miniature silver trees.

My child, I feared, would not know any of these delights. Not for him the abundance of France—only the sparse pleasures of chilly Scotland. But he would have my love, of that I felt certain. Whether he would have any affection from his heartless father I couldn't imagine.

I invited Jamie to my court for Christmas and he came, along with his sister Jean and a much weakened Cristy Ricarton, who walked slowly and uncertainly with the aid of two sticks and looked as though he had aged ten years since I last saw him.

Jamie seemed subdued, and I asked him why.

"In six weeks I will cease to be a free man," he said. "I cannot put off my marriage any longer."

"Don't assume the worst, Jamie," I said. "In time you may come to love and value your wife-to-be. Jean Gordon is said to be a fine strong woman."

He shrugged. "But she is not the woman I would have chosen. We both know that."

I let this pass. There was no point in calling to mind what could not be.

"She cannot possibly be worse than my spouse." And though I had sworn to myself that I would never reveal what had happened on the night my child was conceived, I confided the entire awful episode to Jamie—and only Jamie.

He jumped up from where we had been sitting and reached for his sword.

"That whoreson bastard! How dare he treat you so knavishly, so cruelly! I'll kill him!"

"Keep quiet, or he may do worse!" I said through clenched teeth. "He has ignored me and stayed away from court for months. I don't want him to return. Don't give him a reason to."

After much swearing and pacing Jamie managed to calm himself, though I could tell how angry he was—not only because of what Henry had done to me, and to his friend Cristy, but because of an even more urgent matter he proceeded to tell me about.

"Are you aware that your husband is conspiring against you? That he has persuaded the Protestant lords—including your brother James, and the reverend Knox, and many others—to join him in seizing the throne from you?"

"No. I did not know he had gone that far."

"They even approached me to join them. Can you imagine? Me? The last person in all Scotland who would ever desert you, no matter what anyone may say."

"Yes, Jamie. I know that."

"At first, when they came to me, I wanted to laugh in their faces and denounce them. But then I thought, I can serve you better by pretending to be part of their plan. That way I can warn you in advance when they mean to strike."

"Perhaps I should strike first."

"How?"

"Your sister casts spells. I could ask her to put a spell on Henry."

"You could, but if anything were to happen to him, his allies would then have even more reason to dethrone you. You would be accused of causing his death. No, it is better that you wait for Henry to reveal his treachery. Then your guards can take him and deal with him."

Christmas came and went. A month passed, and then another, and still the conspiracy Jamie had warned me about had not led to any action. My belly was becoming uncomfortably large, the baby had begun kicking me and I often had an upset stomach after I ate. Mistress Asteane watched over me, assuring me that all was well, and Dr. Bourgoing too came to examine me once a week. Meanwhile Jamie's wedding plans went forward and he was married in February, but almost as soon as the ceremony was ended he was back at my court, with his sister—and, I could not help but notice, without his new wife.

"You must take the greatest care now," Jamie told me soon after he arrived. "Do not leave the palace, for any reason. Keep your guards around you. I will stay nearby, and Jean as well."

I assured him that I would do as he said.

"Your husband's diabolical plan is worse than I had thought. He has paid Red Ormiston ten thousand English crowns to attack you, along with his gang of felons. When and where I don't yet know. You need to be ready."

"What if I offer him fifteen thousand not to do it?"

"Ah, but he has given his word. Mere money will not convince him to break it."

I remembered how Jamie and the outlaw had once joined forces. Surely there must be some tie of allegiance between them, even in the murky world of everchanging Scots loyalties.

"You know him well. Could you persuade him not to go through with this murderous attack, for the sake of his loyalty to you, and yours to me?"

"I have already tried. I am still trying. I will add your promise of fifteen thousand crowns to my persuasions."

Day after day passed, Adrien and my guardsmen remained in attendance on me, and my other servants, sensing danger, were visibly wary and seemed to draw physically nearer to me when they were in my presence.

One morning my baby gave such a lusty kick that I cried out, and fell to my knees. At once the guardsmen were all around me, my servants came rushing in to my small dressing room and in the corridor outside there was such a loud hue and cry that I thought the very walls would shake.

But I was fine, I assured everyone that I was in no danger and Jamie's sister Jean sat beside me until all was normal again.

"I've been meaning to give you this," Jean said as we sat together. She drew out a large round stone from her pocket and handed it to me. To my surprise, it felt warm. It was a piece of rock crystal, set in silver and meant to be worn on a chain around the neck.

"This is a charm stone, a gem of power," she told me. "It carries the blessings of many generations of healers. It will protect you, and ease your pains, when your time comes."

I thanked her and hung the stone from a silver chain, and wore it along with the portrait of my mother which I nearly always had with me.

Perhaps, I thought, these worries that prey on me will come to nothing. Mistress Asteane kept telling me that pregnant women are always worried, and often for no reason. I did my best to believe her. I drank my tea, and said my prayers for the best outcome of all the anxieties that assailed me. And all the while I fingered the charm stone that hung around my neck, doing my best to take comfort from its rough warmth, hoping that my child and I would be protected, no matter what dangers we might face.

TWENTY-THREE

WHAT I have to tell now is only a jumble of memories, all of them ghastly. I remember being in a familiar room, surrounded by friends, feeling safe there because Adrien was nearby and Jamie's sister Jean was sitting right next to me and my equerry Arthur Erskine, who always carried his dagger, was sitting right across the table.

We were dining. I remember the rich smell of the food, and the taste of chicken in my mouth, and feeling my baby kick, and hearing David laugh.

But then Henry came into the room—he was not a welcome guest at my table, and I did not want him there, but he sat down anyway and then Jean said "oh no, not now" and then before I knew it there were more men coming into the room, the tall, fearsome-looking Red Ormiston among them. And then Adrien stood up and reached for his sword and one of the men hit him and he fell and my heart started to beat too fast and I thought I was going to faint.

Instead I tried to stand up and that was when Henry pushed me back against the wall and held me there so that I could not move. I thought, dear God, is he going to violate me again? But he just continued to hold me, there against the wall, and I felt the cold metal of a pistol against my temple and then I was aware that someone was clutching at my skirt. Pulling on it, tearing it, and at the same time crying out, "Save me! O madam, save me!"

Henry's sour breath was in my face and someone was screaming and then I felt a strong tug on my clothes and at the same moment there was a cry—hardly more than a breath—and a sort of sighing, and then I felt something warm and wet on my shoes and I managed to look down and saw, first, David's face, and then blood. Red blood, and lots of it, staining my carpet and David being dragged away from me but reaching out with his hands toward me.

"Justice, justice, justice" he kept calling out, his voice more and more faint. Someone was dragging him by the heels across the floor, away from me, and the fur on his coat was red with his blood.

"Call the guard" I kept saying but my voice was no more than a whisper. Then I wanted to shut my ears because there were loud, agonizing screams—a man's screams—coming from just outside the room.

And then, in the midst of all the confusion, in my horror, in my bewilderment, with my heart racing so fast that I could barely think at all, something very strange happened. Red Ormiston, who is a big, wide, hulking man, taller than any of my guards and probably much stronger, and who was wearing a yellow and red plaid with a sprig of heather in his cap, came up to Henry and me and with one hand swept Henry aside. Just swept him out of the way, as if he were nothing more than a dog eating scraps under the table.

I thought, he's going to kill me. I know he is. And I began repeating the words of the Lord's Prayer and shut my eyes.

There was a great commotion in the room all around me. I heard the clink of metal on metal, shouts and curses, women screaming, running feet—and then, all of a sudden, the alarm bells began ringing to arouse the whole city and I thought, my people will come and save me.

Yet it was not my subjects who saved me, but the immense man standing before me, towering over me. The outlaw Ormiston, who fixed me with his dark eyes and held one immense hand in front of my face.

He put his mouth to my ear and muttered "You owe me fifteen thousand crowns."

And then, still thinking that I was going to die, I gave in to the fear and the roaring in my ears and my knees buckled under me and I sank down, down, into oblivion.

TWENTY-FOUR

I was in Jamie's arms. I was being carried in his arms as he ran through the corridors of the palace, bumping along, amid a chaos of noise and crowding and shouted voices and, above it all, the sound of the alarm bells ringing throughout the city.

He swerved. He yelled at people to get out of his way. I opened my eyes but felt dizzy so I closed them again. Was I hurt? Was my baby hurt?

I opened my eyes again but now we were in the dark, and I could see nothing but stone walls. He was carrying me down stairs, into the cellars. I could smell the damp, the green slime that grew down the old stones of the walls on either side of us. Faint torchlight glimmered as Jamie reached the bottom step and made his way along a corridor to a small room nearly filled with piles of wood and barrels and hogsheads.

Jamie set me gently down. I was dazed, but I could stand, holding onto his shoulder for balance.

"We must get away, before they come after us, before there are any more murders. Can you ride, do you think?"

I nodded. "If I must."

"You are not injured?"

I shook my head. But my head hurt. Perhaps I was injured. I decided to ignore it.

"Then we must try to get to the stables. Do you think—"

With a crash one of the barrels tipped over.

"Don't kill me!" came a voice—my husband's voice, tremulous with fear. "I swear it wasn't my doing! They made me! They used me!"

In my weakened state it was all I could do to swat the air and say, "No, no, don't let him near me!"

Henry was cowering in a corner of the storeroom, his clothes covered in blood. Jamie quickly went to him and seized his pistol and the long knife he had stuck into his belt.

"It was all your doing," Jamie said to Henry, his voice cold with rage. "Every bit of it. I know your purposes, and so does the queen your wife. I ought to kill you here and now for what you did—and what you meant to do."

"Oh, Jamie, it was horrible. All the blood, and poor David, they hurt poor David—"

"He is dead. They meant to kill you too, but Red Ormiston protected you."

"He did. I remember now. He said, 'You owe me fifteen thousand crowns.'"

"Please, you must save me," Henry pleaded. "Don't let them find me. They will torture me!"

"And you deserve it. Preening little princeling! Worthless swine! Whoreson cur!" Jamie kicked Henry then, who began blubbering and once more pleading for his life.

"We've got to get to the stables," Jamie said to me. "It will be faster if you can run. Can you?"

Some clarity was returning to my dazed mind and senses. "I'll try."

"Don't leave me!" Henry begged. "Take me with you!"

"Then come along, if you must," Jamie called out over his shoulder as we made our way as quickly as we could through the maze of hallways and storerooms, slipping on the slick stones and listening for the sound of pursuers.

"We've got to get to Dunbar," Jamie was saying. "I have loyal men there. We will be safe there in the castle."

I was feeling ill but once we reached the stables Jamie was able to lift me up onto a strong horse and we rode together, the poor horse straining and snorting under our weight, along the road that led out beside the abbey, avoiding the crowds and hubbub. Henry rode behind us, I could hear him cursing as he fell farther and farther behind.

We were soon out of the town though I could still hear the alarm bells ringing when we were miles away. We rode as swiftly as the overburdened horse could carry us, but it still took us nearly four hours to get to Dunbar. All the way along Jamie kept looking back, watching for fast riders trying to overtake us. But the only rider behind us was Henry, whipping his poor mount along, though we did share the muddy roads with other travelers, some with carts, and with flocks of sheep being driven to market, all of which slowed us down a lot.

Finally we crested a hill overlooking the sea, and there, looming vast and forbidding, was the ancient castle of Dunbar. The castle that had belonged to Jamie's family for generations. I welcomed the sight. Behind those thick stone walls we would be safe, I thought. Except that my husband would be within the walls, and I feared him. I wished that Jamie had dispatched him, there in the cellars of Holyrood. I wished that I had never seen him, and been bewitched by the sight. But what was done was done, and in only a few months there would be a child to carry our blood, to bear our likenesses, to succeed me on the throne.

I took my chamber at Edinburgh Castle toward the end of May, and prepared for my delivery.

The terrible events that had taken place at Holyrood, and that had led me to take refuge in Dunbar Castle, were two months behind me, and I had returned to Edinburgh with an escort of hundreds of loyal men, the conspirators who had assaulted me and killed my servant David Riccio having fled and my treacherous, cowardly husband having once again retreated into the shadows of my life.

When my labor began three weeks later I hoped that the charm stone Jamie's sister Jean had given me would preserve me from suffering. And perhaps it did—to an extent. But the gripping, clamping pains that made me cry out hour after hour caused me more suffering than I imagined any one woman deserved. I strained against each renewed, agonizing onslaught, hoping that it would be the last. I looked to the midwife Mistress Asteane for help and reassurance. But there was very little she could do, other than to remind me, rather drily I thought, that thousands of women since time began had sweated and cried out just as I was doing, and that if they could bear the agony of it, then so could I.

After ten hours of misery she gave me a posset to drink that she said would ease my agony, but I could not keep it on my stomach. I vomited it up, and the retching only made my sufferings worse.

In the end I cried out for death, I was so wretched, and Margaret Carwood sent for the priest who was waiting in the next room, ready to give me extreme unction in the event I did not survive my ordeal.

He prayed over me, and made the sign of the cross, and I thought, will I die before my son can ever know me? I had never known my own father; would my son too be a child of bereavement?

Was this what Michel de Notredame had meant when he said my life would be baleful?

By the time Mistress Asteane told me that the birth was near and that I ought to try my hardest to push the child out into the world, I had no energy left. I was exhausted. She bore down on my stomach and pinched me so hard that I became angry and this energized me. More pinches, more anger—and then I heard Margaret say, "Here comes the little prince," and I gave a last groan and forced my shuddering body to yield up its burden.

I heard a muffled cry. Then whispers.

"He has a caul."

I looked at the tiny red child the midwife was holding up, and saw that he was indeed a prince and that there was a pink bubble around his face. The women in the room shrank back from the sight, but Mistress Asteane took it in stride. Expertly she cut the bubble open, letting fluid spill out, and then my son began to wail as she carefully removed the pink membrane from around his head.

"Hear him now, the little caulbearer!" Margaret cried out, and reverently touched one small arm with her finger. The others rushed up to touch him as well.

"He's a blessed one," someone said. "He will have the second sight, as all caulbearers do. He will know the future."

"I will call him James," I managed to say, though I could hardly speak, my throat hurt so. "Prince James Stuart, and in time King James of Scotland, the sixth of that name."

I began coughing then, and kept on coughing for most of the night, while outside my windows I could hear the guns thundering their salute and my subjects shouting their joy at the news that I had been safely delivered. Little James slept in his cradle beside my bed, swathed in sheets of fine Holland cloth embroidered with the royal arms.

"Prince James," I mused when at last I fell into a deep sleep. "Jamie. My favorite name. Jamie." And I reached out my hand to touch the blessed face of my newest love.

TWENTY-FIVE

MY recovery was slow and full of difficulties. I was nervous, my nails were a shameful sight and I chewed on bits of leather and even on the ivory binding of my prayerbook. My teeth marks were all over it. I never knew when I might feel dizzy and there were times when I shook and shook and could not stop.

I never felt safe. Someone in my household kept playing fearsome tricks to remind me that I was in danger. One night when I went to bed I found blood stains on my pillow. Someone was turning the flowers in my bedchamber upside down in their vases, or replacing them with nettles. When I put on my slippers I found sharp thorns inside them, so that they hurt my feet. Sometimes, when I was eating, I imagined—or was I imagining?—that the food tasted strange, and I spat it out, fearing poison. I had never forgotten what little King Charles told me in France, that my mother-in-law was intent on poisoning me. Quite possibly my enemies in Scotland had the same goal.

Every time I received one of these ugly reminders of danger I felt faint and ill. I knew that I was being watched, that someone—no doubt someone being paid by my husband—was determined to destroy my peace and drive me into a state of terror.

Henry was nowhere near Holyrood, he had gone to Glasgow to be close to his father whose Lennox lands and possessions were nearby. He had spoken of leaving Scotland, of going to Norway or France, and I heartily wished he would go. But then he had changed his mind and gone to Glasgow instead, and he was said to be plotting against me once more, and telling lies about me to whomever would listen, stirring up old resentments and criticisms and even saying that our son James was not his but the child of another man.

I was in low spirits much of the time. I had always been slender, but now became very thin. Far too thin and spare for a woman not yet twenty-five. When I heard that Henry too was ill, and with the dreaded French disease, I worried that he might have passed it on to me, and that that might be why I was fast becoming a wraith.

"You're much too thin, lass!" was Jamie's greeting when he came to my court a scant month after my son was born. "You want feeding up! Come to Ainslie's Tavern and we'll have ourselves a feast!"

I went, under close guard, partly because I felt the need of convivial company and partly because Jamie had told me that Red Ormiston would be there, and I wanted to speak with him.

I had not dined well since the fateful night when I nearly lost my life and David Riccio was killed. The large noisy tavern room was full of the rich odors of roasting fowls and onions, flavorful broth and gravy, freshly baked bread and spiced wine. I ate my fill, sitting across the table from Jamie who watched me eat with inebriated benevolence, nodding his head in satisfaction.

"Where is your wife then?" I asked him while we ate our syllabub.

"She sulks at home."

I raised my eyebrows.

"She seems to think that I am keeping company with another woman," Jamie went on.

"And are you?"

He shrugged. "When I can find one." He winked.

"Surely your marriage will be happier if you don't go with other women."

"My wife allows me no liberty at all."

"She is not your jailer."

"It often feels as though she is."

Sitting there in the noisy tavern, albeit surrounded by Adrien and at least a dozen others of my guard, I began to feel at ease. Just having Jamie nearby reminded me that I had a champion. A champion who was unhappily yoked to Jean Gordon, and who could not seem ever to be free of troubles with women.

"I came here tonight because it is high time I settled my debt to Red Ormiston," I told Jamie. Together we found the huge, bearlike brigand sitting across the room with several companions, all of them drinking from immense tankards. They got to their feet when I approached but I urged them to be seated again.

"Master Ormiston," I said, "I want to thank you for saving my life and the life of my son. If you will come to the palace tomorrow at noon, I will show you my appreciation."

"You owe me fifteen thousand crowns, Your Highness," was all Red Ormiston said. "And my friends here know it. John of the Side," he said, indicating a younger man across the table from him, "and the Lord's Jock, who used to be a preacher before he took to outlawry."

"To outlawry!" John of the Side cried, and the three men drank from their tankards.

"To the queen's health!" Jamie cried, and they drank to that toast as well.

"Until tomorrow," I said, and left the table, the men struggling to get to their feet once more as I departed.

Red Ormiston came to the palace a little after noon on the following day, dressed just as he had been the night before, in worn black trews and a patched leather vest, high boots and a shirt that had once been white, and with a sprig of heather in his cap. With him were the two men he had called John of the Side and the Lord's Jock, both with cleaner faces and hands than when I had seen them last.

I had the men ushered into the throne room, where I waited with Jamie at my side and a dozen guardsmen in attendance.

"You may approach the throne, Master Ormiston," I said. He was clearly alarmed by his surroundings. I thought he might run out of the room.

"I have brought you here to offer you a full pardon for what you did on the night my servant David Riccio was killed."

His look of alarm gave way to one of relief.

"It was Your Highness we were hired to kill," the outlaw said in his deep rasping voice. "I want that clear."

"My husband Lord Darnley hired you?"

Ormiston nodded. "He said the English soldiers would protect us. But there were no English soldiers. We could see that for ourselves. And Lord Bothwell there"—he pointed to Jamie—"he said there weren't going to be any. He was right. He's always been true and square with me and me with him, and he told me, there are no English, not within a hundred miles.

"Look here, he says, Lord Darnley says he will pay you but he won't. The queen will give you fifteen thousand crowns if you save her life. Take it, he says. Take it and save her. So I did."

"Why did you kill my servant then?"

Red Ormiston shrugged. "We had to kill somebody. Just not you." He paused for breath, and looked around the room, then at me.

"Now you owe me my money."

At a gesture from me two guardsmen brought forward a chest and, setting it down in front of the outlaw, raised the lid. It was full of shining gold coins.

Red Ormiston and his friends rushed to the chest, wide smiles on their faces, and dug their hands deep into the hoard of gold.

"Kneel, Master Ormiston," I commanded, and he obeyed. I reached out and took a sword from one of the guardsmen. As he knelt before me, head bowed, I touched the outlaw lightly on both shoulders.

"Arise, Sir Ormiston," I said. And then, as he got to his feet, somewhat dazed by the unexpected honor I had done him, I added, "Arise, and meet your bride."

"My bride?"

The Scottish wife, who until then had been in an adjacent room, now entered the throne room and walked proudly toward us. At my request Margaret Carwood had dressed her in a gown of russet velvet, with a high steepled headdress like those I myself wore. There were pearls at her neck and gold in her ears and on her fingers, and she looked, I thought, like the woman she had once been, the woman who had been the daughter of an admiral and the fiancée of a young nobleman. The woman she had been before she had the misfortune to be won by Jamie in that fateful game of cards.

She was far from beautiful, but she was clean and dignified and she walked toward us with pride, and a glow of happiness I had not seen on her face until then. She looked like a fine, sturdy, respectable wife—a wife any newly knighted outlaw would be proud to have for his own.

"Sir Ormiston, this is Anna. It is my wish that the two of you should wed."

They looked at one another, he taking in her expensive clothes, the pearls and the gold, her plain features, her strong, solid body, her steady gaze, she assessing his tall, bulky frame and countryman's well-worn clothes, his shaggy black hair and uncombed beard.

They looked at one another, and they grinned.

In the briefest of ceremonies—not a nuptial mass as neither the bride nor the groom was Catholic—Sir James "Red" Ormiston and Anna Thorsen became man and wife, with Jamie standing up for the outlaw and Margaret Carwood for Anna.

After the vows had been exchanged, Anna practiced her newly learned Scots. "I haf nefer been so happy as this day I am," she said. "I vish you all so happy."

And I heard Jamie say, under his breath, "Amen."

TWENTY-SIX

No one had ever seen such storms. No one had ever heard such wind. The harsh weather that swept down from the north to freeze the crops and blight the harvest in that winter and the early months of the following year was far worse than even the oldest among my subjects could remember. Cold rain beat down ceaselessly and the merciless cutting wind, high and swift and with a fearsome singing, sliced the air like a knife.

My people blamed me for the fierce storms and the ceaseless wind, saying that I was accursed because I did not adopt the reformed faith and because I was a light woman who had married a man of low morals. I was accursed—and therefore my people were suffering. They did not want to suffer any longer. If I were no longer queen, they murmured, then their sufferings would be at an end.

Now I began to worry that the mischief-makers in my household might not be in the pay of my husband. They might be part of a general upwelling of anger and discontent coming from all my subjects, or many of them. I had no way of knowing—unless someone was caught in the act of trying to taint my food or cut my clothes to ribbons (Margaret had found several of my fine gowns lying in their baskets, destroyed in this way) or substitute wormwood syrup for honey in the big yellow pot that sat on my table.

I knew that I was in danger, but I could not guess from which source the danger might come. And I continued to worry that in becoming thinner and thinner I might be succumbing to the French disease, and that I might die of it.

Thick snow smothered the palace on the January morning my council met to advise me on what action to take to protect myself and my son. Ice covered the windows of my council chamber and I had to have extra logs put on the fire to keep off the chill.

"You will never be safe, Your Highness, until you rid yourself of this man you married." My brother James, whom I had restored to favor (though he did not have my full trust) as I needed and valued his advice, was holding forth as we warmed ourselves in front of the blazing hearth. "You ought never to have chosen him, but the time for altering that has come and gone. Now you must treat him as you would a venomous spider."

"Or a snake in the grass," put in Jamie.

"I have sent two men to Rome to consult with the papal court about a divorce. After all, the pope never granted a dispensation for us to marry."

"And your husband has never forgiven you for failing to obtain that dispensation," said George Gordon, who had taken his late father's place as leader of the Gordon clan. "He accuses you of deceiving him."

"Never mind what Lord Darnley says, or thinks," came another voice. "I have just heard that his plan is to kidnap the baby prince James, take him to the Scilly Isles and proclaim him king (with himself as regent, of course), then invade Scotland with a force of English ships and depose you, Your Highness."

"Can he do that?"

"Not if he should have a terrible accident first," said Jamie. "There are so many ways a man can die: a fall from a horse, a choking rheum, a surfeit of lampreys, a misdirected arrow while he is hunting." He counted these off on his thick fingers as he spoke. "He can tumble off a high cliff. He can run afoul of a gang of thieves. He can drink too much and partake of too much hashish—"

"Hashish? Where would he get hashish?"

"From the sailors. They carry it from port to port, and sell it, and enjoy it themselves."

"No wonder so many ships go aground," remarked another of the councilors.

"What I am saying is," Jamie went on, "Lord Darnley may not be long for this earth."

"I would not be sorry to see him gone," I admitted. "But won't he die soon, if he has the French disease?"

"He could last for years," said my brother. "He would be mad, of course, but he would not be dead. And madmen have led rebellions before now."

As the dark subject of my husband's hoped-for demise was being discussed, snow continued to fall, whirling in columns outside the frost-rimed window, the fallen flakes mounting higher and higher in the courtyard, the snow mounds rising faster than the grooms could shovel them away.

"We will be prisoners here if the snow gets any higher," I remarked. "Just as I am a prisoner of my marriage."

"There is always divorce," came the voice of Lord Argyll, head of the Campbell clan.

"The church prevents it."

"Exceptions have been made," Argyll continued. "Your own grandmother Queen Margaret divorced her second husband, the Earl of Angus."

"Those Tudors trust to divorce overmuch, I fear," was brother James's response. "Many people still say that the English Queen Elizabeth is a bastard because her father divorced Queen Catherine in order to marry her mother."

"All the English are bastards," was Jamie's sardonic comment. "Whether their parents are legally married or not."

"An annulment, then. Surely the best course, short of accident or murder, is to persuade the pope to issue a document saying that the marriage was never valid. Then Lord Darnley cannot claim the throne, either as regent or as your husband."

"But an annulment would make the little prince a bastard, would it not? No one wants that."

The discussion and debate went on for an hour or more, the voices rising at times to shouts in order to be heard above the mournful, vaguely menacing singing of the wind. I bit my nails and listened, aware that Jamie was watching me closely and even more aware that it was up to me to decide what course to take against Henry. It was action that was needed, not words.

And so, despite the snow and wind, I made the decision to ride to Glasgow where Henry was. Partly because I took forty guardsmen with me, and partly because he was ill and weak, I persuaded Henry to return with me to the capital. I needed to keep him nearby, so that whatever scheming he might try to do could more easily be detected and thwarted.

I let him choose his own lodging and he chose a comfortable small house with a garden less than a mile from Holyrood, right next to the town wall. It was in a compound known as Kirk o'Field, a small enclave with several other houses and gardens. I furnished the house for him with hangings and tables, linens and kitchenware from the palace storerooms.

Despite the information I had that he had been conspiring and telling lies about me, Henry seemed quite docile in his new lodgings, and made no demands on me other than that I come to see him during what he hoped would be his recuperation from the French disease. Perhaps he knew, perhaps he denied to himself the knowledge that there was no recovery possible. The dreaded scourge brought with it only increasing weakness, pain, and eventually madness, as my brother James had said. I cringed at the thought of Henry's suffering to come; despite his treachery, and his attempt on my life, despite all the hatred I had felt toward him, I could not wish him the agony of a lingering death.

I went each day with my escort along the Canongate and down Blackfriars Wynd to the little house at Kirk o'Field, and stayed there for several hours while Henry played his lute, and sometimes gambled, and met with Dr. Bourgoing who did what he could to soothe the skin eruptions and ugly rash on the soles of Henry's feet and the palms of his hands. He was growing bald, his once luxuriant blond hair falling out in patches. I brought him knitted caps to wear and mittens for his rough red hands, and concoctions from my apothecary for the headaches that plagued him.

Then came very good news: Dr. Bourgoing told me, in private of course, that he was certain I did not have the French disease, and that my loss of weight was simply the result of low spirits and a poor appetite. And my tirewoman Margaret Carwood told me that she was soon to marry, and asked me if I would attend the ceremony.

"I will do better than that," I said. "I will give a ball at the palace. Shrovetide is nearly upon us, and we ought to celebrate. It has been such a long and dreary winter, we deserve to rejoice and amuse ourselves before Lent comes."

My mood lightened by the day. I ordered my cooks to prepare a lavish banquet for three hundred guests and told my servants to decorate the palace with bright colors and greenery, hundreds of wax tapers and my best gold and silver plate for the banqueting. For the first time since James's birth I felt a return of my old energy, my old lightness of mood, as I prepared for the merrymaking to come.

But outside the palace windows the terrible storms continued, and with them, the racking wind that set my teeth on edge and turned the entire town into a giant icicle. Even the poorest of my subjects were glad to hear that a celebration at the palace was being planned, for they knew that would mean scraps of meat and bread for them and extra charitable gifts given out at the palace gates. But still they grumbled about the worsening weather, and blamed me, and were overheard to say that they wished the accursed queen was no longer on her throne.

TWENTY-SEVEN

MASTER Fullerton!"
I had just walked into my bedchamber, intent on readying myself for the ball which was to begin in only two hours, when I saw my groom, Adam Fullerton, bending over the hearth and throwing something—something—

I cried out in horror as I saw that he was throwing my favorite portrait of my mother in its elaborate gilded frame, into the fire.

I rushed toward the hearth, heedless of my skirts which threatened to ignite from the sparks that flew upward from the blaze. Snatching the tongs, I managed to pull the portrait out of the flames. It was singed but not ruined. My mother's young face, the face I loved more than any other, still gazed out at me from the painting.

My groom had taken to his heels but I ran out into the corridor and called for my guards to catch him. It was Jamie who swiftly brought Adam before me, ashen-faced, his hands secured behind his back.

"So this is the mischief-maker who has been terrorizing you," Jamie said.

"Look! He almost burned my mother's portrait!" I held out the singed painting for Jamie to see.

"Evil swine! Who paid you to do this?" Jamie tore off his belt and wrapped it around Adam Fullerton's throat, tightening it. "Who paid you? Tell me or you'll never breathe again!"

The groom choked, trying to talk. The belt was loosened slightly.

"Was it the king?" I demanded. "Was it my husband?"

The boy shook his head.

"Who then? Which of my traitor lords?"

He continued to shake his head, until Jamie slapped him.

He coughed, then managed to spit out a few words.

"No, not a lord—a—"

"A what?"

"A reverend."

"Don't lie to me, boy," Jamie said menacingly.

"I swear. It was—Reverend Knox."

Jamie loosened his belt and the groom fell to the floor, grasping his throat and coughing.

"He says—you need to know—the fear of God."

"I'll teach that churl Knox to fear—to fear me!" Jamie swore. "And as for this insolent, thieving knave—" He did not finish his sentence, but his intent was clear.

Staring down at the gasping groom, I did my best to remember when the chain of frightening, unsettling events in my bedchamber began. It was soon after my son's birth. And Adam Fullerton, along with several others, had been added to my household at about that time.

"I'm nothing. I'm no one," the boy was saying. "Others are doing much worse things."

Instantly Jamie had him by the throat again.

"What things? Is it that blasted whoreson Knox again?"

Adam shook his head. "No. It's the others."

"What others?"

"I swear I don't know. They are dressed like laborers. I've seen them go into the cellars. I watch them, at night. Nearly every night for the past week they have gone in there—"

"And done what?"

Adam blanched. "Go into the cellars, and you'll see."

"Take me there! Show me what you are talking about!"

"No!" Adam pleaded. "No, it's too dangerous!"

Jamie kicked the groom, knocking the wind from his lungs. I had to look away.

"Show me or you'll be in real danger," Jamie was saying. "From this sword." Swiftly he pulled his sword from its scabbard and held the sharp edge of the blade to Adam's throat.

Trembling with fear, the boy led us down into the storerooms where I had gone with Jamie on the night David Riccio was killed. Past storeroom after storeroom. Past the dim room where we had discovered my cringing husband.

At last, in a storage room filled with piles of discarded lumber and broken furniture and leather trunks that looked centuries old, the boy showed us a hidden entrance to a narrow tunnel. The wall had been breached, and recently, to judge from the jagged edges of the tunnel mouth and the piles of freshly dug earth beside it.

Jamie lifted a torch from the wall and entered the tunnel, holding the torch in front of him. I followed.

"No!" screamed Adam Fullerton. "No fire!"

Reluctantly, Jamie retraced his steps and put the torch back, then cautiously began walking along the tunnel as before.

"Wait here," he said to me.

I heard his footsteps, then a long, low whistle, and an exclamation. "Of all the—"

In a moment Jamie came running out. He seized my hand and hurriedly led me back upstairs, tugging Adam along with us. His face was set in a grim rictus.

"What is it? What's in there? I demand to know."

He put his finger to his lips. "Not here," he said. Only when we were safely back in my bedchamber, and the groom had been handed over to the guardsmen to be locked away, did Jamie speak.

"Now, Mary, listen to me carefully. This is very important. I want you to do your best to pretend that nothing happened here tonight. I want you to get ready for your ball now, and not to let on to any of your household that there is anything amiss. Promise me you will stay calm when I tell you what you need to know."

Wide-eyed, I promised.

He took my hand. "There is enough gunpowder in that basement room to blow Holyrood Palace into the Firth of Forth."

I gasped. I felt faint.

"And all the means to ignite it. I'm going to go now and gather my men and take them down there and get rid of it. All of it. Every last barrel. But you mustn't let on that you know about this, or whoever put the powder there will light the fuses, as sure as anything. Now, are you going to be all right until I come back and tell you everything is safe?"

I gulped. My heart was racing. Jamie squeezed my hand reassuringly.

"Oh Jamie, what if they see you? What if they prevent you?"

"Then we'll die together, Orange Blossom. And we'll meet in heaven—or some hotter place. Now, let me get on with it."

How I managed, my hands shaking, my knees knocking, to dress for the ball I cannot remember. I know that I drank cup after cup of willow bark tea in an effort to calm myself, and that Margaret had to rub my stomach to keep me from vomiting, I was so frightened. I did not tell her or anyone else the awful secret I knew, but she sensed that something was terribly wrong. When she began to question me I cut her off roughly.

"Hold your peace, Margaret, and say your prayers," I said sharply. She did as I asked. I could see her lips moving silently as she helped me dress and arranged my hair and headdress.

"Where is your husband?" I asked when I was fully gowned, my hair faultlessly gathered under my headdress, my pale cheeks faintly rouged with vermilion. (I never rouged my lips or cheeks, but on this night, to hide my fear, I made an exception.) It had only been two days since Margaret's wedding. Her new husband was a member of the night watch, the constables who patrolled the Edinburgh streets after dark.

"Sleeping, Your Highness. He sleeps in the afternoons, so that he can keep the watch all night."

"Go and wake him up. I want you to go with him tonight, on his rounds."

"But Your Highness, the ball—"

"Do as I say, Margaret."

"Yes, Your Highness."

"And stay warm. It is a cold night."

For the past two hours, ever since Jamie left me, I had been in a state of dread. With every passing second I feared that there would come an explosion, a sound like the cannonfire I had heard on the battlefield when we fought the Gordons and my brother James's men. Every minute that passed and brought no explosion was a relief—yet I thought, as the seconds ticked away, perhaps the gunpowder will go off now, or perhaps in another minute, or in five minutes more. I felt my muscles clench as if to ward off a blow that might come at any time. Without being aware of it I found myself frowning, and lowering my head and shutting my eyes tight, gritting my teeth, as if to armor myself against disaster.

It was midwinter, and darkness came early. My guests arrived, the musicians began to play. Where was Jamie? Why hadn't he come to tell me all was well? Had he been captured or killed by my hidden enemies?

An hour passed, and then another. Nothing happened. We danced. We dined. We celebrated the Shrovetide. I began to believe that everything would be all right.

After nearly four hours Jamie appeared among my guests, resplendent in a black velvet doublet trimmed in silver, a glittering diamond in his ear, his jeweled codpiece winking in the candlelight. Only the grime on his hands betrayed (to me alone) what he had been doing. He had been saving my life, and the lives of everyone in the room.

He came up to me and whispered in my ear, "The danger is past. There is no longer anything to fear."

Until then I had managed to control myself. But when I heard that there was no more danger my knees gave way under me and I sank to the floor, and might have hurt myself had Jamie not caught me in his strong arms and carried me, fainting, to the nearest couch.

TWENTY-EIGHT

A thunderous, ear-splitting boom rent the night, shaking the walls of the palace and setting everyone in it, including me, to screaming.

Were we under attack? Were the walls going to come tumbling down around us? Terrified, I leapt out of bed, struggling to shake off the drowse of sleep. Then I remembered. It had to be the gunpowder. The gunpowder Jamie promised me would not harm us.

Expecting more explosions, I hurriedly put on my furred bedgown and slippers while my guardsmen rushed in to my bedchamber, uncertain where the danger lay but determined to save me from it.

"It's the Cowgate," I heard someone shout. "They've blown up the Cowgate!" I went to the window and looked out into the night. My subjects were pouring out of their houses and into the streets, in their nightclothes, carrying torches. There was a clamor of voices. Before long I thought I could hear, in the distance, the tramp of boots. I imagined it was the sound of soldiers coming along the Royal Mile from the castle on its height.

Then a messenger came.

"Your Highness," he said, kneeling, "I have been sent by the constable of the watch to tell you some very bad news."

"Yes?"

"I am sorry to have to tell you, Your Highness, that the body of the king your husband has been found in the garden of the house where he was staying, the old porter's lodge in Kirk o'Field."

It took me a long time to respond.

"He is dead then?" I said at length.

"Yes, Your Highness."

"And the explosion we heard?"

"The lodge exploded. The constable believes it was a mine."

Just then Jamie came into the bedchamber, wearing his nightclothes and looking perplexed.

"What is it? What's happened? Somebody tell me what's happened!"

Others in my household were rushing in, my equerry Arthur Erskine, some of the tirewomen, sleepy-looking grooms.

"Is a search being made for more mines?" I asked the messenger. "Have the guilty men been caught? And is my husband's body being treated with the honor his rank deserves?"

"The men of the watch were in charge when I left," he replied. "I do not know whether they have captured anyone, or what is being done with the king's body."

"Take an escort and go back to Kirk o'Field. Tell the constables that the queen sent you with these instructions." I went to my desk and wrote a few lines, ordering that Henry's body be brought to Holyrood and laid out in the chapel, and that a coffin be prepared immediately to receive it. I folded the paper and handed it to the messenger, who got up from his knees, bowed and left the room.

"Now then," I said to the others, "leave me, all of you, except for Lord Bothwell. Guards, stay in the corridor. Arthur, let no one in except my brother James, if he should wish to see me. Kindly tell him the dire news, if he has not already heard it."

Everyone left my bedchamber, except Jamie, who sat on a bench near the fire, yawning.

I sat also, looking at him but saying nothing. I kept expecting to feel something, anything. But I was numb.

"So he has been dispatched," I said after a time. "And with the gunpowder you found in the cellar. Am I right?"

Jamie nodded.

"It was a sudden decision. After I left you I rounded up Red Ormiston and his brothers and about thirty of my men from Liddesdale who were in Ainslie's Tavern, and we managed to get the barrels out of the cellar, every one of us fearing for our lives all the while. If one of us had dislodged a torch, or struck a spark from a bit of metal, or if, Lord forbid, there had been a stray coal from the kitchens or even straw lit in the stables for warmth, and a wisp of it blown out into the courtyard—" He shook his head at the dangerous thought.

"We got it all into carts. All those heavy barrels. But what were we going to do with them? We didn't dare take them up toward the castle, we would have been seen for sure and challenged. People would have been frightened. Then I thought, if it was Darnley who was plotting to destroy you and your palace, then why not use his own weapon against him? What could be more just?

"So I told my men to get black felts from the storerooms and we covered the carts to look as though we were a funeral procession, and put on our own black cloaks and had Red Ormiston walk in front of us, carts and all, holding up a silver cross we borrowed from your chapel—mea culpa, mea culpa—and in that way we were able to go unhindered down into Blackfriars Wynd and across Cowgate and so to the old porter's lodge."

"No one saw you?"

"The watch, naturally. But don't forget: I am the sheriff of Edinburgh!"

"So you are."

"When we got to the lodge there were lights on inside but the men waiting there (all murderers, I am certain) must have all had guilty consciences—or a want of arms, more likely—and so they fled like rats—like rats, I swear!—out into the night as soon as they saw us. We broke in and set our barrels in place and our fuses. Some of the neighbors came up to the edge of the garden but they didn't dare bother us. Besides, we were swift.

"Darnley must have been hiding somewhere inside. I know he wasn't in his bed, I looked. We lit the fuses and left. But I wanted to make sure the house went up so I stood and watched from a cow pasture a little ways away. I heard shouts and a challenge, coming from the garden of the lodge. Some of my men were still close by, but so were some Campbells and some Hamiltons, and even a few Douglases.

"Then the house went up and I thought, good, that's the end of all Darnley's scheming. He wanted you dead, and now he's dead instead. Then I hurried back to the palace and put on my nightclothes and pretended I had never been away."

"Keep pretending," I said. "What a long day this has been! There is no peace anywhere any more."

But Jamie was grinning. "There is for Darnley," he said, with a malicious twinkle in his eye. "The peace of eternal rest."

TWENTY-NINE

THE wolves were howling, the wolves were closing in. All Edinburgh, it seemed, was convinced that I had ordered, perhaps even carried out, the murder of my royal husband.

My people, lords and commons alike, Catholic and Protestant alike, were united in condemning me.

The most daring among them accused me of being an adulteress, of plotting with my lover Lord Bothwell (for was he not my chief counsilor, and was I not often in his company?) to carry out my husband's murder. They asserted it to one another, and the priests and pastors among them shouted it from their pulpits. Artists drew perverse sketches of me consorting with my paramour. My enemies devised a banner showing my late husband's corpse, and our child, little Jamie, lamenting his dead father, and the word "JUSTICE" in large bold letters. Whenever I left the palace, or looked out of my windows, I saw this banner waving aloft.

And I felt guilty, for in fact I was guilty. To be sure, I had nothing to do with the placing of gunpowder in my palace cellars, which had put me in peril of death. Nor had I given orders that the gunpowder be moved to my husband's dwelling. Nor had I been the one to strangle him as he fled the house (for he had not in fact died in the explosion, as it turned out, but had been strangled, by a person or persons unknown, as he tried to get away). But I had compassed my husband's death, as the legal phrase goes. I had discussed with my advisers how he might be eliminated. I had become one of the wolves, the feral Scottish wolves that turn on each other and rend each other with their sharp teeth. I did not mourn my husband, but neither did I rejoice in his death. Rather I blamed myself, and fell into melancholy.

Jamie was determined to raise my spirits.

"Listen to me, lass, and free your mind of these morbid imaginings!" he said, taking me by the shoulders and all but shaking me like a child. "What happened to Lord Darnley was not your fault—or mine, for that matter. It was entirely his own doing. He had made many enemies. It was only a matter of time before one or another of them killed him. David Riccio's brothers were plotting to poison him. Nearly all the Scots lords hated him, even though they found him useful at times. And remember, the explosives that led to his death were his, he got them from the English (so I have heard). The crime was his—only at the last moment it was turned against him, by the hand of providence, or justice, or whatever name you choose to give to luck."

On a sudden impulse I turned to Jamie. "Take me away from here," I said. "Take me on board the *Black Messenger*. Let's sail away. Far away. And never come back!"

"That's my lass! That's the spirit!" And he laughed his hearty laugh, and swept me up into a dance measure—only there were no musicians to play for us at that moment, more's the pity, and we had to beat out the measure with our own kicking, flying feet.

The island loomed up before us, green and vast and empty, as we rounded the Ross of Mull and pulled into safe harbor. The *Black Messenger* had brought us safely around the northernmost tip of

Scotland and through the rough waters off the coast of Argyllshire, wetted under squalls of rain and buffeted by shifting, unquiet seas that slapped against the ship's hull and threatened to overturn her.

"I've a friend with a cottage here," Jamie said as we entered a protected bay and made safe anchorage. "Bit of a pirate, actually. At least he used to be. Oh—and he also used to be a bishop, but don't mention that. It's a bitter memory to him."

"And how do you know this pirate who used to be a bishop?"

"He sort of brought me up. He was my tutor. He taught me my catechism—and other things."

"Oh."

The aging, white-haired man who met us as we climbed out of the dinghy was spry despite his years. He walked with a limp yet his voice was strong as he greeted us and the look he gave Jamie held the faintest hint of a leer. The leer of a man of the world, not a bishop.

"This is the lady you wrote me about," he said, extending his hand to me in friendship. So he does not know who I really am, I thought. Otherwise he would bow and call me "Your Highness." Or perhaps he does know, but has agreed to pretend ignorance.

"This is my lovely Orange Blossom, yes."

"So mysterious!" the old man said with a wink.

"And this, my dear, is my godfather Archibald Skerriton, who owns most of the land hereabouts."

"I thought this was Maclean country," I remarked, remembering what I had learned of the Highland clans and their territories.

"It is. My mother was a Maclean—and then she married a Skerriton, and I was the sad result." Jamie and Archibald both laughed loudly at this, and I smiled amiably.

"We have had a rough wet journey, and are in need of food and rest," Jamie said.

"And your crew?"

"They stay on the ship. They fend for themselves. They are Norwegians."

"Ah!" Archibald's single syllable was eloquent. Evidently Norwegians were as respected for their self-sufficiency as they were for their ability to sail.

He led us to a small, isolated whitewashed cottage on a hillside, overlooking the inlet. The sun came out from behind the clouds to sparkle on the turquoise waters of the shallow bay.

"Here we are then, Mary," Jamie said after Archibald left us and went back down the hill, whistling.

"Here we are then." We looked into each other's eyes, as we had so many times before. Only now, in the quiet of the cottage, there was no one to interrupt us, there were no demands to distract us.

I laid my hand on Jamie's arm. His shirt was rough under my touch. I could feel the warmth of his strong arm beneath it. Slowly I moved my hand up his arm toward his broad shoulder, then on up to his neck. The cords of his muscles stood out prominently. He swallowed, keeping his eyes locked with mine.

As if in a dream I touched his bristled cheek—and then, as naturally as the rain that began to fall on the cottage roof, we came into each other's arms and our lips met.

We kissed for hours, thirstily, until my lips were red and bruised with so much kissing. So much loving. We lay on the small bed with its sweet-smelling straw mattress, replete with lovemaking, drowsing in each other's arms, murmuring softly to each other. So this is love, I thought. No wonder the poets make so much of it. But they do not do it justice. And I kissed him again.

We hardly left the little cottage for two days. Food appeared at our door—homemade loaves and fresh milk in a pitcher, oat cakes and salmon and seaweed prepared as I had never before eaten it, cheese and a paste made from pungent scarlet berries and—much to Jamie's satisfaction—a jug of the potent spirit called, in Gaelic, the water of life.

We ate and drank, made love, slept, then ate and drank again. I lost myself in pleasure, I gave myself up to it body and soul. Jamie became all to me: the sight of him, the feel of him, the taste and smell of him became my world, and when I slept, I dreamed of him and woke to find him smiling down at me tenderly, eager for our two bodies to become one yet again.

We said little, we who had always had so much to say, and had always said it so plainly. Instead, after the first few days had passed, we walked hand in hand, in silence, along the narrow stony paths that wound along the shore before rising into the mist-shrouded headlands of our island. We crossed the falling burns and skirted the small lochs that lay between green hillocks. Jamie frisked like a young animal, sniffing the air like an eager hound and turning his face to the showers that passed over us, leaving us damp and refreshed. Eagles flew above us, from tree to tree and across the open spaces between them. Their effortless soaring spoke to me in a language more eloquent than mere words: it said, come soar with us on love's wings, come free yourself from the harsh bonds of earth, from all that entrammels you.

I lost count of the days, of the hours even. There was only the moment, one golden moment giving way slowly, lingeringly, to another. I could not bear the thought that it all might end.

One afternoon as a low mist closed in around the cottage windows and the only sound was the surge and splash of the waves against the jagged rocks on the shore below, we sat by the fireside and talked.

"My love," I said, taking Jamie's square, calloused hand with its short stubby fingers and thick palm.

"I know. We must decide what to do now. Now that we know—what we have always known."

"Oh Jamie, my dearest Jamie, how I wish it had been you I married."

"I was promised. And you were stubborn."

I shook my head. "How I regret my foolishness!"

Jamie let go of my hand, got to his feet and stood by the fire, holding out his palms to its warmth.

"I think that we should marry now. You are going to need a protector more than ever."

"I'm afraid I am going to need a whole army of protectors."

He knelt down and took me in his arms. "But only one who loves you. Who would give his life for you. Who wants you here, in his arms, forever."

THIRTY

IT was while we were sailing back to the capital aboard the *Black Messenger* that we made our plan. We had agreed to marry—how could we not?—but knowing that there would be much opposition to our marriage, and that Edinburgh was in a state of turmoil, we had to proceed with care. I was in disgrace, in my subjects' eyes; now I was going to marry the man with whom I had conspired—so many of my subjects were convinced—to murder my husband.

Jamie was determined to spare me as much scandalous talk and condemnation as possible. So we agreed to act in such a way that it would seem as though he was forcing himself on me, taking advantage of me in my widowhood. We would make it look as though he was thirsty for the crown, eager to be king in my late husband's place. As though I were nothing more than an incidental element in his scheme. That way I might arouse my subjects' sympathy instead of their scorn.

"Let me and my borderers storm the palace and seize it," Jamie said, already eager for the action. "Then I can seize you, and insist that you marry me."

"No. There would be bloodshed and I don't want any of my guardsmen killed—or your men either. No bloodshed. Better that you should come upon me while I am on the road, with an escort but not a large one. Suppose I ride to—to Stirling, to visit my son. Suppose I stay with him for a few days, and then take him back with me to Holyrood, and on the way, you and your men can encircle my party and force me to go with you to one of your castles. Then we can be married."

"Yes. Better that it happen while you are out riding—only you must not have young James with you. He has lived at Stirling for most of his life. To move him now would be a sure indicator that we planned the entire escapade beforehand."

"There is one other thing," I added. "What about your wife?"

Jamie cleared his throat. He was uncomfortable, he did not look at me. "I have never spoken of this before, but in fact my marriage is flawed, just as yours to Lord Darnley was."

"You never told me this."

"I didn't realize it until a few months ago. When I knew you were unhappy, and hoped to free yourself from your husband, I went to see a man of law and also took counsel with the church commissioners who rule on marriage. I told them that when I was seventeen, I promised myself to a girl, Janet Beatoun. We swore to love forever, our wrists were tied together in the old way. We were handfasted. We lived together for nearly a year before her father came and took her from me.

"I was advised that my marriage to Jean Gordon was not valid, because of my prior contract with Janet. So I am not a married man after all."

"But even if you are free of Jean Gordon, you are still married by handfasting to Janet."

He sighed. "No, I am a widower. Janet died last spring bringing her fifth child into the world."

"I confess I am confused."

He put his arm around me and squeezed my shoulder. "Don't be. All will be well. The law will rule in my favor—in our favor. I will soon be declared a widower and free to marry any woman I choose, even the queen." He kissed me on the forehead, and I decided not to worry about the entire subject any more. Instead I decided to soar like the eagles, all worries laid aside. I was in love, unlike any love I had ever known. I would trust that love, and let the rest go.

Three months later I was riding along the little stream near the Bridges of Almond, almost within sight of the capital, on my way back to Holyrood from a stay in Stirling. The time had come to put our plan into effect, and I knew that Jamie and his men would be coming for me. But when we heard the horsemen approaching, I was overwhelmed by the sound. There had to be hundreds of mounted men, their horses' hooves resounding like gathering thunder.

I turned my horse and spurred him and began to go back the way we had come, but then Jamie and his men came into sight, and I dropped the reins and gave up, feigning terror and submission.

He had an entire army with him, far outnumbering my small band of guardsmen. He had told me he would be bringing a hundred men, but it looked to me as though there were nearer a thousand, coming on in force, armed as if for battle, and my few men scattered before they could be swept aside and trampled by the oncoming horde.

My horse reared in fear and Jamie rode up at once and calmed her, shouting as he did so.

"Your Highness! You must not enter the capital or you will be seized and imprisoned by the citizens! They have denounced you and will take your throne!"

He took hold of my horse's bridle and led me away, and throughout the long ride to Dunbar Castle we maintained the illusion that he was kidnapping me—in the interests of my safety—and that I had no choice but to do as he said. We continued to maintain it after we arrived at the castle. Jamie held me captive, and I submitted to him as my captor. To all outward appearances I had no choice but to submit, and I gave in to his superior force.

But in truth I was no captive, rather an eager, willing lover. Glad to be with him, rejoicing in his love. And looking forward with the greatest happiness to our wedding day.

For as I confided to Jamie, we had more than one reason to rejoice. Not only were we to be wed, and join our lives together forever, but we were to be parents. My monthly flow had ceased, my face had the roundness and glow of motherhood. I was certain, as certain as I could be without a midwife's accord, that I was pregnant with Jamie's child.

CHIRTY-ONE

THERE was an uncomfortable shuffling of feet and murmuring of voices in the great hall at Holyrood on the morning of my marriage to Jamie.

It was the fifteenth of May, in the year 1567, and as everyone knows, May marriages are unlucky. Ours, I hoped, would be an exception. I could not help thinking back to my first wedding day so many years earlier, when I was only fifteen and marrying the dauphin of France, and my greatest worry was that I was so much taller than my groom! Now, as I looked around me at the scowling faces of my nobles and courtiers and the prominent men of Edinburgh, I had to admit to a far greater concern: my very kingdom was at stake.

On my first wedding day I had worn a beautiful ivory silk gown with yards and yards of intricate lacework. Now I was wearing mourning black (as I had when I married Henry), and so was everyone in the hall, for by my order the entire court was in mourning for my late husband. On that long ago day when I was married for the first time, my uncle the Cardinal de Guise had performed our nuptial mass; on this day there was a Protestant service, and because no pastor in the capital had been willing to marry me to Jamie (both of us being considered in a state of sin for having committed murder), the service was conducted by none other than Archibald Skerriton, Jamie's former tutor and our host on the island of Mull. He had once been of the Roman faith but now, Jamie told me, he made no particular profession of faith at all. But he was still a clergyman, of sorts, and so was able to marry us.

I wore my mother's portrait miniature around my neck for luck, and as Jamie and I joined hands and he slipped the gold wedding band onto my finger, I wished that mother could be there to see us wed. She had been so very fond of Jamie, I was sure that had she been there to see our wedding, she would bless us and understand all.

Yet no sooner were we pronounced man and wife than we began to be reviled. Hisses of scorn and muffled jeers greeted us as we left the hall. Stones and clods of earth were thrown at the windows of my apartments from the courtyard below. The torture (I came to see it as such) of the nightly hymn-singing outside our bedroom windows was revived, and my nemesis John Knox, who had recently become my distant kinsman by marriage, took it upon himself to chastise me loudly and publicly as Jezebel incarnate and the most wicked of all the queens ever to rule on the earth.

It was intolerable, especially in my delicate state. Apart from Jamie, no one but Margaret Carwood (now Margaret Hargatt, since her marriage to Ned Hargatt of the night watch) knew that I was pregnant—she was about to become a mother herself—and I wanted to keep my secret for as long as possible. My baby was small, I had only the most modest swelling of my belly, which made me think that she must be a girl. I hoped so. The thought warmed me. I tried not to dwell on what the future would bring for my children.

For within days of my marriage to Jamie the storm of rebellion broke over our heads. The Lords of the Congregation rose up against us and put themselves under arms, joining with those nobles who declared themselves united in opposition to the throne. We had some supporters, to be sure, but the majority of those able to fight and in command of followers were against us, especially against Jamie, who was now their despised king.

It was clear we would have to take the field against the rebels, and Jamie, who was an energetic commander, gathered our fighting men to a hastily prepared camp at Carberry Hill east of the capital. The enemy gathered on a hill opposite us.

What I remember most about that memorable day the two armies met, June 15—exactly a month after our wedding—is that we were so very, very thirsty. The sun glared down on us mercilessly, we were exposed on our hilltop and there was no shade anywhere.

The other, much more important thing is that there were so few of us, and so many of the enemy! They grew in force even as I sat on our hilltop, mounted and battle-ready, watching the activity on the opposite hill. More and more men kept coming to join our enemies, men on foot and horseback, men driving carts with supplies, men carrying those accusing white banners that bore the images of Henry's corpse with baby Jamie kneeling beside it, and the single accusatory word: JUSTICE.

As I watched their numbers grow, I heard the disconcerting sound of our own men galloping away. My army was deserting me. Jamie did his best to rally them, but there was no denying what was happening. Our army was shrinking before our eyes.

Then Jamie boldly rode down the hill and out onto the field between the two hills.

"I challenge you!" he shouted. "Who will answer my challenge?"

When none of the enemy rode out to meet him he continued to taunt them, shouting "Come out, cowards! Come and fight me! Who among you is man enough to fight!"

But the enemy soldiers remained where they were, their leaders silently watching Jamie waving his sword, wheeling his horse back and forth in a futile effort to rouse a response.

I watched also, licking my lips, trying to moisten my dry mouth. I watched in pity.

What was I to do? What could I do? In the end I sent a messenger to tell Jamie to return to our hilltop. His challenge was being denied.

What purpose did it serve for him to continue to make it? He only looked vain, and foolish. Somewhat to my surprise, he obeyed.

What could we do now, I thought to myself. What was our best course? I could not send my loyal men into slaughter. That might have preserved their honor, tragically, but it would not have preserved my throne.

We were beaten. I knew it, as certainly as I knew that my throat was parched and I had to get a long, cool drink.

Then I saw that one of Jamie's most vociferous enemies, Sir William Kirkcaldy, was coming down from the opposite hilltop, riding alone, and in our direction.

"Hold!" I called out to my men. "Let him come in safety."

I spurred my horse and rode down the hillside to meet Kirkcaldy.

At first I feared that he might produce a pistol and shoot me, or that a lance or an arrow might fly through the air and strike my breastplate. Instead Kirkcaldy was respectful. Even, as I thought then, magnanimous.

He proposed terms: he promised that if Jamie would leave, with his own men, and I would agree to disband the remainder of the royal army, then I would be taken under the protection of the rebel lords and would not be harmed. I had to give my word that the lords would be restored to full favor and not punished for their threat to my throne, and that I would not see Jamie again.

Not see Jamie again! I could never agree to that, I thought. No, not in a thousand years. But if it would bring a temporary truce, just until I could rally enough force behind me to strengthen my throne—our throne—then I would be willing to agree to anything.

"And my son?" I asked. "What of my son?"

"He is quite safe in Stirling Castle. Naturally he will be protected as well. We mean him no harm."

"He will remain my heir."

Kirkcaldy nodded.

"And the Earl of Bothwell will not be harmed."

"He will be allowed to return to Dunbar. From there he may leave the country in safety. Unless, of course, Your Highness wishes to hang him as a traitor. He has dishonored you greatly."

I did not argue with that, even though I knew the opposite to be true. Far from dishonoring me, Jamie had given me the precious gift of his love—and his child.

"And if I should choose not to agree to these terms?"

"Then we shall assuredly prevail over you in battle today."

"And cut off my thumbs?" I could not resist asking.

"It would be difficult to restrain our men from cutting off your head," was the chilling reply.

At this, despite the intense heat of the sun and my great thirst, I actually felt as if a clammy hand had grasped my heart.

"If we were to join battle," I said, trying to keep my voice firm, "and the royal troops were to lose, then I imagine you would execute Lord Bothwell."

"Most assuredly."

I saw, then, that I had no choice but to agree to whatever the rebels asked of me. It was the only way to preserve what mattered to me most, after my own life and that of my son: the life of the man I loved.

I squared my shoulders and held my head high.

"Very well then. As your anointed queen I command you to disperse your troops. I will do the same, after I speak to the earl. Then I give you my word that I will return and place myself under your protection."

I turned my horse and cantered back to the sweltering hilltop, where Jamie was waiting for me within a circle of his trusted men. We dismounted and embraced, without embarrassment, in front of the soldiers.

"They are going to let you go, Jamie. You must go now. Don't let them find you."

"But what about you?"

160

"I will be safe."

"Don't trust them. Especially not that villain Kirkcaldy."

"I must. Now go!"

"My love!" he cried and embraced me again, then swiftly mounted his horse and rode away.

I watched him go, I saw that he did not turn to look back, not even once. I knew why. It was because he could not bear to. Then I mounted my own horse and made my way back down the hill toward where Sir William waited, escorted now by at least fifty men. None of them bowed or reverenced me in any way as I approached. But Sir William had something in his hand. As I came closer he held it out to me. It was a flagon of water. I drank it off at a single draught, the cool, sweet liquid a balm to my throat, my great thirst for the moment assuaged.

CHIRCY-CWO

I trusted the rebels—but they lied. Jamie had been right to warn me.
As soon as I reached their camp they swarmed around me,
nobles and commoners alike, snatching at the bridle of my horse and
hooting and jeering at me as if I were a woman of the streets and not
an anointed queen.

"Whore! Husband-killer! Foul slut! Bitch!"

Every ugly word was thrown at me, and ugly looks as well. The
men kicked dust over me until my dress was brown with it, and my
face and hair too. My clothes were torn and stained. I looked like a
filthy streetwalker, and in my low-spirited state I slumped, my head
hanging down and all my pride gone.

I could not help but weep—in sorrow and in anger, anger at the
rebels but also at myself for imagining that I could trust them. My
only consolation was that Jamie was by now far away, riding his swift
horse, and surrounded by his loyal men. I reminded myself that if I
had made a bad bargain, I had made it for his sake.

I was taken to a small room in a house near the Tollbooth and left
there, with two guards to watch my every movement. I had no
tirewoman, I had to do everything for myself. I could not wash, as I
had no privacy. To relieve myself in the cracked chamberpot, in the

presence of the two mocking guards, was an agony. I was unable to sleep and the food that was brought to me did not tempt me at all. I ate nothing.

Mostly I missed Jamie. I had no defender any more, no loving husband to hold me in his arms. I could not go to sleep knowing that I would wake secure in our bed. Nothing was as it had been. I was still Queen of Scots but was treated as if I were lower than the meanest kitchen maid.

After several days of this misery Kirkcaldy informed me that I was leaving Edinburgh and that I would be allowed to take one tirewoman with me and a few of my oldest and most trusted servants, and a small number of guardsmen. I asked that Margaret be summoned from Holyrood to attend me, and that she be allowed to bring some clothing for me and some of my most precious things.

"What of my son?" I asked. "Will he be with me?"

My captor shook his head.

"When will I see him again?"

"That I cannot say."

That was the worst blow of all.

We left the capital at night, in secret, to avoid being seen and accosted by my wrathful subjects. We rode north to Kinross shire, to Lochleven with its four wooded islands, the waters of the lake gleaming in the moonlight. Boatmen were waiting to row us out to Castle Island, where Sir William Douglas had his semi-ruinous donjon. I was given a small tower for myself and my servants, a dirty, reeking place without so much as a stick of furniture inside.

I stamped my foot and demanded that a bed, at least, be provided for me but the louts who had rowed us across from the shore ignored me and slammed the thick oaken door of the tower in my face.

I slept wrapped in a blanket on the cold, dirty stone floor.

Sir William Douglas owed allegiance to my brother James, now regent for my son and effective ruler of my kingdom while I remained in rebel hands. I could hardly expect mercy or kindness from Sir

William or any other Douglas. Indeed I knew I had to be on my guard to prevent him from worsening my reputation further.

As I lay shivering on the sharp stones, I began to understand just how dire my situation was. My brother James ruled all (though he had no right to) and had no intention of restoring me to my throne. I was the captive of his allies. My son was under his governance. An accident could happen, I could drown in the lake, or die from catching a chill, or even fall from the top of the tower and break my neck. I was reminded of the conversations I had had with my advisers about what to do about Henry. They all agreed that he had to be eliminated, and Jamie had recited all the various ways his life could end by accident. Now I was the one who was unwanted. Would I die, just as Henry had? In the dark, cold room my imagination took flight. What if Sir William Douglas were to fill the basement of my small tower with gunpowder, and blow it up?

If that happened, not only would I die but my unborn child would die too, and that, I knew, must not happen. I loved her already (I always thought of her as a girl), and I knew only too well that she might prove to be the savior of the Stuart line. For I imagined that my scheming brother James might well eliminate my son as well as me. It would be only too easy to do: my brother would simply say that little Jamie was ill, that the physicians could not cure him, and that he wasted away (as so many babies did) and died. Then the throne would be entirely and solely his. He would be James VI of Scotland, and it would be as if I had never survived my own babyhood—as Michel de Notredame had once said was my true fate.

And indeed I had not been living in my tower prison long before my brother and his allies began to carry out their plans to destroy me and my blood line.

On a sad day toward the end of July I was informed by my captor and half a dozen dour nobles (I shall not do them the honor of listing their names) that I had to renounce my throne. Documents were presented to me and I was told, in the harshest and most blunt terms, that I had to sign them. If I refused, my life would be forfeit.

So, after praying for forgiveness, I clenched my teeth, and wept, and signed.

But I told myself afterwards that my signature meant nothing, because it was obtained by force. It was wrong. The men who forced me to sign had no authority. And in any case no earthly power could cancel the supreme sacred authority conferred on me at my coronation. I was Queen of Scots, now and forever.

Who could I rely on now? My cousin Queen Elizabeth, I felt sure. She would not let me languish in rebel hands, treated with such a humiliating lack of courtesy. (I did not let myself imagine that she might have encouraged or supported my traitorous brother and his confederates. That was too disconcerting a thought. But I did remember what Jamie told me, that the gunpowder Henry had placed in the cellar at Holyrood had been supplied by the English.)

I wrote to the queen and told her all that had happened, and entreated her, for the sake of our common blood, to arrange my release and my restoration.

Then I wrote to my grandmother Antoinette in France. We had written to each other throughout my years in Scotland and she knew of my hardships and my fleeting joys. We had developed a sort of code to convey the most private information, the messages we did not want anyone else to read. I wanted her to know that I needed her now, and that I was carrying a child—a child I hoped would be a girl.

But how was I to convey this letter to France?

Late one afternoon shortly after my arrival at Castle Island there was a loud knocking on the main door of my tower.

"Don't let them in!" I said to Margaret.

She shrugged. "They will surely break down the door if I don't."

But it was not my jailer Sir William Douglas or any of the rebel nobles or commissioners knocking on my door. It was a blond, pink-cheeked young man holding a reel in one hand and a string of freshly caught trout in the other.

"For your dinner," he said, smiling and holding out the trout toward me.

"Thank you, but I have no place for my cook to prepare these. We have been eating nothing but the bread we brought here with us and the fruit we are allowed to pick."

While I said this the young man was looking around the bare room.

"And we have no furnishings," I added, "as you can see."

He frowned. "No doubt my brother has his orders, and is following them." Then his face lightened. "But I have no orders. I will do my best to bring you what you need. In the meantime, we can build a fire and cook the fish. It is going to be a lovely warm evening. We can have a picnic." He smiled and bowed. "Geordie, at your service."

I extended my hand and he took it and kissed it.

"It isn't often we have a guest as lovely to look at as you, milady," he said. "We must do what we can to make her stay a pleasant one."

THIRTY-THREE

IT was becoming harder to hide my growing belly. Margaret and I did our best to alter my scant few clothes, making the skirts fuller and wider and lengthening my cape so that it covered me nearly to my knees. But my condition was becoming evident to anyone with a sharp eye, and so I decided to seclude myself in my tower room, complaining of pains in my head and side and saying that I feared I was suffering from dropsy, as my mother had. I was determined to stay in my seclusion until my baby was born.

Fortunately I was able to benefit from the fact that both Margaret and I were well along in our pregnancies, so that when the midwife from Lochleven village on the lake shore came to examine Margaret she was also able to examine me—and was well paid to keep silence about what she knew. For though I was in want of possessions I was not penniless: Margaret had brought one of my jewel boxes from Holyrood when she joined me in my captivity, and it was full of precious gems. In appreciation of her silence I gave the midwife a large pendant ruby that had belonged to my great-grandmother.

My growing daughter was small, but kicked lustily inside me. I imagined her dancing in my womb, and the thought delighted me, loving to dance as I do. Some day, little girl, we will dance together in our own palace, I told her, and your father will be there too to dance with us.

I clung fiercely to such comforting daydreams, for the reality of my situation continued to be dismal. To be sure, the handsome Geordie, who was Sir William Douglas's young brother, brightened it considerably, bringing food to me and my household by boat from the village, providing me with a bed and one for Margaret as well, supplying us with cushions and straw pallets, tables and even a threadbare carpet to cover the sharp stones under my feet.

That he did this out of calf-love I was well aware, and I am somewhat ashamed to say that I allowed him to flirt with me and attempt to woo me, knowing that as long as I appeared to favor his wooing he would continue to give us things we badly needed. He knew, as everyone did, that I was married to Jamie, but Jamie (so I was informed) had been outlawed, and my marriage to him was considered to be illegal. To me it was perfectly legal, and in any case Jamie had my heart and I felt quite certain that no one else ever would. But I allowed Geordie to imagine that I was eligible to remarry, and that I might consider his suit.

Geordie was of the greatest use to us, as he went across the lake from Castle Island to the village on the lake shore daily, sometimes twice a day, and brought us back news and such useful things as soap and sweet-smelling Hungary water from France and clean laundry in wide baskets, washed for us by the village washerwomen.

He also took our letters and brought us letters in return, hiding them in the hollow scabbard of an old sword he strapped to his waist. In this way I was able to correspond with my grandmother, for there was a community (no longer a convent, but a large mansion) of former Poor Clares just outside Lochleven village, and they were in frequent touch with their religious sisters in France. Grandmamma Antoinette had been a benefactor to the nuns of the Poor Clare convent near her estate for as long as I could remember, and my mother had favored them too as among the most dedicated and least self-regarding of the religious orders.

Wet weather and strong winds ushered in the fall, and still I stayed in my tower room, seeing no one but Margaret and the midwife and, of necessity, the persistent Geordie, who would not be turned away.

"I have news for you," he came to tell me on a stormy morning in October as I lay in bed. "There is a message from Lord Ricarton," he said, handing me a folded paper with a wax seal. "And there is a French lady staying at the Clares house. A very grand lady, with silken gowns and jewels at her throat and a cane with a golden tip. Everyone is wondering about her."

I could not conceal my joy at this news. I was strongly tempted to get out of bed and cavort a little, but managed to restrain myself.

"If I tell you a great secret, can I trust you to guard it?" I asked Geordie, who looked quite shamefaced.

"Have you ever known me to betray your trust? You know I would do anything for you, Your Highness—I mean milady."

I smiled at this. "Well then," I whispered, "the French lady is my dear grandmother, and she has come here to help me."

Geordie nodded. "Yes. Family. That is what you need now."

"I want you to take a note to her." I wrote a few lines in haste, then handed the note to the young man.

"I'll take it to her right away."

"Good. Bless you Geordie." And I held out my hand for him to kiss.

As soon as he had gone I broke the seal and unfolded the message from Cristy Ricarton. I knew that he had lands in Kinross shire, though I had heard nothing more about him since his serious injury at the hands of my late husband Henry. I knew that he was an invalid, and that his injuries had kept him from taking any part in the warring between my supporters and those of the rebel lords. I had not expected to hear from him.

"Your Royal Highness Lady Bothwell," he began, which I thought was an odd but amusing way to address me—a reminder of Cristy's humor—"I have the honor to inform you that a gentleman of your acquaintance has recently come to stay with me, a gentleman known for his forthright manner and his liking for jeweled codpieces. He sends his regards and assures you of his undying loyalty and his hope that you may find your way to the top of a certain tower at dusk so that he may salute you in person."

Overcome with joy, I read and reread the message, marveling that after so many months of wretchedness I had at last, on a single day, learned that my beloved husband and my dear grandmother were both near by, and that I was no longer so alone. They were near by, they were safe. I swore that with luck I would soon see them both— or die trying.

THIRTY-FOUR

I made my way up the rickety, half-ruined stairway that led to the top of the tower just as the sun was dipping below the horizon of Lochleven. Clinging to the railing with one hand I clutched a small lantern in the other, its feeble light gleaming dully against the old stones of the tower, stones that had been put there, so Geordie had told me, by builders two hundred years earlier.

Dusk came early at that time of the year, the soldiers of the watch changed at six o'clock each evening and I hoped that they would be busy settling into their evening routine and would not scrutinize the top of my tower too closely, knowing that the light was failing and that before long it would be difficult for anyone to send or receive signals.

Not that I was under suspicion. Up to that time I had not been a difficult captive, rather the opposite. When I had first come to the island Sir William had inspected my quarters every few days to see what I did there, and to uncover any escape attempts I might try to make, but in recent months he had come much less often, and he did not interfere with Geordie's goings and comings from the lake shore, even though he knew very well that his brother was doing errands for me.

I suspected, though I did not know it for certain, that Sir William hoped that I might marry Geordie; the regent was known to approve the match and the Douglas family would surely benefit. For though my Scottish throne had been taken from me, I had strong (albeit disputed) rights as heir to the English throne and if Queen Elizabeth did not marry and have children, I might well succeed her. If Geordie married me he might one day become King of England—something Sir William would be very glad to see happen.

I grasped the loose handrail and pulled myself up the final step. My body had become unwieldy now that the time of my delivery was near, I moved much more slowly than usual and going up and down stairs was a challenge. However, I managed to heave my bulk up onto the leaden roof of the tower and took my first eager look out across the lake, its color faded to a dull gray in the crepuscular light.

There was a small rowboat, painted black so as to be difficult to see, hovering near the shore of the island, partly screened by a line of trees. A tiny flame flickered in the bow, then disappeared.

Jamie! It had to be Jamie! I squinted in an effort to see who it was, to assure myself that it was indeed Jamie and not some spy hoping to entrap me. I could not make out the face of the person in the boat, but his body had the strong, compact shape of Jamie's body and I trusted that I was indeed looking at my husband. I grinned and held up my lantern for the briefest of moments.

As I watched, the boat began to move away, back toward the shore. I stayed where I was until I could no longer make out its contours in the dimness. Then I made my way back down the stairs.

My little Marie-Elizabeth came into the world just before dawn on a cold November morning. I had been in labor all night, and for such a small baby she certainly gave me a lot of pain and trouble! The midwife helped me through it all, dosing me with opiates to ease my pain and prevent my crying out. Mine was the second baby she had delivered, for Margaret had just given birth to her son a few days earlier and the midwife was still in attendance on her, making sure she was healing and that the boy was thriving.

I had been certain my little one would be a girl, just as I had been sure of the names I wanted her to have: Marie for my mother and Elizabeth for the English queen, who I hoped would be a benefactor to us both in the future. She was perfect in every way, slim and long-limbed like me, with a small tuft of soft light hair and blue eyes and a tiny red mouth.

Because her birth had to be kept secret, I had no wetnurse. I nursed her myself, and did my best to keep her from crying by rocking her in my arms and singing to her. She slept beside Margaret's boy Edward—named for his father—in a cradle Geordie brought from the village, a beautiful hand-wrought cradle woven out of reeds from the lake. There they were, two tiny infants together. I watched over their cradle by the hour, often with Margaret beside me. We said our rosaries over them and prayed for their good health and happiness.

I loved looking at my daughter—but I knew that I would have to part from her, and soon. She belonged with Grandmamma Antoinette, who could guard the secret of her birth and make sure she grew up protected from the danger and turmoil that swirled around me.

We had only six days together, Marie-Elizabeth and I. Six days for me to hold her in my arms, feed her, talk and sing to her, smell her sweetness and tell her how much I loved her. Then, on the seventh day, as Margaret and I had agreed, she wrapped my darling child in our warmest blanket and put her in the laundry basket that Geordie took to the village. They set out in Geordie's rowboat, and once again I went to the top of the tower to watch them start out across the lake, praying for my daughter's safety and hoping that it would not be long before I would see her again.

THIRTY-FIVE

ALL that long winter my arms felt empty, and I longed to feel my dear baby girl within them again. I missed my little boy too, of course, but I had become used to seeing him only rarely—and if the truth be told (I know this is a terrible thing to confess), I loved him less because he was Henry's child, conceived by force, and being raised by my enemies. It is a hard thing to write, but it is true. I strive not to hide the truth from myself—when I perceive it.

All that long winter too I felt my hopes rising within me, knowing that Jamie was near (I often saw his boat at dusk, and we signaled to one another, though he was never able to come ashore because of the risk that he might be captured) and that Grandmamma Antoinette and Marie-Elizabeth were living at the Poor Clares mansion in the village across the lake.

And I had another reason to hope. For wonder of wonders—or perhaps not really so wondrous, given the swift and unpredictable ebb and flow of Scottish loyalties—the tide of popular favor had once more turned, and my people, lords and commoners alike, were returning their loyalty to me. Not all of them, to be sure: my brother the regent and the others who had forced me to abdicate still had many Scots on their side. But my party, if I can call it that, was swelling its ranks once again, according to the messages I received from Cristy Ricarton.

And so, for the first time since my captivity on Lochleven began, I began to think seriously of how I might escape from the island and take refuge in a secure fortress where my own army (the same army that had melted away the previous year) could protect me and defend my cause.

I had a secure fortress in mind: Cristy Ricarton's castle, which I knew to be a thick-walled, battlemented fortress, only a few miles from Lochleven village. If only I could get there, I would be safe.

As it happened, there was a death on the island early in May, when I had been there for the better part of a year. Sir William Douglas's steward, a Catholic cousin of his named Duncan, fell over and died during a feast and his wake was held the following day.

Boatloads of mourners began arriving early in the morning to attend the wake, and more boats went back and forth from the island to the village throughout the day for meat pies and bannocks, black buns and crowdie and tayberries and venison and whisky for the many guests. Duncan had been a much loved man, and the mourning, like the drinking that went along with it, was vocal and prolonged, with speeches and sung laments and dancing far into the night.

I waited until dark and then, after a hurried word with Margaret and another with Geordie—ever eager to help me in any way he could—I slipped on my plainest skirt, bodice and sleeves and tied a cloth cap over my hair to hide my golden-red curls. I borrowed Margaret's scuffed slippers and, with a basket over my arm and a small knife, went out of the tower and down to the lakeside where the acacias grew. It was essential that each mourner have a sprig of acacia to throw into the grave, and the trees were being stripped bare of their branches in order to supply the tributes.

Hundreds of men and women thronged the open space between the main tower where Sir William and his relatives lived and the smaller tower that was allotted to me and my household. The singing, fiddle-playing and buzz of talk made for a confused scene as I moved inconspicuously among the gathered folk, keeping my head lowered, intent on reaching the little copse of trees by the lakeside. Once I reached it I began cutting small branches to fill my basket—while watching for Geordie and his rowboat. No one, it seemed, was watching me, for the guards were as intent on their mourning as the visitors from the village, and I could not see Sir William anywhere.

Before long Geordie appeared and I climbed into the rowboat, concealing myself beneath the thwarts and holding my breath out of sheer apprehension as he skillfully rowed the little vessel out onto the lake, the oars scarcely making a sound as they dipped in and out of the dark water.

Freedom! I thought as I lay in the bottom of the boat, listening for voices, for pistol shots, for anything that might signal my recapture. Soon I will have my freedom once again, and my dignity and my authority, and then let us see what my brother the regent can do! I was filled with excitement, and could not wait for the boat to touch the shore. When I felt the bump of our landing I wriggled free and, with Geordie's help, stepped out onto wet sand that did not belong to Sir William Douglas, but to lords and villagers faithful to me, their anointed queen.

I threw my arms around Geordie and kissed him, and let him lead me to where our horses awaited us.

CHIRCY-SIX

I should have gone to France. I know it now, I shall regret it forever. I should have gone, then and there, as soon as Geordie and I came in sight of the gates of Cristy Ricarton's castle, and saw that it was surrounded by soldiers.

I should have gone, but I was stubborn, and so we turned our horses around and went back to the lakeside village, to the mansion where the Poor Clares lived, instead. Where my grandmother Antoinette was staying, with my little Marie-Elizabeth.

Even though, once we reached it and I embraced my little girl and my dear grandmother with a fervor I cannot describe, I found myself unwelcome.

"What can you be thinking, child?" Grandmamma cried when she saw me. "You must not be seen here! There are soldiers everywhere. Your escape is known. Your only hope is to flee to France as quickly as you can. Now, tonight. Go!"

But I did not leave. Instead I went inside my grandmother's small, sparsely furnished suite, and made myself at home—after telling Geordie to guard the door, of course.

"There is no need to go. No one knows who you are, grandmamma, or who Marie-Elizabeth is. The soldiers, if they come, will not look for me here. Now then, where is Jamie?"

"He did not expect you. He is off on a raid, on the *Black Messenger,* with his friend Red Ormiston."

I was crushed, but I realized that I had no reason to expect Jamie to be waiting for me in the village. I had not been able to send word to him in advance about my escape. I had made the decision to leave the island too quickly for that.

"Are you aware that he raids the English ships? Sometimes the French ones too?"

"I know he has been outlawed—even though as my husband, he is rightfully King of Scots."

Grandmamma's disapproving features softened at this, and she chuckled. "King Jamie, is it? I admit that he is quite a man, dear, and he has been very good to us these past months, but I hardly see him as a king!"

"Oh, grandmamma, I don't want to quarrel with you! I am so glad to see you! I have missed you so much!" I embraced her again, and was alarmed to feel her trembling. Then I realized, she was not trembling, she was weeping.

"Stubborn girl!" she said through her tears, her voice breaking. "You must leave! I tell you this for your own protection! For the protection of your child!"

"Grandmamma, things are changing. My subjects are giving me their loyalty once again. Cristy Ricarton has written to me, telling me of all the lords, all the important commoners, and even bishops, who are swearing to defend me and restore me to my throne!"

"And all these men, will they fight for you? I know what is being said, what is being whispered—perhaps better than your friend Ricarton. I have been here in Scotland quite a while now. My servants overhear the village gossip, and watch what is happening. From what they tell me I know for certain that you will never be safe anywhere but in France."

Marie-Elizabeth began to cry, and I picked her up and rocked her in my arms as we talked. My grandmother was relentless. She continued to press me to ride on, that very night, toward the seacoast where I might find a ship to take me to Calais.

"Listen, my dear, your brother-in-law King Charles remembers you very well and likes you, even favors you. You remember him as a boy, but he is a grown man now. It displeases him that you have been so ill-used in your kingdom of Scotland. He invites you to return to your own true country, where your family is. You still have your dower lands there, and the income from them; Charles will add to those lands, if only you will return. Think, my dear, of the secure future you can give your little girl, and perhaps your son too one day, surrounded by loving relations, far from the dangers of constant warfare and strife. A life of ease in the beautiful French countryside."

"Tell me, grandmamma, if the king is so concerned about me, why hasn't he sent any soldiers to help me? Not a single one!"

"And have the English helped you? No! They have been sending money and men to your enemies in Scotland! At least King Charles has not done that!"

We continued to quarrel, while I rocked my daughter and Geordie stood guarding the door. In the end my grandmother realized that she could not dislodge my stubbornness, and I rested on her bed, with Marie-Elizabeth's cradle beside me.

It was the last full night's rest I was to have. For from the day following my escape from Lochleven onward my life became a chaos of jangled emotions and frustrated hopes. I literally had nowhere to lay my head (the Poor Clares mansion being invaded and ransacked by soldiers soon after I left), so while I tried to gather what troops I could, intent on fighting my brother James and his forces, I was always in hiding and never at my ease. I did have supporters—and oh! it was so good to hear my people cheering for me again, instead of shouting curses at me—but no sooner did they assemble to fight for my cause than they fell to quarreling among themselves, and when I tried to do battle against my brother's men my ragtag forces could not mount an attack. There may have been treachery among my commanders, or it may have been that the dire fate that has haunted me since I was born put an end to my futile efforts. I will never know.

Had Jamie been there to guide me I might even then, in defeat, have listened to him and chosen the wiser course—the course my grandmother saw so clearly. But Jamie was at sea, and I could not seek his counsel.

So in the end, beaten and abandoned by all but a few dozen of my loyal men, I simply fled for my life, southward through the rough border country, fearing pursuit from hour to hour and snatching what sparse food and sleep I could.

I sent a messenger to my cousin Elizabeth with a hastily scrawled note. "After God, I have no hope save in you." In my distracted state I imagined that my only chance to preserve my life, to prevent my enemies from capturing me and locking me up again, was to reach the safe haven of England, where my royal cousin would shelter me.

Such is the blind hope born of weariness and despair, fed on daydreams and the imaginings of half-starved nights sleeping on the wet ground, wrapped in some kind soldier's plaid. I was tired and hungry, bone-weary from the effort of crossing streams where there were no bridges and riding down through pathless glens where the way was blocked by trees and scrub and it took hours to go a single mile. My stomach rebelled at the crowdie and haggis, the oatmeal and sour milk that were all I had to sustain myself. My mind too rebelled: I saw, with the terror of the beast mortally pursued by the hunters, that there was no safe place for me.

It was with infinite relief that at last, toward evening on the sixteenth of May in the year 1568, I embarked on a boat half the size of the *Black Messenger* and sailed in her across the wind-swept waters of the Solway Firth, out of Scotland and into my cousin's domain. Into England.

THIRTY-SEVEN

*T*HE orchards were all in bloom outside my windows, acres and acres of apple and pear orchards fragrant with pink and white blossoms, when I was moved into Wingfield Manor in the spring of 1569.

The violent weather that had ravaged the countryside for several years was over, the skies were blue and the spring winds mild, and when I walked amid the blooming trees, watching them shed their petals like a delicate fall of pastel snow, I felt, just for a moment, as if I had returned to the France of my youth, where Francis and I had walked hand in hand as children in the fragrant gardens of the Louvre and Chambord.

I could not help but admire the rooms prepared for me at Wingfield, rooms of modest size but quite adequate for my immediate needs, and those of my household of thirty. My cousin Queen Elizabeth had sent some of her own gold and silver plate all the way from the Tower of London for my use, along with dozens of Turkey carpets and handsome tapestries for the walls, beds and cushions and hangings. She had made me a generous gift of baskets filled with her castoff gowns, gowns made of velvets and silks and other stuffs that were perfectly usable once the stained sections were discarded and the clean unsoiled lengths restitched and fitted.

Fitting was a challenge, for I was growing plump, the bodices, skirts and underskirts of my gowns all had to be cut on more generous lines than in the past. My hostess and frequent companion Bess (who was really my warden but I did not like to be reminded of that) liked to bake, and her delicious cakes and meat pies were my downfall.

"More pudding?" she asked me, offering me a tray, an ingratiating smile on her round face. She sat opposite me, resting her bulk on a bench piled high with embroidered silk cushions. At least, I thought, I am not getting as fat as Bess. I took a pie and sampled it, the rich sweet smell of the honey and cinnamon mingling agreeably in my nostrils as I ate. There was delicious cider to wash it down.

My warder Bess, Countess of Shrewsbury, had reached the advanced age of forty-one, the age (so everyone said) when women turn to lard and lose their beauty. I was then in my twenty-seventh year, though my admirers were swift to tell me I did not look that old. I had a long way to go before I reached the dreaded age of forty-one.

I glanced down at the diamond ring I wore, a gift from my newest admirer, Thomas Howard. (I did not for a moment forget my dear Jamie, or my vow to be ever faithful to him, but Thomas was very sweet and a little sad, having lost three wives in a row and being quite besotted with me.) I wondered how many pies I would have to eat before Thomas would regret having given me the lovely ring.

I noticed Bess's eyes on my ring and quickly looked out the window at the flowering orchards. I could tell that she was trying to read my thoughts. We had spent so very much time together in the year since I first arrived in England, we knew each other well—altogether too well, it seemed to me. My cousin Elizabeth had appointed Bess and her husband George Talbot, Earl of Shrewsbury to be my hosts and to make certain I did not escape the queen's carefully circumscribed hospitality. They housed me in their various manors and mansions.

They made certain that I did not stray, or try to escape—and made certain too that others, Queen Elizabeth's enemies, did not try to kidnap me in order to make me the focus of their conspiracies.

They were spies—and yet at the same time potential subjects of mine, for was I not the next in line for Elizabeth's throne? Bess and her husband knew only too well that, if Elizabeth died and I became Queen of England, I would remember every detail of their guardianship. They knew that they had to be very careful in all that they said and did. Frankly, I thought theirs a thankless job.

"I believe that is the ring the duke sent you, is it not?" said Bess, her words somewhat indistinct as she was munching on a meat pie.

"Yes. It belonged to his great-great-grandmother. She must have been a tiny woman. The ring had to be made larger to fit me—and I have slender fingers." I held up my hand to admire the ring—and to admire the hand as well, for I have beautiful hands with long graceful spidery fingers and they have been much commented upon throughout my life.

"Has he asked you to become his wife?"

I looked at Bess, unsmiling, my gaze even.

"I have not had the honor of a proposal." I was aware, as I said these words, that had Thomas asked me to marry him and had I agreed, I would have been quite capable of giving Bess the same answer. I was learning to lie, although I suspected that I was not as good at it as Bess was.

"No doubt he will need to request the queen's permission." Bess spoke casually, as one who spent a good deal of time at the royal court and was comfortable in the presence of the much feared Elizabeth.

"I believe she would favor a match between us." I did not mention Jamie. I had learned not to.

Bess sighed and put down the tray of sweets and savories. "It would certainly solve many a problem for you, if you were to marry him. You would have a definite standing in this country. You would have a husband who dotes on you—yes, I've seen it in his eyes, he is in love. You would cease to be looked on with—shall we say suspicion?—as a Frenchwoman."

"I am of course much more than a duchess. I am a queen, and heir to the throne of these realms, as my cousin Elizabeth herself has acknowledged."

"There's many who would dispute that, as you know," Bess retorted, suddenly tart. "I don't have to remind you how much our Parliament dislikes Catholics. England will never have a Catholic ruler again, not after the disaster with that acolyte, that zealot, that semi-nun, Murdering Mary." I knew that she meant the late Queen Mary, Queen Elizabeth's fanatically Catholic half-sister and my cousin. "Nor do I need to bring up the claims of others besides yourself to Queen Elizabeth's throne."

"One less claimant now," I shot back. Lady Catherine Grey, another Tudor cousin, had just died, strengthening my own succession rights.

I was growing weary of this familiar ritual of provocative remarks and rejoinders; Bess was not the worst of companions but her conversation had become depressingly predictable, and in truth I suppose mine had too.

I got up from my bench and walked to the hearth, then to the long high windows with their beautiful orchard view. The sky was beginning to fill with gray clouds coming in from the west, as often happened in the afternoons. In my many months of confinement I had learned the habit of watching the weather, appreciating the sweep of wind and cloud, the rising of warmth and the sudden sensation of a chill in the air. Bess too was like this: her tempests were swift to arise though they did not always come from the same quarter, and her shifts of mood, from warmth to chill and back again, were as sudden and as quicksilver as the ever-changing weather.

"Speaking of rings, as we were, I'm sure you have noticed that I always wear two of them: the duke's diamond and the one my cousin Elizabeth sent me as a token of her love and regard." I held out my hand to display the sparkling ring the queen had sent me a few years earlier, with its large heart-shaped diamond. I kissed it fondly.

"She has shown me so many marks of her affection and good will—the plate and furnishings she sent me to use while in this house, her graciousness in agreeing to serve as godmother to my son James, and the costly christening font she sent him, her messages conveyed by officials of her court. I have received many such signs of her love and esteem over the years."

Bess said nothing, merely raising her eyebrows slightly.

"Indeed I often wonder," I went on, "whether she has used and enjoyed the gifts I sent her in return. The five strong hawks from Orkney, for example. Has she ever mentioned them?"

"I don't think so. She likes to ride, especially with her Robin, but she leaves the hawking to her fewterers."

Bess loved gossip, and it gave her pleasure to allude to the queen's closeness—many said intimacy—with Robert Dudley, Earl of Leicester, whom she called her "Sweet Robin."

"I wouldn't count too much on her affection," Bess was saying as she fanned herself—overeating invariably made her hot—"as she has sent men she loves and regards highly to the executioner's block more than once. Though as it comes to that, her sister killed many more men than our good queen Elizabeth could ever contemplate doing away with."

Bess's loud voice trailed off as her husband George came into the room through the high double doors, rubbing his hands together briskly, his whole body aquiver with agitation, the deep lines in his forehead and between his eyes a clear sign of his anxiety. "My love, my love," he said, coming over to Bess and giving her a quick kiss on her plump cheek, "where is that balm the peddler brought us? I need it today. Whenever the weather changes, you know—"

"I lent it to my groom, for the lame mare," Bess said.

"You gave my medicine to a horse? Don't you know that it is made with larks' tongues, and each pot we buy costs a fortune?"

"The peddler cheats you. He knows you are in pain, and that you will pay whatever he charges."

"But not so that the precious stuff can be wasted on nags and hacks!"

"Carlotta is my favorite mare."

"She's the only one strong enough to carry you," I heard George Talbot grumble.

"What was that you said?"

"Never mind. We bore our guest with our quarrels." He smiled at me, an innocent, kindly smile with no hint of the lechery I so often saw in the smiles of men.

"I should like to walk amid the blossoms before the rain comes," I said. "I will leave you to talk."

"Wait for your escort." Bess went out into the corridor and summoned the phalanx of guards who accompanied me whenever I left the manor.

"Bring our guest's cloak," she said, addressing no one and everyone of servant rank in the room. "And make certain she does not catch a chill."

"Sir George," I began while waiting for my cloak to be brought to me, "I need to speak to you about the furnishings supplied to me here and certain other matters. I must have a cloth of state over my chair. I was promised one months ago at my last lodging but so far none has been provided. I also require horses and grooms for riding. I have only ten now, and need at least twenty. And I wish to send my son James in Scotland a pony and saddle. He is nearly three years old and I have not been able to see him or send him letters or even send someone to tell him I love him and have not forgotten him. Surely, as a mother, I must be allowed to do all those things."

George shook his head and continued to rub his hands together.

"I must get permission," he said, without looking at me, "and that is likely to be very difficult. My lord Cecil—"

"Will say no," Bess interrupted. "He says no to everything we ask."

"He is a hard man, an uncompromising man," George agreed. "But then, his aim is to protect his royal mistress. As it should be."

"And he sees me as representing a danger to her."

"Which you do," Bess said. "You covet her throne, and you could be very useful to her enemies—I mean the Spanish and French—should they decide to invade us."

"And as long as we are speaking frankly," I put in, "it is no secret that my birth is legitimate and my cousin's is not. Therefore my claim to the English throne is legitimate and hers is not."

"Ah now, my girls, let us have none of this!" George Talbot put up his hand and stood between us. "Lady Mary, you must guard your tongue, for I am duty bound to report your words to the queen. And my dearest Bess, you too must be slow to argue, and quick to mend any quarrel that may arise. Let your words be made of honey, not gall."

"I'll speak my mind, when and where I choose," Bess asserted with a snort. "And I won't have any mollycoddle old man telling me when to speak and when to be silent!"

Sensing the onset of further quarreling, I slipped on the cloak I was handed by Bess's tirewoman and went out for my walk.

In the pear orchard, the air was brisk for May, but the sun warmed me and it was a pleasure to make my way along, my spirits lifted by the beauty of the blossoming trees and the vigor of my walking. I put aside my worries as best I could and turned my mind to the fresh grass under my feet, the rich sweet scents in the air, the bright green leaves above me and the drift of white petals that floated on the wind.

The gray clouds I had seen earlier had gone. A good omen, I thought, as I crested a low hill, my escort close behind me. From the top of the little rise I could see the narrow road that led from the nearby village to the manor. There was a man on the road, his clothes dusty, wearing a soft hat with a broad brim. He had a thick walking stick in his hand and a large pack on his back. Wanting a rest, I stood where I was and watched him approach.

As he came nearer I thought there was something familiar about him. His gait, his muscular body, the ruddy beard I glimpsed beneath the low brim of his hat . . .

Could it be? How could it be? I stared. I held my breath.

He came closer, and lifting his head, caught sight of me, and of the soldiers standing around behind me.

I could tell that he took in the sight of us in the briefest of glimpses, then lowered his head again.

I swallowed hard. I forced my muscles to stay rigid. I did not let myself shout for joy. But I knew. And I thought my heart would burst from my chest.

Jamie! It was Jamie! My own dearest. My love.

"Good sirs," he said to the soldiers when he reached us, "can you direct me to Wingfield Manor? I am a peddler of apothecary goods, come from Oakerthorpe with remedies for milord of Shrewsbury, to ease his aches and pains."

CHIRCY-EIGHC

J AMIE was made very welcome in the manor house as
Holp the peddler, supplier of balms and potions, and in no
time he had won George Talbot's trust for providing him with his
much needed larks'-tongue balm. Bess too was won over when she
saw that the peddler could keep her supplied with cosmetics to red-
den her aging sallow cheeks and when he offered her a pretty cap
sewn with lavender flowers which, he said, would prevent the
headaches that often caused her agony.

"I have a terrible pain in my side," I told the peddler once he had
satisfied George. "Have you anything that might ease it?"

He turned limpid eyes on me. "Have you consulted a physician?"
he asked in his most professional tone—always aware, of course, that
Bess and George were overhearing every word, and listening for
every nuance.

"Yes. In Scotland. But he wasn't able to help me at all. The pain
comes and goes. Sometimes it is so sharp I cannot sleep at all."

"If you would permit a brief examination, perhaps with your
tirewoman present?"

I looked over at Bess, who appeared skeptical at first, searching our faces, but finding nothing suspicious, dropped her reluctance and shrugged. "Why not?" she said. "What harm can a dirty peddler do?"

A guardsman accompanied Jamie and me to my bedchamber where he left us, with Margaret Hargatt as chaperone. As soon as he had gone Margaret, smiling, retired to a small antechamber, leaving us alone.

At once we came into each other's arms with such fervor that we might have been apart for a hundred years, and not just one.

I had not thought that I had such kisses in me, or such deepgoing need for Jamie's mouth and arms and hands—for every muscular inch of him. Knowing that we dared not take too much time to assuage our passion, and that at any moment we might be interrupted by the guard or my wardens, only made us more fervent.

But at length, in response to Margaret's discreet knock, we had to let each other go and do our best to recover our self-control.

"We will meet again, and very soon. I need to talk to you urgently," Jamie said. "I will find a way. There are many Catholics in Oakerthorpe who support you and are sympathetic to you. I will be staying there. You'll see me again before you can miss me, I promise!"

And then, straightening our clothes and composing our flushed faces, we returned together, along with the guard, to where Bess was waiting. I held my side (which in truth did often give me pain) and Jamie went on about how I needed to use the oil of vetiver he provided and take long walks as often as possible and avoid draughts. Then, with a bow to me and another to Bess (George having left during our absence), he strapped on his heavy pack and took his leave.

I could hardly sleep that night—not because of the pain in my side, but from excitement. He had come to me! He would see me again—and soon. Elizabeth would restore me to my throne, and Jamie would be near me, where he belonged. Yet Elizabeth wanted me to marry Thomas. And the Scots, or at least the current ruling group of them, had banished Jamie from the country.

Oh, the complications! How would I ever find my way through

them? I didn't think it would be possible to regain my throne without the armed might of Elizabeth's soldiers. Yet I did not want England to conquer my realm of Scotland, and place me on its throne as a mere puppet of my cousin.

If only I had an army of my own again, a loyal, stalwart army that would not melt away when attacked but stand and fight, and prevail.

I went for a long walk that afternoon, following Jamie's advice and hoping that once again my guards and I would meet him coming along the road from Oakerthorpe. But we did not see him, nor did he find a way to send me a message. I ate my supper in dejection, went to bed early and tried to sleep.

I was awakened in the middle of the night by Margaret, wearing her nightdress and holding a candle.

"Milady! It is—it is Holp the peddler again"—I had made Margaret swear never to refer to Jamie by his real name or title, or as my husband. "He is in the still room, waiting for you."

The large, dark still room of Wingfield Manor, where flowers were preserved to be made into perfume and fruit was made into jam and grains were fermented, was adjacent to my apartments. I hurried there without being seen or stopped (the guards being notably inactive at night) and found Jamie, crouched against the wall that separated the still room from my antechamber, scraping at the old bricks with his knife.

"How did you get in?" I asked him. The manor stood on a steep hill, the cliffs sloping sharply away on all sides, and the apartments Bess and George lived in were directly above the wide arched entryway. Everyone who came in and went out of the manor could be seen from their vantage point, or so it was assumed.

Jamie turned toward me and smiled. "The Master of the Household likes his cards and dice," he said. "I challenged him to a game. He let me in through the trap door to the old dungeon. He says they used to keep witches and heretics there, in the days of Henry V. Or was it Henry VI?"

"Never mind, one Henry is the same as another."

"At any rate, the dungeon has a passageway to the kitchens, and from the kitchens it is only a few steps and a stairwell to the main house. The master brought me up here, to the still room. This is where they play cards after the household goes to bed. No one uses the still room at night." He went on scraping at the bricks as he spoke, the aged mortar crumbling and falling to the floor as he chipped away at it. Presently he stood up and put the knife back in his belt, wiping his hands on his vest.

He grinned and came over to me.

"Imagine this, Orange Blossom," he said, cupping my face in his hands, his voice low. "The still room has a cupboard for curing meat. In the cupboard is a place where we can take our ease."

He kissed me and, taking his candle, let me into the dark cupboard. Wooden tubs took up much of the space, but there was room for a straw mattress and blankets.

"Now," he said, "no one will disturb us here. Of that I'm certain. The meat in these tubs won't be cured until Michaelmas."

We lay on the soft yielding straw, wrapped in each other's arms, for the whole of that happy night, the sharp scent of salt in our nostrils and the sweet familiar warmth of our bodies balm to our lonely hearts.

THIRTY-NINE

THE jennet Thomas sent me was as sweet-tempered a horse as I had ever ridden. She arrived one day, brought to Wingfield Manor by two messengers wearing the Norfolk livery of green and silver.

All the grooms and stable boys gathered around to admire her, stroking her velvety coat, rubbing her nose, admiring the way her tail was braided, remarking over her hooves, which were striped black and white.

She was small, a woman's riding horse rather than a man's, and she seemed to favor me as I approached her and held out my hand. She nuzzled me and made soft snuffling sounds. I could not wait to ride her.

I had ridden many horses, but had not had a favorite since my dear Bravane had grown old and broken a fetlock and had to be shot. How I had mourned him that day! Now, I thought, here is another favorite to love.

Presently my warders George and Bess came out into the courtyard.

"Another gift from your admirer," Bess said, glancing at the messengers in their Norfolk liveries and then down at my hand to assure herself that I was wearing Thomas's diamond ring.

"A fine jennet," the earl remarked, his eyes agleam, taking in at a glance the little horse's pinto coloration, her mostly white body and brown legs, her deep chest and broad, muscular loins, her beautiful proportions and quiet disposition.

"She comes from the Asturias," one of the messengers said. "Her blood line goes back twenty-seven generations."

"And has she foaled?" Bess wanted to know.

"I believe so. She belonged to the duke's late wife."

Hearing this I felt a twinge. Did Thomas imagine that if and when we married, I would inherit his late wife's possessions—not only her jennet but her servants, her jewels, her wardrobe? And, of course, her husband? Was that how he saw me, as a mere replacement?

Dismissing these unpleasant thoughts, I continued to pet the horse's soft muzzle.

"Bring a saddle," I said to the grooms. "I must try her out."

"Yes, do," George urged. "The sooner the better."

The horse was promptly saddled and I put on my riding boots and gloves and mounted her. She stood quietly while I mounted, but responded with instant spirit when I urged her forward. In no time at all we were out of the broad stonework gateway and onto the old wooden bridge that spanned the moat, then off down the dusty road that led to the orchards and the patches of woodland beyond them.

I shall never forget that first ride on Mignonne, the name I decided to give her that very afternoon. Her gait was smooth and rhythmic, she cantered beautifully and had a swift gallop that I longed to measure against one of Jamie's horses—until I remembered that Jamie no longer had a stable of his own, but was a mere peddler riding a bony nag with a drooping tail.

We flew along, leading my soldier escort a merry chase, Mignonne remaining surefooted even when we crossed streams and rode along narrow, rock-strewn paths where less careful mounts might have stumbled.

After half an hour's ride I paused by a little brook to let the horse drink, and to stretch and catch my breath, the soldiers coming alongside and joining me in my respite.

Before long, the sound of pounding hoofbeats made me alert, and I saw, in the distance, a group of riders approaching. As they came closer I realized that the rider in the forefront was Thomas, gorgeously plumed as usual in a scarlet riding coat and velvet cap with a long white feather; even when out for an afternoon's ride, I noticed, he wore diamond buckles and had the shine of gold at his neck and lace-covered wrists.

On second thought, remembering how Earl George had urged me to try out my new horse, I realized that my meeting with Thomas was no coincidence, and that in fact he had arranged this meeting and had dressed more elaborately than usual because he knew he would be seeing me.

Thomas looked his best on horseback; once he dismounted his short stature and small frame diminished him and reminded me of poor Francis, my ill-fated first husband, except that Thomas was better looking and much more purposeful in everything he did and said.

He smiled, showing yellow chipped teeth.

"I see that my gift is being put to good use."

"Indeed, and thank you milord. I can tell already that she is a gem among horses. I call her Mignonne."

"Still a Frenchwoman at heart, aren't you, giving your horse a French name? Well, that is no bad thing, as it happens."

"I am attempting to perfect my English, and to lose my French and Scottish lilts and rhythms. Listening to Bess hour after hour helps me—a little."

"I too have been listening for hours and hours—not to Bess Shrewsbury, but to the dolts and dullards at the court in London— and to Elizabeth, who is no dullard, but who does tend to screech when provoked, as she so often is."

I had to laugh at this. "I was not aware that the queen screeched."

Thomas gave a shrug, as if to say, she is a woman, and all women screech, and it is of no consequence whether they do or not.

"Of far greater importance, I have been conferring with others at court—men of the north, most of them—who feel as I do about our present governance. Men who desire change and look to me, as England's only duke, to lead them."

His small gray eyes darted about here and there as he spoke, coming to light on my face now and then but never resting there for long. So unlike Jamie, who, when he looked at me, gave me the feeling that he could not take his gaze from my face, my throat, my bosom—as though he were captive to my womanly beauty.

"What sort of change, milord?"

Thomas looked around warily at the soldiers standing nearby before he spoke. "I think we both know what change I mean," he said in a low tone, adding "Let us walk a ways."

We strolled along the edge of the brook, stopping when we were safely out of earshot.

There was a new vitality about Thomas, it seemed to me. He had altered since our last conversation. Something had quickened his disposition, he was less inclined to lapse into melancholy than usual, more animated and at the same time more impersonal toward me. I had the feeling that in a way, he wasn't really talking to me, to the woman he admired and hoped to marry, but to a fellow player in a vast chess game. He was knight, I was rook, and the personage we were speaking of, the powerful queen, was the dominant player but also the one in greatest danger, for whoever toppled the queen won the game.

"Did something happen on your visit to court, Thomas? Something that has changed your expectations?"

He smiled. "You women! You are always jealous. No, my dear, I did not meet anyone else or dally with anyone else." He reached for my hand and assured himself that his diamond was on my finger. "You alone wear my ring. You are the one I am pledged to."

"We are not pledged, Thomas," I reminded him. "You have merely given me a gift, which I wear as a token of our friendship. I forbid you to tell anyone that we are pledged, or that I have given you my promise."

He made a dismissive sound, and dropped my hand. "As you wish. For the moment."

"And when I asked whether something had happened to change your expectations, I did not mean to ask whether you had become enamored of another woman."

He gave me a sharp look, then went on a few steps farther from the soldiers, who continued to watch us but did not follow us. Mignonne stood cropping the grass at the brook's edge, looking as if she were heedless of all but the sun on her back and the fresh taste of the green blades on her tongue.

"There is something I must tell you," Thomas was saying. He was addressing his words to me but his eyes never left my guards. "No, two things. First, the pope's bankers are raising funds to support a rising in the north, which will happen very soon, and second—" He broke off, aware that one of the soldiers was walking toward us.

"If you will pardon me, milady, I have orders to return you to the manor within the hour," the guardsman said.

"But when your orders were given, I did not know that I would have the pleasure of meeting up with my lord of Norfolk."

"Nevertheless, your ladyship—"

"I will answer for her lateness," Thomas said. "Now leave us alone."

The soldier made no retort, but merely bowed to Thomas and retreated, saying "As you wish, Your Grace."

"Now then, second," Thomas said to me after a time, his voice somewhere between a mutter and a whisper, "there is something about Elizabeth that has come to my knowledge. Something that will bring her down, as surely as any army."

My eyes wide with surprise, I listened.

"The scandal alone could dethrone her—and will, if I have my way."

"But I thought—"

"Yes, I know. You rely on earning her favor. I have relied on it too—in the past. But we must do what serves our interests best. Elizabeth may fall—and soon."

Now it was my turn to whisper. I whispered into Thomas's ear, avoiding being tickled by the white feather that dangled from his cap.

"What is it that you know?"

"She wrote letters. Letters to her paramour Robin Dudley. Letters that prove she knew when and how Dudley's wife Amy was going to die. And I know where those letters are."

"Where?"

"In Amy's casket."

FORTY

I𝒯 was not yet dawn when I heard the hounds baying in the kennels of Wingfield Manor, awakening me, and took fright from the loud tumult in the courtyard. The next thing I knew men were tramping through the corridors of the old manor house, loud voices were shouting and heavy oak doors were being thrown open amid screams of alarm.

My faithful Margaret, courageous as she had always been despite her nearly forty years, came into my bedroom from the antechamber where she slept, holding a cudgel that she kept underneath her trundle bed in case of danger, and stood in front of my door, feet planted apart, ready to defend me.

Jamie had given me a pistol which I kept well hidden, but I had no time to take it from its hiding place and load it before I heard the loud thudding of boots outside my door and then, with a crash, the door was forced open.

Margaret was swept aside as if she had been made of featherdown, her cudgel plucked from her hands. Armed men poured into my bedchamber, ransacking my desk, my chests, the little shelf where I kept my rosary and prayerbook, rifling through my linens and even ripping my mattress to shreds with their knives, making an utter shambles of my bedchamber while I stood shouting at them to stop.

Where were the guards, I kept thinking. Where were George and Bess? What was going on? Would these men harm me?

Then, as quickly as they had come, they left, marching noisily out of the room and clustering in the corridor outside. I saw that they had taken some papers and my prayerbook, but had left my clothing and lace and the valuable trimmings for my gowns untouched. My jewels were not in the bedchamber, Bess kept them under lock and key in the manor's treasure room. I hoped they were safe.

I knelt down beside Margaret, who was lying on the floor, dazed and breathless, and did my best to raise her up. She shrieked when I touched her left arm, and I saw then that the bone was poking out through the cloth of her nightdress, below her elbow. The foul ruffians had broken her arm.

I went out into the corridor, where the men were, and called loudly for my servants. No one came. I waited, but still no one came and the house was oddly silent, though I could hear horses clopping and stamping outside and I thought I heard, as if from a distance, Bess's loud, querulous voice raised in argument.

I went back into my bedchamber and tried to shut the door but it had been torn from its ancient hinges. Not knowing what else to do, I stayed beside Margaret, doing my best to comfort her, wishing with all my might that Jamie would come.

Finally I heard a slight commotion in the corridor and in a moment a man appeared in the open doorway. He was tall, almost regal in his bearing, yet his clothing was somber in hue and rather plain, save for the stiff white ruff at his neck. He was clean-shaven, and though I judged him to be quite elderly—at least forty-five or fifty years old—he did not look at all feeble and his face was surprisingly unlined. It was the face, not of a nobleman, but of a farmer. I might almost have said, of a Yorkshire farmer—a good honest plain English face, though the eyes were shrewd and the mouth unsmiling.

I took all this in, though my heart was pounding and the ravaging of my possessions left me feeling as though I had been ravaged myself, my dignity torn from me and my anger rising because of the injury to Margaret.

I saw that the man in the doorway had a silver walking stick, and leaned on it slightly, as if he too had an injury or a weakness that needed propping up.

"Mary Stuart, I am ordered to detain you in a state of arrest for aiding the rebel Thomas Howard, Duke of Norfolk, and to inform you that the duke is in prison and will be put to death."

I drew in my breath in fear, but at the same moment I instinctively, unobtrusively, turned Thomas's ring so that the diamond was on the inside of my hand, and began slowly working the ring down from my knuckle, over the joint and off my finger, holding onto it with my fingertips and wishing I could drop it out the window.

"And I demand," I answered in my firmest voice, "that my servant Margaret be treated at once by a physician. Your churls have injured her."

"Sit down," said the intruder. "You will answer the questions put to you and add nothing further in your responses. If you are fractious or argumentative you will be confined in the dungeon."

Fighting my strong urge to refuse this command, I forced myself to sit on a bench—the one undestroyed piece of furniture in the room. I managed to slip the duke's ring into the ruins of my mattress.

"Have you sent letters to the Duke of Norfolk?"

"No."

"You have! I have seen them! Such letters were in the duke's possession when he was seized! You are a prevaricator!"

He reminded me of John Knox, yet he was not a preacher.

"Are you pledged to the duke in marriage?"

"No."

"You are a liar. You wear his ring." He reached for my hand, but the only ring I wore was the one the queen had sent me several years earlier.

"Where is the ring?"

"The only ring I wear is the one you see on my hand, the one the queen was gracious enough to send me."

"The ring will be found. And your treason will be exposed. Have you written to the pope in Rome?" he went on.

"No."

"Liar!"

"Have you written to the King of France?"

"Yes. He is my brother-in-law."

"Treason! To communicate with the enemy of England!"

"I may surely communicate with my relatives."

"It is not for you to decide what you may and may not do. You are guilty of treasonable behavior. You may well follow the duke to the executioner's block. In the meantime, your household, which I believe numbers some forty-one servants, will be reduced to ten, and you will be confined to the manor."

"But what about my exercise?"

"You may take exercise by walking upon the roof."

"And what if I should fall off?"

His pause was brief—and eloquent.

"Then England, and England's queen, and I, Baron Burghley, shall be greatly relieved."

FORTY-ONE

I was in very grave danger.

I was formally accused of plotting against the queen's government, of being a traitor, of lying about my treason—in short, of being an enemy of England, deserving of death.

"Cecil—I mean Baron Burghley—wants to cut off your head. He'll do it if he can," Jamie told me bluntly when we met in the still room after he came back to Wingfield Manor from his excursion to London and the south.

William Cecil, Lord Burghley, the queen's principal adviser and secretary of state, was doing all he could to eliminate me as a rival to my cousin Elizabeth.

"Burghley is in command now more than ever," Jamie said, "because the queen is ill. She hands over her authority to him when she has one of her fainting spells. She faints when she gets angry, they have to revive her with vinegar. Sometimes she stays in bed for days afterwards. And she gets terrible headaches, that keep her shut up in her room. And they say she is consumptive. Oh, the list of her ailments is long, believe me. The court is full of rumors about it. She isn't yet forty, but she has the ailments of an old woman. All her physicians say so, though they do not dare say it to her face."

"If she is really that ill, then maybe she will finally name her successor. Maybe she will name Baron Burghley to succeed her," I said wryly.

"No chance of that. He is too hated—and he belongs to the Puritan sect, the Protestant extremists. Parliament would never stomach a Puritan in the seat of royalty. But one thing is certain: Burghley will use whatever power he has to rid England of you. He is afraid of you. He knows what a threat you are to the queen's security. He'll see to it that you are condemned to die, if he can, under any pretext."

"If only we could find Amy Dudley's casket, and the letters Thomas told me about."

Jamie shook his head. "I did my best to find the casket on this trip. There is no casket in her tomb at St. Mary's Church in Oxford. That I discovered for certain. But no one would tell me where else it might be. No one would even talk to me. Of course, I could hardly expect anyone to confide in me, I'm only a peddler of remedies and potions. No one important. And even to discuss Amy Dudley is to raise the question of whether the queen might have had her murdered."

"If only we had those letters, I could try to bargain with my cousin," I mused, half to Jamie and half to myself. "I could trade the letters for my freedom."

"Don't talk foolishness, Mary," Jamie chided me. "Surely you realize that if Queen Elizabeth knew you had documents that could prove she ordered Amy Dudley's death, your life would be worth less than nothing."

Month after month, following my formal accusation, I waited to receive word that like Thomas, I would be executed for treason. Yet the months passed, and no announcement came. I was kept confined at Wingfield Manor with my much reduced household—including Margaret with her imperfectly healed left arm—and was not allowed to leave the manor house or communicate with the outside world. But Jamie, in the guise of Holp the peddler with his larks'-tongue balm and other medicinal remedies so necessary to George Talbot's wellbeing, came and went freely under the eye of Baron Burghley's men, as freely as did the suppliers of foodstuffs and even the occasional cloth merchant bringing silk or lawn for new gowns. (The time was long past when I was wearing gowns made from the queen's castoff clothing; I was allowed a dressmaker, and a clothing budget.)

I was not without news of events in the outside world, or of events at the royal court. I learned, somewhat to my horror, that my brother James had been assassinated in Scotland, as had his successor as regent, my former father-in-law Lord Lennox. I was made aware of the dread aftermath of Thomas's failed rising in the north: men hanged for treason in every village and town, heavy fines levied on the villagers, grain stores seized by the queen's officers, which in a region of lean harvests meant a very real threat of starvation. And I was aware of the most enduring legacy of the rebellion, the fear that lingered on after the brutal reprisals had ended. The queen's message was clear; rebellion would be harshly punished, the rebels hanged and their communities devastated.

After many anxious months of waiting for my own reprisals to descend, I was sitting one afternoon in Bess's chamber, embroidering a cushion, my needle in my hand, when Bess surprised me by saying that I would soon be leaving the manor.

"George is going to take the waters at Buxton," she said. "You are to go with him. He is sure the waters will help to relieve the pain in your side. You can take your tirewoman with you. The mineral baths may help her arm to heal."

The hot, sulfurous pools that welled up from deep in the earth at Buxton spa were known to have healing properties, and the sick had sought them out for centuries. Bess's husband went to bathe his arthritic hands and gouty feet and legs in the medicinal waters from time to time, but he had never before taken me with him. I was frankly astonished at the suggestion that he meant to take me now, given the far stricter confinement that had been forced on me since Baron Burghley's invasion of Wingfield Manor and the fearsome accusations made against me.

I did not question the plan, but was somewhat apprehensive. Was this proposed visit to the spa part of some diabolical scheme to get rid of me? Would villains attack me and kidnap me on the way to Buxton? Was this Baron Burghley's insidious way of ridding himself and England of the danger I represented?

Then I learned the startling truth behind the proposed visit. The queen, who traveled extensively every summer, going on progress from one splendid manor house to another, visiting her nobles and obliging them to feed and lodge her enormous retinue for many days or even weeks at a time, was coming with her household to Buxton. As Jamie had told me, Elizabeth was plagued by illness. She sought relief at the healing waters of the spa.

And, I strongly suspected, she wanted to see me. She must have sent an order to George Talbot to bring me to the spa.

We were not due to leave for Buxton for another three weeks, and during that time I devoted myself to making a gift to present to my cousin when we met. I knew that she had a taste for extravagant, magnificent clothing and jewels, and that she indulged her desire for these luxuries on a grand scale. She was vain, Bess said. She liked to believe that she was beautiful. Any gift that flattered her vanity would be welcome.

I set to work designing the most beautiful garment I could afford to make. I chose a swath of blue satin for a cloak, cut and sewed it with care, making sure my stitches did not show (careless seamstresses always fail to conceal their stitches), and when the cloak was finished, I embroidered it with extravagant red and pink roses, bold yellow and purple tulips (tulips being then in vogue, having only recently begun to appear in English and Scottish gardens), blue gillyflowers and delicate white and green anemones. I lined the cloak with peach and gold satin with gold spangles, and when it was finished I thought it a unique and charming thing, sure to capture the queen's reputedly wayward fancy.

When I showed the finished cloak to Bess I saw nothing but admiration in her shrewd, often wary eyes. She rarely gave me compliments, but on seeing the cloak she said, "Now, that would look far better on you, milady, than on the bony queen Elizabeth. How it would set off your hair and eyes!" She held the cloak up to me and looked me up and down admiringly.

"You've a fine skill with a needle," she added before handing the garment back to me. "When you get back from the spa we shall have to make an altar cloth together."

Buxton lay in a green valley whose remarkable mineral springs had been discovered and visited often by the Romans many centuries ago. The waters appeared to arise from an ancient well dedicated to St. Anne, and when our coach reached the town and passed by the well George Talbot insisted that we get out and drink the hot, sulfurous water, which tasted bitter and burned my throat slightly as it went down.

When we reached the baths we found them crowded with men and women, their bodies swathed in opaque drapings similar to Roman tunics, only longer. There was no immodesty, or none that I could detect. There was no distinction of rank either; common folk bathed alongside highborn folk, and the earl splashed happily alongside men of business and their rotund wives.

Margaret helped me undress and put on my own shapeless tunic, then dressed herself in her spa attire and together we eased ourselves into the near-scalding water.

We were in a large pool, rectangular in shape, bounded on all sides by old Roman stonework with the remains of statuary at each corner. A rooflike canopy shielded us from the weather. Steam rose from the hot water in thick sheets, and the odor of the waters was so strong it almost made me choke. Yet when I slid under the hot liquid and let it penetrate into my skin, down to my very bones, I began to feel a delicious sense of relaxation and wellbeing.

The earl had been right; the pain in my side, which was everpresent, began to diminish, and as it did, my cares too seemed to melt away. I had been so very anxious about the accusation of treason made against me that I had almost forgotten what it was to feel free of worry and fear.

Now I felt that freedom slowly creeping over me, as my body yielded to the heat of the waters and I let myself float buoyantly on the tide of peace.

I slept well that night, a long dreamless sleep, and woke refreshed. We were staying in one of the earl's many houses, this one only about a mile from the heart of the town of Buxton. The earl came to me soon after I finished my morning tea, rubbing his arthritic hands together as if he felt no pain, his sad eyes brighter than usual.

"Now then," he said, "I need to have a private word with you." The room was cleared of servants and we went to sit in a window embrasure.

"Her Majesty the queen requires you to bathe this evening at ten o'clock. The waters are reserved for her use at that hour. You may take your tirewoman with you, but no one else. Be prompt. And be prepared. Her Majesty is easily provoked, and, as Bess may have told you, she can be violent when provoked."

"I shall endeavor not to provoke her."

The earl sighed. "Your very being provokes her, milady. She heartily wishes she were rid of you, as do I, if the truth be told. But you are her blood kin, and a queen born. She cannot bring herself to treat you as she did poor Norfolk. To do away with you would mean pointing a dagger at her own heart, as I have often heard her say."

"Ten o'clock then. I shall be ready."

The earl leaned toward me until his face was very close to mine. "Be on your guard, madam. That is all I have to say. Be on your guard."

FORTY-TWO

PROMPTLY at ten o'clock I arrived at the great mineral pool and walked slowly along its stone perimeter. The moon had risen, a nearly full moon that shone down on the still waters and silvered them with its bright reflection.

A lone figure was entering the pool, a woman, so thin she was almost wraithlike, her sparse gray hair floating unfettered around her shoulders and down her back. She entered the water, her simple spa gown spreading out around her as she submerged. The moonlight drained her of color; she looked ghostly, the planes of her face harsh and sharply etched.

I knew the woman had to be my cousin Elizabeth, yet it was not the Elizabeth of her formal portraits, which I had often seen since Bess possessed copies of several of them. This was not the rouged, high-colored, youthful woman whose picture I had seen so often at Wingfield Manor, but a different creature entirely, an aging woman who looked ill, and whose bony arms, wrists and chest revealed a physical vulnerability that startled me and made me draw back, for a moment, into the shadows.

It was no wonder the courtiers said she would not have a child, I thought. She did not look at all like a woman of childbearing years, with the ripe, abundant flesh of a mother or a mother-to-be. She looked like a slight, fragile woman on the threshold of the dreaded years, the years over forty when women's flesh becomes repugnant and what beauty they possess drains away. I wondered what she had looked like at twenty, or at twenty-five. Despite what her vanity told her, I knew that she had never been beautiful, nor had she resembled her dark-haired, seductive mother. It was her sister Mary who had been the beauty, blond and sweet-faced (though her face, people said, had become drawn and lined soon enough). Elizabeth was the quick-witted one, it was said, though always nervous and fearful.

And why not? She had had much to fear, throughout her life.

I watched as my cousin moved languidly through the hot waters, then I entered the pool myself and joined her.

"So, my brave little cousin, we meet at last." Her body appeared frail, but her voice was low, masculine and commanding. She scrutinized me for a moment, and I met her gaze. "My friend Cecil," she went on, "wants me to cut your head off. I think he would do it himself, if I'd let him."

I was frightened, more by the wry laugh that accompanied her words than by the words themselves, or her acidulous tone. Despite the scalding water, I shuddered.

"I have restrained him. That is the only reason you are alive. Now the question is, what am I to do with you? By God's death, I do not know."

"I cannot solve that dilemma, Your Majesty," I said, hoping my voice was not tremulous, but unable to prevent myself from thinking, does she mean to drown me?

"When I was very young, in France, a wise man read my fortune, and told me that I had disordered the cosmos by surviving, as a child. I was not meant to survive, he said. Yet I have."

"In this we are alike. My survival too was rued by many—though never, thankfully, by my remarkable father. The Lion of England."

Suddenly she swam away from me, her movements more swift and athletic than I would have imagined. Evidently her frail appearance was deceptive.

When she returned I asked her, "And what would the Lion of England have advised you to do?" I was aware, as soon as I said the words, that I had spoken recklessly.

"Ha! All the world knows his ways. He removed all inconveniences from his path, without mercy. He would say, 'Off with her head!' But I am not my father."

She looked at me, searching my face, evidently wanting to see fear there, or shock, but seeing none.

"There is a likeness between us, is there not?" she asked presently. "We are both tall, we are both slender—" (You are skeletal, I wanted to say, but didn't.) "We both have lovely hands, and are thought to be beautiful." I held my peace, returning her steady gaze. "Only you have a son, and I have not." (And I have a daughter as well, I wanted to say, but of course I did not.)

For a time there was no sound but the lapping of the waters against the stones, and the splashing made by my cousin's restless hands. I could not help but feel more and more relaxed, as the heated waters bathed me, while she appeared to be becoming more and more agitated.

"You could still marry, Your Highness," I said at length.

She shook her head violently, making the drops fly from her long gray hair.

"Never. I would be a fool to marry. And you may as well know, even the physicians say it is unlikely I can have children. By God's holy bones, there is enough gossip on that topic!"

"I'm sorry." And I was, in that moment, genuinely sorry, thinking of my own beloved little ones.

Elizabeth tossed her head. "I'm not—except for the devilish question of the succession, of course. In truth I don't like children. Dirty, unruly things. A curse and a worry, most of them."

Her tone was bitter. Why, I wondered. Was it because the one man she had wanted to marry, Robin Dudley, was denied her?

I thought back over what I knew of her life. She had been born into great controversy, as Henry VIII's daughter by his love Anne Boleyn. But Anne was executed when little Elizabeth was how old? Two or three, I think Bess had told me. Only a tiny child. Did she even remember her doomed mother? Then she was declared a bastard, and made to feel an outcast at her father's court. After the Lion of England died, her young brother King Edward had restored her to favor, but her Catholic sister Mary, when she became queen in her turn, had distrusted her half-sister Elizabeth and put her in the Tower. Poor Queen Mary, who everyone said had had a sad life and had been brokenhearted because she could not bear a child. And then, at last, Elizabeth had become queen, against all odds—only to find herself thwarted in her desire to marry her beloved Robin—a thing she desired so greatly that she ordered the murder of Robin's wife Amy. Or so it was widely believed.

Perhaps she is bitter out of guilt, I thought. Is that what keeps her from allowing Baron Burghley to have me executed? The fact that she does not want more guilt on her conscience?

But in the course of these musings my cousin had swum to the edge of the pool and was climbing out. I heard her muttering "A curse and a worry. Yes, by God's death, a curse and a worry." Then she shouted for her women, and in an instant three of them appeared, carrying blankets to throw around the queen's spare shoulders, and lanterns to light her way to her waiting carriage.

I knew that Margaret was waiting for me, and that she would come if I called for her, but I delayed. Instead I continued to lie in the hot soothing waters, pondering my cousin's words and reminding myself that as Jamie always said, it was actions, not words, that counted. And Elizabeth's actions, though somewhat puzzling, were not hostile. She had come to the vicinity of Wingfield Manor to see me. She had kept me alive. She had spoken, on the whole, civilly to me and had even confided that she disliked children and most likely could not have any.

Or had all her actions been false? Had our entire meeting been a ruse, designed to deceive me or distract me from some larger and more sinister plan? Did she know that Thomas had told me of the letters hidden in Amy Dudley's casket? Was she hoping to find out whether I had them, or what other scheme I might be involved in?

The moon had risen higher, and its pale white light bathed all in beauty. But for me there was to be no peace that night. For hours I lay awake, haunted by images of my thin, wraithlike cousin with her bony body and blunt words, her wry laugh and acid tone, her talk of a likeness between us and her sudden, abrupt leavetaking. What was I to make of it all? Did she mean me well or ill? And was she, despite the latent strength in her frail body, unlikely to live much longer?

FORTY-THREE

THE queen left Buxton on the night of our encounter in the mineral baths. I never received a thank you for the lovely blue cloak I made for her, or even an acknowledgment that she had received it. There was no further word from her on any subject. Only silence—and her abrupt departure.

On the day after she left, however, I received a gift that was more precious to me than any communication from the queen—except, of course, the communication that I most longed for. The news that I would soon be freed.

Jamie was at Buxton, staying at George Talbot's house, in his constant guise of Holp the peddler. He was very welcome there, as the invalids and semi-invalids who frequented the spa were eager to buy his medicinal remedies and he could be very charming and persuasive when he chose, as I well knew.

And Jamie had another service to offer. Like many peddlers, he made small loans. From time to time he had loaned modest sums to the immensely rich George Talbot (who always felt poor and needy), and Talbot was usually in arrears in his repayment, which made him inclined to do favors for Jamie. Others at the spa owed Jamie money also, in fact he had quite a clientele of wellborn people who were in debt to him, just as they were in debt to their dressmakers and tailors, their jewelers and coach-makers. Jamie encouraged these debts—and charged high rates of interest, just as the Italian moneylenders did. He confided to me that he was building a small fortune.

"When I have enough, I'll buy us an army and invade Wingfield Manor and take you far away, someplace where the English can never reach us."

"Oh, if only you could!"

"We could sail to the Orkneys or the Faroes, or perhaps southwards to Africa where the monkeys and the parrots come from. How would you like that?"

"Please, dear Jamie. Please."

He kissed me, then said that he had a surprise for me.

"Talbot has given me permission to take you riding." We went out to the stables and there I found Mignonne, and gladly mounted her. She whinnied softly as soon as she saw me, and I petted her soft neck.

"Where are we to go?"

"Oh, not far. Out into the countryside."

The hill country around Buxton was rough, the riding paths no more than narrow tracks overgrown in many places with brambles and scrub. We rode without an escort, until we had gone perhaps five miles from the town of Buxton. Then we reached a cottage with a barn attached, a very modest place indeed, so modest that I couldn't imagine how Jamie had happened to find it or who could live inside.

But when the cottage door opened and I saw my beloved grandmother Antoinette standing in the doorway, smiling, her arms outstretched, I let out a cry of joy and ran to her. She had grown more gray in the years since I had seen her last, her face more lined but still very handsome, the elegance of her garments a sharp contrast to the bareness of her surroundings.

She stepped back into the dark room and called out, "Viens-tu, ma poupette, viens voir ta maman!"

In response to her words a sweet-faced little girl came up to me, her dimpled hands held out, her small mouth turned up in a grin, her plump cheeks pink with excitement.

"Maman maman maman," she cried, and I swept her up into my arms and wept and swung her around and around for sheer happiness.

"She's a bonny Scots lass, is she not?" Jamie said proudly. "Even if she does speak French and call me papa."

I could not get over the sight of my dear Marie-Elizabeth. I had seen a miniature portrait of her, painted when she was about three years old, but I had not seen her in the flesh since she was a tiny infant. I held her in my lap and would not let her go, while my grandmother told me all about the farm in Normandie where they lived, Saint-Cheron, and the healthful life they enjoyed there, with fresh eggs from the hen house and fresh cream from the dairy, home-grown barley and oats for baking bread and apples and pears and cherries from the orchards in season.

"I have a pony, maman," little Marie-Elizabeth told me, looking up into my face with a beguiling smile. "And there are kitties in the barn and grandmamma gave me a bird that talks. When are you coming to live with us?"

At this I could only shake my head. "I don't know, dearest little girl. If only I knew."

"Recite your Latin for maman, poupette."

I smiled to hear Marie-Elizabeth pronounce the words of a few lines from Vergil in Latin, her Latin heavily accented with French.

"Her tutor is very pleased with her," grandmamma said. "And her dancing master as well."

"You should see her ride," Jamie said. "I helped teach her. She has a good seat for a child who is not yet six years old."

Jamie explained that as soon as he had heard I would be coming to the spa, he sent Red Ormiston in the *Black Messenger* to bring Marie-Elizabeth and my grandmother to England, hoping they could see me during my weeks away from Wingfield Manor. Ormiston smuggled them ashore at a deserted cove unguarded by Baron Burghley's spies.

"The coast is well guarded these days. They are watching for the Jesuits, who are swarming ashore in dozens, coming to take back England for the pope."

"I know. The French ambassador writes to me. He sends his messages through the cobbler Johannis, in the cork heels of my shoes."

Jamie held out his hand to Marie-Elizabeth. "Come, my bonny." She slid off my lap and took his hand. "I know your grandmamma wants to talk to you alone, Orange Blossom. We will go and see the garden."

I watched my daughter's retreating figure with longing.

"Anyone can see how you love her," grandmamma said. "You should be with her. It could be arranged, you know. You have only to tell us when and where, and King Charles's soldiers will come for you. This Baron Burghley I hear about has eyes everywhere—even on this cottage, I have no doubt—but your Jamie is clever. He could find a way to get you to the coast, and King Charles will bring his ships to guard you on your return to France."

She knelt at my feet, the folds of her long black gown spreading out over the dusty floor.

"Your little girl needs you. She cries for her papa, she sees him so rarely. And now that she has known you, she will cry for you too."

I could not help but be moved by this plea, it was so heartfelt—and so unlike my self-possessed, wise grandmother.

"I weep for her too, grandmamma," I said. "And for you."

A silence fell, then my grandmother spoke again, in a far firmer tone.

"Don't imagine that Queen Elizabeth will just hand you her throne," Antoinette went on, rising shakily from her knees and beginning to walk around the small room. "Don't imagine that she is your friend. She is ruthless. Everyone knows it. She is even more ruthless than your mother-in-law Catherine, who I have never liked or trusted and who ordered the murder of so many innocent souls on that terrible St. Bartholomew's Day."

My former mother-in-law had shocked all of Christendom the year before by ordering the slaughter of thousands of Protestants in Paris, a slaughter that continued for nearly a week and left untold numbers dead. The victims had been killed for no other reason than that they were Protestants, not Catholics; the queen feared that they meant to destroy the supremacy of the Catholic church in France.

"Ever since the pope excommunicated Queen Elizabeth there has been war brewing between the Catholics and Protestants here in England," my grandmother was saying. "You are the Catholics' heroine. Secret Catholics, fearful of the Protestant queen and her Parliament, hang your picture in their homes, along with the crucifix. They hope that through you, the country can be brought back into the fold of the true church. But you know what will happen. There will be war, and more slaughter, and you and your son will be in danger—and Marie-Elizabeth too, if—God forbid—it becomes known that she is your daughter.

"Do not risk it, petite reinette," she pleaded, suddenly abandoning her calm tone and showing her emotions once again. "Come home to France, as you should have when Marie-Elizabeth was first born. Don't make the same mistake as you did then! Come home to France, where you are loved, and forget all that has happened since you left. Let us all start afresh at Saint-Cheron. You have a husband and a daughter, and it may even happen, God willing, that one day your son will be reunited with you as well.

"The path you are on cannot lead to anything but destruction. You cannot really expect to ever be queen in either England or Scotland. Your claims are just, but they can never be realized. The Scots despise you and even if Elizabeth dies, she will not leave her kingdom to you, but to your Protestant son—or someone else entirely.

"I beg you, dearest Marie, listen to your wise old grandmamma and come to us in France!"

You should have been a lawyer, I thought to myself. You are very persuasive—and I would like nothing better than to live with Jamie and Marie-Elizabeth and you in your rural paradise. But no matter what you or Michel de Notredame or anyone else may say, I know where my destiny lies, and it does not lie on an estate in Normandie. I am a queen, a queen of two realms, not a dairymaid or a farmer. I must seek my thrones. Once I reign, I will bring my family to court. All will be as it should be. I must be patient, and courageous, and in the end, I shall have it all.

FORTY-FOUR

MY network of friends and supporters was broadening. Hour after hour I sat at my writing desk at Wingfield Manor, reading and answering letters and messages from the French ambassador and King Philip of Spain, my uncle the Duc de Guise and secretaries at the papal court in Rome. We corresponded in codes and ciphers, the messages concealed in a wide variety of receptacles, everything from herring-baskets and jars of candies to jeweled medallions with hollow centers and boxes of scented gloves. I bribed the rat catchers that came regularly to Wingfield Manor to conceal letters in their traps, which were fitted out with false bottoms under Jamie's supervision. Some of my correspondents sent me books in which they had written extra words and sentences between the lines on certain pages, marked with green ribbons. Others wrote in tiny script on bolts of white taffeta brought to me by my dressmaker.

In the months following my strange interview with my cousin the queen, the messages all tended to say the same thing: that the power of the true church, supported by the armed might of Spain and France, was growing in England and that it would not be long before my cousin was forced to give up her throne and I would reign in her stead.

My hopes rose, especially when I learned that Pope Gregory XIII himself was a strong advocate of my royal rights, and that he had a plan to end my captivity and bring about a glorious future for me as his favored daughter. I rejoiced in the pope's support and approval; unlike so many others in my past, he did not condemn me as a murderess, as both the Scots and the English did, or as a traitor, as Baron Burghley and many others in England did, or as a Jezebel with a wicked heart as John Knox did. Instead he lauded me as a faithful daughter of the church and the rightful queen of both Scotland and England.

It was no wonder I began to look forward each day to receiving my secret mail, which I shared with Jamie when he was not out raiding Spanish treasure ships with Red Ormiston or smuggling goods from France.

By favorable chance there were major changes under way at Wingfield Manor. George Talbot and his wife were quarreling more and more often, and Bess was gone for weeks at a time, supervising the building of her grand new mansion at Chatsworth. George moped and bellowed in rage; when upset with his wife he tended to gorge on sprats, and then became dyspeptic and had to stay in bed, sometimes for days on end.

All the commotion and confusion benefited me, as the earl was less scrutinous than his wife, and I was given more latitude once again, as in the days before Baron Burghley made his first frightening appearance at the manor and constrained my liberties so severely.

The baron continued to appear at infrequent intervals at Wingfield Manor, and sometimes even imprisoned and tortured my servants in an effort to force them to confess that I was guilty of treason. But I was fortunate; my servants were loyal, and no threats or pains could make them betray me. In time the baron came to realize that his efforts were in vain, and his visits ceased.

Besides, as my correspondents told me, the baron was needed in London, for the royal court and council were said to be divided and the queen's power was under threat. There were rumors of renewed discontent in the north country, discontent which was spreading and causing unrest in the midlands and south as well. England was once again in turmoil.

I had learned, during the years of being Queen Elizabeth's enforced guest, that when there was turmoil in the country, my warders tended to be lax.

Jamie was away when the rat catchers brought word from the Spanish ambassador that Pope Gregory had a special plan for me, and would be sending his messenger to inform me of it. This happened in the year 1575, a year of unexpectedly mild weather which caused the villagers of Oakerthorpe to say that I was bringing good fortune once again, and that good crops were sure to follow, since I was helping to return England to the true faith. Most of the villagers were Catholic, though they dared not profess their faith openly; by law all subjects of Queen Elizabeth had to attend Protestant services. They welcomed the priests who were arriving from France and Rome and Ireland to work among them; they hid the fathers in their cellars, or in secret rooms of their houses with secret entrances. They waited for the day when England would be Catholic again, and I would be queen.

"Beloved daughter of His Holiness," the ambassador's message to me read, "I greet you in the name of Him whose holy purposes we both serve. A courier will be sent to you. Be prepared to go with him."

I knew nothing more than these few cryptic words, but they were enough. They were more than enough. Suddenly I was all excitement. When would the courier come? Would he take me directly to London, and would I find a Spanish army there, doing battle with the forces of my cousin Elizabeth? Or perhaps two armies, one Spanish and one French?

At last, I thought, I am to receive the treatment I am entitled to by birth. The great ones of Europe, who had neglected me for so long, are about to exalt me to my rightful place among them.

I packed a small bag, taking only my rosary, my pistol, my prayerbook, my medallion of my mother and the small portrait of

Marie-Elizabeth Jamie had given me, along with a few necessities. I would not be needing much, I told myself. Soon I would be living in a palace again, with my every want provided and my every need supplied.

I hid the bag in the still room, beneath the bed where Jamie and I had spent our happiest hours. Then, telling no one but Margaret what my purpose was, I settled down to wait for word of my destiny.

FORTY-FIVE

$\mathcal{T}$HE Spaniards came stealthily, in the longest watches of the night.

I had been told to await a messenger, but it was not a sole messenger that stole into Wingfield Manor through a broken pane in the scullery on that dark night but several dozen. I did not wake but Margaret, who was always more alert to sounds than I, was awakened and came to tell me that there were strangers in our midst.

Feeling certain it was the messenger I had been expecting, I dressed hurriedly and with Margaret's help was soon ready. Meanwhile the visitors were rousing the household. I could hear the brawl starting in the guardroom where the soldiers slept and in no time at all, shouting and the slap of swords filled the manor. There was a knock at my bedchamber door and Margaret admitted two handsome, dark-haired gentlemen who made me the briefest of bows.

"Come quickly, Your Highness," one of them said in thickly accented French, using a term of address I had not heard in many years. "We must move you while we can."

They led me onto a balcony that overlooked the small kitchen garden. It was dark, far too dark to see the ground below me.

"God help me!" I heard myself say as they secured a rope to one of the stone pillars. They meant to lower me to the ground, like a beast being lowered into the hold of a ship by a pulley. I was terrified.

"You must be brave," one of the men said. "A queen must be brave. Shut your eyes, and trust us."

I would not relive the next few moments for any amount of gold. I tried not to think. I closed my eyes and felt the rope being secured around my waist.

Then I felt myself being lifted, gently, and then, suddenly, there was nothing solid under my feet. It was not a smooth descent. I swung helplessly from side to side, and with each downward tug of the rope I thought I would fall to my death. I tried repeating the words of the Lord's Prayer but could not concentrate.

After what seemed like an hour I felt hands clutching my feet, and I was helped to the ground. I opened my eyes then, and saw by torchlight several men who bowed to me and indicated that I should mount one of the waiting horses. I did not hesitate. I put myself into the hands of these strangers—these liberators—and rode off beside them into the night.

I held tightly to the wooden railing as the *Black Messenger* crested the swells of the Sleeve, as the French call the English Channel, and did my best not to give in to the urges of my heaving stomach. Ships and I did not agree well; if I went below, into the tiny cabin I shared with Jamie, I was sick within minutes. Only by staying on deck, and holding onto the railing as if for dear life, was I able to keep my food down.

It was not only seasickness that kept my stomach in turmoil, it was excitement. For Jamie had informed me that at Pope Gregory's request I was being taken to Rome, to the Holy See, and this thought thrilled me. His Holiness the pope was honoring me with his favor, and upholding my royal rights. At last all that I had been fighting for was within my grasp. Day after day, as the ship made its way along the coastline of France, Portugal and Spain, as we passed through the Pillars of Hercules into the Mediterranean, I kept this vision of papal support and protection before my eyes. By the time we reached the papal lands and the ship made its way up the River Tiber, I was convinced that my life had taken a new turning, and that nothing would ever be the same for me again.

I had never seen anything as magnificent as the audience chamber of Pope Gregory at the Vatican in Rome, with its rose marble colonnades and high domed ceiling, its great wide vestibule with statues of ancient warriors and near-naked goddesses, its gilded doorways and bronze eagles (a reminder of Rome's pre-Christian past) and, in the center, the raised, high-backed thronelike chair in which the lean, lively Gregory himself sat, engaged in conversation with the men around him.

Everything in the Vatican, it seemed, smelled strongly of stale incense, though the environment was certainly not one of worship. This grand room was far from being a place of quiet sanctuary, where worshippers were invited to pray; on the contrary, it was a place of worldly affairs and material concerns. Of money and power—and those who controlled both.

For the great audience chamber was full of people: cardinals and bishops, moneylenders with their books of account, officials of the papal treasury and chancery, ambassadors and emissaries from abroad, workmen making repairs and cleaning women scouring the floors and sweeping. Supplicants, favor-seekers, embattled enemies shaking their fists at one another and shouting—all created a din louder than that of any open-air marketplace.

The noise was almost deafening, like the buzzing of hundreds of bee hives, filled with angry bees. When I entered the great room, surrounded by my escort of Spanish soldiers, and with Jamie at my side, the din did not subside, but the crowd did part to let me walk through to the Holy Father's high thronelike chair.

He rose at my approach, and stepped down from the raised chair onto the marble floor so that we were on the same level (though as usual, with most men I stood near, I was quite a bit taller).

"Daughter," he said, holding out his arms in welcome. I gladly walked into his embrace, then kissed his ring. His hands, I noticed, were like a woman's hands, soft, the nails carefully manicured.

Leaving the great audience chamber he led me and those with me into a much smaller, darker and cooler chamber where we sat on cushioned benches and were served delicious sherbet and fresh pears.

"These are from my own garden," the Holy Father told me, indicating a verdant courtyard visible through an archway. "I like to pick them myself, early in the morning, before the world descends on me." He laughed. "It really does feel that way sometimes."

"Your Holiness—" I began, "I cannot thank you enough for my— liberation. It has been so long since I was a free woman—"

"And high time. You should have been freed years ago. That ill-born wretch that calls herself Queen of England should have been thrown down and trampled underfoot for the bastard that she is. And you, beloved daughter, must take your rightful place upon her throne."

"The powers of Catholic Europe have been slow to support Queen Mary's rights with anything stronger than words," Jamie said boldly from where he stood, behind me and off to the side.

The pope looked at Jamie, taking in his truculent statement and his even more truculent stance, feet planted apart, one hand on the hilt of his sword.

"My lord Bothwell, is it not? You are welcome here at the font of all Christendom, even though I am told you are a heretic."

"I follow the true religion—"

Fearing an argument, or worse, I reached out to put a restraining hand on Jamie's arm.

"As do I," said the pope, smiling. "We will leave it at that, since I see you enjoy the favor of Her Highness the Queen. As to the support the Holy See offers Queen Mary, more will be revealed tonight, at the banquet Cardinal Colonna is giving in her honor."

"What news from England, Your Holiness?" I asked.

"The bastard Elizabeth has put your former jailers in the Tower, and no one knows of your escape except the members of your household and hers. It is better so. While we marshall our forces for our assault, the bastard Elizabeth is saying that you have been arrested and are being held in a secret prison. We could not have wished for a more favorable situation. Except for a very few, the English do not know of your escape."

All the lords of Rome, it seemed, both spiritual and temporal, were gathering in the Colonna palace to honor me. I lacked a gown suitable for a banquet but the cardinal's sister Olivia, a warm, matronly woman whose French was heavily spiced with Italian, offered to provide what I needed.

From her many trunks and baskets of gowns she produced three suitable for me to wear—one in a glowing midnight blue, one in peach satin and one (the one I chose) in a fragile shade of parchment with delicate lace around the bodice and sleeves. While her dressmakers made the necessary alterations she brought out a variety of headdresses for me to try, and ropes of pearls to adorn my neck and ears.

It had been a very long time since I was dressed as a queen—or even as a fine lady. I sat before a tall pier glass as Olivia Colonna supervised the combing out and dressing of my long red-gold hair, the anointing of my cheeks and forehead and neck with oil of lavender, the rouging of my lips and the blanching of my skin. My eyes were brightened with herbal drops, my teeth scrubbed with twigs and my bitten nails covered with thin, soft gloves.

I marveled at the change in my appearance. I looked ten years younger—or at least five, if I am truthful. It was as if the worries and hardships of the past had fallen away, or been covered over with a soft flattering veil that masked the deepening lines and shadows of my face. Instead of an anxious prisoner I had become, in the space of an hour or two, a lovely woman, a woman no longer young but beautiful with the ripeness of her years, her beauty faintly tinged with the melancholy of worldly experience. I looked at myself in the mirror, and smiled.

I can still enchant, I thought. My charms have not deserted me. And with that smile lingering on my lips I accompanied Olivia Colonna into the great hall of the Colonna palace, where the lords of Rome awaited me.

FORTY-SIX

LIVELY music beckoned from the great hall of the Colonna palace, and even before I entered I could smell the delicious scent of the garlands entwined along the staircases and the bowls overflowing with red roses on every table. Frescoes in vivid hues of russet and cobalt, aquamarine and yellow ochre shone from every wall—masterworks, as I supposed—and caged birds sang in tuneful melody from windows and alcoves and niches in the graceful pillars that rose to the high painted ceiling.

In the Colonna palace I was at the center of the rich Roman world, a world far older than that of the French court and far grander than the petty splendors of Holyrood. The Colonna family, as the cardinal's sister told me with pride, could trace its descent to the days of Nero and Augustus; long before the bishops of Rome had begun to rule the church, the great families of Rome had dominated the city, and often controlled the cardinals as well.

Admiring glances and voices greeted my entrance into the room in my beautiful borrowed gown. All around me I heard "Your Majesty," "Your Highness" and the words were welcome to my ears.

I could not help but notice that Jamie, who followed me at a respectful distance (for we were advised to follow royal etiquette, and not enter side by side), was greeted with stares and curious glances, and even a few smirks. No doubt he appeared very provincial in his somewhat worn northern finery, I thought. Yet I could hardly imagine him draped in the languorous silks worn by the Roman men, costly garments but far too effeminate to suit Jamie's virile, martial spirit.

I moved deeper into the room, approaching the long banqueting tables with their thick embroidered cloths, flower-filled vases and gleaming silver. Then I suddenly smelled a strong musky scent and heard a voice at my ear.

"Come! Hurry! You are in danger!"

A firm hand closed over my arm and I felt myself pulled away, toward a window embrasure partially hidden by a padded hanging sewn in complex patterns of gold and silver threads. My rescuer concealed me, then spoke in a low, musical voice to one of the guardsmen in Spanish. The guardsman left, and my rescuer joined me once again.

I looked at him. His light hazel eyes were as tender as a girl's, the dark lashes long and thick and curling, yet his expression was determined and commanding, his thin mouth set in a firm line, his high forehead uncreased by the deep marks of worry that were so often prominent in strong men's faces.

He was younger than I was, and not as tall (alas!). But his bearing and air of confident superiority made it clear that he was highborn. He did not look like an Italian, or a Spaniard either. I was both puzzled and fascinated.

"Your Royal Highness, it was not my intent to alarm you," he said in his musical voice, "but I had to remove you from harm. There was a man near you who I recognized. He is an agent of Baron Burghley. A hired assassin. I have had him seized and eliminated."

He spoke French with an accent I did not recognize. His words alarmed me.

"So the wicked baron pursues me even here, in Rome," I said with a shiver. "Where there is one assassin, there must be more."

"I'm glad Your Highness is aware of the extent of your danger."

"I was safer in captivity." I confessed it mournfully.

"So it would seem."

At this I sensed a commotion in the room.

"Where is she? What have you done with her?" It was Jamie's voice, and I felt a catch in my throat, hearing it. His tone held an edge of panic.

I started to move away from our protected enclave, to join Jamie, but my rescuer restrained me, gently but firmly. My body yielded easily to the feel of his hands on the soft, lace-trimmed sleeves of my gown.

"Please, Your Highness, do not put yourself at risk. Let me."

He stepped out into the room.

"Who seeks our royal guest?"

I heard an uneasy murmuring among the guests.

"And who are you?" Jamie challenged.

"I am the man who has protected her against the English assassin."

"What English assassin? Where is he?"

I needed to see what was going on in the banqueting hall. Searching the hanging that hid me, I found a worn patch and a small hole. I looked through it, and saw Jamie, truculent as ever, challenging my rescuer, with one hand on the hilt of the short sword he wore at his waist. Oh Jamie, I thought, please don't cause trouble. Not here. Not tonight.

Facing Jamie was the younger, stronger, less challenging other man, balancing lithe and catlike on the balls of his feet, a faint dismissive smile on his thin lips.

"The assassin has been removed. There is nothing more for you to be concerned about, old father."

Laughter greeted this rejoinder, the laughter of the sophisticated Italians ridiculing the sputtering, belligerent Scotsman in their midst— the Scotsman with graying hair at his temples and a noticeable limp in one knee. Jamie was about to enter his fifth decade, and though he was as tough and combative as ever, his arms were weaker and slower than they had been when I first met him, his eyes less keen, his breath shorter and his balance less sure.

With a roar like that of an old bull Jamie drew his sword and lunged at the younger man, only to find his blow swiftly parried and to suffer the humiliation of being caught tightly in the younger man's arms, and disabled from fighting any more.

"Take this gentleman back to wherever he is quartered," I heard my rescuer say as two guardsmen came forward to seize Jamie. "Keep him there until the banquet is over."

I watched Jamie being taken away. I wanted to intervene and help him, above all to spare him the loss of his dignity, but I knew it would not be prudent for me to try to change the situation. Jamie was my husband, yet I had to pretend otherwise—to pretend that, as Pope Gregory and all the Catholic sovereigns believed, my marriage to him was not valid and I had no romantic ties to complicate my political life.

Besides, my common sense told me that Jamie did not belong in the hothouse world of Roman society. He was too brash, too quick to show his feelings; he was not practiced in cloaking his purposes and deceiving his enemies. For years I had heard stories of the treachery of Italians, who were said to conspire in the shadows and hide their nefarious doings by using slow-acting poisons and concealing venomous serpents in their enemies' gardens. They smiled while they stabbed, it was said. With Italians, nothing was as it appeared, all was a game of smoke and mirrors.

I heard Jamie swearing and protesting as he was led away, and felt my heart sink.

My rescuer had returned to my side, and once again I smelled the strong, almost overpowering scent of musk.

"Your Highness," he said, "you ought not to be abroad tonight without a large escort to protect you. Who knows what traps Baron Burghley may try to set? I should like to offer my services to you as your guide. I have many men to call on, we can assure you safety. Will you come with me?"

He held out his arm, and I felt no reluctance in placing my hand atop it. He led me out through an arched colonnade into the garden, where moonlight shone down on leafy trees, their branches stirred by a warm breeze off the river. Surrounded by a phalanx of armed men, poleaxes in their hands, their boots crunching the ground and pavingstones beneath our feet, we walked onto a winding roadway and past fragrant walled gardens enclosed behind ancient gates, and once again I had a sense that my life had reached a new turning, and that nothing in it would ever be the same again.

FORTY-SEVEN

ALL Rome was spread out before us, the lights along the riverbank flaring and twinkling, the windows of the great palaces ablaze with firelight, the lanterns in the tall churches lit like beacons amid the gloaming of the poor districts with their twisting narrow lanes and dim alleyways where thieves lurked.

My companion had led me up into the highest tower of the Castel Sant'Angelo, the Angel Castle, which offered a magnificent panorama of the city.

"There is the Trastevere district," he said, pointing to a cluster of low buildings across the river. "And the Ripa. Don't ever go there without dozens of men to defend you; the only people you are likely to meet are murderers and drunkards. Better still, stay away entirely."

He pointed to another area where the houses were larger and the gardens more spread out behind their forbidding stone walls.

"Don't go into that district either, unless you want to risk danger. That is the quarter of the courtesans: Niobe, Charis, Demetria—"

"You sound as if you know them well," I ventured, half teasingly, unsure how this handsome young man, who I did not know at all, would react.

"I know them well enough," he responded with a look that was half mischievous, half rueful. "Tullia, Aulea, Penthesilea—" His voice dropped to a low monotone. "If you must know, I have known them from childhood. My mother was one of them."

"And your father was not her husband."

"No."

"I see. But you are a personage of note. A captain of men. I saw how the banquet guests were looking at you. They respect you." I did not know who this man was (and in truth I was enjoying the adventure of not knowing) but he was clearly an important man.

I had a sudden chilling thought. Was he one of those I had heard of called condottieri, private warlords who obeyed no laws and lived as they pleased, bullying and threatening and terrorizing anyone who opposed them?

"Should I be afraid of you?" I asked, ashamed of my naïveté yet unable to prevent myself from asking.

He smiled. "Remember, Your Highness, I am the man who removed you from the path of the assassin. I have your welfare at heart." He took my hand and lifted it to his lips. "I am not the one you ought to fear. Baron Burghley and his men, yes. The thugs of Rome, yes. The marsh fever that rises in the summer and sweeps away thousands of Romans every year, yes. Even the heat and dust, that will sap your strength and make you cough and wheeze. Rome is a very unhealthy place, as you have already discovered. Yet it can also fulfill your dreams, whether they are spiritual or material."

He paused, and looked into my eyes. "Which are your dreams, Your Highness?"

Bells rang from the numberless churches all around us, a thunderous peal of bells so loud it clouded my senses and so long I thought it would never end.

"I want my son," I managed to say as my head cleared. "And I want my throne back. The throne of Scotland."

I wanted to add, "I want my daughter as well," but I didn't dare; Marie-Elizabeth's existence had to be kept secret.

When the clamor subsided we came down from the tower and resumed our walk, glad for the everpresent escort of halberdiers as we passed along streets where troops or gangs were shouting and skirmishing, horses galloping, tavern brawls erupting and quarreling voices filling the air. Rome was a very noisy, captious city, I thought, compared to Edinburgh, where there were feuds and quarrels aplenty but where the night watchmen kept a rough order and the only sounds after midnight, as a rule, were those of voices raised in dirgelike hymns.

"Rome is far noisier than Edinburgh," I remarked as we came to a square with a cascading fountain, water spouting from the generous breasts of long-haired marble maidens and the gaping mouths of scaly stone fish. "The stinks are the same, and the quarreling. But the air here is far softer, and the language much lovelier to listen to, even though I don't understand it. And the monuments—surely no other city has such monuments."

Our way led to the Colosseum, a huge amphitheater, long since ruined yet still recognizable for what it had once been, a great open-air theater where shows and exhibitions of all kinds were held. Cats roamed its old stones, their eyes gleaming yellow, their yowls eerie in the shadowed night.

"Here is where Nero threw the Christians to the lions. In his day it was pagan against Christian, now the battle is between the true church and the Lutheran heretics."

"And the Calvinists," I put in. "Many Scots follow the Calvinist teachings and would not want them forgotten."

"Who are the lions now, I wonder?" my companion mused aloud, disregarding my comment. "The troops that are unleashed against the heretics, or the heretics who roam the world, seeking whom they may devour?"

We heard, in the distance, the tramping of boots and the sound of many horses.

"Those are my men," my companion said, "returning from a raid on a village in the Campagna where heresy has taken root. They had orders to kill every heretic, or suspected heretic. I have no doubt that every man, woman and child in that village has been duly punished for their heresy." A cold sneer crossed the thin line of his lips, making his handsome face turn almost ugly.

"Heresy can and will be stamped out, you realize," he said with new confidence in his voice, "and corruption along with it. My father sacked and burned this city, long before I was born. They say his horsemen stabled their beasts in the great cathedrals and pillaged all the ill-gotten treasure from the papal chests."

"Your father was a prominent commander then?"

"Yes."

"Was he a condottiere?"

At this my companion laughed aloud, the first time I had heard him laugh.

"I'm sure the Romans saw him in that guise, yes."

We said no more for a time, but began the long walk back to the Colonna palace. My companion asked if I would prefer to ride back, and offered to summon a carriage, but I said no, that I preferred to continue our walking tour, even though my delicate golden slippers were ruined and the skirt of my lovely gown stained and torn.

I was in love with the balmy night, with the squalid, splendid city set amid the reeking marsh. I had not walked so far in years. My body sang with the sheer pleasure of it. And I could not help but be intrigued with the mysterious, fascinating man who had revealed it all to me. A man I had never seen before that night. Whose name I did not know, or seek to know. Who exerted a strong influence over me, though I could not have said how, or in what that influence consisted.

A man who, as I mulled these things over in my mind, was moving closer to me as we entered the ancient Forum, with its crumbling temples and fallen pillars, its ancient walls and courtyards now reduced to heaps of slag.

"Some day, Your Highness," he was saying in his musical voice, "these old stones will breathe again. Rome will be restored, renewed. New monuments, even larger and more beautiful than the old ones, will rise here, and Christendom will once more be united under one church. And one Holy Father."

His voice gathered urgency as he spoke, and I began to see the panorama of the new Rome, resplendent in its newfound glory.

"It is become my life purpose to see this dream come true," he was saying. "I have shown you the city, Your Highness, because one day, in its resurrected form, it may belong to you—to us—when heresy is quelled and all the heretic kingdoms of the world are reconquered and truth reigns supreme."

He spoke as one uniquely inspired—yet his words seemed suddenly hollow, and his allusion to our possessing the city together verged on madness.

Is he mad, I wondered. What does he mean? What can he mean?

I hesitated. Was I being drawn into a lunatic's obsession? Yet the longer I stood there, amid the old stones bathed in moonlight, the easier it was to believe in the regenerative power of his dream. I could almost see the new Rome rising from the old, like the New Jerusalem of the Bible. Almost—but not quite.

Common sense and curiosity took me over.

"Who are you," I asked the man of great dreams, "that you weave such spells?"

He turned to me and swept me a bow.

"Don John of Austria, Prince of Guelderland and Knight of the Golden Fleece, Scourge of the Turk and Defender of Christendom, at Your Highness's service."

FORTY-EIGHT

"SCOURGE of the Turks indeed!" Jamie blustered. "Scourge of the brothels more likely! By all that's holy, Orange Blossom, when are you going to show some sense!"

I had told Jamie all about my nighttime excursion with the prince Don John, and about his vision of a revitalized Rome. I did not tell him about the prince's enigmatic reference to our ruling the new Rome together, however. Jamie, for his part, had informed me that Don John ("the emperor's brat") was the natural son of the late Emperor Charles V, which made him the half-brother of King Philip of Spain and a candidate for the imperial throne.

"You're only angry at him because he humiliated you in front of all those people at the banquet," I said in response to his outburst.

"Of course I am—what man would not be? Notice I said man, not infant. Your Don John is how old? Twenty? Twenty-two?"

"He's twenty-five, and he did defeat the Turks, in a great naval battle at a place called Lepanto. Everyone here speaks of it, I am told. He is a miracle-worker."

"And what has he done since working his last miracle? Sit in church and tell his beads? Kiss the pope's holy foot?"

"He is rooting out heresy in the Campagna."

"Hah!" Jamie's derisive snort was explosive. "There is no heresy in the Campagna. A few pallid agitators preaching to the farmers! Is this the best the great hero can do, slaughter defenseless peasants?"

I had no answer to that. "I am to have another audience with Pope Gregory next week," I told Jamie. "I hope to learn more then."

Jamie wiped his face with his silk neckerchief.

"It's a wonder any of us can think at all, with this heat. Does it ever stop?"

I was discovering the drawbacks of Rome in August: the enervating heat, the flies, the dust clouds that rose from the roadways making everyone cough. The stench of the dank marsh. Romans believed in closing every shutter and bolting every door in an effort to retain what coolness they could. The airless rooms were stifling. I longed for the damp gray mists of Scotland.

Jamie and I were both irritable and out of sorts when Pope Gregory summoned me once again to his audience chamber—this time in order to make an important announcement, he said.

Once again we entered the vast high-ceilinged chamber crowded with clerics and petitioners, moneylenders and men of business, cleaners and repairmen and hundreds of hangers-on. This time, however, there were three high-backed thronelike chairs raised off the floor, not just one. The Holy Father sat in the first, I was escorted to the second and the third remained empty.

At Pope Gregory's command grooms began clearing the room, pushing the highly vocal crowd back toward the pillared walls where they continued to clamor for attention until he silenced them with a wave of one soft white hand.

"My children," he began, "it is no secret that we shelter among us one who has been wrongfully removed from the Scottish throne. The widowed Queen of France, and rightful Catholic Queen of England."

I held my head proudly at these words. It was good to hear my right proclaimed, and my royal self named without equivocation. Despite all that had happened to me over the many years since Francis died,

I was who I was. Who I was born to be. I was and would always be a queen.

I let my glance wander to where Jamie stood, at the forefront of the crowd, looking uncomfortable and shuffling his feet. I knew it was galling to him never to be thought of or recognized as my consort, or by his own title. He was ignored, a mere prop in the stage-set of my drama. Yet he sought his own stage, his own play. I often wondered, was I depriving him of the admiration and respect he deserved, by casting my larger shadow over him? The older we both grew, the more I asked myself this question, though it was only one of many things that occupied my mind.

"Her presence brings us luck," the pope was saying, "for we are about to embark on a great crusade. A crusade to rid our world of heresy and error. One man will lead this crusade—"

Here the crowd interrupted the Holy Father with cries of "You will lead us, papa," and "You, blessed one." But the pope held up his hand once again to silence these partly sincere, partly flattering cries. Smiling, he shook his head.

"Not I but one far more accomplished than I in the art of earthly warfare. One who will stand by the queen's side as her champion, her conqueror—her husband!"

A curtain was drawn back and Don John strode rapidly into the immense room, agile and athletic, a bright purple cloak swinging behind him jauntily as he walked. The onlookers cheered, loudly and lustily, and he bowed to them, right and left, looking both pleased and accustomed to the acclaim they offered. He did not look at me. When he took his seat in the empty large thronelike chair he swirled the beautiful purple cloak around him in a practiced theatrical gesture, and I smelled once again the strong musky cologne he wore.

My husband! I nearly laughed, but checked myself. The Holy Father meant what he said, I realized. Don John had had the pope's plan in mind when he spoke of sharing the new Rome with me. All fell into place in my thoughts; I had been rescued from my captivity and brought to Rome in order to play a key role in Pope Gregory's scheme to reverse the spread of Protestantism and mend Catholic Christendom. I was to lend the weight of my royal blood to Don John's conquests. Just as my cousin Elizabeth had wanted me to marry Thomas Howard, so the Holy Father had a marriage partner of his own in mind for me, Don John.

I was shocked into silence.

The applause for Don John was dying down, when I heard a deep male voice mutter, "It smells like a dead animal in here."

"Did someone speak?" the Holy Father asked.

"I said, it smells like a dead animal in here." Jamie stepped forward, his words loud and challenging. "Either that or some fool has put on too much bad cologne."

"Not again, old father." Posed elegantly in his tall chair, Don John barely looked at Jamie. "Haven't you learned your lesson yet?"

Titters greeted these mocking words, and I started to rise to defend Jamie against them, not knowing how I would do this.

But Jamie was too quick for me. He covered the distance between himself and Don John so rapidly that the latter did not have time to react. In an instant Jamie had tipped over the tall chair, sending the prince in his purple cloak sprawling.

"Stinking son of a mongrel bitch! I'll see you dead before I watch you marry this woman!"

Don John scrambled nimbly to his feet.

"Enough of your petty insolence!"

"Bastard! Whelp! Jumped-up knave!"

The younger man lunged, but Jamie quickly took refuge behind the pope's huge bulk and high miter.

"Puking puppy!"

A cry of "Canes! Canes!" came from the crowd. The repeated word became a chant.

Spanish and Italian knights, I knew, liked to joust with long sticks, or canes. The cane combat could also be on foot.

Long stout sticks were thrown to both men from out of the crowd—Pope Gregory dodging between them—and in a moment battle was engaged.

The sticks slapped and struck one another in an intricate rhythm while the two men, the one quick, the other slower to react but stronger and angrier, thrust and parried their blunt weapons, spicing their blows with insults.

"Old father, old father," came the encouraging chant from some in the crowd. "Don John, Don John" came the answering cry, much louder and full of mirth. Jamie's face was red, and I knew it was not only because of his exertions but because of his anger at being teased and taunted.

Pope Gregory tried in vain to restore order and stop the mayhem, but his voice was lost in the din; the grooms quickly escorted him to safety, out of range of the scything sticks.

Then Jamie's cane snapped in pieces, leaving him hopelessly vulnerable to his opponent's blows and unable to land any blows of his own.

"I am betrayed!" Jamie roared, holding up the remains of his cane. "Who threw me this splinter?"

Don John, with what I thought was commendable gallantry, had stopped fighting when Jamie found himself defenseless.

"Show yourself!" Jamie was demanding. But no one responded.

He threw the pieces of wood down on the marble floor and with a great oath, began to walk out of the room, then turned back toward me.

He held out his hand toward me.

"Are you coming, Orange Blossom?"

I started to get up to follow him, then heard Pope Gregory's voice, gentle and fatherly yet firm. The voice of the father I had never had.

"No, Mary."

"But I must."

"You must do as I say. I am God's vicar on earth."

"God's vicar in hell!" Jamie burst out, and then he had to take to his heels, for nearly all the men in the room, save the pope and Don John, who sat in his thronelike chair and wrapped his purple cloak around him, were running after him.

With a last despairing cry of "Mary!" Jamie dashed along the wide corridor that led from the audience chamber into the hall beyond, the furious Romans in urgent pursuit. I got up and tried to follow, but my feet were leaden, and besides, I could not possibly reach the sprinting Jamie. And had I caught up with him or his pursuers, what would I have done then?

I stood where I was, shaking my head in sorrowful disbelief. I had just witnessed my dear but hotheaded husband creating havoc in the audience hall of the pope himself, the Bishop of Rome. He had disgraced himself beyond redress. I was his loyal wife, my place was at his side. But my future, and the future of my children, surely depended on Pope Gregory's good will.

What should I do?

I turned to look back at the Holy Father and Don John, sitting in their tall chairs, absorbed in talking with one another. I hesitated, sad and more than a little bewildered, then slowly walked back toward them and took my place in the third chair.

FORTY-NINE

JAMIE was gone.

I wept, I grieved for him. I wished with all my heart that he would come back to me, or at least send me word where he was and how to relay a message to him.

It was as if the earth had simply swallowed him up, and left me desolate.

Not knowing what else to do, I stayed on in Rome, outwardly playing my role in the grand design of the papal crusade, allowing it to be assumed that I would marry Don John, though Pope Gregory, greatly to my relief, spoke of our future marriage as an event that would not happen for some time, not until the armies and the great fleet he was preparing were all in readiness, and the invasion was under way.

As for Don John, he seemed to have little interest in me as a woman. He was always courteous and gentlemanly, but distant and preoccupied. There were no more moonlit trips through the monuments and ruins of Rome, no words of love, no tender exchanges. I was merely a part of his arsenal. His passion, I soon discovered, was all for his ships, the two hundred and seven immense galleys that, with a horde of lesser vessels, formed the armed fleet of the Holy League. Again and again I heard him talk at length of the power of the galleys, their cannon that shot straight and true, the crews that the prince trained himself (he had learned gunnery as a boy), the vast enemy losses his ships had inflicted.

"We annihilated them!" he said, his handsome face alight with the happy memory of one victory or another. "We lost a few men ourselves, perhaps seven thousand, but they lost ten thousand, or even twenty! It was a very great victory."

He stayed in Rome, or in the nearby port of Ostia, throughout the surprisingly cold winter (I had not realized that it snowed in Rome, just as it did in Scotland and France), but when spring came he sailed north, to Flanders, where a huge force of Spanish infantrymen, supported by thousands of German and Walloon troops, were being readied to invade England.

My spirits were low, yet I could not help being excited by the thought of the coming invasion. I remembered with keen pleasure my brief, exhilarating experience of warfare in Scotland, what it was like to gallop across the fields and meadows in pursuit of the rebels, how it felt to be victorious over them, even the ghoulish satisfaction of watching trophies being collected on the bloody battlefield and thrown carelessly into a reddened basket.

My cousin, my enigmatic, maddeningly elusive cousin Elizabeth, was to be conquered while I would be exalted. My children would be reunited with me and given due honors. All the old wrongs would be righted, all broken faith restored. And surely, I thought in my most optimistic moments, surely Jamie would come back to me then, and sit at my right hand as my beloved consort, all his peevish quarreling forgotten.

My happy daydream did not include Don John—except as the commander of the great invasion force. For that, I needed him. But once I was Queen of England and Scotland again, I could treat him as I liked.

I tried to make the best of my situation, but in time I began to sour on Rome. The extreme heat enervated me, and the cold of the drafty papal palace when harsh storm winds blew gave me a rheum in my chest that would not go away. I could not safely leave the protection of the palace, as I feared to encounter more of Baron Burghley's agents or assassins—and besides, the streets were full of hired ruffians and brawlers, drunken louts and thieves. Although I continued to venerate the papal city as the center of the true faith, and to heed the words and trust the good intentions of the Holy Father, the great monuments of the past no longer allured me; they reeked of age and decay, while I longed for the vital and new. New beginnings, new hope. Don John's new and revitalized Christian world.

Months passed, then more months, and still the grand invasion force was not launched. When I tried to find out why, I was given evasive answers or told that such things were not the proper concern of ladies.

I sputtered. I smoldered. I endured.

I had been in Rome nearly two years when I decided I could take no more of the tedium of waiting for the grand invasion to be launched. Don John had returned to the Eternal City from Flanders, not because of any pious obligations—he was not the sort of man to undertake a pilgrimage—but because he was running out of money.

Rome was full of moneylenders, and he appeared to patronize them all.

"It is a very costly venture, this crusade," he remarked in my hearing. He was signing his name to documents as he spoke, and gold coins were being counted into a small chest on a table next to him by a roguish-looking man wearing a long brown robe with deep pockets.

"His Holiness has been generous," Don John went on, "and so has my brother King Philip. Yet more is needed. Much, much more." He looked and sounded weary, his voice a dull monotone. Gone was the Don John I had first met on the night of the banquet at the Colonna palace, the inspired visionary, the flamboyant actor on the grand stage of the papal audience chamber.

"When will the invasion begin?" I asked him bluntly.

"When the men and ships are ready," he said without looking at me, keeping his eyes on the coins going into the chest one by one.

"You must have some idea how soon that day will come."

He was silent.

"If I were to go to Flanders with you," I said after a time, "I could speak to my bankers there. I could raise funds I imagine. But only if I could say when the armies and fleet will be fully trained and equipped."

I lied. I had no bankers in Flanders—though at one time, when I had been married to Francis, there had been hordes of bankers eager to make loans to the French court at extremely high rates of interest.

Hearing me say that I might be able to take out some loans Don John looked up at me from under his beautiful long lashes, and I thought I saw a flicker of hope in his eyes. But when he spoke his tone was full of disdain.

"And would you have me provide information about our plans to our enemies? They have ears everywhere, you know. They are listening even now, most likely," he added glancing over at the man in the brown robe, whose face remained impassive, and on around the room where many financial transactions were taking place. "No one is to be trusted."

"Surely you don't distrust me."

"Less than others, perhaps. But this room, this palace, is full of listening ears."

At length, using all my powers of persuasion, I convinced Don John to agree to allow me to come to his camp at Vlissingen, promising to borrow as much money as I possibly could, as soon as I possibly could, from any bankers who would lend to me, on the strength of my claim to the thrones of England and Scotland. I did not believe Don John to be mercenary, exactly. I did not feel that he was intent on exploiting me. Rather it was clear to me that his fleet and his army were of such vital importance to him that in his view, any source of funds could be tapped to support them.

With my promise of financial help, a newfound spark of optimism seemed to animate the commander, and he began to speak of launching the invasion in a matter of weeks.

"We are nearly ready, after all," he confided to the men around him, as I stood by. "We only need a few more men, more horses and arms, spare sails and ropes—" He seemed to carry a long list of requirements in his head, a list so long I wondered whether it would ever be completely filled. "If only we had the funds . . ." His voice trailed off, his expressive face all at once bleak.

"Will you be able to get the funds I need, Mary?" he asked me. "Do you think you will?"

FIFTY

WHEN I first arrived at the huge, sprawling army camp at Vlissingen, with its endless long rows of tents and its mounds of refuse, its stench of horse manure and gunpowder, spoiled food and unwashed bodies mingled with the more appetizing odors of roasting meat and beer, I was impressed with the armies Don John had assembled. Clearly he was, as everyone said, a miracle worker when it came to amassing men, although he was having a great deal of trouble paying them. The camp was alive with activity. Overloaded carts came and went along muddy pathways, whips cracking over the backs of the tired horses and bullocks that pulled them along. Everywhere soldiers lounged alongside the tents, eating around campfires, shooting at improvised targets, sparring with one another, grinning at the full-lipped, swaying-hipped camp followers in their boots and dirty petticoats.

Visible in the harbor just beyond the camp was the enormous fleet of galleys, rocking in the swell, small boats coming and going amid them. Flying from each masthead was the yellow banner of the Holy League.

Don John had prevailed upon his half-brother King Philip to lend him a dozen chests of Spanish gold, enough to get the expedition under way, but the funds had not yet arrived. I had been at the camp for three weeks, and still no final orders had been given. Because of the promised Spanish loan nothing more had been said about my attempting to raise funds from the moneylenders in Bruges or Amsterdam, and this came as a relief to me. But other issues were weighing heavily on my mind— beyond the most serious issue of all, Jamie's absence, which I tried my best to push aside, out of my thoughts, at least during the day.

The armies at Vlissingen, I had discovered during my weeks there, were assembled into tercios, groupings of thousands of pikemen and musketeers who were expected to fight together in precise formations. I had been hearing the colonels of the tercios complaining to Don John that they did not yet know their places within the brigades, which meant that they had no idea where to go or what to do once battle loomed.

What was worse, the commander had not informed the colonels which ships they and their men were to travel in once the army embarked. Each of the two hundred galleys was capable of transporting hundreds of men, and the embarkation had to be carefully planned and executed or there would be chaos in the harbor.

When I ventured to ask Don John where the fleet was to land once it was launched, he bristled.

"Why, on the enemy shore, of course," he said.

"Yes, but where? England has a long coastline."

"Where they least expect us," was all he would say, but as we were conversing I noticed another odd thing: Don John had no pilot's charts in his tent, no maps of southern England. No maps of any kind, in fact, or charts of the Sleeve such as sailors invariably consult in order to choose their best routes.

Where were his charts, his battle plans, not to mention his messengers and secretaries? Who was keeping track of what went on in the camp?

One day I heard shouting and a gun firing. I rushed outside to find an altercation under way.

Two wretched-looking men were being tied to posts in preparation to receive a whipping. They were jabbering in Spanish, pleading piteously for their lives, insisting that they had done nothing wrong.

Soldiers were collecting in clusters, some taking the side of the men to be punished, some crying for their blood to be spilt. Guns were drawn, harsh words were flying back and forth. I asked what was going on and was told there had been a spill of oats—precious fodder for the horses. The two men were blamed.

Don John strode up to the posts and viciously slapped each man's face.

"Who paid you to do this evil thing?" he demanded.

The men, wincing from the blows, managed to shake their heads. "No one," they said. "No one. We did nothing. We swear it on the cross of Our Saviour."

"By the beard of Christ! You are liars. Oats do not spill themselves. You are spies. The English baron pays you." He kicked one of the men, who cried out with pain and begged for mercy.

Turning his back, the commander ordered the whipping to begin.

I could not watch. I have never been able to witness cruel punishments without feeling terrible distress. I began to walk away, murmuring a prayer for the two men, when I heard another outcry.

"Your Lordship, there has been a mistake." It was a mature man's voice, low-pitched, the voice of one in authority. I turned back and saw one of the colonels, evidently an experienced officer, striding toward Don John.

"These men are not responsible for the hole in the oat sack, Your Lordship. I will vouch for their innocence. There were rats in the tent. They gnawed the hole. There has been no bribery, no spying."

Don John stared at the man suspiciously.

"I don't believe you," he said, and ordered the punishment to proceed.

Something about Don John's behavior was troubling me. I was impelled to intervene. I approached the colonel and Don John, holding my skirts out of the mud in what I hoped was a modest gesture and walking toward them with my head lowered. I was intensely aware, at that moment, that I was the only woman in a growing crowd of unruly men.

"My lord prince," I said to Don John, "will you, for my sake, show your mercy and release these good Christians? I will take them into my service, if you like. It is the rats that serve the enemy, not these men."

I looked into his eyes, but I saw no mercy there, only resentment. I saw then that I had put him in an awkward position; he was gallant, and he would not allow himself to behave other than in a gallant manner. Yet his distrust of the men had not been dispelled, either by the colonel's explanation of what really happened or by my generosity toward his prisoners.

He bowed to me, though I could tell that his muscles remained stiff.

"Take them then," he said curtly, and left. The men were hastily untied and at once they fell at my feet, weeping with gratitude.

"Come with me," I said to them, and they followed me until we were at some distance from the others. Don John was nowhere in sight, and the colonel who had tried to save the men from punishment had also disappeared.

I drew a coin from my pocket and gave it to the men.

"Take this," I said in my halting Spanish, "and leave the camp. Go as far away as you can. You will not be safe if you stay here."

With fervent cries of thanks they ran off, down the path that led out of the camp and toward the highroad to Bruges, leaving me to ponder the incident and worry over Don John's state of mind and health.

Had the incident with the spilled oats been the only one of its kind I might have seen no reason to worry further. But there were others. One evening, in a burst of righteous anger, Don John swept through the camp, searching for men playing cards or gambling with dice—a very common pastime among the soldiers. "Blasphemers!" he shouted when he found gaming going on, overturning the tables and throwing the cards and dice into the fire and ordering the men to be shut in deep underground pits and deprived of food.

(I could not help but think of Jamie. Where was he? Was he gambling in some noisy tavern? Was he surrounding himself with unworthy women? Had he forgotten me?)

Not long after this the German armament-makers, men who provided the soldiers with their weaponry and were, along with the provisioners, the most vital suppliers in the camp, laid siege to the commander's quarters and demanded to be paid. I watched as Don John received them, solemnly handing one man after another a ripe orange drawn from a basket beside him.

The armorers, heavyset, barrel-chested men, their arms knotted with muscles from years of lifting and twisting and pounding masses of resistant metal into weaponry as artful and beautiful as it was deadly, were dumbfounded by the prince's eccentric behavior. They looked at one another from under thick brows, spat on the oranges and threw them to the ground, then stalked out.

Word of this bizarre incident spread through the camp, and made the soldiers restive and suspicious.

"Is he going to pay us with oranges too?" I heard men say, some with an uneasy laugh, others with disgust. "We haven't been paid for months. Is this what we are going to have to show for our labors? Fruit?"

I could not help but remember what I had heard about the odd behavior of Don John's relatives, when I was a widowed queen in France and my grandmother was persuading me to consider King Philip's son Don Carlos as a prospective husband. The crippled, hunchbacked Don Carlos, she told me, was said to keep to himself and was suspicious of everyone; he amused himself by watching small animals being roasted alive. His father King Philip was reputed to be morose and withdrawn, a terrible husband who persecuted and tormented his wives. And Philip's grandmother, Joan the Mad, had been infamous for refusing to let her late husband's body be buried and keeping it with her, ordering the coffin opened from time to time so that she could embrace his stinking remains. Even Joan's grandmother was rumored to have been insane.

Did Joan the Mad give people oranges instead of coins, I wondered. Had Don John taken leave of his senses? Ought I to write to Pope Gregory, to tell him what was going on in Vlissingen? Or should I heed the advice that I had been given, and remember that such things were not the proper concern of ladies?

I found that I had no need to answer these questions, for just as the men of the invasion force were losing faith in their commander's sanity word arrived from Rome that the Turks, Don John's old enemies and the enemies of all Christendom, were once again sending a huge fleet to invade the Mediterranean. Rome was threatened; if the Ottoman fleet was allowed to prevail, all Europe might come under Muslim rule.

The commander was needed. He had won a great victory over the Turks years earlier. Surely, with the aid of divine providence, he could turn them back once again.

Filled with a newfound sense of purpose, his puzzling eccentricities overcome, Don John went aboard his flagship and sailed for the south, after announcing that he meant to destroy the entire Turkish fleet so thoroughly that the Ottomans could never menace the Holy League again.

He said nothing to me at his leavetaking, so swift was his departure and so urgent its purpose. I watched as his galley was carried out to sea on the outgoing tide, sails unfurled, dipping and rising as it met the swells, banners waving in the freshening wind.

A part of me longed to go with him, for the start of a journey is always exciting and the prospect of remaining in the camp, with its increasing reek and filth and its air of neglect, deflated my spirits. Even before the galley was over the horizon and lost from view I could see the campfires being doused and the soldiers striking their tents and packing their possessions.

The dream of a great invasion had dissolved, leaving me stranded on a cold and unfamiliar shore, with nothing but my courage and my hopes to sustain me against the storms to come.

FIFTY-ONE

PULLING a soldier's hooded cloak over my untidy red hair and biting my nails from nervousness, I joined the long slow exodus from the military camp. No one seemed to be in charge, now that Don John had left; the heart had gone out of the enterprise and since the soldiers and armorers, the provisioners and carters had not been paid (the promised Spanish gold had never arrived), there was no reason for anyone to remain in the forlorn settlement. The few servants Don John had assigned to me during my stay in the camp—my own servants having been left behind in Rome—were among the first to depart. I was on my own.

I found a half-starved nag, saddled but lacking a rider, that had been tied to the back of a wagon. When no one was looking I untied her and mounted her. Together we began the plodding trek toward Bruges.

The road seemed long, the skies leaden. On we went, rain-sodden mile after weary mile, the old horse and I, sustained by the bread, hard cheese and oats I found in her saddlebags and by the hospitality of Walloon villagers who offered us the shelter of their barns to sleep in, amid the animals' stalls.

At first I was fearful, as a woman traveling on my own (though I did my best to ride near officers or clusters of musketeers, acting as if I were one of their party). I kept my cloak pulled down over my face, spoke little, and hoped that I would be taken for a thin young man rather than a woman. No one scrutinized me too closely. After a few days my fear and wariness began to go away.

I crossed into France, intent on reaching my grandmother Antoinette's farm at Saint-Cheron in Normandie. My last letter from her, which I had received while still in Rome, had come from Saint-Cheron, and I hoped she had not moved on to another estate and that the warfare then troubling France had not forced her to abandon the farm to seek safety.

I saw much evidence of conflict on my journey. Burned houses, barns and churches, scorched fields and destroyed orchards told much about the prevailing warfare between Protestant and Catholic factions. Grandmamma Antoinette had written me of this ugly contention, and of the many villagers made homeless by it, but until I saw the wreckage with my own eyes I could not realize what widespread harm had been done.

It was a relief to discover, when I finally reached Normandie, that the lovely valley surrounding Saint-Cheron was unblemished by the fighting, the stretches of lush meadow and thick forest just as I remembered them from my childhood, the view of the river still idyllic.

The farm too was as I remembered it: the thick-walled old buildings, their walls of soft mellow limestone, their roofs of red tiles drawn from a local quarry. The stone cottages where the farm laborers lived, each with its small garden neatly kept. The old well in the courtyard of the main farmhouse, its wood dark with age. And the comforting sounds of the horses whinnying in their paddocks, the ducks quacking softly to one another, the goats bleating to be milked. Sounds far different from those I had been hearing for many months—musketfire and the pounding of guns, raucous laughter and shouted quarrels, the rough music of the army camp and the tortured squeals of animals being butchered for meat to feed the soldiers.

When I reached the brow of the little hill above the farm I reined in my bony mount and paused, savoring the tranquil scene, then touched her thin flank and eased her down into the courtyard to where a groom was waiting to help me dismount. He touched his cap in greeting, and I startled him by bursting into tears and embracing him as if he had been a long-lost relative.

"By all that's holy, will you look at yourself!" Grandmamma Antoinette cried when I was shown into the house by a maid who gave me a dubious look before admitting me.

"Marie! Where have you been? Why are you wearing those filthy clothes? Why hasn't Margaret arranged your hair?"

Her questions flew, but before I could answer them I caught sight of my lovely daughter coming into the room, and rushed to take her in my arms.

Laughing and crying, I admired Marie-Elizabeth, who had grown into a tall, slender child with my reddish hair and creamy skin, and with the look of her father in her large dark eyes and well-shaped nose, her pointed chin with its hint of defiance, her air of strength as well as budding beauty.

I could not speak, I shook my head in wonder at the sight of her. I had thought of her so very often, and prayed for her, and sent her messages to say that I loved her. But we had had so little time together. We barely knew one another.

She smiled at me and took my hand.

"Come and take some refreshment, mother. You look weary and hungry." She led me into the large, warm farm kitchen that smelled of fresh-baked bread and spices and sat me down at a table before the fire. She brought me wine, and a bowl of thick clotted cream, a delicious compote of pears and quince apples and a savory meat pie.

I had not realized how hungry I was. I fell on the food like one starved, ignoring my manners completely and reverting to animal instinct. I stuffed myself, then sank into a drowse. I was so tired I was barely aware of being led into a darkened chamber and put to bed.

I awoke to the sound of my grandmother's tart voice.

"Come now, enough of this! You've been asleep for two days. Did you know that?"

I sat up, dizzy and disoriented. I was in a strange room, but grandmamma, sitting on the bed, her keen searching eyes peering into mine, was familiar.

"Now then, it's time you remembered who you are and how you need to present yourself to the world." She beckoned to two maids who took off my nightgown (I had no memory of putting it on) and helped me into a big wooden tub full of water more cold than warm. I shivered, but it felt good to have the women lather me and scrub me and wash out my long neglected hair.

"Where on earth have you been, child?" my grandmamma wanted to know.

"With Don John's army, in a place called Vlissingen, waiting for him to invade England."

"Then what are you doing here?"

"Don John had to leave. The camp disbanded. I didn't know where else to go. Where is Jamie?"

"In Scotland. He is safe—for now. He sends letters and money every month to Marie-Elizabeth. She adores him, you know."

I adore him too, I wanted to say, but I did not want to discuss what had happened with Jamie in front of the servants, so I waited until after I had had my bath and my hair had been combed out and was drying in front of the fire. When Grandmamma Antoinette and I were alone, I told her all that had occurred, how Jamie had left Rome and I had been drawn into Pope Gregory's grand plans—plans for the conquest of England, and for my marriage to Don John and my accession to the throne still occupied by my cousin Elizabeth.

"At least you are no longer the prisoner of that hateful woman,"

Grandmamma Antoinette said, referring to my cousin. "She has not only robbed you of your throne, she has robbed you of your youth."

She handed me a small looking-glass and I was shocked at how much older I looked than when I had last contemplated my image, in Rome, dressed in my finery and feeling admired and full of hope. Then I was still in the glory of my womanhood, or so I fancied; now I looked like a scrubwoman, my complexion dulled by neglect and anxiety, my hair limp and lusterless, the clean but simple garments I had been given to wear making me look like a poor villager rather than a queen.

I gazed into the looking-glass for a long time, then handed it back to grandmamma with a sigh.

"And to think I imagined that I could ever mount a throne again!" I remarked. "What foolish dreams!"

"None of that!" grandmamma snapped. "Remember who you are speaking to! A daughter of the Bourbon royal house. You may fancy that your standing in the world has changed, but I assure you mine has not. I live quietly here in the country for the sake of your daughter and my granddaughter, whose true identity I have kept hidden. I say that she is the orphaned daughter of a dear friend, and no one questions me further. No one wants to know the truth about her. As long as she stays here, in obscurity, we remain untroubled by Her Self-Importance, the dowager Queen Catherine. Your former mother-in-law."

"Those days seem so long ago," I mused. "How Queen Catherine loved Francis! How sad she was when he died!"

I continued to lift my damp hair and air it out in the warmth from the fire, lost in my memories.

"None of her children please her. My friends at court tell me that she has grown more hardened, more difficult as she ages. Poor weak Charles, when he was king, broke under the weight of his sorrow when all those innocent Protestants were killed, that horrible slaughter the queen dowager ordered. He claimed he was haunted by the screams of the dying Protestants, poor boy—and when he complained that he was suffering, she called him a lunatic and walked away. No wonder he died so young.

"She liked his brother Henry better—until he began dressing in women's clothes and dying his hair purple. Since then she has practically disowned him, but he is still king, after all, and has all the power a king can command. No one knows better than she does what a nasty side he has to him; she doesn't dare shut herself off from him completely. What matters most to her, after all, is that she retain some power for herself.

"And now there is the youngest of her boys, Francis the Frog (or so your cousin Elizabeth calls him). He has courage, that one, and he's not afraid of his mother. Your cousin likes him. He may become the next King of England, you know. But his mother spits when she sees him, because like her, he's ugly. A poxy face, a puny body. The runt of her litter. All mothers despise the runt."

I listened to my grandmamma's shrewd, unsparing comments on the royal family and felt a rare calm come over my weary body. I was in good hands. We were in a rural enclave not far from the sea. I imagined that I could escape by boat if the worst happened, and agents of either Baron Burghley or Queen Catherine descended on Saint-Cheron. We were far from Paris, and the royal palaces that clustered nearby.

And Queen Elizabeth, it seemed, was intent on wooing Prince Francis the Frog. No one had any illusions about her true intentions, of course; it was not the puny, poxy Francis she wanted, it was an alliance with France itself—her way of counteracting the power of the Catholic Holy League, the might of Catholic Christendom.

But the great hero of Christendom, Don John, was no more.

I had not been at Saint-Cheron long before I learned that he had gathered his ships and led them into battle against the Ottoman fleet—and that for the first time his forces had been defeated.

The heroic Don John, champion of the Holy League, mighty

commander, had lost a major battle—and had not long survived that loss. According to what Grandmamma Antoinette's informants at court wrote to her, he had retired to his camp, caught a fever, and died within sight of his beloved galleys, the name of the Holy League on his bloodless lips.

He was mourned. His death seemed to many to represent a major reverse to the Catholic cause, for there was no one to replace him as leader of that cause—no one, that is, except his dour half-brother King Philip of Spain. And no one expected King Philip, then entering his fifties, to lead an army, let alone a fleet. He was no commander, he knew little of ships, and above all, he was disliked, while Don John had been revered, indeed almost worshipped.

Although I had not loved him, I too mourned Don John, despite his arrogance and his excessive self-regard. For among the men I had known, he was the one with the broadest and highest vision. He was inspired, and inspiring. Jamie was my love, and ever would be. But Don John, for a brief time, had been my hero, my champion.

Who would be my champion now?

FIFTY-TWO

We began to embroider a tapestry together, Marie-Elizabeth and I, as August gave way to September and then to the frosts of October. Grandmamma Antoinette had been teaching her embroidery since she was five years old, so she was no novice, but there was much more that I could show her and besides, our tapestry was more than a work of art: it was a record of our lives.

Each morning after we had gathered the eggs (my daughter had to teach me how to avoid being pecked by the indignant hens) and harvested the late fallen apples for the pigs we took off our mud-spattered farm aprons and went into the sewing room. There, beside Grandmamma Antoinette's loom with its brilliant pattern of white lilies and red roses, was the embroidery table with its skeins of silk in a bright rainbow of colors, along with trays of needles, inks and pens.

As a girl in France I had been fascinated by calligraphy, and had learned to form letters in the old fashion of the monks, each letter a small art work complete with decorative banners and curlicues and twisting tendrils of color. So now I took up my pen and carefully fashioned a motto for our wall hanging: ONE LIKE THE LIONESS. We began by embroidering these letters, careful to cover the marks of my ink while following their curving outlines as exactly as we could.

As we sewed, we talked.

"My wonderful mother was a lioness for courage," I told Marie-Elizabeth, who was trying hard to emulate my small, even stitches, her tongue between her teeth, her brow furrowed in concentration. "I have never known another woman like her. My father King James died when I was only a few days old, as you know, and so it was up to mama to reign in his place. She fought hard to keep her authority—and she kept it, despite all, right up until the time she got sick." I paused, the memories were painful and it was hard to go on. "Your father helped her all he could. She loved him very much."

"He has told me a lot about her. How she had a strong will, just as you do."

I had to laugh at that. "Do I? I sometimes wonder. I think I give in too easily."

"I have seen a painting of her," Marie-Elizabeth was saying. "And of my other grandmother too."

"You have rich noble and royal blood in your veins, little one. The blood of the Stuarts, and the Hepburns, the Tudors and the Guises. Like me, you are heiress to two thrones." I smiled at her, with what I hoped was a benign smile rather than a sad one—though I suddenly felt sad, speaking of a destiny that seemed unlikely to be fulfilled.

"But my brother James will inherit those thrones, not I."

At the mention of my son James I sighed and put down my sewing.

"James!" I shook my head. "If only you knew how many times I have tried to send letters to him—and not only letters, but gifts. But he refuses to receive them—or those who claim to speak for him do. I feel he is lost to me."

"He follows the heretic religion."

"He was baptized into the true church when he was a baby, of course. But he has been raised as a Protestant—and all that he knows of me comes from the Protestants around him who hate me.

"He is a caulbearer, you know," I went on. "He was born with special powers. The Scots believe that caulbearers can see the future. I have no doubt he will grow up to be someone remarkable."

"Does he know about me?"

"No, dear. No one knows about you but your father and Grand-mamma Antoinette and my servant Margaret. I have kept you a secret."

"Why?"

"To protect you."

I could tell that she wanted to ask me more questions, but was unsure whether she should. I did not want to frighten her by telling her about Baron Burghley, who had sent an assassin to Rome to kill me, or about my enemies in Scotland, or indeed about any of the dark forces in the world. She was too young, as yet, to have to cope with that knowledge.

"If my brother can see the future," she said after a time, "won't he be able to see me in it?"

It was a perfectly logical question, only I had no answer to it.

"Possibly," I said, "but I don't think he knows about you yet."

As the weeks passed and winter approached I was aware that my health and wellbeing were improving. I was sleeping soundly for the first time in years, my body sinking deep into a pile of featherbeds. I ate good healthy food from the farm, reassured by the knowledge that the granary was full of oats and peas and millet put aside for the winter and that the barn was stocked with fruit and preserves and cider made from it, that the pigs had been slaughtered and their meat salted down. On the farm, life was secure and regular in its patterns; it followed the seasons, and the seasons were predictable. I had nothing to fear, there was no uncertainty, no need for trepidation about the future.

The pain in my side that had plagued me for years was less acute, and the headaches that sometimes sent me to bed for days did not come at all at Saint-Cheron. My body felt lighter, my mind suffered less from worrisome thoughts. I loved being with Marie-Elizabeth and Grandmamma Antoinette. My only real sorrow was that Jamie was not with us. On my best days I felt hopeful that in time he would join us at the farm; on my worst days I mourned him, and prayed that he would soon return to me.

Much as I savored my life on the farm, I could not suppress a nagging sense of ennui. The very sameness and certainty that gave me peace of mind weighed on me like a smothering blanket. My days lacked variety, life lacked spice and vigor, the agreeable sensation of unpredictability.

Often, in the long afternoons, I would gaze at the hills surrounding the farm and long to ride beyond them, to end the sameness that had begun to draw a shroud over my everyday existence. I began taking long walks, venturing out beyond the boundaries of the farm, risking the dangers of the forest where at any moment I knew that I might, if unlucky, encounter bands of thieves or gypsies, or uncouth half-wild charcoal men who lived in squalid dens like beasts and were covered in black dust. There were spirits in the forest, so it was said; in invading the realm of the spirits I was tempting fate.

Nothing escaped Grandmamma Antoinette's shrewd notice and she commented on my restless state of mind and body.

"Your problem, Marie, is that you have seen the world, or a great deal of it, and you cannot seem to settle into a small place after knowing the larger one. Don't you realize that most people spend their entire lives on one little plot of land, in one village, never even seeing the nearest town? Traveling to another country would be unimaginable for them—and unwelcome.

"Be content with what you have here, Marie! You are not a young woman any longer. Make the most of what life is offering you, and do not pant after what cannot be!"

I tried my best to follow my grandmother's advice. I thought, if I must spend the rest of my life here at Saint-Cheron, it will be well. It will be well enough. Better to spend it here than in an English or Scottish prison, or enclosed by the decaying walls of Rome. But no matter how hard I tried, I could not shake off the uncomfortable sense of constraint that weighed me down.

A year passed, then two, and the embroidered tapestry Marie-Elizabeth and I had been working on was all but finished. We had poured all our skills into it, and left something of our souls in its colorful panels as well. There were scenes of my birth in Scotland and my upbringing in France, my marriage to Francis and my widowhood, my discordant years as queen, my unhappy marriage to Henry and the birth of James, then my second widowhood and my happy union with Jamie. I did not weave his departure into the tapestry; I continued to trust that our separation was temporary, and that we would eventually be together again.

Marie-Elizabeth's birth was given a prominent place at the center of the hanging, her life with grandmamma on the farm, my unhappy years of imprisonment in Scotland and England, followed by my escape and my time in Rome and Vlissingen. All was depicted: the court splendors, the battles, the brief triumphs and the long years of despondency mingled with evergreen hope. A final scene was a dual portrait of Marie-Elizabeth and me, sewing together happily, a heartwarming family image.

"You see?" Grandmamma Antoinette said as she gazed contentedly at our handiwork. "You see what beauty you can create when you stay in one place, and make a good life for yourself?"

But I knew that it was no use. I had not been born to be obscure, to live a hidden, quiet life. I had the blood of kings in my veins, and so did my daughter. There was more for me to do in the world. I felt certain of it. Besides, while I had been rusticating in Normandie, Christendom had undergone fresh convulsions.

While I had been gathering eggs and tending the livestock, listening to Marie-Elizabeth practice on the lute and virginals, and amusing myself in the evenings playing backgammon and chess with Grandmamma Antoinette, while I watched the seasons change, and the land grow green, then golden, then sere and white with frost and snow, there had been fresh battles. The Catholic cause had strengthened, and King Philip and the might of Spain now stood between the marauding Turks and the Christian lands. My cousin Queen Elizabeth had abandoned her flirtation with Francis the Frog and it was clear to everyone that she was too old to marry and have a child; she needed to name a successor, and I knew that that successor ought to be me.

The wall hanging was nearly finished, but Marie-Elizabeth and I decided not to complete it, but rather to leave room for scenes to come.

"This is about our lives, mama," she said with a sweetly solemn smile. "We have much more living to do."

I nodded. "We do indeed." During my time at Saint-Cheron, Marie-Elizabeth had grown from a pretty child to a young woman. In another year or two she would be old enough to marry, as I had at only fifteen. Her lithe, slight body was taking on a woman's curves, her bright eyes, soft lips and lovely fair complexion would be alluring to any man. She stood tall and straight and proud. When I looked at her I thought, here is another young lioness, bearing the blood of kings, and with a royal courage.

But the world knew nothing of her, and I was only too aware that the only way I could keep her safe was to allow her to stay hidden, far from the swirling intrigues of princes, until it was time for her to be woven into the tapestry of power.

FIFTY-THREE

ON the day that the spare, white-haired, limping Archibald Skerriton came to Saint-Cheron with a letter from Jamie and stunning news for me, I was digging in the kitchen garden, preparing the rows for planting beans. My kerchief was askew, my hair untidy and my hands were brown with the rich loamy soil I had mixed with outscourings from the kitchen and manure from the stables and pasture. I heard men's voices in the courtyard and, brushing off my hands on my apron, went out to see who had arrived.

The old man walked toward me, his gait brisk despite his limp.

"It has been a long time, Orange Blossom," he said with a smile and a wink. "But you have weathered the years well."

It took me a moment to recognize him, but once I did I was overjoyed. Archibald, Jamie's godfather from the island of Mull, the very worldly former pirate who had once been a bishop. I greeted him warmly, then my questions tumbled out: how is Jamie? Where is he? Is he safe? Does he miss me?

Rather than answer, the old man reached into his trouser pocket and pulled out a folded paper.

"This will let him tell you all," he said, handing it to me then putting a finger over his lips. "But do not read it here. Take it to a private place."

I went quickly into the house, leaving the groom to tend to Archibald's horse and Grandmamma Antoinette to welcome him.

"My dearest one," the brief letter read, in Jamie's large sloping hand, "I think of you night and day. I trust our fortunes are changing. My messenger will tell you more. I send my heart with this letter."

There was no signature, and no need of one.

Filled with joy, I washed my hands and face and took off my apron and then went to find Archibald, to find out what "our fortunes are changing" meant.

It was thought best not to speak of important matters in Marie-Elizabeth's hearing, so we waited until she had gone to bed. Then Grandmamma Antoinette and I sat with Archibald in the spacious candlelit kitchen with its smell of spices and candle wax, and he told me the exciting news.

"Jamie has had word about the location of the letters hidden in Amy Dudley's casket."

I was so stunned that I had to grasp the table to keep my bearings. I shook my head in amazement. Such very welcome, unexpected tidings.

"But I thought Jamie had tried his best to find Amy Dudley's casket and failed. I remember him telling me that no one would even say a word to him about it, let alone confide in him where it might be hidden."

"True enough. But there has been a change. Amy's half-brother John Appleyard has loosened his tongue about the letters—and the casket. Always before, Appleyard was a great admirer of Robin Dudley, his brother-in-law. Because of his admiration, he concealed what he knew of Dudley's guilt—and the queen's. Appleyard had been at odds with his sister before her death and felt no loyalty to her—also he has a venal side. He kept his secret in part because he wanted preferment at court—lucrative wardships, offices, sinecures. Anything Dudley could procure for him.

"For years he knew where the letters were, but he refused to tell anyone. Now, however, he is angry with Dudley (who is out of favor with the queen, and less powerful than before) and wants to injure him. He is willing to reveal the location of the letters—for a price."

"How much does he want?" I asked, so quickly and so bluntly that I made Archibald laugh.

"Jamie told me you would be eager. Too eager."

"Of course I am eager. And from all that I heard when I was in Rome, the English people are eager too—impatient to rid themselves of their barren Protestant queen and to see Catholicism restored."

Grandmamma Antoinette had been sitting silent, listening intently to all that Archibald said, her intensity eloquent. Eventually she spoke.

"My friends at the French court say that Elizabeth's throne is slipping rapidly out of her grasp. Her enemies are growing stronger than ever. More and more Catholic priests and missionaries of the Society of Jesus are being sent into England. New converts are being made every day."

She turned her searching gaze on me, and I nearly flinched, the look in her eyes was so piercing.

"They are full of enthusiasm to see the true church restored. They look to you, Marie, as their rightful queen."

Archibald nodded. "Your name is on many lips, Mary. And not all of them Catholic. You are the hope of many a rebel. But precisely because of that, you must be more careful than ever to protect yourself—and Marie-Elizabeth."

I felt a chill.

"The English don't know about her, do they?"

"No," Archibald said. "But if she were to leave Saint-Cheron, especially in your company, and return to England or Scotland they might well guess. For that reason Jamie wants her to stay here on the farm, while you come with me, aboard the *Black Messenger* which is waiting in the harbor near Caen."

"And go where?"

"To Mull, where he has assembled a force of a hundred men. Where he can keep you safe from Baron Burghley and from the Scots who are in the pay of the English."

"I can contribute enough to pay another hundred men—and I have no doubt our French King Henry will contribute even more," Grandmamma Antoinette said.

"And I still have my jewels, or at least some of them," I put in. "I should have enough pearls and rubies to satisfy Amy Dudley's brother."

"Leave that to Jamie, Orange Blossom. You can talk all over with him when you arrive on Mull."

With the aid of Grandmamma Antoinette and two of her tire-women, I packed a few things for the journey. I did not allow myself to dwell on my sorrow at leaving Marie-Elizabeth; had I indulged that awful feeling, I might never have left.

"Never fear, my dear, I will explain to her that for your sake and hers, you had to leave suddenly. I think she is always aware that at any moment, you could be snatched away, or called away."

As softly as I could, I entered Marie-Elizabeth's bedroom and, without waking her, kissed her cheek and whispered that I loved her. Then I embraced my dear grandmamma and thanked her for all that she had done for me and for her great-granddaughter.

"Godspeed," she said as she watched us mount our horses. "Be cautious, Marie. Do not be hasty. Remember all that is at stake."

It would not be dawn for several hours. A light rain had begun to fall, and the air was chilly.

"With luck, we should be able to make the outgoing tide," Archibald said as he scanned the eastern horizon. "I told Red Ormiston that I might be back before it was light. He said he would have all in readiness for our departure."

"You knew I would not want to lose any time leaving Saint-Cheron once I learned of the possibility of finding the letters, didn't you."

Archibald looked sheepish.

"Let us say I was forewarned—by Jamie."

With a final glance back at my dear grandmamma, and a final wave, we were off, finding our way by starlight along the narrow path that led toward the coast, and the rough waters of the Sleeve, and the waiting shores of England.

FIFTY-FOUR

ONCE aboard the *Black Messenger*, Archibald wanted to sail directly to Scotland, but we could not do that; a storm delayed us, and swept us northward, and then we broke a spar and ran out of provisions and had to make landfall at St. Leonard's on the south coast of England while the crew went ashore to make repairs and take on fresh water and food.

Though Archibald cautioned me against it, I went ashore as well—I had been ill on the ship and needed to feel solid ground under my feet, without the constant rocking and lurching that made my stomach so upset.

I thought it would do no harm if I walked along the sea front of the small town, and I asked Anna, the woman I had once called the Skottefrauen but who for many years had been the wife of Red Ormiston and his companion aboard the *Black Messenger*, to accompany me.

We strolled together along the quay, I breathed deeply of the sea air and tried to adjust my rolling gait to the unmoving pavingstones beneath my feet. The slanting rays of the late afternoon sun shone down on the old jetty and the fishing boats that were coming in with their catch. We had just paused to watch one of the boats unload, the men carrying baskets of still wriggling fish up the stone steps to display them for sale, when a man came up to me. He was tall and broad, with the large hands of a laborer and the high domed forehead of a man of middle years. Yet he gave an impression of strength and vigor.

He looked at me carefully—quite rudely, I thought—scrutinizing my face.

"Sir?" I said, my voice curt. "Sir, it is churlish to stare."

A look of astonishment came over his features at the sound of my voice, and instead of answering me he reached out to grasp my arm.

"By all that's holy," he cried, "you resemble the Queen of Scotland, Queen Mary! And your voice is the same!"

I suppose I should have shaken my head, wrenched my arm free from his grasp and passed on. Instead I smiled—a small smile.

"It is the queen!" he cried to those nearest him. "I saw her when I went north with Lord Reidpath. It is the queen herself!"

The man knelt at my feet, and I saw that he had taken a rosary from his pocket and was fingering the beads. It all happened very quickly. I did not know what to do.

"We are Catholics here at St. Leonard's," he was saying under his breath. "Where is your army? I am an armorer. I would like to join your forces."

I was recovering from my surprise.

"I assure you, you are mistaken, sir. Please let me pass."

"Of course," I heard him whisper as I went on by. "I will say no more. Just be aware that we are with you, and we are many!"

Because of the noisy crowd on the quay the man's sudden outcry and display of reverence to me had not caused a great deal of notice, though some heads had turned in our direction. I took Anna's arm and we hurried to leave the quay and were soon back aboard the *Black Messenger*.

But once aboard, I could not stop thinking about the incident. What if there were indeed many Catholics in the town of St. Leonard's, and what if there were others—perhaps many others—in the area? Indeed throughout southern England?

My thoughts whirled. I could hear my dear grandmamma's voice saying, do not be hasty, remember all that is at stake. But her cautions were lost amid my rising hopes. Perhaps, I thought, there is a secret army of Catholics in the Weald, perhaps men and munitions are being amassed there just as they were in Vlissingen. It gave me hope to imagine that possibly all was being done in secret, in defiance of the queen, and Baron Burghley and his spies.

And if, as I hoped, my many supporters were taking active steps to rebel against my cousin Queen Elizabeth then it was all the more imperative that I find the late Amy Dudley's brother John Appleyard without delay and buy the information he was offering: the location of his sister's casket and the crucial letters it held.

John Appleyard was well known to Londoners, his house in Bishopsgate was among the grandest in the parish (so Archibald learned from patrons of the Black Bull Inn in the neighboring street) and he was said to feed sixty beggars every day outside the door to his kitchens and to provide alms for sixty more. He had once been Robin Dudley's steward, Archibald was told, but no longer held that lucrative office. Still, he had many more court appointments that made him a rich man.

Why then, I wondered as I wrapped my gleaming, sparkling necklaces and rings, jeweled ornaments and diamond buttons in silken pouches and placed the pouches carefully into a velvet bag, did he want still more money? So that he could feed a hundred beggars and give out even more alms? Somehow I doubted that benevolence was his motive. He knew that the letters hidden in his sister's casket could ruin my cousin's repute and bring the old scandal of Amy Dudley's murder back to life. He knew how valuable they were to the queen's enemies, and he was greedy.

After much argument and persuasion I had convinced Archibald to come to London so that I could sell my jewels and buy the information that would lead me to the letters. He argued strongly that we should sail to Mull and leave all such decisions to Jamie, but in the end I won the argument. I was the more stubborn, I was younger (though feeling my years), and I was, after all, the true claimant to the English throne. Archibald threw up his hands and agreed to do as I wanted.

The first thing I had to do was convert my valuable jewellery into coins, and for this task Red Ormiston—Sir James Ormiston, as I had dubbed him—was ideally suited. He had after all been selling valuable goods, nearly always stolen or smuggled goods, to dealers who trafficked in such merchandise for decades. I entrusted my heavy velvet bag to him (not for a moment worrying that I might never see either Red or the bag again) and within a few hours he returned, leading two horses, their saddlebags filled with gold coins.

After securing the chests of coins in a safe hiding place (which to this day I have never revealed), I sent Archibald to confer with John Appleyard.

Even though the aging Archibald was a self-confident man, I saw clearly that his knees were shaking when he set off to strike a bargain with John Appleyard. I did not envy him his task, indeed I pitied him.

Presently he returned to us, his face ashen, and said simply, "He wants more."

"But there is no more!" I cried. "I have no more!"

"Unless we can find more money, he will not tell us what we need to know. He is a hard man."

"Perhaps he is afraid of the queen," I wondered aloud. "He may not be greedy, merely frightened."

"Or both," Archibald suggested. "Yes, I would say he was definitely frightened. He kept watching his servants, as if he couldn't trust them."

"Maybe one of the servants knows where the casket is," I ventured.

"And there may be another way of finding out, rather than giving any more money to John Appleyard."

Early the following morning I went with Anna Ormiston to the meanest shop I could find where old clothes were sold. I outfitted myself in a threadbare gown and ragged cape full of holes, trailing both garments through the dirt of the street until when I put them on I looked as though I had been sleeping in the street or in a dirty doorway. I took off my boots and covered my head with a thin black shawl, darkening my face with soot and pulling the shawl down over my forehead.

"By all the saints, Orange Blossom, your own grandmamma would not know you now!" Archibald exclaimed when he saw me. "What in the name of heaven are you going to do, got up like that?"

"I'm going to take advantage of John Appleyard's hospitality," I said. "I'm hungry, and I hear he feeds all the beggars in the neighborhood."

And with Anna Ormiston and two of the strongest Norwegian sailors from the crew of the *Black Messenger* following me at a distance, I set off, hobbling on my bare feet, for the grandest house in Bishopsgate.

FIFTY-FIVE

I felt bony fingers clamp down on my arm and yank me toward a much weathered stone wall.

"Hush! Hold your tongue!"

The old woman was bent and grizzled, with stiff white hairs protruding from her determined chin. Like the rest of us in the crowd waiting at the gate of John Appleyard's tall gabled house, she wore rags and had a feral air.

"Do not say that name! The queen's men are everywhere!"

"What—" I began, but she shushed me again.

"You know the name! Hold your tongue!"

The name I had been saying was that of Amy Dudley. I had joined the crowd of those waiting for alms at the gate of the large house, and while waiting I had been asking, quietly and discreetly as I thought, about whether anyone knew where Lady Amy had been laid to rest. Though I had persisted in asking for some minutes, no one had answered me, I had been shunned.

I looked down into the alert, suspicious eyes of the old beggar woman. "I am ready to pay anyone who can tell me what I want to know."

"Don't speak of that here!" She tightened her grip on my arm and pulled me into a crevice in the wall, a declivity where the ancient stones had fallen or been pried away by thieving hands. Rain had begun to pour down and our voices were drowned out by the sound of its splashing and thudding against the uneven pavingstones. The old woman raised one thin arm in a vain effort to shield herself from the downpour.

I leaned close to her. "Do you know where Lady Dudley's casket is?"

"I know all there is to know," she said, speaking more to the wall than to me. "Wickedness. Every sort of wickedness. What they did to that poor girl! They tried to hide it all, by moving her here and there. Moving her poor broken body . . ."

"Moving it where? Where is the casket now?"

The old woman looked around, but there was no one near enough to us to overhear.

"Right next door, at St. Ethelburga's!" she whispered. "In the crypt!"

"Do you know this for certain? Have you seen the casket?"

Suddenly she was angry. "Have I seen it? Have I, Rose Pinto, seen it?" She drew herself up to her full height, which was far below mine. "I prepared her body. I saw her die."

There was pride in her tone.

"You were in her household then?"

"I was her maid. But the others saw it as well. All the old servants. Mistress Odingcells, Mistress Owen—we saw her writhing on the floor after she ate those stag pies. We saw the terrible pain she was in, from the poison."

"But I thought she died from a fall!"

"Nonsense! After she was poisoned, her poor body was thrown down the stairs by that wicked Richard Smythe, the one the queen bribed to keep her secret! And Appleyard was there too—" Here the old woman looked around again, hastily, before returning to her story. "It was Smythe that bribed the jury afterwards, that swore she had an accident and fell down the stairs, and that no one was to blame. Oh, he has much to answer for in the next life, that one!"

"But you never came forward with the truth?"

"We were all told to keep silent. If we kept silent, we would be taken care of. That's why Appleyard feeds us. And there's silver for us too, every Lady Day and at Eastertide."

I reached for the bag of small coins I had brought with me—all I had left from the money Red Ormiston had gotten for my jewels. All that I had kept back for my own modest costs.

"This is yours, Mistress Pinto," I said, handing her the bag. She snatched it from my hand and darted out into the rain, joining the cluster of dripping beggars waiting at the gate.

St. Ethelburga's, I thought. Right next door, at St. Ethelburga's. I was so excited I ran, splashing through the filthy puddles in my wet feet, nearly colliding with Anna and the Norwegian sailors, so eager was I to tell Archibald what I had discovered and to make our plans.

By nightfall the rain had turned to a cold drizzle, the beggars had long since gone to their places of shelter and I had taken off my ragged clothing and put on a clean dry gown. The cold rain had given me a chill, and I sneezed and coughed as I sat talking with Archibald and Anna and her husband.

"What if the crypt is locked?" Archibald said.

Red Ormiston laughed. "There's not a lock in England I can't pick—or break."

"But the noise, that would draw attention."

"I can be quiet."

"What if there are guards?" I put in.

Red pointed to a thick cudgel leaning against the wall. And Anna drew the long sharp knife that she always carried and laid it on the table with a heavy thud.

Archibald sighed and shook his head. "I wish Jamie were here. But if he were, he would cause a commotion. That would bring Burghley's men for certain, and nothing would be accomplished.

"No, we are better doing this alone. Just ourselves. Besides, if we waited for Jamie to arrive the casket might be moved."

In the end we decided to wait for midnight, then go to St. Ethelburga's and break in. Archibald would bring a chest to carry the letters we expected to find inside the casket. It was the crudest of plans, but we would not be suspected. Not if Rose Pinto, Amy Dudley's faithful former maid, did not betray us, and I did not think she would.

Sneezing and drinking chamomile tea to calm my fluttering nerves, I tried to drowse as I waited for midnight and the long-awaited culmination of my hopes.

FIFTY-SIX

We went along the wet street past John Appleyard's house with its flaring torches, sputtering in the rain, to the small old church of St. Ethelburga's. On the side away from the house, a narrow set of steps led downward into darkness. It was the entrance to the crypt.

Red Ormiston went first, prepared to have to use force or stealth to move the ancient door. Archibald followed, carrying a torch that provided very little light, its flame burning low. But to our surprise the door yielded to Red's touch, and we crossed the threshold into a room that smelled of dust and mold and time-ravaged bodies.

Archibald raised his torch and we saw at once that the room was full of stone tombs—and that we were not alone.

I hardly had time to gasp in surprise before I felt my arms pinned behind my back and saw that Red Ormiston, with a deep cry of outrage, was being overpowered by three strong men. Archibald dropped fainting to the floor while Anna, knife raised, held two attackers at bay but was not quick enough to threaten the others that grasped her from behind and soon disarmed her and tied a cloth around her mouth.

I felt and saw all this, yet amid my shock and fear I could not take my eyes from the thin figure that stood in the center of the room, a wooden casket on the stone floor in front of her. She was taking papers out of the casket one by one and setting them alight from a burning brand she held. So absorbed was she in her task that she seemed to ignore our presence, though Red Ormiston continued to struggle and kick out against his captors and swear strong oaths and Anna too did her best to scream, though the cloth that bound her mouth shut reduced her screams to weak grunts.

It was Elizabeth who was burning the papers, wearing the shining blue satin cloak I had made for her years earlier, its bold design of red and pink roses, yellow and purple tulips glowing vibrant in the torch-light. When she moved I could see the gleam of gold spangles on the underside of the cloak. She, or her tirewomen, had gone to much trouble to preserve that carefully made garment, I thought, even as my heart was pounding and I was also thinking, she's going to kill me now for certain.

As if to confirm my dark imagining I saw Baron Burghley standing in a corner of the room, and beside him, sitting heavily on a bench, her arms and legs bound, her posture forlorn, was another familiar figure: Bess Shrewsbury!

Elizabeth paused in her work of destruction and said in the low, commanding tones I remembered hearing at Buxton spa, "So my friend Rose Pinto has brought you to us, as I trusted she would."

She regarded me coolly from across the room, and I did my best to gaze steadily back at her, taking in the gray hair streaked with white, the masklike face drained of color, the sharp bones that stood out from the deep wrinkly mesh of her neck. How she had aged! And not only aged, but withered; there was so much less of her than on the last occasion when we met.

"I congratulate Mistress Pinto," I managed to respond, all too aware that my voice shook a little. "She is a fine actress, even if she does betray the memory of her mistress Amy Dudley."

"She is loyal to her sovereign."

"Her present sovereign, not her true sovereign."

At this I saw Baron Burghley take a step toward me, and I flinched.

"He does wish you ill," Elizabeth said with a wry smile, meanwhile setting fire to each paper in turn, then dropping the burning ash into a wide-mouthed urn. "Had I left your fate to the baron, you would not be here now."

I heard the sound of crying, and realized that it was coming from Bess.

"Ah, Mistress Shrewsbury, all this talk of death upsets you. Yet you were eager enough to prepare those stag pies you made for our good Amy on the day of her dreadful accident, were you not? The pies with an added ingredient in them—a deadly ingredient—"

Bess shook her head violently, sobbing. "I didn't know," she cried. "I didn't know."

"Of course you knew! And one day you will pay for all you knew, and for letting my little French cousin slip through your fingers and be taken off to Rome, where she plotted against me, and planned my death, just as Baron Burghley now plans hers."

I felt faint. Had I not been held firmly by the men on either side of me—men who reeked of beer and sweat—I would have fallen to the floor.

"Oh yes, she has been plotting my death for years," the queen went on, as if musing to herself, in her menacing low monotone. "My spies have kept me well informed of all she has said and done. Where she has gone, whom she has been with—"

Oh God, I thought. Not Marie-Elizabeth. Not Grandmamma Antoinette. No!

"There is a little farm in France, I am told. A charming place, tucked away where no one would be likely to find it. No one but the baron's men, who are there even now, waiting for a message from me. I wonder what message I ought to send them?"

It was too much for me. Trembling, I wept—and at the sound of my weeping, Bess joined me.

"Come now, ladies. Where is your courage? If I did not weep when my mother was taken from me, and shown no mercy, and killed by my father—if I did not weep when I was raped by the man I loved and trusted most, the tall, handsome Thomas Seymour—if I did not give in to tears when my bloody sister threw me in the Tower—why then, surely you can show some restraint now."

Somehow I found my voice.

"Do not make us pay for the wrongs you have suffered."

"Bravely said. But now, revenons à nos moutons, as the French expression goes. There is, as I was saying, a little farm in France, where a child lives, a child who bears my name along with her mother's. I was not asked to be the godmother of this child when she was born—indeed I did not know of her existence until quite recently. But now that I do know, I must decide what should be done with her."

With every word out of the queen's mouth I felt my dread rise. It was hard for me to breathe. I prayed silently, frantically, desperate for help.

"It would be easy to remove her; no one knows who she is, or where she is. You and your clever grandmother have kept her a great secret. But you ought to know by now, nothing can be kept secret from me, not for long."

"Except one thing," I whispered. "The secret of happiness."

"What was that?" Her voice sharpened.

But I was silent.

"Make her speak!" she cried, and I cringed, waiting for blows to fall.

"No—not yet." She was clearly agitated. She stopped burning the papers and, with an impatient gesture, kicked shut the lid of the wooden casket.

"You have a choice, cousin," she resumed after a time. "You can preserve the life of this unknown girl by swearing to give up your treasons, or you can continue to conspire against my throne. If you do that, the girl will die."

"How do I know that any of what you say is true?"

At a nod from the queen, a large cloth was brought forward into the light. It was the wall hanging Marie-Elizabeth and I had worked on for so many months, the carefully embroidered intertwined story of our lives. The words ONE LIKE THE LIONESS stood out in the dimness.

At the sight of the embroidery something within me gave way, and I felt the heavy weight of despair. There is no hope now, I thought. It is Elizabeth who is one like the lioness now, not my mother, or me, or my lovely daughter. And she has us all at bay.

I was distraught. I hung my head. Lord, into thy hands I place my fate. Save me, O Lord, from the lion's maw.

"Yes," I said quietly. "I will agree to what you ask."

"Louder! Swear before all those here."

"Yes!" I shouted, my voice shrill, cracking with emotion. "Yes, I vow it! I will not conspire against you!"

My shouting roused Archibald from his faint. He lifted his head, looked around the room, his eyes wild with surprise and fear. "No, Mary, no!"

And then, before my horrified eyes, the guards beat and kicked and pummeled him until his breath was gone and there was no more strength in him.

FIFTY-SEVEN

I went into a darkness on the day the queen recaptured me and threatened me, a darkness from which I did not recover for a very long time.

It was a darkness of the spirit. A sort of little death, as I thought of it later. Something deep inside me, a reservoir of faith and trust, dried up, never to be completely restored. Only those who have suffered such a blow can understand what I mean. If you can understand, I ask you to pity me.

I am told that my hair turned gray quite quickly, and my eyes grew more deep-set and pouched, wary and full of fear and sorrow. I could not see this transformation, I was not allowed any pier glass in the small room where I was kept. My new warder did not approve of vanity. But I am certain that my suffering, my disillusionment, was carved into my face, the pain evident in the tightening of my mouth, the curving of my spine that had once been proudly straight, the hunger—a hunger not only for food, but for hope—evident in my sunken cheeks. My once white skin became sallow and puckered, my teeth fewer and yellowed. The breath that came from my mouth, at one time as sweet as apples and honey (so Jamie told me) became rank, and my words, once honeyed, were often bitter and sharp as knives.

My physical pains increased and multiplied: the stabbing pain in my side, the soreness in all my limbs that worsened when the weather turned foul, my weak, injured knee that buckled under me when I tried to lift anything—all cried out for succor. I needed the larks'-tongue balm that Jamie had provided for George Shrewsbury. I needed ease for my tired flesh and above all, healing for my wounded spirit.

I bit my nails until they bled. I read my Bible. I fastened a heavy gold rosary around my waist and told my beads many times a day, sometimes kneeling (when my knee allowed), sometimes standing at the small barred window which gave me my only view of the outer world, and sometimes, in the worst hours of the cold night, lying in my hard bed, sleepless and beset by dejection, impatient for the dawn that never seemed to come.

It was only when I learned, through the French ambassador in London, that my cousin was thinking of putting me on trial once again that I began to come out of the fog of pain and despair that surrounded me for so long and attempted to grapple with the world again.

My imprisonment was so harsh and so isolating that I had very little news, but I was allowed to communicate with the French ambassador, who was then the Baron de Châteauneuf. He informed me that my cousin Elizabeth was becoming more and more frightened, so frightened that her fainting fits were increasing and she had acute stomach pains. She was convinced that the Catholic powers, especially King Philip of Spain, were filling England with spies. It was only a matter of time before these spies found their way into her own council, and betrayed her. There was no one she could trust, no one except Baron Burghley, who had been telling her for many years that she had to put me to death, because I was her principal rival for power.

If only she would die, I said aloud as I read the ambassador's message. If only she would catch the plague, or eat one of Bess Shrewsbury's special stag pies, or just succumb to the consumption her physicians say will carry her off before long. Once she died, the ambassador assured me, my son James would be king. There was a firm agreement between the royal councils of England and Scotland that the throne would pass to James. Once Elizabeth was in her tomb and James ruled in England, surely he would liberate me from my captivity and let me live out my life in comfort. In my dejected state I no longer aspired to rule myself, it would be enough that my son should govern both realms, and leave me to live out my remaining years in peace.

My aspirations had changed, but so had my cousin's plans for me. I was to be tried, and judged, and swept away, like the irritating piece of chaff I had become.

One morning I had just completed my toilette, putting on the black gown and white veil that had become my daily apparel, and fastening the gold rosary around my waist, when I was rudely interrupted by my warder and informed that I was to be moved to Fotheringhay castle in Northamptonshire. My servants hastened to pack my few possessions and load them onto a cart. Then, under heavy guard, I was escorted to the castle where I was shut in a small plain room and told that my trial would soon begin.

I never forgot the peril I was in—and the danger in which my growing daughter Marie-Elizabeth stood. I had sworn not to conspire against my cousin the queen, yet I could not control the conspiring of others, and I had been warned that if any plot against the queen's life came to light, whether or not I knew of it or was involved in it, I would be put to death and my daughter would disappear. I lived each day, indeed each hour, with this dread knowledge in my thoughts and pressing on my heart.

So it was with the greatest anxiety that I learned, just before my departure for Fotheringhay, that several young men had been executed for undertaking to kill the queen, and executed in the most cruel and brutal way possible, suffering the pain of having their bowels cut out and their privates cut off before being hacked into bits like dying animals at a slaughterhouse.

This gory news struck me like a blow, frightening me so that I had difficulty breathing and had to reach for one of the servants to steady me. I had visions of terrible recriminations to come, of Marie-Elizabeth being stabbed and mutilated and even my dear grandmamma having her aging body violated by cruel men with axes and bludgeons. It had happened before, I knew. I had read in my history books—I spend much time in reading now, to pass the time—about the execution of Henry VIII's poor elderly relative Margaret Pole, who was nearly seventy years old when she was charged with treason, her head and neck hacked repeatedly by a bungling executioner, her death an excruciatingly painful ordeal.

The recent revelations of conspiracy against the queen my cousin were not the first such plot that I knew of; my Guise relations in France had attempted, in vain, to cause a rising in England and one Francis Throckmorton had been executed for his part in this conspiracy. The Baron de Châteauneuf had implied, in his infrequent messages to me, that other plans and plots were constantly forming and unraveling in the murky world of Catholic intrigue.

Yet the cruel executions and the decision to put me on trial convinced me that with each plot, the threat to my cousin's throne was being taken more seriously. I wondered whether the revelations about the most recent plot were true. Did the young men who had been put to death really mean to carry out the murder of the queen? Or was it all just a devilish invention of Baron Burghley, eager as always to create a reason to order my death?

Like the queen, I had little trust in anyone, save the Lord who had preserved me and continued to preserve me. I was praying on the afternoon my warder and three of the queen's privy councilors came to tell me that my trial would soon begin. I was to be judged, they said, by a commission of twenty-four peers of the realm and government officials and men of law. These men would determine whether there had indeed been a plot to kill the queen, a plot undertaken in my name. If they determined that such a plot did exist—and they assured me they had proof that it did—then I would be put to death. I was not to be permitted any advocate of my own, I was told, nor any witnesses to swear on my behalf.

They did not say "you must prepare to die," but there was no mistaking what they meant. I was being told that my time had run out. I was to be sacrificed for the sake of the queen's peace of mind. There would be no leniency for me, as a condemned traitor to the throne.

The men left, and before long my supper was brought to me. I could eat nothing. I sat before the fire in my small cold room, staring into the low flames like one deprived of sight and hearing, speech and thought.

I was to be condemned to die. There was to be no escape. No hope of escape. The baleful destiny long ago predicted for me had come upon me at last.

FIFTY-EIGHT

A S I sat before the fire, numb with shock, I heard the door of my small room being opened. My warder came in with a short, gray-haired woman—a woman I had not seen in many years, but whose face was more welcome to me, at that moment, than I can possibly convey.

"Margaret!" I cried, getting up from my bench and holding out my arms to my dear tirewoman and friend. We embraced for a long, lingering time, both of us in tears.

"Look at you, Your Highness," Margaret cried. "Still my lovely queen!"

"Much altered, I fear."

She took my hand and patted it. "Not so very much, to those who love you." She smiled, then went on. "The queen herself sent me. She told her messenger to say to me that you would have need of my help tonight and in the days to come."

I shook my head in disbelief. "The queen? Are you in the queen's service now?"

She nodded, then whispered "I thought I might be of use to you if I joined the royal household. My husband Ned was taken on as a constable of the watch, and I am head laundress in Her Majesty's palace at Richmond."

"But why should she retain you, knowing your loyalty to me?"

"I think because there is a part of her that has a regard for you."

"Even after the way she has treated me?"

Margaret shrugged. "You are still alive. Without that regard, you wouldn't be."

"Margaret! You are not her spy, are you? Come to add to my suffering in my last days?"

"Indeed I am not. I am what I have always been—and what the queen knows me to be. I am your loyal servant, who honors and loves you. I am sure she means me to ease your days."

I threw up my hands. "She is beyond my understanding. But not beyond my hatred," I added under my breath.

Margaret and I supped together—I was suddenly very hungry—there in the narrow room, before the fire, and as we ate, she talked, her voice bright, almost shrill. I could tell she was using the voice she meant the guards just beyond the door to overhear.

But at times she lowered her voice to a near whisper, and talked of matters of the greatest importance to me. I hung on her every murmured word.

"I have seen King James," she said softly.

"How is he? Did he speak of me? Did you tell him I love him?"

"I may as well tell you the hard truth."

"You always have."

"He did not show any love or concern for you. He did not want to speak of you at all. I saw his eyes darken when I said your name."

I said nothing for a time. "I did hope he might have some affection for me," I said at length.

"The men who nurtured him and raised him crushed any feeling he may once have had for you."

"Yes, I suppose I knew that."

"He is nothing like what you would expect," Margaret went on. "He staggers, because his legs are weak and malformed."

I nodded. "I was always worried about his legs. They never straightened out the way they should have, when he was a baby."

"He stammers."

"He had a large thick tongue. His nurses all remarked on it."

"He is ill-favored, not at all like yourself or his late father Lord Darnley, whom everyone detested but who was, it must be said, a beautiful man. James is nearly a grown man now, but weak and cowardly, afraid of every shadow, like a timid boy. He clings to older, stronger men and loves them in the way the Scripture says he should not. He cringes when anyone except his special favorites come near him. They say he has a very able mind, but no heart."

"My dear son, the caulbearer! The child gifted with the second sight!"

"If he has the second sight, I have not heard of it. He writes poetry, a great deal of it, and keeps poets near him. But only handsome ones, according to his doorkeeper, who is a friend of Ned's. And he drinks. He drinks a great deal."

I shrugged. "He is Scottish."

"Even for a Scot, he drinks a great deal. And when he drinks, he calls in his minions, and they grow wild, riding on each other's backs, and shouting and swearing, and falling down as drunkards do. He has no sense of how a king ought to behave."

"Has he no virtues?"

Margaret thought awhile. "He loves books," she said at length. "He is said to wish that he lived in a library and not in a palace."

"Ah! He is a scholar. But scholars do not make good kings."

A servant came in and put a log on the fire, making it crackle and spreading a little more warmth in the room.

"Margaret, James could save me, if he chose. He could persuade my cousin to cancel the trial and release me. Will you go to him and plead for me? Ask him to intervene with Elizabeth?"

"I already have. I spoke to him when he was at court. He received me, even after he was told that I had been your servant while you were still Queen of Scots."

"And what did he say?"

"He couldn't say very much. We were not alone. Clearly he was unsure what to do, and it was also clear to me that what he cared about was inheriting the English throne from Elizabeth. I think he will do whatever Elizabeth tells him to do, about you. He has no memory of you, you know. The one thing he did say was, that you have chosen your own path, especially when you had his father murdered. You have determined your own fate, and cannot evade it."

"But I did not order the murder of Darnley!"

"Your son and many others believe you did. He says you deserve to suffer for your sins. He is a strict Protestant, after all. A man after the late John Knox's heart. As a Protestant he does not dare anger his Protestant subjects by defending and helping a Catholic martyr (which is what you have become, in the eyes of many), even if she is his mother. His Protestant subjects force him to show you no mercy, while his subjects who are secret Catholics condemn him for doing nothing on your behalf. Do you know, he cannot leave the palace, the people clamor so loudly for him to use his influence to have you released. He is under siege!"

"And I will never see my son again," I said softly. "My dear boy. May God watch over him, and protect him."

FIFTY-NINE

O N the day of my trial my hands were shaking and I was trembling. It began the moment I entered the great hall on that October morning, leaning on Dr. Bourgoing's arm, and went on until I left many hours later, dragging myself along, my strength exhausted.

I tried not to show my fear as I walked slowly past the men brought together to judge me, impatient, grim-faced men, ordered by my cousin to pronounce sentence on me as a traitor so that I can be put to death.

They took off their hats as I passed, out of respect, but they did not do me the honor of giving me a throne to sit on—only a plain chair, as if I were an ordinary woman and not a queen born.

I had not wanted to appear at my trial at all. I knew it would make no difference to the outcome whether I was present or not: I would be condemned either way. And yet, as I sat in my plain chair, looking into the solemn faces of the men appointed to condemn me, I was glad that I had agreed, after much coercion, to take part. At least by being present, I could refute the lies told about me. I could confront my accusers and accuse them, in turn, of lying.

When the Lord Chancellor asserted that I had plotted to kill the queen I was able to say, as loudly as I could, that the court could not judge me because I am a queen and not a subject. I could shout (though my voice was no longer very loud, and broke whenever I strained it) that all the evidence brought against me was fraudulent, all the documents fabricated, all the witnesses coerced into telling lies. I said, again and again, that I had been betrayed by my cousin the queen, who had offered me her protection and given me long years of imprisonment instead.

Not long into the trial my head began to ache with all the exertion I was making. I could feel the blood pounding in my ears, at times it was hard to breathe, and even harder to try to shout louder than my angry accusers. Dr. Bourgoing advised me that I was overstraining myself, that I ought to ask for time to rest. He brought me a restorative cup of wine and advised me to say my rosary quietly, fingering the gold beads I wore at my waist, as a way of calming myself. I did my best to follow his advice, yet I kept hearing the harsh words shouted out against me— "wicked Jezebel," "traitorous woman," "murderess," "villainess"—a long litany of ugly words. The echoing voices rolling around the vast chamber made me dizzy, as if the words were bludgeons and I a struggling victim reeling under their blows.

Gradually the many voices blurred into one strident accusing voice, and then, as if in a sudden explosion of sound, all at once there were many shouts, a chorus of shouts, all saying the same thing: Guilty! Guilty! Guilty!

I cowered, I pulled the white veil I wore over my face to hide my fear. I heard myself growl—yes, growl, like a cornered animal. I heard Dr. Bourgoing say, "It is enough! Can't you see how you are wearying this poor aging woman!"

At his words I seemed to find fresh energy, and managed to get up from my chair and stand before my accusers, drawing aside the veil so that my face could be clearly seen.

"I forgive all those who have been coerced into giving false evidence against me," I said. "I forgive the men who wrote false messages, and created false ciphers. I know you are all under sentence of royal displeasure, unless you do as you are told."

"Do you dare to impugn the veracity of the queen's court?" demanded the Lord Chancellor in a voice so thunderous I feared it would pierce the high painted ceiling.

"I forgive all my judges," I went on, "and all those in exalted office"—here I looked directly at the Lord Chancellor, who flinched under my gaze—"and pardon you all here present, for presuming to judge one of higher birth and greater right than yourselves."

And with that, amid renewed shouting, I reached for Dr. Bourgoing's arm and felt the reassuring grip of another arm on my other side, and began to make my slow way out of the room.

I was dignified, I did not falter, nor did I look back with indignation at those who were shouting at me, though some of the words they used were gutter words, not fit for a highborn lady, much less a queen.

But as I reached the door my legs felt weak, almost as though they would collapse under me. I tightened my grip on Dr. Bourgoing's arm, and he murmured, "Courage!" which helped me, though I was trembling.

The trembling in my hand that began that day has never gone away. It became difficult to keep my poor hand steady as I tried to write. The words I have written since that day have had an unsure, awkward look to them, with wide wriggles and tall spikes quite unlike my usual handwriting which, if I do note it myself, is exceptionally well formed and quite lovely. I hoped that after I slept my hand would stop shaking and I would be able to write in my usual fashion. But the change was permanent. The harm was done.

I was condemned, as I knew I would be. I spent my days in prayer, and reading my Bible, shriving my conscience and preparing to die.

But it did not happen. No one came to tell me that I was to be moved from Fotheringhay, or that the day of my execution had been determined. Nor was Margaret recalled to Richmond. Instead she was allowed to remain with me, a great comfort and support to me. And after several weeks she was allowed to receive a visitor: her husband Ned Hargatt.

She spent several hours with him, and afterwards came to me, her thin face full of smiles.

"Ned has seen your Jamie!" she said, handing me a small object wrapped in white silk. "He sends you a miniature, and much news. King Philip is gathering a great fleet, he calls it the Most Fortunate Fleet, to bring an army to invade England. Lord Bothwell is to be captain of one of the carracks, the *San Marco*, with fifty guns and three hundred men. The fleet gathers at Lisbon, they sail for Portsmouth and the south coast any day!"

"Ah," was all I could manage to say, at first. Then, "Ah, Lord, let them come soon! Give them fair winds and a following sea!"

Margaret and I embraced, my heart leapt. When Don John died, I had lost my champion; now I had found him again, only this time it was my true champion, my dearest love, who would sail into battle to save me, and bring me safely back into his arms again.

SIXTY

WEEK after week went by, and I heard nothing further from my warders, or my judges. Daily I hardened my courage to face the dread announcement that I would be brought to the block, to kneel before the executioner's axe. And nightly I was thankful for yet another day's reprieve.

My trial had been in October; by November I was beginning to imagine that I might after all be saved, either by the mighty Spanish fleet or by the half-sincere, half-reluctant clemency of the queen, who, it seemed, was staying Burghley's hand. In my heightened state of nerves I could not help but become superstitious; I imagined that the gift Jamie sent me, a miniature of himself and Marie-Elizabeth, was a good luck charm, that as long as I wore it on a chain around my neck, I would continue to avoid death.

"She has a regard for you," Margaret had said of the queen, and in my most optimistic hours I imagined that this was true. In my worst hours, however, a contrary logic tormented me. If King Philip was sending his Most Fortunate Fleet to invade England and Elizabeth knew it (for how could she not?), then would she not, in her dread, make certain of my death before the fleet arrived?

And if, out of regard for our common blood, she could not bring herself to give the order for my execution, then would she not do as I had read King Henry did when he flinched from ordering the death of his friend Thomas Becket and called for his servants to do the murderous work for him? Would I die a secret death, as Amy Dudley had, from eating poisoned food or touching poisoned letter paper, from drinking a cup of lethal wine that would put me to sleep forever, or from being taken in secret to a house where there was plague, and shut inside until I died?

While I wrestled with these anxious thoughts another month passed, and Christmastide arrived, and with it, a token from the queen: a ring bearing her seal.

When I showed the ring to Margaret she nodded solemnly. "You see, she wants to preserve you. Why else would she send you her very own signet? It is a message—a very hopeful message."

Or could it be a trap? I was fearful of putting the ring on my finger. I had often heard that Italian poisoners hid deadly poisons in rings and other jewellery; when the wearer wore the jewel, they died.

Margaret snatched the signet ring from my hand and slipped it over her forefinger.

"No Margaret, don't take the risk!"

But after several minutes she was still breathing, and I had to concede that the ring had not been devised to kill me. I wore it, allowing my hopes to rise a little more each day.

And each night I dreamed of the Most Fortunate Fleet, hundreds strong, great galleasses, their sails spread like wide wings, oared galleys and broad high hulks, swift pinnaces darting in and out from among the large ships, the entire fleet standing out to sea, close hauled to a northerly breeze, making for the shores of England.

My dreams were precious to me—and they almost came true. But alas! My cousin's fears grew too strong, and she faltered and grew faint, dreading the coming of the Spaniards and the terrifying ships. And at the last, she gave in to the men around her, that advised her ever more strongly to order my death.

In the end, she did as they bade her.

SIXTY-ONE

THEY came for me tonight, after I had supped and said my prayers and retired to bed, to tell me that I am to die tomorrow morning.

There were four of them, four men I had never before met or seen, sent by Baron Burghley to make their dire announcement.

They did their best to harden themselves to their task, and tried to keep their faces solemn, but I could see that they were all in tears, and it was not long before my servants too were weeping, overhearing what was being said to me, and even some of the guards.

I crossed myself and asked for a priest to be sent to me, but the men said no, the queen would not allow it.

"I want you to know," one of the men said, "that the queen suggested that we ought to put an end to your life privily and in secret, sparing her the guilt and blame. We all refused." They nodded.

I looked from one to the other, and saw that their faces were pinched and full of sadness.

"I thank you, my loyal subjects," I said, allowing myself the luxury of saying what I so often thought, that in truth, I was their queen, and not that other, who had suggested that they murder me.

Hearing my words, they did not demur, but knelt.

"It is a good thing Baron Burghley is not here to see you now," I said, with a smile.

"Baron Burghley can go to the devil," one of the men said, and another responded, "Assuredly he will."

"At what hour am I to die?"

"At the hour of eight."

I sighed. There was much to think of, to prepare for. I went to my small desk and took out a paper that I had been keeping there for months.

"Here are my instructions for what is to be done with my body. I wish to be buried in France, in Saint-Denis, as a Catholic, and not in Scotland, with a Protestant service."

"Condemned traitors are not given honorable burial," said one of the men, as all four got to their feet. "But there is still time for you to repent, and to recant your Romish faith. If you do this, you can be buried as a member of the Church of England, though the burial will have to be in unconsecrated ground."

"And do you think me likely to do that, after all that I have endured for the sake of the one true church?"

No answer was necessary.

I held up my hand, displaying the queen's signet ring.

"Is there no hope of clemency?" I asked, already knowing what the answer must be.

"Her Majesty will be pleased to receive her ring, if you will be so good as to return it," one of the men said, holding out his hand. "She told us that it had been lost, and that you might possess it."

I took off the ring and dropped it into the outstretched hand. Then, after assuring me that they regretted their most irksome and sorrowful duty in informing me that I was to die, the four men bowed to me and took their leave.

My poor servants, I thought. Who will look after them or hire them after I am gone? I did what I could to find a gift for each one—a miniature, or a book, a small keepsake, a bit of embroidery or a token from my small store of clothing. I blessed them and kissed and embraced each one, doing my best to smile and wipe away their tears, then asked them all to drink one final toast with me.

"May you all keep warm in your hearts the love I bear you," I said, my voice trembling, "and may you find new lives of peace and hope after I am gone. Remember me in your prayers." Then we recited the Lord's Prayer together, and they filed out, weeping quietly, leaving me to my own solitary meditations, and to pondering how best to use my last hours.

Try as I might to keep my thoughts on heavenly things, to pray for those I love best and to be thankful for the joys I have known in this life, I find that I am distracted by the tramping of the soldiers' boots outside my window. So loud a noise! So many men coming and going!

And I realize, when I look out through the high bars, that many more soldiers are being brought on to the castle grounds. Hundreds more. And not only soldiers, but carts and guns, bowmen and halberdiers.

All is becoming clear: the commander of Fotheringhay is preparing not only to fortify the castle, but to defend it. An attack must be expected. An effort to rescue me!

When will they come? At dawn? Has the Most Fortunate Fleet already landed, and are the Spaniards on their way here?

Perhaps the Catholics of England have risen in rebellion even now, and London has fallen to their overpowering numbers, and the queen has been captured and thrown into her deepest dungeon, her crown and her kingdom taken from her, her authority cast off.

Is it possible that I am already queen, only I don't yet know it? Or are these the midnight ravings of an old woman condemned to die, and unable to accept her fate?

I cannot know, but I must keep a close watch on the courtyard below, so that I will be sure to see Jamie when he comes for me, shouting, as he used to do, "All for risk, Orange Blossom! Arise and away!"

Whatever the truth of this moment, I end my record here, as the bells chime the midnight, in hope of rescue, or, if not, in hope of the life eternal promised by our dear Saviour, wishing any who read these words the blessings and the mercies of God, for all your lives long.

Marye the Queen

NOTE TO THE READER

Just a reminder that in this historical entertainment, authentic history and imaginative invention are blended, so that fictional events and circumstances, fictional characters and fictional alterations to the past intertwine. Fresh interpretations of past personalities and events are offered, and traditional ones laid aside.

As far as is known, Mary Stuart and the Earl of Bothwell never went together to the island of Mull, Mary never shared a mineral bath with Queen Elizabeth at Buxton spa, and the explanation offered here for how Lord Darnley died is an imagining. Readers eager to uncover the factual truth of the past, that ever elusive goal of historians, must look elsewhere than in these pages, where "thick-coming fancies" crowd out sober evidence and whimsy prevails.

Yet in whimsy, at times, is to be found a richer truth than in the tantalizingly fragmented, often untrustworthy historical record. And even though there is reason to believe that in actuality Lord Bothwell met his end in a Danish prison in 1578, and did not live to know of Mary Stuart's ultimate fate, some have questioned the identity of the remains of that long-ago prisoner. Perhaps, just perhaps, the real Lord Bothwell escaped, and hid himself away, to live out his life in contented obscurity.

A Reading Group Gold Selection

MEMOIRS OF MARY QUEEN OF SCOTS

by Carolly Erickson

About the Author

- A Conversation with Carolly Erickson

Historical Perspective

- "Back in the Day":
  An Original Essay by the Author

- *Mary Queen of Scots:* A Time Line of Events

Keep on Reading

- Reading Group Questions

For more reading group suggestions,
visit www.readinggroupgold.com.

 ST. MARTIN'S GRIFFIN

Why do you think Mary Stuart holds such perennial fascination for readers?

Her story has so many compelling dimensions: tragedy, political conflict, romantic passion, even suspected crime. She reigned as Queen, she took the field in battle against her enemies, she held her own against the legions of those who were staunchly opposed to women wielding power.

Yet she was at the same time a wife and mother, a tender lover (at least, as portrayed in this historical entertainment), a beautiful woman whose cause many thousands found compelling. To us, as to her contemporaries, Mary was a woman for all seasons. Hence her enduring appeal.

"Mary was a woman for all seasons."

Given the circumstances of Mary's life, she must often have found herself in extreme emotional distress. Occasionally, she must have felt as if she were in the hands of a remorseless fate. Yet she coped. How do you think she managed that?

There was an inner core of resilient strength in her that surfaced time and again. A physical and mental robustness—perhaps the same elemental robustness that caused her to survive as a tiny infant when those around her thought she would not live. When seeds are planted, and tiny plants break through the earth, some thrive while others wither. Mary seems to have had what it takes to thrive, not to succumb to fear or illness, though she certainly suffered from both.

In Mary's time, the era of the Protestant Reformation and the Catholic revitalization and reform that is sometimes called the Counter-Reformation, a person's faith was a vital determinant of his or her path through life. What role do you think Mary's Catholicism played in shaping her life experience?

Mary's claim to the English throne, and her rivalry with Queen Elizabeth, rested on her Catholicism. English Catholics, supported by the papacy and the Catholic powers of Europe, hoped to dethrone Elizabeth and make Mary Queen of England. In Mary's personal life, as her behavior on the day she was executed makes clear, she remained a staunch daughter of the Roman church, and her unwavering faith sustained her. Historians and novelists may attempt to look into the heart and read its secrets, but they remain locked away. The depth and sincerity of Mary's Catholicism can never be truly known, only surmised from her actions.

It has been said that the authentic past is no longer accessible to those of us living in the twenty-first century, because we are doomed to view it through the narrow lens of our own life experience and through the mythic distortions of movies, epics— and the whimsical creations of superannuated novelists. What are your views on this issue?

I think the distortions caused when one age looks at another are both inevitable and fascinating. When we look back at the lives of women who lived hundreds of years ago, we are asking questions that were unknown, indeed undreamed-of, at the time. We scrutinize Mary Stuart's life looking for evidence of independence, strength of purpose, her sense of her own identity and rights. But in Mary's time no one would have envisioned these issues at all—these were issues for men to grapple with, not women. Most of Mary's female contemporaries lived short lives, in strict and often harsh subordination to men—subordination enjoined by laws and religious teachings—and inhabited a twilight mental world (one imagines) bereft of literacy or aspirations. Not that they were lacking in intellectual capability, merely that whatever capability they possessed was rarely awakened or encouraged. Discussions of the way our present-mindedness distorts our understanding of the past can make for lively talk!

Would you like to have lived in a previous century?

Questions like this turn history into a parlor game, and both sanitize and trivialize the past. While it is understandable that we seek diversion wherever we can find it, and reading about past times can certainly be diverting, the risk is that we will lose our authentic history while seeking to use it as entertainment.

I am well aware that in saying this I ought to admonish myself for writing historical entertainments! However, for most of my writing years I wrote nonfiction, that very demanding task of attempting to re-create the authentic past through scrutiny of existing records and through a sort of sixth sense scholars develop that (we hope) guides us and sensitizes us as we create an approximation of what really happened, and how.

"When we look back at the lives of women who lived hundreds of years ago, we are asking questions that were unknown, indeed undreamed-of, at the time."

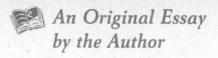
An Original Essay
by the Author

"Back in the Day"

Are we losing the past?

Are we forgetting what made one era different from another, each century distinct?

The catchphrase "back in the day" invites a view of previous centuries as an undifferentiated, over-romanticized blur instead of an intricately evolving, multilayered story whose chapters deserve to be delineated with care.

A story, yes, but one perhaps increasingly seen as "full of sound and fury, signifying nothing." Or rather, full of error. For who is there to serve as an overarching authority for all the "historical data" on the Internet—some reliable, much unreliable.

There is a careless ring to that phrase "back in the day." A sense that what has gone before ought to be tossed aside as irrelevant to present concerns. What really counts, what really matters, is now, not then. Not back in the day.

Present-mindedness is alluring; it smacks of the fresh, the new, the current—and therefore the best. Surely there is virtue in discarding what has become out-moded and stale, what might drag us down in our quest for progress.

We rejoice, after all, in having left so many wrongs behind: the evils of legal inequality, slavery, patriar-chal attitudes that hampered women and prevented our advancement. The multiple sins of life back in the day send a frisson of horror down our liberated spines. Who would willingly reenter a world in which life was "solitary, poor, nasty, brutish, and short," as the very present-minded Thomas Hobbes wrote more than three centuries ago.

Yet Hobbes, and his educated contemporaries, were very aware of the great time line of Western history, as then envisioned: from the stirrings of classical rationalism in the Athens of the fifth century, before Christ; to the spread of Roman law and eventually of Christian faith and values in the later centuries of the ancient world; to the long medieval twilight to the dawn of the Age of Reason and the rise of critical thought.

The past, for Hobbes, was a cautionary tale, useful, if in no other way, for showing what to avoid. The present-mindedness of our own time is of a different order; it seeks to discard the outlived centuries without paying them the slightest heed.

A hundred years from now (assuming the doomsayers predicting the end of the world in 2012 are wrong), our era may be thrown out as useless. By then, of course, the phrase "back in the day" will have been long out of fashion: a quaint epitaph for a forgotten past.

Time, some physicists now propose, may itself be an illusion. We may in actuality occupy a timeless multiverse in which past and future meld into an eternal present. If so, I may be occupying the same space as Julius Caesar and Mae West—to conjure an image of an improbable couple.

"The day," such as it is, may go on forever, making phrases about the past meaningless.

Confusion beckons; can madness be far behind? For
surely, in some guise or other, sequentialness (is that a
word?) is a basic human need. We crave to orient ourselves in midcourse of our common journey from ape
through sentient thinker through Caesarian conquests
to Hobbesian rationalism to—Mae West and beyond.

Even if "back in the day" turns out to be "full circle,"
we will nonetheless yearn for the lost centuries, the
long and slow slip of time, the ancestors and the
memories, the unfolding story of who we are and
where we have come from across the generations.
And we will mourn the loss.

*Historical
Perspective*

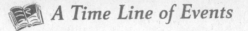

December 8, 1542	Birth of Mary Stuart
December 14, 1542	Infant Mary becomes Queen of Scotland
September 9, 1543	Mary is crowned Queen
April 24, 1558	Mary marries the French dauphin Francis
August 19, 1561	Widowed Mary returns to Scotland
July 29, 1565	Mary marries Lord Darnley
March 9, 1566	Murder of David Riccio
June 19, 1566	Birth of Mary's son James, future James VI of Scotland, James I of England
February 9, 1567	Death of Lord Darnley
February 8, 1587	Mary is beheaded

1. Why do you think Mary Queen of Scots is such an iconic historical figure? What is it about her that continues to fascinate lovers of history?

2. Why do you think Mary had such a difficult time ruling over her Scottish subjects?

3. Fate, enchantments, and the power of the otherworldly lay over the characters in this novel. To what extent do you believe fate rules our destinies? How do you imagine sixteenth-century attitudes on this issue differed from those of our more secular age?

3. In the novel, Mary regrets that she did not return to France after escaping from Lochleven. What might the course of her life been if she had returned to France?

4. Had Mary become Queen of England, do you imagine that she would have been swiftly dethroned by a popular rebellion?

5. Mary's nemesis John Knox wrote a treatise condemning the "Monstrous Regiment [Rule] of Women." In your view, have women rulers, over the centuries, proven him wrong in his condemnation? Or have women and men been equally adept (or inexpert) at wielding power?

6. In the novel, Mary says that she "was not born to be obscure, to live a hidden, quiet life." "I had the blood of kings in my veins," she says, "and there was more for me to do in the world." Was this conviction her blessing—or her curse?

7. Mary asserts at one point that Queen Elizabeth, for all her power and cleverness, never found "the secret of happiness." Do you believe that Mary herself found it? Have you?

Turn the page for a sneak peek at
Carolly Erickson's new book

Rival to the Queen

Available in October 2010

ONE

FLAMES crackled and rose into the heavy air as my father's servants piled more bundles of brushwood on the fire. Smoke rose grey-black out of the flickering orange tongues, the heat from the rising fire making my younger brother Frank draw back, fearful that we too might be singed or burned, even as the stench of burning flesh made us put our hands over our noses and recoil from its acrid, noxious reek.

I did not step back, I held my ground even as I heard Jocelyn's agonizing cries. I held my breath and shut my eyes and prayed, please God, make it rain. Please God, put the fire out.

It was a lowering and cold morning. The overcast sky was growing darker by the minute, and I had felt a few drops of rain. I thought, it wouldn't take much rain to douse this fire. Please, let it come now!

A large strong hand clamped onto my shoulder—I could sense its roughness through the sleeve of my gown—and I felt myself pulled backwards.

"Get back, Lettie! Can't you see the fire is spreading? Stand back there, beside your brother!"

"But father," I pleaded, my voice nearly lost amid the roar of the flames and the sharp snapping of twigs and branches, "it's Jocelyn. Our Jocelyn. I am praying that the Lord will send rain and save him!"

I looked up into my father's anguished face and saw at once the ravages of pain on his stern features. His voice was hoarse as he bent down and whispered "I'm praying for him too. Now do as I tell you!"

The fire was growing hotter. I was sweating, my flushed face was burning though the day was cold and once again I felt a spatter of raindrops on one cheek. I moved back to join my brother, who was weeping, sniffling loudly, and took his hand. At first he had tried his best to be manly, to resist the strong tug of emotion that we all felt. But Jocelyn had been his tutor, our tutor. He taught us our letters, and our writing hand, and, later, gave us our lessons in Greek and Latin. I had studied with him for seven years, Frank for nearly six. We loved him.

And now we were being forced to watch him die.

He was being burned for heresy. For professing the Protestant faith, as we did. For refusing to obey Queen Mary's command that all her subjects attend mass and revere the pope and renounce the church of Luther, the church her father Henry VIII and her late brother Edward VI had officially embraced, in sharp opposition to the age-old Roman belief.

Many felt as Jocelyn did, but most hid their convictions, and attended mass despite them. My father, who was always a practical man, did as Queen Mary ordered and told us to do the same.

"What we do outwardly does not matter," he told us. "It's what we believe in our hearts that makes us members of the true faith. The Lord sees what is in our hearts, and protects and favors us."

But Jocelyn, who was very brave, and very learned, a scholar from Magdalen College and a student of the ancient texts of the church, was not satisfied. To pretend allegiance to the pope and the mass was wrong, he said. To disguise the truth. And so he had spoken out against the queen and her Catholic mass, and had been seized and thrown into a dungeon. And now, on this day, he was condemned to die.

I had watched him, looking thin and gaunt, as they made him walk across the damp grass to where the reeds and split branches were being piled knee-deep. In the center of the pile was a three-legged stool, and he had been made to stand up on it. But before he did so he reached down to pick up some of the reeds and kissed them reverently.

"See how he blesses the reeds! See how he embraces his martyrdom!" I heard people in the crowd exclaim. "Surely he will be with the Lord in paradise!" But they kept their voices low, for they did not want to be put in prison or forced to submit to punishment, and we were all aware that there were guards and soldiers everywhere, listening for blasphemous words against the church of Rome.

Then the torch had been put to the twigs and branches, and the fire had blazed up, and Jocelyn, praying loudly for the queen who had condemned him and for my father and the servants who had built the fire, had at last been overcome by pain and began screaming.

I heard my father, in anguish, call out to Jocelyn, asking his forgiveness. But the only response was a loud wail of agony, and hearing it, I saw my proud, stern father shed tears.

Young as I was, only sixteen on the day Jocelyn was condemned to die, I realized that my father was being punished alongside our tutor. Queen Mary was making him suffer. She knew well that he had been a faithful servant of the crown ever since he was a very young man, serving in King Henry's privy chamber and, after the old king's death, serving King Edward as an envoy and councilor. He was unwaveringly faithful to the monarchy— but he did not, in his heart, profess the old religion, and she resented him for this. She was vengeful, everyone said so. Now she was taking vengeance against my father by forcing him to carry out the sentence of death against the young man she knew he was fond of, Jocelyn Palmer.

All of a sudden a strong wind blew up, I felt it lift my skirts and draw its raw breath against my neck. I let go of Frank's hand for a moment as he pulled away from me, escaping the glowing sparks that blew toward us.

The wind was putting the fire out. I dared to look at Jocelyn. His hair was burnt away as was most of his clothing, and the skin of his face was scorched and blackened, but his lips were moving.

He was singing, a hymn tune. His voice was scratchy but I recognized the tune. Others joined in the singing as the fire died to embers.

"Dear Jesus, Son of David, have mercy upon me," Jocelyn cried out. "Let it end!"

Soldiers approached my father and spoke to him, standing so near to him that I could not hear what they were saying. I looked up at the darkening sky. Surely it would rain soon, a hard rain. The sign of God's mercy.

Then my father was giving orders and fresh loads of brushwood and branches were being brought and the fire rekindled. But not before a burly guard had reached up to strap two swollen sheep's bladders around Jocelyn's waist.

"No," I cried to my father. "Spare him! Let him live!"

Once again my father grasped my arm, bending down so that he could speak to me, and to me alone.

"I must do as the queen commands. Otherwise we all face Jocelyn's peril. But there is one last mercy I can show him. The bladders are filled with gunpowder. When the fire reaches them, they will explode, and he will die. He will be spared much agony."

Torches were put to the wood and the fire began to blaze up, though I could feel drops of rain falling now, the rain I had prayed for, and smoke rose with the fire, black, choking smoke that was blown into our faces, and with it, the stink of Jocelyn's flesh. I thought then, I cannot bear this.

I felt my gorge rise. I doubled over. My legs felt heavy, and it was hard to breathe. Minutes passed. All around me I could hear people weeping and sighing and coughing from the thickening smoke. I glanced at Frank. He had closed his eyes and bowed his head. His fists were clenched at his sides.

With a bright flash and a loud crack the bladders of gunpowder exploded, but there was to be no mercy for Jocelyn. The blasts went outward, tearing away part of one of his arms but leaving his blackened torso intact.

How I found the courage to look at Jocelyn then, in his last extremity, I will never understand. His legs were burnt, blood seeped from the fingers of one arm and his eyes were charred sockets. Yet his swollen tongue moved within what was left of his gums, and I knew that he prayed.

"Lord Jesus," I heard my father say in a broken voice, "receive his spirit!"

Then with another loud crack the skies opened and rain began to pour down in thick sheets, flooding the grass and quenching the fire and turning the ground to thick squelching mud underfoot.

It was the rain I had prayed for, but it came too late. What was left of Jocelyn's body hung limp and lifeless, the flesh of his face—a face I had loved—so burned away that I could not have said whose face it was.

I felt Frank reach for my hand and we clung to each other, standing there in the drenching rain, until the crowd scattered and my father gave the order to wrap the body in a burial cloth and take it away.

TWO

WE left England shortly after Jocelyn died. We had no choice, father said, and mother agreed. England was no longer a safe place for the Knollys family.

It was not just that my father, Francis Knollys, could not bring himself to preside over any more cruel executions of fellow Protestants—or of Catholics either, for that matter—for he was, deep down, a tenderhearted man. Or that Queen Mary was growing more and more vengeful, ordering more and more men and women to their deaths because they would not conform to her Catholic beliefs. Or that some said she was mad, crazed by anger and sorrow over her inability to give birth to a living child to succeed her on the throne.

It was more than all these things, a deep-rooted taint of blood that made us vulnerable to the queen's wrath. For we were related to Queen Mary's half-sister Princess Elizabeth, and Elizabeth, just then, was imprisoned in the Tower of London, accused of treason.

My beautiful mother Catherine was Princess Elizabeth's aunt, and I and my brother and sister were the princess's cousins. Queen Mary believed that everyone related to her half-sister was suspect, and probably dangerous to her throne and to the peace of the realm, and certainly immoral.

My mother had explained our family history to my sister Cecelia and Frank and me when we were quite young. It all began, she said, early in the reign of our famous King Henry VIII, many years before we were born.

"You see, our late King Henry, when he was married to Queen Catherine, his Spanish wife, needed a son to inherit his throne. But all Queen Catherine's baby boys died, and nearly all the baby girls too, all except for Mary, who is now queen.

"If only Queen Catherine had died!" she went on, a little wistfully. "Everything would have been so much easier. But she did not die, she just went on having more and more babies, and they kept on dying. The poor king thought that God was cursing him, and maybe He was. So in time King Henry honored other women and let them become the mothers of his children. One of those women was my mother, your grandmother Mary Boleyn."

Our grandmother Mary Boleyn had died when I was a very small child, far too young to remember her, but I had seen portraits of her, painted when she was young. A lovely girl, with light brown hair and blue eyes. An innocent girl, or so one would have thought from the look of the portraits. Yet I knew from what my mother said that she had the reputation of being far from innocent.

"She had a husband, William Carey," mother was saying. "Yet she also had the king's love. And his was the stronger." The last words were almost whispered, as though mother were confiding to us a precious secret.

"So you are the king's daughter!" I cried. "And we are all his royal grandchildren!"

My mother smiled, an enigmatic smile.

"Some people say that, but only my mother knew for certain. And she would never say. I think the king made her swear to keep everything about our birth a secret. Certainly King Henry always favored me, and your uncle Henry too."

Our mother's brother Henry was a frequent visitor to our family home at Rotherfield Greys. He was a tall, muscular man, an exceptional horseman and fine athlete. Yes, I thought. Uncle Henry could very well be the son of the late King Henry, who had the reputation of being able to match or exceed any man at his court for height and strength and was a champion riding at the tilt.

"So you are a princess, and Uncle Henry is a prince," I said. "You should be granted royal honors."

My brother and sister nodded enthusiastically. "You should, mother," they urged.

But mother only laughed. "I am no princess—at least I was never acknowledged as such. I am plain Catherine Carey, daughter of Mary Boleyn Carey and Will Carey of the privy chamber. And brother Henry is of the same lineage—officially. In truth I do not know who my father was, the king or my legal father Will Carey, who died when I was very small. Or possibly some other man, for my mother was said to have other lovers. I have no desire to make exalted claims to the throne, or to be a rival to Queen Mary."

"Yet you look like him," I insisted. "You have reddish hair and blue eyes and are very fair, just as he was." I knew only too well what King Henry had looked like, all the royal palaces were full of his portraits, and there was a sculpture of his head and shoulders in a place of honor in our family home.

At this my mother nodded, but then she went on, in quite another tone.

"Whoever my true father was, there is a far darker aspect to our family story. It concerns your grandmother Mary's sister Anne."

We all knew of Anne. The witch. The harlot. The evil woman who had cast a spell on King Henry and used her magic to force him to divorce good Queen Catherine and marry her instead. The wicked queen who had been beheaded.

I had heard the servants gossip about Queen Anne for as long as I could remember. They often crossed themselves—in the Catholic fashion—when they spoke of her, as if to ward off her potent evil that lingered on, even though she had been dead for many years. My parents never spoke of her at all—at least not in my hearing—so mother's mention of her made me pay particular attention to her words.

"My aunt Queen Anne Boleyn never liked my mother. They were very different. Mother was a soft and comforting sort of woman, who liked to laugh and dance and had a sunny nature. She loved to eat and drank more wine than was good for her."

Hearing this I glanced at my sister, and caught her eye. We quickly looked away again, but each of us knew what the other was thinking: our mother also drank more wine than was good for her.

"My aunt Anne was a shrewd woman," mother was saying. "I liked to think that she saw the world through narrowed eyes. She thought Mary was a fool—though in truth I think it was Anne who was, in the end, the more foolish. My mother was happy most of the time, while Anne, for all her shrewdness, never was. At least I never saw her when her face was lit with happiness."

Smiling, she reached down and cupped my face in her two hands, then Cecelia's. "That is what I wish for you girls," she said. "That your pretty faces will be lit with happiness, all your lives long."

"Did you watch Queen Anne die?" Frank asked mother, "like we had to watch Jocelyn die?"

"No. Brother Henry and I were away, living in the country. We were in disgrace, as were all the Boleyns. As we still are. But it was Anne who mattered. Anne and her brother George and all those in their households. Oh, that was a horrible time. Everyone I knew was frightened, and my mother most of all."

"Was Queen Anne really a witch?" Frank asked.

Mother looked thoughtful. "It was said that she practiced alchemy. Mother told me about a room she had, where she kept potions and powders. The servants thought she was turning lead into gold, though if she did, she never gave any to us. She may have made poisons. But as to witchcraft—" She broke off, shaking her head and looking dubious. "It was said the king loved her with an uncommon hunger. But I think it was the hunger of great lust, and not of witchery. In any case," she concluded, "Queen Mary never forgave her stepmother Queen Anne for being so alluring to the king that he divorced her mother. Mary hates all Boleyns, and no doubt she always will."

Mother's words were much in my thoughts as our family boarded the *Anne Gallant* at Dover, leaving Queen Mary's Catholic England and bound for the safety of Protestant Frankfurt, where my father had acquaintances who he said would take us in. I held my head high, convinced, as I was, that I had the royal blood of the Tudors in my veins. And I remembered what my mother had said, that it was far better to be happy than shrewd, and above all to be wary of the wrath of kings and queens.

THREE

WHETHER it was because of my newfound certainty that I was of royal ancestry or simply because, at sixteen, I was coming into my years of promised beauty, I was much admired when we arrived at our new home in Frankfurt.

I had been a beautiful child, everyone had always agreed on that, though my father had frowned on all talk of my loveliness and said "You'll make her too full of herself" or "Too much praise makes the devil's playground" when my mother and others spoke admiringly of how pleasing my looks were. My younger sister Cecelia, my father's favorite, tended to burst into tears and leave the room when I was the center of attention; this made him vexed at me, though it was hardly my fault that my hair was the rare red-gold of autumn leaves and my skin as flawless and as translucent as the finest ivory. (Cecelia's hair was a mousy brown and her skin, while smooth, tended to be the color of sand. But she had very good teeth, as I often reminded her.)

We were lodged in the grand house of Jacob Morff, a member of the Consistory and an elder of the Lutheran church, the dominant influence and authority in Frankfurt. The four-storey gabled house was near the Old Bridge, where a few Catholic sisters continued to operate a foundling home and to take in unwanted infants. We heard the babies crying at all hours, in fact it seemed to mother and me that their numbers were growing with each passing day. But beyond this nuisance all was comfortable in the Morff household, and we were shown a courteous if impersonal hospitality.

It was the custom for Protestants to shelter one another, for as our numbers grew we were persecuted mercilessly, and there were many English Protestants coming to the continent, fleeing Queen Mary and her burnings, when I was a girl. Herr Morff had several English families living in his large house, though he was not a genial host, rather he kept a grave distance, as though unsure what to make of us foreigners. In time I was to understand why.

At first I quite enjoyed myself in our new town, a large and bustling place, its narrow streets crowded with horses and carts and peddlers on foot. The sprawling marketplace was bursting with commerce, except on Sundays, when all business transactions were forbidden by the Consistory as were all amusements. The ancient cathedral with its tall spire towered over all other city structures, and the massive stone bridges that spanned the Main river, the thick brick walls that surrounded the town and the weighty, many-storied houses centuries old gave the entire place an air of solidity, if not of grandeur. London was older than Frankfurt, father said, but Frankfurt was richer—and much more moral, now that the Consistory governed all.

That it was a moral place we knew from the abundance of hymn-singing that went on, not only in church, where the

337

services were long and tedious (though no one was allowed to complain about this out loud), but in the streets and squares. When we went out in the afternoons, we often walked or rode past group after group of townspeople who had gathered to sing hymns or other pious songs.

"We must join in," father said. "We must not appear strangers in their midst." So we learned to sing "How lovely shines the morning star" and "My trust in Thee can nothing shake" and "From depths of woe I cry to Thee" in our English-accented German and we tried our best to imitate father's expression as he sang, his heavy-lidded eyes sad, his lined, narrow face full of a dark longing.

We did our best to look and act pious, but true religious feeling cannot be feigned, and in truth we were young and full of pent-up energy and had few outlets for our restless physical vigor. Hymn-singing was not the activity we needed.

But the elders made and enforced strict rules about what we could and could not do. We were not allowed to swim, lest it lead to "promiscuous bathing" with men and women, boys and girls all joining in together. Long walks were forbidden, because they made the blood flow more rapidly and heightened the passions. Athletic feats promoted pride in the body, and the body was the prime portal of sin. Dancing, which led to frivolity and flirtation, was condemned with especial rigor.

One Sunday there was a scuffle in the square near the Old Bridge, in front of a tavern called the White Lion. I had often seen men quarreling and fighting in our village of Rotherfield Greys and on our visits to London but until that afternoon I had never seen men attacking one another in hymn-singing Frankfurt. Then I noticed that at the center of the brawl was Jacob Morff's sturdy, blond son Nicklaus, a boy I liked for his jokes and a way he had of imitating the cleaning women in the

Morff household. These maids walked with their knees together, taking short steps and always looking down at the floorboards, never at each other or objects in the room or other people. They were not shy, nor furtive, merely inconspicuous to an extreme degree. Nicklaus Morff, despite his girth and strong young muscles, could squeeze himself down and assume the appearance and carriage of one of these maids, pressing his knees together and walking in a way that made me laugh out loud, and Cecelia too if she was nearby.

Now, however, Nicklaus was pounding the head of another boy onto the rounded stones of the square, and shouting "No, you won't! You can't!" as the cluster of squabbling men and boys grew larger, drawing a crowd.

"Stop this at once!"

It was the voice of a big man I had seen once or twice at Jacob Morff's house, a senior member of the Consistory who, as he began to speak, seemed to cleave a path through the crowd until he stood amid the fighters, pulling them apart and shouting at them. Several other older men joined the leader in putting a halt to the violence. The brawlers, disheveled and dirty, several of them bloody, stood stiff-limbed and scowling. I heard Nicklaus swear angrily under his breath at the boy he had been scuffling with.

"Each of you, take note! This is your warning. If you are seen lifting your hands against each other again, you will be publicly denounced by name. Come out, saith the Lord, lest the body be cankered by its weakest members. Now, speak! What is the cause of this rioting and drunkenness?"

At first no one spoke. Then a man was thrust forward by some of the others.

"It is the White Lion, Elder Roeder. It is to be closed!"

"That is correct. There are to be no more taverns in this city from now on. Only Christian eating houses. With a Bible on every table. The Consistory has ordained it."

A loud moan of outrage arose from the crowd.

"Silence!"

But the moan of protest went on, and there were shouts of "Beer! Beer!" and a few people began singing a drinking song.

Elder Roeder drew from his long black gown a tablet and a charcoal-tipped stick, and began writing down names. Meanwhile I saw, somewhat to my amazement, that Bibles were being flung out of the door of the White Lion, landing on the cobblestones and raising small puffs of dust. I thought to myself, are these the same citizens of Frankfurt who meet to sing hymns in the streets? Or are there two Frankfurts, the city of the pious and the city of the others, who do not sing hymns and who drink in taverns and, most likely, engage in promiscuous bathing and athletics and card-playing and dancing.

"Sacrilege!" shouted the elder, and he wrote more furiously on his tablet. "You are all denounced! You will all appear before the Consistory!"

"Well, if we must," shouted Nicklaus Morff, "then we must. But we can all get drunk first!"

And before anyone could stop him he darted into the White Lion, and a good many of those in the crowd followed him in, leaving Elder Roeder to his writing and shouted threats.

Father led us all away before we too could find our names recorded on his tablet. But the elder's angry shouts followed us as we made our way along the river, past the bridge and the foundling home, and began to hear, as well, the strains of a raucous drinking song.